THE LAWS OF MAGIC

MOMENT OF TRUTH

THE LAWS OF MAGIC SERIES

THE LAWS OF MAGIC

OF

MAGIC

MOMENT OF TRUTH

MICHAEL PRYOR

RANDOM HOUSE AUSTRALIA

A Random House book
Published by Random House Australia Pty Ltd
Level 3, 100 Pacific Highway, North Sydney NSW 2060
www.randomhouse.com.au

First published by Random House Australia in 2010

Addresses for companies within the Random House Group can be found at
www.randomhouse.com.au/offices.

National Library of Australia
Cataloguing-in-Publication Entry

Author: Pryor, Michael
Title: Moment of truth / Michael Pryor
ISBN: 978 1 74166 309 9 (pbk.)
Series: Pryor, Michael. Laws of magic; 5
Target audience: For secondary school age
Subjects: Spy stories
Dewey number: A823.3

Cover illustration by Jeremy Reston
Cover design by www.blacksheep-uk.com
Internal design by Mathematics
Typeset in Bembo by Midland Typesetters, Australia
Printed in Australia by Griffin Press, an accredited ISO AS/NZS 14001:2004
Environmental Management System printer

10 9 8 7 6 5 4 3 2 1

For the author of the first proper book I
ever owned: Johann Wyss

One

AUBREY FITZWILLIAM WAS ON A MISSION. DETERMINED, unwavering, purposeful, he would not be diverted from his goal, especially since spring was in the air.

Aubrey had decided that he was committed to snaring Caroline Hepworth. *No*, he corrected himself, *not snaring*. Poor choice of metaphor. 'Winning her' wouldn't do either, and he was staying well away from any idea of sweeping her off her feet. He shuddered at the prospect of calling it 'pitching woo', even if it would provoke her extraordinarily attractive laughter.

He would simply tell Caroline how he felt about her. He would be dignified, polite, sincere. He would be clear and forthright. Then he would listen to Caroline's reaction patiently, not interrupting, and he would honour her intention. He would not argue, quibble or pretend that he was joking all along and that he actually had an appointment to hurry to.

He would begin this mission straight away. Almost, anyway. As soon as he had time, really, what with one thing and another. Or, rather, he'd act when the time was right, for these things can't be hurried. Timing was everything, he'd found – or imagined – in these matters of the heart.

Aubrey realised that Commander Craddock was talking and sending rather pointed glances in Aubrey's direction. He composed himself and vowed that he'd pay better attention. Even though he had been in Darnleigh House before, being part of a tour guided by the head of the Magic Department itself was priceless.

Aubrey had been surprised to see Commander Craddock undertaking such a menial task, especially in the tense times since the revelation of Prince Albert's claim to the throne of Gallia. Perhaps it said something about the man's professionalism, his sense of responsibility to the department he had steered for years.

Or it might just have been his turn, Aubrey thought as Craddock ushered the small band of irregular agents through the cryptology section. Aubrey sensed the magic in the large, clattering machines along one wall as they churned through possible solutions to intercepted communications. The rest of the room was taken up with desks – behind which worked an assortment of operatives, frowning and scowling mostly, consulting reference texts and scratching away with pencil and paper – and booths where telegraph operators tapped away on their keys, headphones covering their ears and with the distant gaze that comes from managing messages from far away.

Down two flights of stairs and they emerged into the second underground level. 'Research,' Craddock said shortly, indicating the long corridor. It was the epitome of anonymity, with institutional green walls, frosted glass panels in many of the doors, grey linoleum so unremarkable that it could have robbed any number of banks with impunity – no danger of its being identified. The doors were bare of signs, simply sporting numbers, nothing to give away what was going on inside – but closed doors didn't stop magical awareness. Aubrey gritted his teeth as he sensed complex spellcraft at work. He had a typically disconcerting confusion of sensation – his skin prickled with colour, hues that flickered between green and blue with immense rapidity – but the shifting and intersecting nature of the many spells at play made it difficult to determine exactly what sort of magic was being undertaken.

Several others were also affected, to judge from the shifting stances and grimaces. A serious-looking fellow – Woodberry, Aubrey remembered after a moment's groping for a name – put his hand up. 'What sort of research, sir?' he said, in a voice that broke in the middle of his question. No-one laughed.

'I can't tell you that,' Craddock said. 'You could be a spy.'

Woodberry went pale. 'I –'

Craddock held up a hand, stopping the protest before it had begun. 'A joke, Woodberry, a very mild joke. I can't tell you because I don't know if you're going to be involved in our research activities. That's something we'll know by the end of the week.'

'Sir?'

'While you're here, you'll be undertaking testing to see what talents you have that we can use.'

Aubrey was intrigued but, despite his curiosity jabbing him, kept his hand down. He was trying to remain inconspicuous. While he was pleased at the invitation for special training, since it was a vote of confidence from Commander Craddock, he also didn't want the others to think it was only because he was the son of the prime minister.

This sort of thing was almost a reflex by now. Every time Aubrey thought he was being foolish, that no-one cared, an officious busybody would raise eyebrows and remark obliquely on some action or other of his and how it must be useful to have such a famous father.

As much as he respected and admired his father, being the son of Sir Darius Fitzwilliam, PM, was a constant trial.

Craddock led the small band along the corridor. Aubrey smelled iciness and heard a low-pitched hum that descended into a rumble that made the floor vibrate. Just before they reached the intersection at the end of the corridor, a door on the left opened. A scowling operative stepped out of the room marked B6, and Aubrey was immediately taken aback. From his appearance the operative had to be a specialist, and an important one at that. Craddock's operatives were almost always immaculate in their black uniforms, professionally discreet, unobtrusive to the point of being almost invisible. This man, however, had a shock of grey hair that showed signs of constantly having hands dragged through it. He had glasses, flaming red cheeks, and he wore a baggy grey jumper over a uniform that looked as if it were grappling with him. He was glaring at the sheaf of papers in his hand, so totally taken up with his exasperation that he didn't see Craddock and his band of curious irregulars. He turned around, shook the papers at someone inside the office and – to Aubrey's soaring interest – shouted out a torrent of ancient Sumerian.

Then the specialist saw Commander Craddock and he froze. Aubrey could almost see him running a mental finger down his list of correct procedures before he finally stood at something like attention and brought his hand to his forehead in a salute-like action.

Craddock took this in for a moment, then addressed his small band. 'Tonkin here has been brought in to head our Ancient Languages section. Having a problem, Tonkin?'

Tonkin's grip on his papers increased. They began to crumple. 'There'd be no problem, sir, if only those idiots would remember . . .' He gathered himself and straightened his eyeglasses. 'A slight disagreement of interpretation, sir.'

Deep as he was in his own studies of Ancient Languages at Greythorn University, Aubrey was well aware of how easy it was to have multiple interpretations of old script, especially when the subject matter was magical.

'A disagreement that compromises security, Tonkin?' Craddock said.

Tonkin blinked. 'Sir?'

'You work in a top secret section. On a highly sensitive project. One that could affect the security of the realm. And yet, the door behind you is open.'

Aubrey was in the grip of an internal struggle. Part of him thought that the best thing was to look away, embarrassed, and allow Tonkin some dignity. Another part of him said that any security operative, even an irregular one, had a duty to gather intelligence whenever and wherever possible.

Which was, he realised, a long and tangled way of admitting that he was dying to see what Tonkin and his crew were up to. Ancient Languages? A top secret project? Safety of the realm? It was as if someone had specifically designed something to tantalise Aubrey Fitzwilliam, packaged it in irresistible wrapping and pasted a 'Do Not Open' sign on it.

After a split second or two, he succumbed. He stood on tiptoes and looked over Woodberry's shoulder, past the disapproving Craddock and the dismayed Tonkin, and the world went away as he realised what he was seeing.

The room was long and windowless. A row of electric lights illuminated a bench in the middle of the room. On three sides, it was surrounded by tables where operatives were hunched, sweating over papers and peering through magnifying glasses.

One operative was standing near the central bench. She was staring at the open door, mouth open, while one white-gloved hand held what looked like a parchment and the other pointed at the man-sized, irregularly shaped stone on the bench. Its black surface shone dully under the electric lights.

The Rashid Stone, Aubrey thought, stunned. *That's impossible. It can't be here.*

Eventually, Tonkin remembered himself. He flailed at the knob behind him before he managed to drag the door shut. It closed with the heavy solidity of doughty steel reinforcing.

'That's better,' Craddock said to Tonkin, then he turned to the goggling band of irregulars. 'Security applies to everyone in this building. Even researchers. Isn't that correct, Tonkin?'

Tonkin swallowed again. 'Yes, sir.'

'Do not forget it. Even though there appears to be a dearth of experts in this field at the moment, I'm sure we can replace you.'

Tonkin stood still while Craddock swept off toward a distant set of stairs. Aubrey was nearly left behind because he was still astounded by what he'd seen – in fact, he couldn't have been more astonished if the room had held a pair of elephants arguing over the latest battleship plans.

The Rashid Stone. What was it doing here? The last Aubrey had heard, the Rashid Stone had disappeared on its way back to its rightful owner, the Sultan of Memphis. Had Craddock diverted it from returning to its home? If so, what had happened to the person charged with this restitution: Professor Mansfield, Aubrey's lecturer on Ancient Languages at Greythorn University?

Still off balance, Aubrey tottered after the others. Any feeling he'd had of being the old hand around Darnleigh House had vanished. It had been replaced by an uncomfortable sensation of being a mystery magnet; he had a brief and definitely unsettling vision of enigmas, conundrums and posers being drawn toward him no matter which way he turned, flitting relentlessly through the ether.

Prince Albert, the incorrigible punster, would no doubt say that all this was due to his attractive personality. Aubrey grinned and groaned at the same time, which nearly made his face explode; trying not to draw attention to himself, he hurried after Craddock and the others, massaging his cheeks and wincing.

Two

ALONE, IN THE DARK AND EMBARKING ON ACTIVITIES that were possibly disloyal, probably dangerous and undoubtedly illegal, Aubrey began to have second thoughts about his plans for the evening.

Darnleigh House was not a good place to have hesitations – even if one was *meant* to be in the headquarters of the Magic Department of the Security Intelligence Directorate, something Aubrey was prepared to argue if he was found. After all, he was an irregular operative of the Directorate, on a week of intensive training. He belonged here, if only temporarily.

In the middle of the night, the building was quiet, but not silent. Standing in the dormitory in the dark, trying not to wake up any of the others, he listened before setting off. Clicks and hums, far-off rumblings, snatches of faint conversation and the muffled, indistinct sounds that indicated activity came to him through his mundane senses. Through his magical awareness, he could feel traces of magic coming from all directions, which meant that work was going on throughout the night. He knew that magical surveillance, for instance, was an around-the-clock procedure, and the corps of sensitive magicians in their basement offices would be monitoring for any signs of major magical disturbances. He made a mental note to stay well away from that part of the building.

The other emanations? He had no idea. Darnleigh House was a place of secrets.

Aubrey patted his appurtenances vest. He'd packed a number of helpful items before leaving home on a 'just in case' basis. Two segments of narrow hose pipe, for instance, magically linked, just the thing for underwater work. He imagined Caroline Hepworth's amusement at such a thing and her admonishing him for an overactive imagination.

The thought of Caroline, apart from giving him the usual knot of confusion in his stomach, prompted him to get moving. She was always one for action instead of indecision.

He slipped past the ablutions area, out of the door and into the corridor. Furtively, he flitted past the canteen, where he was intrigued to see a few operatives talking in low voices over mugs of tea, even at this hour. Were they forensic magicians, just returned from examining the site of a magical disturbance? Or were they covert operatives who'd been tracking Holmland spies? From their weary faces, they could be interrogators, trained in sniffing out magical subterfuge, or even researchers who'd been working on the golem machine that Aubrey had brought back from Holmland.

He'd left his jacket behind in the dormitory and was wearing a black cashmere pullover. With his black trousers and softest shoes, he hoped it would make him inconspicuous without looking as if he'd suddenly joined the Burglars' Union.

He strained both his ordinary and magical senses to avoid meeting anyone, while rehearsing his excuse for padding around the building after midnight. He'd left a fountain pen in the library, you see, a sentimental favourite, and he simply had to retrieve it.

Earlier that day, he'd actually primed this excuse by hiding his pen while he and the other irregulars were being shown the Department library. Normally, Aubrey would have been fascinated by the extensive collection, but finding a place to leave his pen so it would be plausible but not too obvious took some time. He had to secrete it near something which would be his excuse within an excuse – a book about the history of golem making. Commander Craddock, for one, would be suspicious about a pen retrieval story and would look for the *real* reason for Aubrey's slinking around. He would investigate where the pen was left and see the golem book – and put two and two together. Aubrey was obviously using the pen as a cover story to obtain the book. This in itself, wouldn't be a serious matter. It would, Aubrey hoped, show that he was intensely interested in magical issues of importance to the country. Craddock may even approve and ask no further questions.

Since being introduced into the murky world of espionage and conspiracy, Aubrey had been a quick learner. A plan was a good and fine thing, but a plan within a plan was even better. Alternatives, feints, fallbacks and ruses were vital tools in a world where appearances hid a thousand plots and countless motives.

He was aware that some people lived their life like this, as a series of ploys and gambits, where each interaction was a struggle for supremacy, each conversation a chance to establish a position of power. Many of these people ended up in politics, and Aubrey's father had had to deal with them. They often prided themselves on being sharp, being tough negotiators. Usually, however, working with them was a war of attrition where gains were made inch by inch. Sir Darius alternated between irritation and despair at this approach, so much time being wasted with such posturing.

At times, this sort of carrying-on made Aubrey question his desire for a life in politics. Not for long, however. His view was that if he could win the confidence of the electorate, he might be able to help change these antediluvian attitudes. Bit by bit, progress would have to happen. Especially if Caroline Hepworth were serious about looking at a seat in Parliament.

As he crept down the stairs, he considered this prospect with a grin. Votes for women were one thing – and his father had assured Caroline that he was about to present a bill to bring this about – but a female member of Parliament? He couldn't wait to see the faces of the more longstanding members. Some of the backbenchers may even wake up.

The Ancient Languages section shared the first basement level with part of the Forensic Squad. Aubrey had considerable interest in forensic magic and had been hoping that the training week would include some time with them. The specialised methods the Forensic Squad used to analyse magical residue were fascinating – and he had a notion that some aspects could be useful in other areas of magical endeavour. Madame Zelinka's Enlightened Ones, for instance, and their battle with neutralising dangerous magical residue, could be interested in some of the machinery the Forensic Squad had developed to help their probing.

He turned left, away from the lure of the Forensic area, and saw the lock on the door of Room B6. A large, smug, Perkins' Invulnerable cruciform lock. He recalled that this was the same model that burglars had nicknamed the 'Don't Waste Your Time'.

Aubrey scanned the other doors in the corridor. Each one was fitted with a cruciform lock – a sign of extreme caution? As if a normal pin tumbler lock weren't enough, the cruciform lock effectively added three more keyways and, if he wasn't mistaken, that wasn't all . . .

Very gently, he probed the lock, a mere feather brush of his magical senses, just in case it had any sort of detection built in. He smiled grimly. The lock was fairly quivering with sensitive magic detection overlays, just ready to go off if any magical methods were used to break the lock.

He straightened and took out his pocket watch. The Brayshire Ruby, inset in the cover, gleamed softly at him. He snapped it open, studying the neat way the hand signified two o'clock, knowing all the while he was procrastinating, putting off having to come to grips with what was bound to be a fiendishly difficult lock.

Aubrey rubbed his hands together. Given enough time, he could sort out the lock. But given enough time, someone was bound to wander along and ask themselves what a black-clad intruder was doing hammering away at a door. An explosion would sort out the lock, for instance, but explosions were renowned for drawing attention, so he reluctantly discarded that option.

No, he needed to proceed with subtlety. While it may be less certain, a subtle approach had the virtue of not immediately landing him in hot water. Accustomed as he was to thermal aquatics, he preferred to avoid them if possible.

From his appurtenances vest he withdrew the slim metal object he'd spent some time working on after dinner.

He knew he didn't have Caroline's delicacy and sureness of movement that made her an uncanny lock picker, so he had to use magic to construct an appropriate tool.

The metal object, for which two butter knives had sacrificed themselves, was effectively a rough blank cruciform key. It would fit into the slot well enough, but, naturally, it wouldn't match the four sets of pins and so it wouldn't open the lock.

Not without some help.

This was the tricky part, Aubrey decided as he studied his blank key and then the lock again. With magic, he aimed to vibrate each vane of the blank. This should jiggle each of the sixteen pins inside the lock until he could turn the blank, and hey presto!

Just to make things harder, he had to set the blank vibrating and then remove all traces of magic residue from it before it came in contact with the lock. Otherwise the magic detection spells would sound an alarm. At the least.

He didn't really want to contemplate the most the spells could do.

The vibration spell was a simple application of the Law of Position. He effected a minute shifting of the edges of the blank, backward and forward. Or was that up and down?

One way to find out, he thought, and softly uttered the spell. Immediately, he grinned as the blank began humming, numbing the bones in his hand. He cast a neutralising spell which removed the tiny residual effects and the key continued humming.

It was a high-pitched, whining noise, hardly noticeable, more a mosquito than a hummingbird. He had to steady himself to insert the blank into the key slot as it wove backward and forward, but in it went. Cautiously, he let it work for nearly a minute, restraining himself from jiggling it just to help, but then the vibrations lessened, dying away until the blank was still again.

He grimaced and withdrew the blank, cast the vibration and neutralising spells on it again, and slid it back in the slot.

Three times he repeated this, asking himself if he was flogging a dead horse, until, abruptly, the lock turned.

It was some time before he realised that his plan had worked.

He scrambled about, pushed the door slightly open, slipped his blank back into a pocket, and stepped into Room B6.

Once he closed the door behind him it was black inside. He stood for a moment, gathering his breath and fumbling in his appurtenances vest until he found what he was after.

He fitted the shell-like cups over his eyes and was immediately rewarded when the darkness disappeared.

He could see clearly. The room was in shades of grey and silver, giving the workaday setting a gloss of moonlit glamour.

At least this modified cat's eye spell was working well. He'd refined the magic he'd used in their Banford Park escapade last year, and had succeeded in eliminating the fishy smell that he'd accidentally incorporated into the hasty first version. With the aid of these useful devices, he was able to make out the benches, the chairs – and the man-sized dark shape he'd come all this way to investigate.

Of course, having entered a secure, top secret area, he now had to do his best to investigate and return to the dormitory undetected. No cover story would be enough now. 'These cat's eyes? I thought they might help me find my pen . . .'

He approached the stone carefully, scanning the floor ahead for any dropped objects, anything that would make a clatter or a crunch.

Then he froze. Arms extended, feeling the air ahead, he stopped dead in his tracks. *Something* was in the room. All was still, but Aubrey had the overwhelming impression that he wasn't alone. His mouth was suddenly dry. Cautiously extending his magical awareness, he probed ahead, but sensed nothing. Then he tried to listen past the thundering in his ears that was his own heartbeat, but nothing came to him. At least, nothing rational. Instead, all he had was a primeval certainty, an impression no doubt formed from a collection of subliminal clues – a minute sound, a shifting in the air currents, a change in the temperature, in the way sounds echoed around the room . . .

Light – sudden, blinding light. Aubrey hissed and threw himself sideways, then realised that he was dazzled because of his cat's eyes. He swept a hand over his eyes and rolled to a crouch, trying to see in all directions at once.

In the corner of the room, leaning against the wall, was Commander Craddock. He held a slim silver fountain pen in one hand. 'You're looking for this, Fitzwilliam?'

Three

*I*T WAS PROBABLY TOO LATE FOR AUBREY TO PRETEND he was only sleepwalking, but desperation prompted him to give it a try. 'Sir?' he said, groggily. He put a hand to his head. *So tired, I'm so tired . . .*

'Your pen, Fitzwilliam. You left it in the library. And that's one of the worst attempts at sleepwalking I've seen all week.'

So much for somnambulism. Aubrey climbed to his feet. He wondered exactly how much trouble he was in. Was his time in the intelligence community over before it had really begun?

'How did you get in here?' Craddock's voice was even. Aubrey detected no censure. Not yet.

'The lock.' Aubrey gestured vaguely.

'Go on.'

Aubrey realised that he wasn't about to get away with a nebulous explanation. He found the blank key. 'I used this.'

'Explain.'

When Aubrey had finished his explanation, Craddock was silent for a moment, then he nodded. 'Ingenious.' Aubrey's spirits rose a little. 'And costly.'

Aubrey's spirits sank. 'Sir?'

'We're going to have to replace all the locks with something more secure.' Craddock narrowed his eyes. 'Can you do this again?'

'I think so, sir.'

'Good. I want to you write down your procedure in detail. We may be able to adapt it for our field teams. It could be quicker than teaching them lock-picking, especially since some of the more fumble-fingered never seem to acquire the knack.'

'Certainly, sir.'

'By Friday.'

Two days. 'Of course, sir.'

Craddock studied him for a time. Aubrey was prepared for this and stood at ease, hands behind his back, and waited. 'You do understand that you're being tested while you're here,' Craddock said finally, 'don't you?'

'I'm fit and well, sir.'

'I'm pleased to hear it. But we're testing for other things. Aptitudes. Talents. Specialisations.'

Aubrey thought of the other irregulars he'd seen that day and wondered where their talents lay. 'Glad to be able to help, sir.'

'From these tests and the tasks you've done for us in the past, it has been noted that you've developed some skills for covert activities. What your father calls unconventional approaches.'

'Sir?'

'You have a flair for coping with the unexpected, and you have the sort of curiosity that is beneficial in this field.' Craddock put his hand on the script-covered stone. 'As such, I suppose you're wondering about this.'

Aubrey's first impulse was to feign indifference at seeing the artefact. He quickly abandoned this. Craddock was no fool. 'I glimpsed it earlier, sir. I thought it had disappeared.'

'That's right. You had some connection with Professor Mansfield, didn't you?'

'She was my lecturer in Ancient Languages. And a friend of my parents.'

'The last report we have is that she is missing. With the Rashid Stone.'

'But what's this then? Sir?'

'Use your magic.'

Aubrey did as he was told, then raised his eyebrows. 'It's a fake.'

'A reconstruction. We worked it up using the Law of Similarity and the Law of Seeming.'

'It looks perfect.'

'With one small problem. Look at this.'

Arms crossed on his chest, Craddock walked around to the back of the stone. Bewildered, Aubrey followed and was agog when the reverse of the stone was completely bare. 'Where's the rest of the script?'

'We don't have it.' Craddock ran his hand over the smooth, unmarked surface. 'The Rashid Stone was in the Albion Museum for a hundred and fifty years. In that time, dozens of people copied the script, from both sides. When the stone was stolen from the museum, we became interested in it. Before we could begin studying it in any serious way, however, every copy we knew about vanished as well.'

'Magic.' It was the only way Aubrey could think of to achieve such a thing.

'Gone. From Albion, from the Continent, from all the world. The only record we could find was a muddy stereographic image which we used for the front.'

'I can only think of one person who could do something like that,' Aubrey said.

'Indeed. And anything that Dr Tremaine is interested in interests us.'

'Have you made any progress?'

'The current thinking is that the Rashid Stone may lead us to deciphering this script.' He pointed at the lowest section of the artefact. 'If our experts are right, it may shed some light on the actual relationship between magic, language and human consciousness itself.'

Aubrey had had thoughts along the same lines, but hadn't had a chance to pursue them. 'Fundamental stuff.'

'Correct. It's entirely possible that someone who can bring these areas together in a unified theory ...' Craddock's calm slipped for a moment and Aubrey was shocked to see something that – in another man – would be called fear. 'Well, such a person could control magic itself.'

AFTER CRADDOCK ESCORTED HIM BACK TO THE DORMITORY, with a blunt word or two about remaining there, sleep refused to come as Aubrey's mind whirred. He lay on his bed in the dark while a thousand thoughts tumbled through his head.

The connection between magic, language and human consciousness was the great unsolved riddle of the age, a riddle that was consuming the entire attention of some of the finest magical minds of this generation. If solved, it promised to open whole new fields of endeavour and to lead to magical applications of untold power.

When a shadowy figure was suspected as being behind mysterious events, Aubrey's first, second and third choices were Dr Tremaine. Professor Mansfield had promised to appear at the Fisherberg symposium when she disappeared. Aubrey had been shocked to learn that Dr Tremaine was actually the organiser of this event – for his own ends, naturally. In the uproar over the revelation of Prince Albert's claim to the vacant throne of Gallia, things like Professor Mansfield's disappearance were overlooked, of small consequence in the days following the bombshell.

Aubrey was now starting to see it as another of Dr Tremaine's schemes within schemes, and the idea of Dr Tremaine controlling magic was a nightmare made real.

He couldn't wait to get home to look at the mysterious stone fragments that had come into his possession – fragments that Professor Mansfield had been sure could help unravel the puzzle of the Rashid Stone. He'd promised himself that he'd give the fragments to the Department after he'd hammered out some new probing spells that he'd been working on but, with one thing and another, he hadn't quite managed it.

One thing and another. He grimaced. *They* always *get in the way.*

THE NEXT MORNING, AS HE SAT IN ONE OF THE DEPARTMENT'S demonstration laboratories, Aubrey went to stifle a yawn, only to feel another coming hard on its heels, so that his head almost burst with the effort. Through tears, he was glad he was sitting at the back, as he was sure his face had turned an alarming shade of red.

The demonstration laboratory held perhaps thirty or forty people, the rows of seats sloping precipitously to provide a good view of the bench at the front. Commander Craddock stood behind it while one of the more anonymous operatives unloaded glassware and batteries from a trolley.

'Good morning,' Craddock said. He was wearing black, as usual, but not his typical long coat and wide-brimmed hat. His white-haired head was bare, and he wore a short, black jacket and a high-collared black shirt. And a tie, black. 'I hope you all slept well. You'll need to be in top form today.'

Aubrey winced, even though Craddock's gaze didn't linger on him. He ducked his head as another jaw-cracking yawn took hold of him, and pretended to fumble around in his satchel. When he was himself again, he looked up to meet Craddock's gaze square on. 'Now, let us consider the work of Lanka Ravi.'

Aubrey's weariness fell away from him. Lanka Ravi. Aubrey had been lucky enough to catch one of the great theoretician's controversial lectures at Greythorn University. He'd been staggered by the insights the young man presented. One after another, Ravi had elucidated new ways of looking at fundamental laws, connections between areas of magic considered incompatible, conjectures about possible future applications for magic. Lanka Ravi's intellect was dazzling, and Aubrey had been shocked to hear of Ravi's death while on his way back to his home on the sub-continent. When Aubrey heard the news, he had a profound sense of loss, an awareness of all that would not be done because Lanka Ravi had passed away before his time.

Aubrey rubbed his hands together, then he quickly opened his notebook. He didn't want to miss anything. Craddock was a fine magician and a deep thinker. If Lanka Ravi's work was of interest to him – and the Department – Aubrey was keen to find out why.

Before Craddock could begin, however, the door to his right opened. A hesitant operative slipped in and was cornered by Craddock's assistant. They had a hurried, hushed exchange. Craddock had stopped speaking as soon as the door moved. He didn't turn; he simply stood, waiting, his face impassive, and Aubrey knew that something was afoot – and it may also explain why the head of the Magic Department was occupying himself with the relatively minor task of taking care of irregulars. This way, Craddock ensured he was at headquarters and ready to respond.

To what?

In the face of the assistant's insistence, the intruder hesitated, then handed over an envelope. The assistant didn't look pleased, but took it to Commander Craddock while the intruder left, closing the door with a palpable expression of relief.

With a minute tightening around his eyes, Craddock took the envelope from his assistant. Then he raised an eyebrow and looked up. 'Fitzwilliam.'

Aubrey was immediately the focus of attention of all the irregulars.

'It's for you,' Craddock continued, not without some satisfaction at Aubrey's discomfort. 'It's marked "Urgent".'

THE POLICE PRESENCE AT NO. 4 CREDENCE LANE HAD increased, Aubrey noted as he was admitted to the Prime Minister's offices. A sign of the times.

He didn't recognise any of the constables on duty, and their business-like demeanour as they scrutinised him discouraged any light conversation. He was ushered to a waiting room near the main stairs. There, under the watchful eye of the constables who popped in every few minutes, he waited. And waited. And waited.

So much for urgency, he thought after the first hour went by, dragging its feet so much it would have left gouges in concrete.

The sole window of the waiting room looked out on a deserted courtyard that featured a pear tree in bloom. Two remarkably uninteresting paintings hung on the walls. Aubrey had his choice of a still life with fruit or a thatched country cottage with – no doubt – a horde of rosy-cheeked children inside. After an hour or so of staring at them, they began to blur together and he had visions of rosy-cheeked bananas inside a thatched cottage, which gave him a start.

Aubrey tried not to let his irritation grow. Having a role in the Security Intelligence Directorate – no matter how peripheral – was good for his ego. Magic was one area where his father hadn't gone before him and any successes were indisputably his own. Being dragged away from it was hard to take, despite the urgency of the summons. Being ignored on top of it was even more nettling.

Aubrey did his best to divert himself from such childish thoughts. He wondered about the hushed tension that permeated the building. He'd visited numerous times since his father had regained the Prime Ministership, and he understood that the offices had never exactly been a leisurely place, but the seriousness on the faces of those who hurried past the open doorway was a sign that something was amiss. Aubrey idly considered possibilities. Someone in the Opposition caught embezzling party funds? Or, worse, someone in Sir Darius's own Progressive Party up to no good? His father had hinted that he was less than impressed with some of the backbenchers. Such had been the Progressives' election success that some had gained seats unexpectedly – and their quality was not all it should be.

A junior aide – a young man several years older than Aubrey – popped his head into the waiting room. 'Sorry, Mr Fitzwilliam. The PM's been caught up again. Sends his apologies. Cup of tea?'

'Did he say how long he was going to be?'

The aide screwed up his face. 'It's hard to tell. There's a lot going on.'

Aubrey noted how the aide hadn't actually answered his question. He could go far in politics. 'Tea would be appreciated, thank you.'

The tea was excellent, as was the light lunch that was brought an hour later. By two o'clock, Aubrey's lack of sleep was catching up with him. Soon, it had caught up, gone past, and was threatening to lap him. His eyelids each weighed a pound. His chin was regularly sucked downward to meet his chest. Blinking was taking seconds to complete.

A cough made him jump. 'Sorry,' he said, automatically reaching for an excuse. 'I was concentrating.'

A short, brisk woman looked over her glasses at him with the sort of polite disdain that only comes with years of practice. 'I see,' she said, clearly unconvinced, but quite happy to allow Aubrey his delusion. 'A motorcar is waiting for you.'

Aubrey glanced at the window to see that evening was drawing in. The gas lamps in the street were glowing cheerfully. 'My father wanted to see me.'

'He sends his apologies. His post-luncheon meeting went longer than expected, then he was whisked into an emergency party session.'

'What should I tell my mother?'

'I believe they've been in communication.' The woman pursed her lips. 'She's expecting you.'

The motorcar was an Oakleigh-Nash and Aubrey cursed its comfort. It made it even harder to stave off sleep as it rolled through the streets, past the Houses of Parliament, over the bridge, and made its way toward the family home in Fielding Cross with the subdued rumble of very expensive machinery, a noise Aubrey decided was purposely designed to send one to sleep.

He staggered out of the motorcar, mumbling thanks to the driver and treating Harris, the butler at Maidstone, to an incoherent greeting. Aubrey had visions of his bed, but he was brought up short at the foot of the grand stairs. 'George,' he said, with a fair stab at intelligibility. 'What are you doing here?'

George Doyle was leaning against the newel-post, arms crossed on his chest. He was wearing a belted, striped Norfolk jacket and looked fit and vibrant. 'I might ask you the same question, old man. Your Darnleigh House jaunt finish early?'

Aubrey tried again. 'Aren't you supposed to be at university?'

George sniffed the air. 'You know, I think dinner is almost ready. Shall we go and see?'

With some bewilderment, Aubrey followed his friend only to run into Harris coming back the other way. 'Dinner, young sirs,' the butler announced. He glanced at George, to let him know that he knew that his summons was superfluous but wanting it understood that it was his job.

When they reached the dining room, Lady Rose was already there. She was wearing a favourite dress, a striking blue, high-necked and long-sleeved. Immediately, Aubrey could see the concern in her eyes. 'Mother. What's going on?'

'Hello, Aubrey. I'm glad you're here.'

There's a wealth of commentary in that simple utterance, Aubrey thought and he began to grow very uneasy. 'George, how long have you been here?'

George drew up a chair. One of the serving staff arranged his napkin on his lap. 'A few hours, old man. Came as soon as I read the telegram.'

'Ah. From my father?'

'That's the one. Said I should join you here. I was starting to wonder where you'd got to.'

His mother smiled a little, but Aubrey noted how she was fiddling with the gold charm bracelet around her wrist – the one his father had given her soon after they first met. 'Your father telephoned and said he wanted you both to stay here until he could talk to you. After he'd received permission from your father, George, of course.'

Aubrey's weariness had vanished. Something was awry, seriously awry. 'Mother? Do you know what's going on?'

Lady Rose was about to answer and the soup was brought out.

'Potato and leek,' George said. 'Capital.'

George finished quickly, and allowed himself to be persuaded to have seconds, while Aubrey dawdled over his. It wasn't that the soup was poor – it was excellent – but he spent most of his time watching his mother.

She barely lifted her spoon. She chatted absently with George about the putting together of the latest edition of the *Luna*, the student newspaper at Greythorn. George had received some favourable notice for his series of articles about the ordinary people of Holmland, and his prestige among the students working on the paper had grown considerably.

Engaging as she was, Aubrey couldn't help but notice that his mother's real attention was on the doorway that led to the entrance of the house. George hadn't noticed this – devoted as he was to Lady Rose – but Aubrey saw the subtle shifts of posture and position that meant that Lady Rose could see the door without having to turn away from speaking to him.

When the doorknocker hammered, Lady Rose stiffened. George's chat drained away when he saw the expression on her face. Harris appeared with a heavy, cream envelope on a silver tray. 'M'lady?'

She held out a hand in the same way one might ask for a cobra and took the envelope and the letter opener that was also on the tray. Her lips were set in a grim line as she slit the envelope with quick, efficient movements.

It didn't take long to read, and Aubrey was dismayed to see all the colour run from his mother's face. 'Mother?'

She didn't respond. She put a hand to her mouth and scanned the letter again. Finally, she folded the letter and held it in both hands in front of her. 'I have some distressing news.' She took a breath. 'Holmland has invaded the Low Countries.'

George smothered an oath. Aubrey clenched his fists and his heart pounded inside his chest. Nearly two years of tension, of plots and counter plots, had led to this moment. He'd hoped that it would never come, that a clever stroke would forestall it forever, but the tide was sweeping over them even as they did their best to resist it.

'At ten o'clock,' Lady Rose continued, visibly growing paler, 'your father is due in the Lower House. He is going to announce that we are at war.'

There it is, Aubrey thought numbly. Such a simple statement: we are at war. Nation against nation, and misery would be the only inevitable outcome.

'Holmland must be aiming to invade Gallia through the Low Countries,' he said and he tried to remember his geography. Racing through the Low Countries would be easier than trying to force through the hilly terrain and fortified areas of north-eastern Gallia. 'Our treaty with Gallia means we have no choice but to support the Low Countries.'

'It was inevitable, I'm afraid,' Lady Rose said, 'after the assassination.'

Aubrey couldn't help but agree. A few weeks after they'd fled Holmland, the Elektor's nephew had been shot while touring the Goltans. Veltranian rebels had killed the well-meaning Duke Josef during a parade. Aubrey knew the loss would strike the Elektor hard. He held his nephew in high esteem, and it had been his idea for Duke Josef to visit the Goltans. It was the Elektor's effort to reassure the Veltranians that Holmlanders weren't all warmongers and barbarians, an effort than bravely ran counter to the more belligerent designs of the Holmland government.

A doomed effort, it would seem.

Immediately after the assassination, Holmland – urged on by its ally, the Central European Empire – had issued a series of demands to the Veltranian government. Some of the demands called for the quashing of anti-Holmland political parties and taking immediate action against the assassination suspects and co-conspirators. Holmland went further, insisting that the Veltran government control the press, which had been notoriously anti-Holmland. With the factions in Veltran, this was always going to be impossible, and Aubrey suspected that Holmland knew this.

Ambassadors from Holmland and the Central European Empire withdrew when the Veltranian response to the ultimatum was deemed inadequate. War was declared soon after – and Muscovia rallied behind its Goltan ally, Veltran, which meant that instead of a small-scale spat, the incident was now a heavyweight contest.

This was the headache the Continent had become. A web of treaties and alliances linked all countries, sometimes in multiple ways, and Aubrey knew that this is what his mother meant by inevitable. One country declaring war on another drew in more countries which dragged in the rest. It wasn't so much a line of dominoes as a fishing net soaked in oil and set on fire, spreading flames in all directions at once.

Once Holmland was at war with Muscovia, its ambitions were given free rein. While it engaged the enemy to the east, one faction of the military generals apparently thought opening a western front, advancing troops through the Low Countries, would be a fine idea. Why have one battlefront when you can try out your new toys on two?

Albion had no choice. It had to go to war – and Dr Mordecai Tremaine was on his way to immortality.

Aubrey spared a thought for Rodolfo, the Veltranian patriot he'd come to know in his guise as a brigand. The last Aubrey had heard, Rodolfo had been going home to try to stop his brother from being swept up in the machinations that were only too rife in the benighted country. Rodolfo had had rumours of assassination plots, rumours that sounded ominous in the light of Duke Josef's death.

George broke the speculation that had seized Aubrey. 'Lady Rose,' he said tentatively, 'sorry to ask, but does Sir Darius say why he wanted me here? Wanted *us* here?'

Aubrey was pleased. George had gone to the heart of the matter.

Lady Rose looked uncomfortable. She turned her charm bracelet for a time, rotating it around her slender wrist and looking at neither George nor Aubrey. Finally, she came to a decision and lifted her head. 'He did. I'm not sure if I agree with his motives, and I'm not sure that you will either.'

Aubrey and George looked at each other. 'I assumed he wanted support for you,' Aubrey said, but his words dried up as soon as he said them.

'And why would he think I'd need support?' she asked calmly. Aubrey thought it was the sort of calm that travellers from the colonies, survivors of tropical cyclones, reminisced about, saying, 'Remember that lull just before the house was crushed by falling palm trees then swept away by the landslide and flood? *That* was the calm before the storm.'

Aubrey backtracked as fast as he could. 'Support each other, I mean. Quite an announcement, that. Strength in numbers, someone to share the load, that sort of thing.'

'Hmm.' Lady Rose narrowed her eyes, clearly unconvinced but willing to let the matter drop. She picked up the letter, which had been lying on the table next to her wine glass, as unobtrusive as buffalo at a wedding.

'Darius was most concerned for you both,' his mother said after she scanned the letter again.

'Concerned?' Aubrey echoed. He didn't understand. If he wasn't safe in Darnleigh House, where on earth did safety lie?

'Indeed. He's worried about you doing something foolish, as he puts it.'

'Ah.' Aubrey sat back. 'I think I see.'

'You do?' George said. 'I'm afraid you've left me behind, old man.'

Lady Rose smiled at George. It was a smile with a touch of sadness. 'He doesn't want you to enlist, George.'

Four

FTER A DINNER THAT HAD BECOME UNDERSTANDABLY sombre, Lady Rose retired to her study. It was George who suggested cocoa in the library while they waited for Sir Darius to come home. Aubrey promised to join him, but with trepidation went via his room to check on his Roman fragment, the cousin to the Rashid Stone.

After he opened the safe behind the portrait of his great-great-grandfather, he found the empty velvet bag. He didn't trust his eyes, so he plucked the bag from under the pile of legal documents. He opened it, felt inside, turned it inside out, then sat on the striped sofa against the wall, his stomach hollow.

Dr Tremaine was an astounding magician. He knew that – but he hadn't imagined the man could cast a spell which would bring him objects *he couldn't possibly have knowledge of.*

It was a pointed reminder of the capabilities of the foe with whom he was dealing.

Making his way to the library, Aubrey was at sixes and sevens, imagining the scenes in Parliament as the rumour of war swept through its halls. His father would be under siege by members of his own party and members of the opposition, all wanting extra information, or favours, or appointments. It didn't matter what the nature of an emergency was; some saw an opportunity for advancement while others wanted to come to the aid of the country in dire times.

Aubrey hoped that his father's Cabinet colleagues – good people, most of them – were able to keep the petitioners away. He knew his father would want to work on his speech.

His father was a fine speechmaker – and speechwriter, when it came down to it. Several of his colleagues used professional speechwriters to hammer out the words needed for the public, but this was an area where Sir Darius was old-fashioned. He insisted on writing his speeches for himself.

At times, he'd used Aubrey as a sounding board, trying out early drafts and asking for criticism. Aubrey liked the way his father used direct language and avoided the circumlocutions that too many others in Parliament were entranced by. Sir Darius loved to salt his speeches with blunt, one-syllable words and phrases that were pithy, commonplace, but memorable.

This speech, declaring that the nation was at war, would need all of his skill and care.

Aubrey wondered, too, what effect the declaration would have on the Magic Department and the Security

Intelligence Directorate as a whole. It had virtually been on a war footing for some time, but the training week had suggested to him an organisation that was ready to move up a gear, to bring all its resources to bear on the twin jobs of gathering information and protecting the nation from espionage.

Of course, the university would need to take stock. Many of its people would be reserve officers, likely to be called up immediately – and Aubrey had heard rumours that many had already been seconded, abandoning courses mid-semester. Deans all over the campus would no doubt be frowning over reallocations, cancellations and amalgamations. The university was likely to become a serious place indeed. Aubrey thought of the days by the Greythorn River, the long afternoon teas and the fun of the cricket matches. It may be a long time before such carefree days ever resumed, especially if Dr Tremaine's plans came to pass.

He imagined Dr Tremaine was feeling satisfied as nation after nation declared war on each other. It was the sort of scale he'd been after all along, the magnitude of war that was needed to complete the Ritual of the Way.

George opened the door to the library. Aubrey could see that, in the warmth of the evening, the windows had been open. The smell of honeysuckle made his favourite room in the house even more inviting. He took one of the large leather armchairs and let his gaze wander over the thousands of volumes on the shelves.

The Ritual of the Way was death magic of the worst sort. It was theoretical, because no-one had ever thought that a sufficient blood sacrifice could be organised. Dr Tremaine, however, was a man who dared do what others recoiled from. He had realised that war was nothing if not an organised blood sacrifice. If he could harness it and orchestrate a battle of gargantuan size, he could achieve his ends.

Immortality. Even the warmth of the summer evening wasn't enough to stop Aubrey from shivering at the prospect of an immortal Dr Tremaine. Given eternal life, could anything stop him?

There was a knock at the door and Harris brought in a tray. George took it from him and placed it on the table between his chair and Aubrey's. He poured, and Aubrey was charmed when he saw that Harris had found his favourite childhood mug. Solid brown earthenware, a smiling cow beamed out at him from it.

George had a more mature mug – a thoughtful-looking duck – and after he sipped he sighed. 'Good cocoa, that.'

Aubrey sipped. 'Harris made it himself.'

'Not cook?'

'Harris prides himself on his cocoa.'

'I see.' George took another mouthful, then placed his mug on the table. 'All right, old man. Now that the cocoa discussion is out of the way, I need to ask you a question.'

Aubrey lifted an eyebrow. 'Mmm?'

George pursed his lips, scratched his chin, frowned and then rubbed his hands together. Running out of time-wasting gestures, he finally fixed his gaze on Aubrey. 'What are we going to do?'

Aubrey put his mug on the table as well. He sat back and crossed his arms on his chest. 'That's a very good question, George. It deserves to have a very good answer, but I'm dashed if I know what it is.'

'Let me throw a few words into the ring: duty, responsibility, obligation.'

Aubrey made a face. 'You don't have to remind me about duty.'

'I know, old man.'

'King and country, that sort of thing?'

'Sounds old-fashioned when you put it like that.'

'If you mean unthinking obedience and loyalty to something as abstract as a country, then I think it *is* a bit old-fashioned.'

George nodded, but Aubrey saw this was potentially upsetting. 'Don't mistake me, though,' he went on. 'I happen to think you can do the same thing for two different reasons. While some people might rally to Albion just because of patriotism, with no questions asked, I like to think that I support Albion because I've asked the questions and I'm satisfied with the answers.'

'Like your magic,' George said slowly.

'What?'

'You keep going on about Rational Magic, where you magic types ask questions and work things out intelligently. Maybe you're doing the same with patriotism.'

'Rational Patriotism.' Aubrey tried it on for size, and was quite comfortable with the fit. 'If I'm rationally patriotic, I can admit that while Albion isn't perfect there *is* a lot to be proud of.'

'Freedom of the press,' George said. 'Freedom of thought.'

'More or less. And there's the rule of law. And Democracy.'

'Votes for women?'

'Coming soon,' Aubrey said firmly. He uncrossed his arms and counted on his fingers. 'Writing. The Arts. Sciences.'

'Charity,' George said. 'Don't forget charity. Albionites know that it's the right thing to do to help those less well off than you are.' He held up a finger. 'And don't forget cricket.'

'How could I? Aubrey said. 'It's a good country. Not perfect, but it's better than the alternative. I'd hate to see it crushed.'

'That's the other thing,' George said. 'We're talking about defending ourselves here.'

Aubrey had visions of invaders marching on Parliament House. Or the Palace. Or Maidstone. He shuddered. 'While I wouldn't want Mother to hear it, I'd do what I could to protect her.' *And George's parents. And Caroline, of course. And Mrs Hepworth. And Harris. Then there's Bertie . . .*

'Of course.' George scowled. 'I'm worried about Sophie and her family.'

George had met Sophie Delroy a year ago, while on their Lutetian escapade. They'd been diligent correspondents ever since, and Sophie had visited Greythorn on one memorable occasion. Aubrey thought they were well matched. The sharp and ambitious Sophie and the clearly smitten George.

'Why not ask them over here for a holiday?' Aubrey suggested. 'Plenty of room here at Maidstone.'

George chewed on this. 'Or I could ask them to the farm. Father would like that.'

'They'd be out of harm's way.'

'If you allow me to leapfrog sideways, so to speak, it's true, what you say.'

'It is?'

'The best way to lessen worry is to do something about it. One of your maxims, that.'

'It is?' Aubrey hadn't realised he'd appropriated one of his *father's* favourite mottos. Not that he minded – he agreed. Doing something – *anything* – was about the only remedy for the paralysis that worry could bring about.

'A favourite,' George said firmly. 'Now, I don't think we've really decided what we're going to do.'

'A question for you, then. How do you feel about being summoned here?'

'Summoned?' George frowned. 'I didn't really see it like that.'

Am I being oversensitive? Aubrey wondered, but he went on. 'Well, what about being described as "foolish"?'

'Steady on, old man. I think it was our possible actions that were described as foolish, not us.'

'Aren't you splitting hairs, George? It sounded to me as if we couldn't be trusted and we needed to be sheltered for our own good.'

'I suppose there was a bit of that . . .'

'I'm not sure how well that sits with me.' Aubrey reached out for his cocoa, but his cow mug was cold. 'I'm worried about this war, George.'

George stood and brushed off his jacket. 'Let's sleep on it. It's too late to do anything now.'

Aubrey glanced at the clock on the mantelpiece over the fire. It was after eleven. He'd wanted to wait for his father, but if he wasn't home by now he may not be home at all. 'Tomorrow morning it is. Plenty of time then to do something rash.'

Five

SIR DARIUS DID NOT COME TO MAIDSTONE AT ALL. AT breakfast – while George stowed away enormous quantities of bacon and eggs – Aubrey thought his mother was doing well to cover her concern, but he saw how she tensed when the telephone rang. When Harris returned, she continued buttering her toast but with the sort of studied concentration that meant she was controlling herself carefully. 'Who was it, Harris?'

'Duncan, m'lady, one of Sir Darius's aides. He apologised and said Sir Darius was unlikely to be home at all today.'

Lady Rose paused in her buttering. 'I thought not.' Then she resumed, scraping the butter over a piece of toast that was already well spread. 'Was there any indication when he may be here?'

'As soon as possible, was the message.' Harris paused. The butler was the embodiment of discretion, but in the minute shifting of his stance Aubrey thought he detected discomfort. 'One other thing, m'lady. Sir Darius asked to make sure that Master Fitzwilliam and Master Doyle remain at Maidstone.'

Aubrey and George exchanged glances.

'Thank you, Harris.'

'M'lady.'

Lady Rose put her toast on a side plate. Aubrey had never seen a piece of charred bread so perfectly buttered. 'Your father is concerned about you, Aubrey. And you, too, George.'

'More concerned than usual?' Aubrey said.

'Apparently.'

'So he's imprisoning us.'

'Keeping you safe, I'd put it. Until he can talk to you, at least.' Lady Rose frowned. 'He has your best interests at heart. Oh.'

'Oh?'

Lady Rose took up her napkin and touched it to her lips. Aubrey couldn't imagine why. She hadn't eaten a thing. 'I just used a platitude. Your father and I vowed we wouldn't resort to such in raising you.'

'I was getting ready for "Your father knows best".'

'That the sort of thing that platitudes lead to,' Lady Rose said.

'I'm sure he does,' George said. 'Have your best interests at heart, old man. Your father.'

'I know,' Aubrey said. 'But when anyone says that, it seems to me, it denies one's own wishes and responsibility. It suggests that they know better than you do yourself.'

His mother considered this. 'He does know you rather well.'

'Granted.' Aubrey toyed with his cutlery. 'I wonder what he thinks I'm going to do?'

'Try to save the world, of course,' George said gruffly. 'It's what you usually try to do in an emergency.'

'This is rather more than an emergency,' Aubrey pointed out. 'What can one person do?'

WHAT CAN ONE PERSON DO? THE QUESTION ROLLED AROUND Aubrey's head as he finished breakfast and excused himself, saying he needed to do some magical research. He went to his room and stretched out on the chaise longue, arms behind his head, and thought.

I'm only one person, what can I do? was an excuse that resounded through the ages, and Aubrey had never subscribed to it. It was the refuge of the half-hearted and it gave comfort to those who preferred to do nothing. He didn't like that attitude but it did mean that he went too far the other way, at times. He acted precipitously, trying to do something when it may have been better to wait for help. When he found a sleeping dog, he found it hard to leave it lie.

And he had a father who thought he knew best.

It rankled. Even though he respected his father and wanted to make him proud, it still rankled. While he wasn't as contrary as Caroline tended to be, he still found it difficult to do something just because someone told him to. If he agreed, it was different. But blind obedience wasn't his forte, despite the spirit of the age – even when the Fitzwilliam family name was at stake.

He laced his hands behind his head and stared at the ceiling. Trapped at Maidstone, he was, confined to quarters. It was frustrating, and he understood the unhappiness of the tiger at the zoo, pacing backward and forward interminably, wishing for the bars to disappear.

He wanted to talk to his father. He *needed* to talk to him, to get the talk out of the way and then embark on action. In dire times like these, actions were necessary.

He sat up and took out his pocket watch. He didn't want to look at the time. He wanted to remind himself of the Fitzwilliam legacy.

He was at a cusp, he realised, a time where many futures beckoned – but only one was the way forward.

Set in the cover of the watch, the Brayshire Ruby glowed like a drop of blood. The ruby had been handed down through the generations, each owner having the responsibility to set it in a way that they chose. When Dr Tremaine took it from Aubrey, he had been distraught at losing a part of his family heritage. On a whim, Dr Tremaine had returned it. Suspicious, Aubrey had spent some time investigating it, using multiple magical techniques, probing with his magical senses to see if Dr Tremaine had invested the watch with any malignant surprises.

To Aubrey's puzzlement, the watch had proven totally clean. Which made him all the more puzzled about the ex-Sorcerer Royal's motives.

He cradled the watch in both hands. Fitzwilliams had been prominent throughout history and he was fully aware of the challenge of living up to the family name.

And where the family name was involved, he knew the perfect person who could offer advice.

LADY MARIA LOOKED UP WHEN AUBREY ENTERED AND frowned over the letter she was reading. She wore a mauve gown with long, black sleeves, and was sitting in a huge leather chair in front of a window in her sitting room. It looked over the potting shed and glasshouse, which Aubrey had once thought odd, as it wasn't the most picturesque vista Maidstone had to offer. His grandmother explained, however, once he asked her, that she liked watching people at work. She approved of busyness – and she also managed to overhear some interesting gossip at the same time.

'Aubrey.' Lady Maria's hair was bright silver, almost white, but her face was smooth and unlined. She held out her hand and Aubrey took it while she studied him. Although she was well into her eighties, Lady Maria had lost none of her acuity. She noticed everything.

'Grandmother.' Unbidden, he pecked her on the cheek and she studied him even more closely as he took a chair opposite her.

'You've heard the news?' she asked.

Aubrey didn't expend any effort trying to guess how Lady Maria knew. She hadn't been present when Lady Rose read Sir Darius's letter, because of her recent habit of taking most of her meals in her room. Her information network – which she preferred to call her 'many correspondents' – was extensive and very well credentialed. Aubrey was sure that Harris had no secrets from her, for instance, and her friends on the Continent included many prominent figures.

'I have. War has been declared.'

'Again.' Lady Maria sighed. 'It was inevitable, but it is never good. Which is exactly what your grandfather said last time, and the time before that.'

'He did?' Aubrey's grandfather was a military man through and through. He'd commanded regiments and been important in bringing about changes which had modernised the army. He was a cavalry man at heart. Aubrey had always thought of him as bluff and straightforward, a man who loved the headlong charge at the enemy.

'Whenever Albion embarked on a war, he wanted it over and done with as soon as possible. What he saw as efficiency, others saw as ruthlessness.'

'The Bloody Duke,' Aubrey murmured absently.

His grandmother stiffened. 'I do not like that name.'

Aubrey could have kicked himself. He knew that. Everyone in the family knew that, and they avoided using it at all times, despite it being in common parlance and even featuring in history books. Lady Maria's view of her husband, Aubrey's grandfather, did not include such unsavoury aspects as nicknames. 'Sorry, Grandmother. I was distracted.'

'By your plans.'

'Rather thrown up in the air by all this, wouldn't you say?'

'They are your plans, Aubrey, not mine. You should know their trajectory better than I would.'

True, Aubrey thought, *so why am I here?*

'So why are you here?' Lady Maria said, echoing his thoughts so neatly that Aubrey winced.

'I was looking for some advice.'

She raised an eyebrow. 'Really?' Then she held up a hand to forestall his protests. 'People come to me for advice on many things, Aubrey, but I cannot remember you doing so since you were very, very young.'

'And what was that about?' Aubrey asked, intrigued.

'Apparently your teddy's parents weren't letting him do what he wanted to do. You wanted to know the best way to help him organise them.'

Aubrey blushed. 'Ah, yes. I remember.'

'And your toy soldiers had a somewhat similar problem with their toy commanders.'

'I see. A long time ago, of course.'

'Of course. And here you are again. Regular as clockwork: once a decade. I'm fairly rushed off my feet, advising you.' She paused and gazed at him until he became uncomfortable. 'I cannot counsel you in much, Aubrey.'

'I'm sorry.' He went to stand. 'Perhaps I should go.'

'Sit,' she said and Aubrey's knees gave way before he was able to give them a conscious command. 'Let me tell you in what areas I may be of some help.' She gathered herself. 'As you know, I am the custodian of the Fitzwilliam family name and reputation, correct?'

'That's true.' True, if an understatement. Lady Maria had devoted much of her time to establishing the Fitzwilliam heritage. She was currently overseeing four separate books on the family's contribution to Albion history, one of them a biography of her husband — the third so far.

'And in wartime, Fitzwilliams have distinguished themselves. When duty calls, Fitzwilliams are first in line, never shirking their duty.'

'I suppose so.' Aubrey's grandfather wasn't the only Fitzwilliam military hero Aubrey was conscious of. His father had been decorated many times for his bravery in combat and his inspirational leadership had won the day on more than one occasion.

'And you're wondering what you should do.'

'I *always* wonder what I should do.' He ran a finger up and down the arm of the chair, absorbed in the way the velvet nap moved. 'I was hoping you might have some more information from Holmland.'

'When undecided, seek more information. Your grandfather would approve. Seek more information then act decisively.' She tilted her head at the letter in her hand. 'I have had some news from Professor Delroy, but that is all that I have had from the Continent in the last week.'

'I hope Holmland agents aren't intercepting your letters,' Aubrey said, mostly to cover his surprise. Lady Maria was in correspondence with the father of George's special friend?

'They always have in the past, but they haven't been so clumsy as to cut off delivery.'

'I beg your pardon?' Lady Maria was lobbing surprises at him like grenades.

'Don't look so shocked. Your intelligence people, the ones you're thick as thieves with, they intercept my letters. Intercept, copy out, then send them on so I'm not aware of their interference. That's what the Holmlanders have been doing for years, too, and a dozen other agencies as well.'

'Aren't you worried?'

'Aubrey, I gave up worrying years ago. A pointless expenditure of energy.'

'But people are reading your letters!'

'It won't do them any good at all. Anything my friends

tell me is couched in terms so allusive and roundabout that I'm the only one who can understand them.'

'The security agencies are very clever.'

'They may be clever, but they haven't lived eighty-four years of my life. That's what they'd need to unravel the hints and implications in my correspondence.'

'I wasn't aware that you knew Dr Delroy.'

'For many years. A fine mind. The Gallian government would be lost if it weren't for his economic guidance. Poor man.'

'Oh?'

'He is most unhappy, Aubrey. Family can do that, you know.'

Personal matters weren't the sort of thing one should be curious about, Aubrey knew, but it was difficult to ignore such a tantalising hint. Besides, he might be able to help George if he knew . . .

Don't, he warned himself. He could see a slippery slope just ahead. Ask about this matter, then he'd need to know a bit more and soon he'd be a prying, unhappy gossip, keen to know about the private lives of others, but never satisfied.

'Thank you, Grandmother,' he said with an effort. He stood. 'You've been most helpful.'

'I'm sure,' she said with a wry smile. 'Don't you want my advice after all?'

'Advice? Of course.'

'Here.' She gestured to him to bend over. When he did, she kissed him on the cheek. 'Do the right thing.'

HE LEFT HIS GRANDMOTHER, FEELING STRANGELY PLEASED BUT still confused. Her final words were cryptic, but Aubrey was accustomed to such things. Cryptic comments, enigmatic observations and puzzling responses were commonplace in Maidstone.

She'd given him more food for thought, but he already had a surfeit of that and could feel mental indigestion coming on.

He wandered along the gallery, toward his room. His hands were thrust into his pockets and his brow was thoroughly wrinkled as he pondered his future.

Magical scholarship was mightily attractive. He loved the thrill of discovery and implementation in this field, using his innate talent and building on it through rigorous investigation. He could make a name for himself, and it would be special. No Fitzwilliam had ever shown much magical talent until he came along, so if he could succeed, it would be unique. He could see a life of magical theory, perhaps a chair at one of the universities, or even the position of Sorcerer Royal.

Magic would always be part of his life. He couldn't deny it, but he understood now that the lure of something else was more insistent. Politics. He wanted to go into politics – but could he succeed in magic *and* politics? To make the matter knottier, he had the possibility of pursuing a magical career via Craddock's people, the Magic Department of the Security Intelligence Directorate.

He stopped in front of a portrait of his grandfather. His grandfather, the soldier, in full uniform, the defender of his country.

It may not be a choice between two options. A third

presented itself, bursting out of the pack and racing to the lead.

He turned on his heel to find George mounting the stairs, with the happy smile that came from having completed a sufficient meal. He looked up just as Aubrey seized his arm. 'George! I know what one person can do!'

'I'm glad. Can another one do it too?'

'Yes, of course. It's something that can make a difference, especially when lots of people do it at the same time.'

'Well, don't keep me in suspense, old man. What is it?'

'We can join up.'

Six

'*J* KNOW I'VE ASKED THIS QUESTION BEFORE, IN OTHER circumstances,' George said as they jumped off the bus the following day, 'but do you really think this is a good idea?'

They skirted a newsagent that was besieged by customers. Posters announcing the declaration of war were plastered all over the small wooden booth, and Aubrey had to struggle through to buy a paper. He read about his father's speech in Parliament and the overwhelming support it received – one hundred million pounds was immediately voted toward the war effort. Huge crowds had gathered at the Palace in the early morning, cheering whenever the King and Prince Albert appeared at the balcony.

In all this optimism, Aubrey was relieved to see that Quentin Hollows, the British Ambassador in Fisherberg, had been handed his passport by the Holmland authorities and was safely on his way home. Aubrey had appreciated the support of Hollows when they were in Fisherberg and had been concerned at his situation in the Holmland capital once war was official.

He was also sobered to read that the Holmland invasion of the Low Countries had begun with a bombardment by airship. This was a modern war, in all its horribleness.

Aubrey pointed at the long line of men stretched along the pavement in busy High Street. Shopkeepers stood outside their establishments and cheered the young men who were coming from all directions, alone and in small groups arm in arm. Whistles and shouts came from the line, attracting attention, and every newcomer was greeted with a roar of acclamation. 'All those chaps seem to think it's a good idea, George.'

George put his hands on his hips. 'For king and country?'

'And for our families. For Caroline and Sophie.'

'Those chaps don't know Caroline and Sophie.'

'They must have their own reasons, then.'

During the bus ride to Harnsby Road, a mile or two from Fielding Cross, Aubrey had told George about Lady Maria and her correspondence with Professor Delroy. George expressed puzzlement over the hint of family trouble, and Aubrey could see that a letter would soon be winging its way from George to Sophie.

They tacked themselves onto the back of the line, to cheers, and Aubrey soon realised that the overwhelming reason for joining up was that it had every prospect of being a smashing lark. At least, that was the prevailing opinion around them.

They shuffled along, slowly getting closer to the doorway of the recruiting office. The volunteers were all young men. Some were very down at heel, others well dressed, but they were all excited, chatting in animated fashion, sharing anecdotes fathers and uncles had told about the last war. Carefully chosen anecdotes, Aubrey was sure, by said fathers and uncles. Plenty of jolly japes among the troops, and not much fear or panic or actual bloodshed.

The standard expression was a broad grin, as if anticipating a football match, and Aubrey wondered where all the sober, thoughtful types were. He refused to think that they weren't volunteering because they knew better, but he couldn't help notice that none of the faces in the line looked to be older than their early twenties.

The chap directly in front of them turned around. He wore a cloth cap, but his suit was well cut and expensive. 'I say, those Holmlanders won't be expecting this, don't you know?'

'Won't be expecting what?' Aubrey asked carefully.

'All these fellows, ready to go.' A broad sweep of an arm. 'We'll show the Elektor what's what.'

Having met the Elektor, Aubrey had the impression that he'd be upset by developments rather than rubbing his hands together. 'I'm sure we will.'

This satisfied their interlocutor, who grinned and went back to discussing horses with someone in front of him.

'Do you think they know what they're getting themselves in for?' George muttered to Aubrey.

'I don't think anyone does,' Aubrey said. 'Not even the generals.'

Aubrey subsided into himself and listened to the chatter about coming to the aid of the plucky people of the Low

Countries. While Aubrey couldn't fault their generosity of spirit, he did wonder about his fellow recruits' lack of worldliness, especially when he heard, more than once, the confident sentiment that the war would be over by Christmas.

It took nearly two hours – and lunchtime was approaching, as George pointed out – when they finally mounted the stairs into the shop front of a building that was clearly inadequate to handle the numbers. The counter was manned by a stern-faced sergeant who was doing his best to keep up. Next to him, a monstrous pile of paper threatened to topple over and Aubrey hoped that the sergeant wouldn't be in the way when it did, thus becoming the first Albionite casualty of the war.

He laboured over forms and lists, and each recruit was then sent to one of the four rooms in the rear of the building. Medical examinations, Aubrey expected, as a stream of young men exited and then ambled out of the back door with papers clutched in hands.

Posters hung on the walls, extolling the virtues of the service. They explained why army life was a good life and that joining up was the only decent thing a man could do. They looked as if they'd been there for decades, to judge from the uniforms and the weapons, and Aubrey knew that deep in the Ministry of Defence a whole team would be working on newer, more appealing ways to coax the hesitant to join up – not that this was a problem at the moment.

On the bus, Aubrey and George had discussed their options. Aubrey had considered the navy, after being impressed with the *Invulnerable* and the *Electra*. George had suggested joining the new Flying Corps, which brought together various military airship and ornithopter squadrons and was rumoured to be toying with the new fixed-wing aircraft.

In the end they agreed on the army. Mostly it was because the nearest recruiting office for any branch of the military was the Caulfield Regiment, one of the great infantry names in Albion Army history. Aubrey had little preference, really, as long as they didn't join the Cliffstone Guards. Joining his father's old regiment was simply too much to contemplate.

'Name?'

Aubrey started. He'd reached the head of the line. 'Fitzwilliam.'

The sergeant grunted. 'First name?'

'Aubrey.'

Aubrey amused himself by looking at the top of the sergeant's head as he scratched away. His salt and pepper hair was cropped short. Aubrey ran his fingers through his own longish black hair and wondered if the shortness was compulsory or simply a preference on the sergeant's part – although he was sure the army didn't encourage personal preferences.

'Fitzwilliam, eh?' the sergeant said, looking up. He had a neat moustache. Aubrey readied himself for the customary confirmation that he was indeed the Prime Minister's son, but the sergeant just frowned and consulted a list. He grunted again and picked up the telephone. 'Over there.'

Aubrey looked in the direction the sergeant had jabbed his pencil. Against the side wall, a bench stood under a window. Three unhappy-looking young men sat on it. 'Over there?'

'That's what I said, sunshine,' the sergeant said.

Aubrey shrugged at George and crossed the room, his boot heels loud on the wooden floor, even over the hum of chatter in the small room. The three others on the bench looked sidelong at him when he sat down. Each of them had their hats in their laps – two bowlers and a straw boater. Aubrey was glad he hadn't worn one or else they would have ended up looking suspiciously like a milliner's showcase. He looked up and behind him to see a sign tacked to the wall over their heads: 'Group W'.

'How long were you in for?' his nearest benchmate asked. He was a sallow-looking chap with a nose so sharp it could be used to open letters.

'In for?' Aubrey frowned, then his eyes widened. 'In prison, you mean?'

The next chap along – small, pugnacious, face like a limpet – leaned forward. 'Nah. In the latest Royal Academy exhibition.'

It was with relief that Aubrey looked up to see George trudging toward him, bafflement on his face. 'They think we're criminals,' he said out of the corner of his mouth once George had sat down.

'And there's something wrong with that? I thought a few criminal skills would be very handy in the army.'

'Are you saying that soldiers are criminals at heart?'

'Soldiers? I thought the criminals would be made officers straight away.'

'Be that as it may, they've got the wrong end of the stick here. We don't belong.'

'Oh ho,' his pugnacious benchmate said. 'Something wrong with Group W? Too good for us, are we?'

'It's not that,' Aubrey said and paused when he realised

he was therefore arguing that he belonged with convicted felons. 'Never mind.'

'I think we should go and explain our situation,' George said.

'Good luck, mate,' Pugnacious said, crossing his arms. 'Tried to tell him that my stretch in the clink was a misunderstanding. He wouldn't listen.'

Aubrey looked at the queue. It still stretched out of the door and past the shop front window. 'I think he has enough on his hands.'

The telephone on the sergeant's counter rang. When he answered, his attention immediately went to the Group W bench and Aubrey swallowed. The sergeant had the look in his eye that Aubrey imagined some commanders had when choosing volunteers for suicide missions. 'You two.' He jabbed his pencil at Aubrey and George. 'On the end. Room 3. Look lively.'

'Both of us?'

'Now, sunshine.'

Aubrey swung open the door to Room 3 to see it was bare apart from two wooden chairs in the middle. George shrugged. 'The army.'

When the door closed behind him, it revealed that a tall officer had been standing behind it. He was tall and lanky and had so little chin Aubrey assumed all his pillows had no slips. 'Right. This way.' He pointed at a door that could only lead outside.

'No medical examination?' Aubrey asked.

'This way,' the officer repeated, as if he were talking to a small child. 'This way.'

Aubrey was strangely reluctant, but guessed that disobeying orders was a bad way to start an army career.

In the lane outside the door, a lorry was waiting, motor running. A private stood at rigid attention by the tail gate. 'In the back,' the officer ordered. 'Hurry now.'

As soon as they scrambled in, the tail gate was banged shut and the lorry lurched off down the lane. A screeching left-hand turn and they bullocked their way into High Street traffic.

'War does strange things to normal procedures,' George shouted over the growl of the engine. Canvas flapped over the rear of the lorry, making it easy enough to see their passage.

'The modern army,' Aubrey said. 'It's all new.'

The driver was in a hurry. He used the horn almost constantly as he threw the lorry from side to side through the busy traffic. 'We're headed toward the city,' Aubrey said as they passed Limner's Hall. 'Maybe they're inducting everyone at the Ministry of Defence.'

'All the criminals, anyway.'

Aubrey sat back at that. Maybe undesirables were shipped off somewhere. He could see them driving straight through the city and heading out into the country east of Trinovant, ending up in a camp that harboured all those unfit for military service, like a boil on the buttock of Albion.

The lorry rounded the Jubilee Pavilion and roared along Hollingsworth Street, past the greenery of Pitcher Park and then into Eastride. It was then that Aubrey threw out his first wild imaginings. When they slowed and turned into Pettypoint Street, he was certain he knew where they were going. Grainger Square loomed ahead. They turned right and drew up in front of a vast, gloomy building, the knocked-together conglomeration that began with a pair of three-storey townhouses and had grown over the years into a vast warren of secrecy.

'Good lord,' George said, staring up at the oppressive façade that loomed over them. 'Darnleigh House.'

The soldier who had loaded them appeared at the rear of the lorry. 'All out,' he said, but his eyes were on the building rather than on his passengers. 'This is your stop.'

COMMANDER CRADDOCK WATCHED AUBREY AND GEORGE from the other side of his desk. 'We can't waste talent, I'm afraid. While you would have been useful in the army, we think you could be more useful elsewhere.'

Aubrey's irritation at being impressed — at being co-opted against his will — was soothed somewhat by this, but he allowed it a bite. 'It *is* called volunteering, isn't it?'

'Unfortunate, that,' Craddock said. He had a small silver paperweight in one hand and he rolled it through his fingers. 'It's not necessarily the best thing for the country.'

'Ah. And you know better?'

George looked uncomfortable at this exchange. 'I say, Commander, I can appreciate why you've got Aubrey here. Top notch magic talent and all that. But it doesn't explain what I'm doing here.'

'I agree,' Commander Craddock said. 'It's remarkable, Doyle, how little magic you have in you. Many people have a touch, even if only an infinitesimal amount. But you seem entirely devoid of magic.'

George smiled. 'That comes as quite a relief, actually, since I've seen the sort of thing magic can do.'

'You do have other skills, but they are of more use elsewhere. Propaganda, perhaps, with your writing. Just follow Tate here and she'll take you to Lattimer Hall.'

Aubrey and George swivelled in their chairs. A black-clad Department operative was standing at the door. Long black skirt, black jacket, gloves. Aubrey hadn't heard her enter. 'Lattimer Hall?' George said. 'Special Services headquarters?'

'Just across the park,' Craddock said. 'We work closely together now that we're united under the auspices of the Directorate, especially when it comes to recruiting.'

'You have your recruiters on the lookout?' Aubrey said.

'We have a list of names,' Craddock said. He placed the paperweight in a small silver saucer. It shone like a beacon. 'If they appear at a recruiting office, we're notified. When you and Doyle showed up, I said we'd take you both in and then get Doyle here to Lattimer Hall.'

'And what if these names don't volunteer?' Aubrey asked.

'They will. Given time.'

'So you don't think the war will be over by Christmas?'

'Do you?'

Aubrey remembered the war build-up he'd seen in Holmland. 'I doubt it.'

'The war will be a horror beyond most people's imagining. When this becomes apparent, it will deter some from volunteering – but others will understand how important it is.' Commander Craddock pushed the paperweight with a finger. It rolled around the saucer. 'And if they don't, we'll have to convince them.'

Aubrey hoped that wasn't as ominous as it sounded. Craddock had made a professional career out of sounding threatening.

George stood. 'Be careful, old man,' he muttered to Aubrey, but he brightened when he joined Tate, the Department operative. She looked at him coolly from under her cap with large dark eyes. 'Are we in any hurry?' he asked her. 'I know a little café, just around the corner . . .'

His voice cut off as the door shut, and Aubrey smiled. George would never die wondering.

'Things have changed, Fitzwilliam,' Craddock continued. 'With the declaration of war, I need every talented individual I can get hold of. I want to bring you on board, not as an irregular, but as a full operative of the Department.'

'I see.'

'I'm organising a special intelligence and espionage corps. I want you to be part of it.'

Aubrey sat upright. 'But aren't I a little young?'

Craddock smiled grimly. 'You're eighteen. Many of our army volunteers are younger than that. Besides, how old do you have to be to die for your country?'

Aubrey swallowed. 'I'd prefer to live for my country. I could get more done that way.'

'So do I, but I want you to understand what's at stake here.' Craddock took a large, leather-bound ledger from a desk drawer. He opened it. 'I'm going to need all sorts of people, young and old. We'll be recruiting women, too, plenty of them.'

'For active service?'

'Of course. We're not going to overlook talent, wherever we find it. The regular army can shilly-shally on such matters, but we can't afford to. I anticipate that members of these special units will have to work in different places, blending in unobtrusively.'

'Overseas?'

'Wherever they're needed. Behind enemy lines, in Gallia, in the Goltans.'

When Aubrey had committed himself to being a soldier, he'd accepted that he would be sent to the front. He'd worked up his courage to encompass this eventuality, and now his expectations were thrown out of the window. This was not what he'd been planning – but it was altogether more exciting.

'I'm not sure what my parents will think.'

Craddock paused. 'That, of course, is up to you. But I had imagined that you'd sorted it out before going to enlist.'

Aubrey opened and closed his mouth. 'What do I have to do?' he said finally.

Craddock opened another desk drawer. 'Sign here, and here.'

With a feeling that his life would never be the same, he took the pen that Craddock offered and signed.

'Now the oath.'

As Aubrey repeated the words after Craddock, promising loyalty to the King and to Albion, he had a sudden sense of the vast machinery of war gobbling him up. He hoped that he was gristly enough and tough enough for it to spit him out in one piece.

'Now.' Craddock handed him a copy of his enlistment papers. 'Go home.'

'Go home?'

'Every recruit gets forty-eight hours before he has to

report.' Craddock smiled icily. 'Consider it your first task as part of the military. If you survive talking to your parents, we'll see you in two days.'

Seven

IT WASN'T COWARDICE THAT MADE HIM SLIP IN A SIDE entrance of Maidstone, Aubrey assured himself. It was simply good tactics. No sense in confronting his mother before his father came home. One scene was better than two.

He stood just inside the door, his back to the wall of the box room. Appetising aromas came from the kitchen, reminding Aubrey that he'd missed lunch. For a moment he considered nipping in and cadging something from cook, but he chose not to press his luck.

He knew the discussion with his parents would be a battle, but he hoped it wouldn't be a major battle. A skirmish would be preferable, with only light wounds on both sides, but he had his doubts. His parents had plans for him and he was sure that signing up for a clandestine espionage unit wasn't one of them.

Scholar Tan's advice came to him: *Make choices before your foe makes them for you.*

He ticked off the usual decisions facing a battle commander. Site? Well, no choice there. He supposed he could try to catch both his parents on neutral ground, but with the uproar over the declaration of war, he'd be lucky to see his father at all. Timing? Again, that was out of his hands. When his father managed to get home, that would have to do. Weather? Troop numbers? Logistical supply chain? Not terribly relevant. But there was one thing he could look for, one thing that any commander would be grateful for.

Allies.

HE STOOD OUTSIDE LADY MARIA'S DOOR AND ADJUSTED his jacket and tie. He pushed his hair back and wished that he'd already had a service haircut; his grandmother would have liked it.

He lifted each foot in turn, rubbing his boots on the back of his trousers, hoping that this would make them shiny enough for her. Finally, he knocked on the door, waited for her invitation, and entered.

Lady Maria looked up, and closed the notebook she'd been writing in. 'Ah, Aubrey. I thought I'd be seeing you again.'

'Grandmother.' He kissed her on the proffered cheek, then busied himself with drawing up a chair. 'I need to have a word with you. Another word.'

Lady Maria glanced at the letter in her lap. Very deliberately, she folded it and slipped it into the open drawer of the table by her side. 'Go ahead.'

'I have something to tell Mother and Father, and I thought I'd talk to you first.'

'And what is this weighty matter that needs such groundwork?'

'I've joined up.'

'Good. When?'

Aubrey hesitated. He'd been expecting surprise. Instead, his grandmother had simply taken his bombshell for granted. 'This morning. Just after I saw you.'

'Which regiment?'

'Ah. That's a little tricky.'

'Don't tell me you joined the navy. Ghastly folk, sailors.'

'No, not the navy. A special section.'

'Military intelligence, then,' Lady Maria said dismissively. 'We can't have that.'

'I beg your pardon?'

'Secret service will do you no good in the long run because it stays secret. The army is the place for you. After you lead your troops successfully and win medals, your future will be assured.'

Aubrey glanced out of the window. Two of the gardeners were trundling out a lawn roller. He'd once heard someone ask Lady Maria how to get a lawn as good as the one at Maidstone. She'd sniffed and explained that it was straightforward: simply sow grass seed, then cut and roll for three hundred years.

'I hadn't thought of it like that,' he said, which was true.

'Of course not. Now, let me talk to some friends and I'm sure I can make arrangements. The Cliffstone Guards, of course. I'm sure they will be needing some good junior officers.'

Aubrey rubbed his forehead. So he had an ally in the joining up business, but it was like seeing your ally appear on your left flank then, without warning, go galloping off without looking at the battle plan at all. He was sure she could arrange a commission. Her network of friends, acquaintances and people who simply owed her favours had been built up over decades.

It wasn't what he wanted.

'Grandmother, I think I might need to explain myself a little better.'

It took some time, and a welcome pot of tea, before Aubrey reached a level of understanding with his grand-mother. At first she was insistent, taking her customary stance of knowing best, but Aubrey didn't give up. He stood firm. He'd never been successful with his grandmother before, and it was like moving a monolith an inch at a time, but he wondered if it wasn't a sign of his growing up that he didn't back down.

Finally, Lady Maria fixed him with a look that Aubrey, with some hesitation, decided held a measure of respect. 'I've never seen you like this, Aubrey.'

'I don't think I've ever been like this.' Aubrey was both exhausted and proud of himself. Lady Maria was like a force of nature as far as getting her own way was concerned, and yet he'd stood his ground.

'Hmm. I'd tell you that you're reminding me of your father at that age, but I'm sure you don't want to hear that sort of thing.'

Aubrey rubbed his forehead. 'How did you feel when he joined up, Grandmother?'

'It was altogether different. He went into the family regiment. The Guards.'

'I understand that. But weren't you afraid?'

'Of course. But he was doing a good thing.'

'And so will I.'

Lady Maria was silent for a time. 'How can I help you?'

Aubrey sat back with relief. 'I don't want you to argue my case for me.'

'Of course not. That would be rather contradictory, since you're making a point about your self-determination.' Lady Maria was nothing if not shrewd.

'You've done what you can, Grandmother. Just talking to you has helped.'

'A rehearsal, you mean.' She tapped a finger on the arm of her chair.

'If you're able, a word or two after I've spoken with them may be useful. They may need someone to talk to.'

'I'm sure I can contrive a chat with them,' Lady Maria said. 'And I'm sure the times when your father took it into his head to go his own way will come up.'

Aubrey's ears pricked up. 'Such as?'

'Another time, dear.' She paused. 'Is that him now?'

Aubrey swivelled. A motorcar had just drawn up out the front of Maidstone. For someone so old, his grandmother had very fine hearing. He jumped to his feet and kissed his grandmother on the cheek. 'Thank you.'

'I'm pleased to help. An ally in time of need is worth more than gold.'

Aubrey was halfway down the stairs before he realised, with some astonishment, that his grandmother had been quoting the Scholar Tan to him.

I live with a family of first-rate surprisers.

He found his parents in Lady Rose's drawing room, amid the ostrich feathers and papyrus tapestries. They were standing close to each other, holding both hands and talking in low voices.

'Aubrey, good, I wanted to talk to you, too.' His father's face was drawn and the skin under his eyes was dull. He had monumental energy, but Aubrey could see that the times were taxing even him. 'You've heard the news, I take it? Sit, sit. No need to stand around.'

Aubrey took an oriental lacquered chair he hadn't seen before. It had a red velvet cushion. 'War? It's hard not to have heard.'

His mother and father took a small sofa directly opposite him. 'Not that,' his father said. 'I've just come from the palace. His Majesty has taken a turn for the worse. After the King appeared to the crowd at the palace, he collapsed. He's been confined to bed again.'

'He has taken the news very poorly,' Lady Rose said. 'He was convinced that his cousin would never permit Holmland's going to war.'

'How's Bertie holding up?' Aubrey asked.

'Stout fellow, Bertie,' his father said. 'He's taken on even more of the royal duties.'

Aubrey was concerned for his friend. At a time like this, the nation was lucky to have Prince Albert, but it would be difficult to rally the nation and to tend to a dying father at the same time. He promised himself he'd visit Bertie when he could – but that reminded him that his immediate future was out of his hands.

He swallowed, circling around the delicate matter at hand. 'And how is the mobilisation going?'

'The fleet has already put to sea,' his father said. 'Every regiment is doing its best to ready itself. I've been promised that by the end of the week, we'll be moving, but we'll need to bring up troops from the colonies as well.' Sir Darius touched his moustache. 'We're going to send an expeditionary force almost immediately – four infantry divisions and one cavalry.'

'To the Low Countries?'

'To north Gallia,' Sir Darius said bleakly. 'By the time we're mobilised, it's thought that the Holmlanders will have sliced through the Low Countries.'

The thought chilled Aubrey. The horror had begun. Towns, villages, farmhouses would already be trampled by the Holmland advance.

'You went out today, Aubrey,' Lady Rose said evenly.

'Hmm,' Sir Darius said. 'I thought I'd asked that you stay here at Maidstone for the time being.'

This is it. He took a deep breath. 'That's what I wanted to talk to you about. I know your time is valuable, Father, but it's important.'

Sir Darius studied him, solemnly. 'You've enlisted.'

Over the gasp of his mother, Aubrey felt as if he were a bowler who had just begun his run up and was tripped by an unseen foe. 'You knew?' Then his earlier irritation returned. Was nothing he did his own? 'How many of your people are watching me? It didn't take long for them to report.'

Lady Rose took her husband's hand. Her knuckles were white. He glanced at her before answering. 'I didn't know. I simply asked myself what I would have done in your place.'

'But you stuck me here to stop my enlisting!'

Sir Darius raised an eyebrow. 'Did I? I thought the message was about stopping you from doing something foolish.'

We're speaking the same language, Aubrey thought, his head spinning, *but I'm not sure I understand at all.* 'Like joining up?'

Sir Darius sighed. 'I knew that we'd have little chance of talking you out of joining up. So I thought what would be best is if George was alongside when you did. I hope he was.'

'Oh.' Aubrey sat back in the chair. The hard wooden back pressed into his spine, but he hardly noticed. 'You *wanted* me to enlist?'

'Well, *I'm* not going to say that,' Lady Rose said. Her cheeks were pale, but her voice was calm. 'I'd prefer to have you safe at home instead of bounding off in search of glory. But if you were happy with remaining behind, you must have undergone a radical personality change.'

Aubrey grimaced. 'So you wanted George and me to enlist together?'

'It seemed the best outcome,' Sir Darius said.

'But we haven't. I mean, I've enlisted. And so has George. I think. The last I saw of him he was going to lunch with a very pretty Department operative.'

'Aubrey,' his mother said. 'You're starting to babble. Slow down. Tell us everything.'

He did.

'I see,' his father said when he'd finished. 'The Magic Department. And you say George has been snapped up by the Special Services. I can't say I'm surprised by either outcome.' He gave a hoarse laugh, one with little actual amusement in it. 'I wonder if they realise what's ahead for them.'

'What? The Department?'

'No. The Holmlanders.'

Eight

FOLLOWING THE INSTRUCTIONS ON HIS ENLISTMENT papers – and still shaking his head at how his parents continued to confound his expectations – Aubrey presented himself back at Darnleigh House two days later.

It's starting to feel like home, he thought as he glanced up at the glowering building. He was quite the veteran, being at the place so much lately. Standing on the pavement in a milling crowd, he probably was – at least, compared to those around him.

It was a mixed bunch, most of them holding papers similar to Aubrey's. Drawing attention to themselves was the only characteristic they seemed to share, which made Aubrey wonder about their future in clandestine intelligence. Most of them appeared lost or befuddled, and not a few of them showed every sign of being daunted by the reputation of the building they were standing outside.

Before he entered, Aubrey allowed himself a wistful moment. Events had conspired against him and his mission to declare himself to Caroline. He was going to have to postpone it, much as he hated to. Although Caroline had no idea of his mission, he felt as if he were letting her down, which was something he'd vowed never to do.

Inside, Aubrey had to wait in line with more bewildered recruits. The entrance hall of Darnleigh House had the remains of its Gothic origins, with a soaring vaulted ceiling and narrow windows high in the pillared walls. It tended to automatically create a hush, once foot was set inside, especially given the rumours that were whispered about goings-on in the bowels of the edifice.

Aubrey took note of how varied his fellows were, even more than the volunteers at the recruiting centre. For a start, nearly a third of them were female, young and old. The males ranged in age, too. Quite a few looked to be Aubrey's age, but others were mature adults, and some were middle-aged and even older. Aubrey saw one grey-bearded man hobbling toward the front desk with the assistance of a stick.

All Aubrey could assume was that Commander Craddock was untroubled by age or sex. Talent was his sole criterion. Although exactly what talents were of utility to the Department waited to be seen.

Doing his best to appear confident and assured, Aubrey presented his papers. They were stamped, filed, his name was crossed off a list, and he was given a sheaf of brand new forms and a slip of buff paper with instructions to go to Room 14a.

Aubrey hesitated, then turned back to the corporal who had processed him, but she was already working through the details of the next recruit. Aubrey nearly interrupted her but at the last moment he had second thoughts. He treated the situation as a test. What good would he be as a Department operative if he couldn't find a room in the headquarters building?

He could use logic, or gather information before setting off, or he could try to elicit instructions from people who belonged, but instead he chose the time-honoured method of wandering around and keeping an eye on people who gave the impression of knowing where they were going – or those who were looking for the same thing he was.

As he wandered, he was reminded that he was in a place that was obsessed with security. Many doors bore admonitions about authorised personnel only, or security clearance required, or the blunter – and unmistakeable – 'Keep Out'.

He had no desire to test how well policed these signs were and he gave them a wide berth.

Aubrey found Room 14a on the first floor. Along with Room 14b, Room 14c and Room 14d, they were in Corridor 14 and Aubrey congratulated himself on concluding the obvious once he blundered into the right part of the building.

He knocked and entered. A depressingly cheery man in a white coat looked up from his desk. 'Forms on the desk, buff slip in the basket, then take off your clothes.'

Aubrey swallowed. He looked around at the screen, the scales and the patient table. His recruitment may be somewhat unconventional, but it looked as if he wasn't going avoid the indignity of the medical examination.

After a chilly time of being thumped, prodded, jabbed and peered at, Aubrey was given a green slip to add to his sheaf of papers and directed to the Quartermaster's section. The bored operative eyed Aubrey for something rather less than a split second, then he glanced at a list on the counter before stalking off and returning with a bundle of black clothing, a pair of boots, and a slip of blue paper. He pushed all of this on Aubrey. He was about to ask where he could change when the operative jerked his head to the curtained booths on the left.

The uniform – trousers, long-sleeved shirt, pullover and beret – was comfortable and fitted surprisingly well, apart from the beret, which was a little tight. Aubrey had difficulty believing that the grizzly man had picked his measurements so well and so quickly, but shrugged it off as a benefit of experience. He pulled on the black boots and they too fitted perfectly – even though the operative had no chance of seeing Aubrey's feet.

Aubrey stood back and looked at himself in the mirror. This wasn't the uniform he'd been accustomed to seeing on Craddock's operatives, so he assumed it was the equivalent of a regular soldier's barrack dress, to be worn while stationed at headquarters. Regardless, he thought the simple black was dashing. Understated but stylish was his estimation. He had a fleeting pang wishing Caroline could see him, and then he was struck by the guilt he'd managed to put to one side.

He hadn't let Caroline know that George and he were going to enlist, and he hadn't communicated with her in the forty-eight-hour home period either.

His motives for this were mixed, and he was still trying to sort them out for himself. To begin with, he wasn't sure of her reaction, and he'd learned enough not to presume where Caroline was concerned. She might be cool about the decision, or outraged, or simply angry about it. On the other hand, she might be supportive. Not knowing, Aubrey had taken the coward's route and avoided telling her at all.

Which is only going to make it worse when she finds out, he thought. He considered sending her a letter, but glumly knew that his mother would let her know before a letter could possibly reach her.

So much for my mission.

Aubrey rolled his civilian clothes into a bundle and fastened his belt around them to keep them together. When he exited, an eager-faced recruit was at the counter, drumming his fingers while waiting for his turn. Aubrey took a moment to examine the place with his magical senses.

He grinned. Right where the recruit was standing, a spell had been embedded in the floor. A little examination showed that it was a passive spell that measured and weighed a body in the vicinity, a neat and minor application of the Law of Dimensionality. The operative must have some connection on his side of the counter that directed him to the correct uniform components for each recruit. Aubrey's tight beret must have been a hiccup in the spell, which was only to be expected with such a complex application.

The slip of blue paper directed Aubrey next door to a large room that was bright with electric light. He winced when he saw the walls lined with mirrors and the half-dozen barber chairs on each side. The rotund fellow in a white coat nearest the entrance pounced. 'A customer! At last!'

His eleven colleagues watched enviously as Aubrey was guided to the nearest chair. 'Now, what would you like?' the barber cheerily said as he tied a smock around Aubrey's neck. The white linen covered him entirely. 'Something along the lines of the latest from Lutetia? Or were after the Venezian look?'

'Venezian?'

The barber barked a laugh. 'Only joking, youngster. Just one style here, so hold still.'

A few minutes of buzzing, clipping and slashing later, Aubrey grimaced at the image in the mirror. Over his shoulder, the barber was grinning. 'Done, and it's not going to grow back while you're sitting there. Next!'

The barber whipped the sheet away. Aubrey was given a slip of yellow paper and pointed toward the door. Automatically, his hand went to his head to feel the closely shorn sides. On top, it was a little longer, but nothing like the luxurious crop he'd become used to. He had a fleeting pang, but he had more important things to worry about. The slip in his hand, for instance.

On his way to the main hall Aubrey found that his beret now fitted perfectly; his admiration of the measurement magic rose.

Everyone was going in the same direction. Most of the recruits were rubbing their arms and – to judge from their expressions – giving every impression that the main purpose of a medical examination was to make one feel quite unwell.

The main hall was enough like a lecture theatre to make Aubrey feel quite nostalgic. At the front was a dais, a long desk or bench, and a pair of lecterns. On the wall behind the dais was a large blackboard, which looked freshly cleaned.

Rows of hard, wooden chairs faced the stage. Aubrey found a spare seat three rows from the front, in between a middle-aged man who looked as if he'd just walked out of his position managing a bank, and a woman a few years older than Aubrey, who glanced at him through her glasses before clutching the bag on her lap as if he'd made a move to steal it. She was trembling and Aubrey had a great deal of sympathy. He'd been in Darnleigh House before. These new recruits must be uneasy, given the reputation of the Department and its chief.

Within a few minutes, the doors at the rear were closed. Aubrey twisted and looked to see that the hall was only a third filled and he nodded, thoughtfully. *A hundred*, he thought, *maybe a hundred and twenty. Not many, but not bad for a couple of days' recruiting.*

Commander Craddock entered. As he strode to a lectern, he swept his gaze over the new recruits. From his face, Aubrey couldn't tell if Craddock were impressed, dismayed or bored with what he saw.

Without any preamble, he began. 'Most of you in this room did not volunteer for the Magic Department. Most of you went to enlist, in good faith, in more regular branches of the service. For that, I applaud you. For being diverted, I apologise. Each of our recruitment centres was given a list of names to look for, but they were also equipped with a device which detected incipient talents, those that will better serve Albion here rather than slogging in trenches or stoking engines in a battleship.'

Aubrey straightened. *That* explained why so many of them were looking stunned. They hadn't known that they had magical ability!

Magical ability wasn't common, any more than a talent for higher mathematics or concert-level music. Hard work and training could make the most of natural ability, but little could be achieved if a person was devoid of it in the first place. Some schools tested for magical ability, but many people never had the chance to find out if they possessed the raw skill. Aubrey often compared it to someone who lived all his life in the desert. He may potentially be the world's best swimmer, but would never, ever know it.

To hear that the Department had a device to detect incipient magical ability, though, that was news indeed. He added it to his list of things to be investigated.

Craddock cleared his throat and Aubrey was jolted from his cogitation to find the commander looking straight at him. 'Others, particularly the ladies here,' Craddock continued, 'were sought out for known talents and skills. I'm afraid the already depleted magical departments of the universities will be under-staffed for some time. I won't apologise for that, for this is a time of crisis. Albion needs you.'

Aubrey rubbed his chin. The already depleted magical departments of the universities? He'd heard rumours that various positions in magical faculties were currently unfilled, with a number of prominent researchers taking sabbaticals while others had simply disappeared. Dark mutterings in the cloisters of Greythorn suggested numerous possibilities, each more outlandish than the last.

'All of you need one thing,' Craddock said after a pause. 'Training. For the next month you will live here at Darnleigh House. All of you will receive physical training. In addition, each of you will receive specialised training according to your skills. Any questions?'

One tall youngster put up his hand and Aubrey had to admire his pluck. 'When will we see service, sir?' he asked in a voice that didn't quaver too much.

Craddock looked down for a moment. When he looked up, he said, 'Before you know it.'

Aubrey was one of the few close enough to hear what Craddock added under his breath. 'And before you're ready, most likely.'

Nine

ONE MONTH. FOUR WEEKS. THIRTY DAYS. SEVEN hundred and twenty hours. Lying on his bunk in the dormitory, Aubrey thought he had an aching muscle or a bruise for every one of those hours.

He had been looking forward to the training because he thought it could give him another chance to investigate the copy of the Rashid Stone. Or perhaps he'd have an opportunity to work with magical suppression, or to inspect the golem-making machine he'd captured and sent back from Holmland.

Instead, with the other Department recruits, he became accustomed to being ferried most days via motorbus to a Directorate facility an hour away. On the edge of the city to the east, near where the Harwell River came down through the hills, in essence, it was a combination parade ground, firing range and hell on earth.

Soon, Aubrey felt as if he'd been sent back to his

cadet training at Stonelea School – or perhaps the school's notorious Physical Education classes. Except that instead of mildly sadistic masters propelling him over vaulting horses, he had instructors made of some bullet-proof material whose main delight, in all weather, was shouting.

So much shouting. Shouting while he ran over broken ground. Shouting while he scrambled under barbed wire. Shouting while he swung from ropes. Shouting while he crawled through mud. Shouting while he assembled and disassembled a variety of firearms and then used them to blast away at targets that were eye-strainingly far-off and – sometimes – startlingly close.

Hand-to-hand combat produced the most bruises and, unsurprisingly, as he was flung through the air again by another shouting instructor, it reminded him of Caroline. Her skills in unarmed combat came from early instruction with a variety of oriental masters, friends of her father. When Aubrey picked himself up from the mats, time after time, he knew that a handful of sessions wasn't going to bring him up to Caroline's standard, but he was willing to do his best. He had a new appreciation for her, as if he needed any extra grounds for such a thing.

The shouting, thankfully, disappeared during explosives training. The instructors here were just as intense – older men, often with a disturbing number of missing fingers – and somehow managed to make their whispers just as effective as the bellowing of the others.

He was thankful that his explosives training was brief, a mere introduction to the discipline, and was sorry for the recruits who showed aptitude for this sort of work.

They were whisked off for more intensive training, the prospect of which made Aubrey shudder.

Another relatively quiet session came from a mild-faced, older man who was the instructor in disguises. When he explained how to change appearances subtly and with a minimum of artifice, Aubrey was embarrassed at his own earlier efforts. With a deft application of tiny strokes around the eyes and some tightening wax inside the cheeks, an effect was created that would have taken Aubrey hours and laborious amounts of makeup. In hindsight, his Tommy Sparks alter-ego was embarrassingly crude.

Aubrey excelled in the communications training. He picked up the telegraphic code easily, tapping away with alacrity, never confusing T and P. His earlier experimenting with ciphers held him in good stead. While other recruits around him spent much time on head-scratching, he knew the theory and practice of one-time pads and was able to encipher and decipher at a rate that impressed the instructors. They whisked him off for advanced training and introduced him to the encoding machine, a recent advance that sped up the process and, if intercepted, made messages even harder to crack. After some familiarisation, Aubrey was able to punch keys and substitute the geared wheels with relentless speed.

Magical training was organised with clinical efficiency. Grim-faced operatives circulated through rooms full of recruits sitting at desks, trying to perform a basic light spell given to them on slips of light green paper. When Aubrey conjured up a shining globe within seconds, one that rotated slowly on its axis thanks to a minor embellishment he'd added, he was herded into a smaller room, with others who had passed through this coarse sieve. A handful were astonished, never having suspected that they had magical talent, and Aubrey wondered where they'd end up. What part of a military service entering a war needed untrained magic users? Could the Department spare the personnel to train them?

One frail youth winced throughout the spell-casting efforts. Even though he stumbled through them, he was treated with some respect by the instructors, and after he'd fumbled a straightforward, if lengthy, Patterning spell, he was taken aside and then escorted elsewhere.

Aubrey wasn't consciously eavesdropping. He simply found the spell undemanding and when the instructors were speaking softly with the frail youth, he couldn't help overhearing one fascinating phrase: remote sensing.

Aubrey knew that the Department had a long-established cohort of remote sensers, sensitive magicians whose job was to monitor for magical disturbances. The best could detect major magic being undertaken thousands of miles away.

The remote sensing team operated constantly, day and night, and it was always looking to build its numbers of operatives.

It looked as if it now had one more to add to its ranks.

After a day of successfully transforming, heating, inverting, manipulating, translating, concealing and amplifying, Aubrey had begun to get bored. The grim-faced operatives weren't chatty and they wouldn't let him read the notes they were taking. They refused to be impressed by Aubrey's enhancements, and he wondered if showing initiative in this area was a good thing or a bad thing . . .

The handful of other talented recruits had dwindled

as the day went on, winnowed out by the increasingly difficult spells set for them. Having reached a level of competence, they were directed to intensive training in their speciality.

Aubrey caught up with all of them over the subsequent few days, though, for at the end of the first day of magical training – Aubrey having performed all tasks with ease – the grim faces consulted, threw their hands up in the air, and directed Aubrey to participate in each of the specialised intensive magical training sessions.

Most were straightforward and almost painfully practical, at least for people who may have to perform magic in battle situations – covert lighting, sound deadening, distraction techniques, spells both offensive and defensive. A few were wrinkles on techniques Aubrey knew well, variations interesting enough to fascinate him and leave him disappointed when he had to move on to the next. Some were completely new applications, profoundly practical again, like the panoply of spells useful for securing a perimeter from intrusion, both physical and magical. Aubrey was intrigued and wanted to spend more time investigating what he suspected was a connection between these spells and the magical neutralising spells he'd been working with.

These sessions were a relief in many ways. A relief from the mud, a relief from the burning pain of tired muscles, but most of all, a relief from the shouting.

The best set of lungs belonged to Sergeant Wallace, the non-commissioned officer in charge of Aubrey's platoon of twenty recruits. Sergeant Wallace was the NCO who roused them in the morning – Aubrey only had to have his bed tipped over once before he understood that now meant *now* – and who chivvied them about from parade ground to classroom to mess hall. Aubrey thought that the sergeant must have some sort of magically enhanced voice box, with the amount of roaring he did, only relaxing when he handed over to someone who took the platoon on specialised instruction, accompanied by more shouting.

Aubrey had never thought it possible to be shouted to sleep, but when Sergeant Wallace's nightly 'Lights off in one, two, three, NOW!' rang from the rafters, he was out like a light.

Right now, however, he had about two seconds to drag himself out of bed before Sergeant Wallace exercised his bed-tipping muscles.

Once the platoon was de-bedded and dressed, they stood in front of their bunks, quivering.

'Right!' Sergeant Wallace bellowed in a conversational manner. 'Although you are far from ready for anything apart from patrolling lonely stretches of coastline, you are apparently going to be let loose on the enemy. God help them. And us.' Hands clasped behind his back, he shook his head in pity. 'You have endured four weeks unlike any you've ever had before, and I want you to remember one thing: don't disgrace yourself. That's all. Don't disgrace yourself. Now, mess hall in ten minutes. Move it!'

In the clatter and bustle of the mess hall, Aubrey found a corner. While he stoked himself with porridge, he considered Sergeant Wallace's announcement.

His training had been hard, no doubt about that. Underneath the aches and pains, his muscles were hardening and he was sure that if he kept up a modicum of exercise he'd enjoy the fitness and it would do him good in the long run.

The other seats at the table began to fill. Aubrey exchanged nods and greetings, but everyone appeared to share the same sombre, thoughtful mood. The end of training meant, as Sergeant Wallace put it, being let loose. And being let loose in a war situation was enough to give anyone pause over their porridge.

Craddock's earlier mentioning of special units had been vague and imprecise. Working behind enemy lines? What exactly did that mean? After the training, Aubrey was starting to have some idea. With the emphasis on such dangerous skills as explosives and firearms, he was heading into dangerous territory.

Aubrey was prepared to admit that he favoured not dying over dying. But he also hoped that he was brave enough not to shy away from danger when he was needed to do the right thing. He couldn't shirk. He would put himself in harm's way, if it meant helping bring the war to a speedy end.

Being the sort of person he was, he reminded himself to minimise risks wherever he could. *Be cautious*, he told himself, *think things through, look for the unexpected, be prepared, stay alert*.

He wished George and Caroline were here. Together, they covered all of those things. Apart, he felt lessened – and more exposed.

He poked at his porridge and was wistful. He missed his friends. He was sure George would be all right, as he had the happy knack of falling on his feet in most circumstances. He was probably neatly ensconced in a propaganda unit, churning out story after story about the cheerful recruits bravely preparing to defend king and country.

And Caroline? Here Aubrey's wistfulness was mixed

with guilt. He would have to do something about his interrupted mission. Sooner, rather than later.

A tray plonked on the table, right opposite Aubrey. Woodberry, familiar to Aubrey from the irregulars tour, looked surprisingly cheerful and well rested. 'Morning, Fitzwilliam. Exciting, isn't it?'

Aubrey pushed his porridge bowl aside. 'That's one way of putting it. "Exhausting" is another, and probably more accurate. Then there's "painful", which is also remarkably apposite.'

Woodberry was a scrambled eggs man. He showered them with salt before plunging in. 'Painful for some. The most painful thing for me was this nasty paper cut.' He held up his forefinger, wrapped in a neat, white bandage.

'Mind it doesn't get infected,' Aubrey said. 'I knew a professor who lost an arm because of an infected paper cut.'

Woodberry's eyes widened. 'Really?'

'Certainly.' Aubrey enjoyed the harmless ragging, but Woodberry's comments only emphasised to him that Craddock had different things in mind for different people. Woodberry was bound for a job in Darnleigh House, Aubrey was sure. Not a field operative, not some-one for the special units. One session on the firing range was enough to convince Aubrey of that. Woodberry's skills were firmly in areas other than pointing and shooting dangerous things like rifles. While he didn't actually hit anyone, it was only due to the instructor's quick reactions in dropping to the ground and to the fortuitous log that happened to be between the instructor and Woodberry's wild round.

Woodberry frowned, glanced at his finger, then pointed

his fork at Aubrey. 'Have you heard? They're bombing Trinovant.'

Aubrey started guiltily. Training had been so intense that he'd felt cut off, insulated from the world, and most particularly the war. Woodberry had been training in homeland liaison and was much more aware of what was going on. 'Already. Much damage?'

'Not so far. Plenty of panic, though. When those airships come over, it's a riot in the streets.'

'Which is probably as useful as actual damage.' Aubrey drummed his fingers on the table and tried to divide his anxious thoughts between worrying about Caroline, George, his parents and everyone else he knew. Bombs falling on Albion? This was war made real. He hoped this would shock the doubters, those who thought that war was either nonsense or a jolly lark.

After breakfast, the recruits were directed – via concerted shouting – to the main hall for the first time since their initial meeting. Aubrey was uneasy, the more so when the hall began to fill with unfamiliar faces, people in uniforms other than the discreet black of the Department.

These strangers looked more like traditional army troopers in their khaki dress and, unlike the novice Department operatives, they all looked brimming with fitness and vigour. None of them was older than thirty, apart from their sergeants, who shared the same shouting prowess as the Magic Department instructors. Aubrey imagined them all catching up at a convention, sharing shouting techniques, and hoped that it was held well away from built-up areas.

Curious and straight-backed, the army recruits filed

into the hall, taking up the seats on the right-hand side of the auditorium.

When George marched through the door, Aubrey nearly fell off his seat. *Special Services!* he thought. *They must be Special Services recruits!*

It was only with a huge effort that he prevented himself from leaping to his feet and hallooing to his friend, but something told him that this may be frowned upon, bad for discipline or somesuch. Instead, he contented himself with trying to catch George's eye – a futile effort, given that George was chatting with a tall blonde girl in the seat next to him.

Aubrey was working through the implications of the appearance of Special Services recruits when something else happened and he did, indeed, fall off his seat.

Amid laughing and good-natured chaffing from those around – and some bored shouting from the nearest sergeant – Aubrey picked himself up and regained his seat, marvelling at how total surprise could make one temporarily boneless, unable to undertake such a simple action as sitting.

He hardly heard the chaffing and the shouting, for he was in a world where his focus had narrowed so all he could see, all he knew, was that toward the end of the file of newcomers was Caroline Hepworth.

Caroline! Suddenly, everything changed. Of course, he would have to explain why he hadn't informed her of their enlisting, but she was here! He would be abject, he would be apologetic and, in the end, he would try to make her laugh.

It was like one of those moments when clouds open and beams of light emerge, crepuscular rays, bright and glorious and changing the entire landscape. Aubrey was allowed this chance to make good.

He could reactivate his mission.

Caroline had been in much the same position as he had been, on irregular detachment, except she was with the Special Services under Commander Tallis. Since the two divisions were now part of the Security Intelligence Directorate, that would explain the khaki-clad newcomers. Magic Department operatives and Special Services operatives officially working together. This was just the sort of thing his father had been planning when he reorganised the security services.

Aubrey crossed his arms on his chest with satisfaction at his own surmising. He was bursting with eagerness. He wanted to get to Caroline and George. He wanted to explain and catch up and share and simply be with them. He craned his neck and he thought he spied her, sitting near the front of the hall, oblivious to his presence.

Almost bouncing on his seat, he realised he'd have to wait. Commander Tallis entered after the last of his people. Aubrey was pleased to see that the stocky man was still glowering and fuming, for it meant all was right with the world. The head of the Special Services went through life as if everything was conspiring to irritate him. If nothing was going right, he scowled. If everything was going right, he smouldered. If some things were going right and others were a complete cock-up, he raged in a state of furious contentment.

Despite this, Tallis was a dedicated and fierce leader. His Special Services operatives were mostly drawn from the regular forces and provided vital, non-magical agents whose bravery and adaptability was renowned.

George and Caroline. Aubrey couldn't help grinning, but when he realised he was drumming his feet on the floor like an excited child, he managed to rein in his pleasure before someone noticed and the shouting started again.

Craddock and Tallis stood together at the front of the hall while everyone settled. Tall and lean versus short and solid. Detached versus fuming. Thoughtful versus abrupt. Opposites in many ways, apart from their dedication to protecting Albion.

Aubrey was interested to see who would speak first, and was amused to see that their longstanding rivalry was expressing itself in painful politeness. Craddock motioned Tallis to the lectern, only to have the Special Services chief decline with a gesture and insist that Craddock begin. With a raised hand, Craddock signed that he was happy to have Tallis speak first, especially since he was the host of this gathering in the Magic Department headquarters. Tallis worked his jaw at this, and stepped forward.

The low buzz of curiosity cut off as if guillotined. Tallis glared for a moment, then began. 'We are at war,' he said. A little unnecessarily, Aubrey thought, but Tallis was rather blunter than the circuitous Craddock. 'While you've been training, Holmland has been moving, pressing into the Goltans and massing for a push into Gallia. Its ally, the Central European Empire, has been driving toward opening a front with Muscovia. Bombs have fallen on Albion. People have died.'

If Tallis had been trying to crush any high spirits, Aubrey decided, he was doing a good job.

Tallis continued once the shocked murmur had subsided. 'The Security Intelligence Directorate has the crucial role of protecting the realm through gathering information about the enemy and preventing the enemy doing the same with us.' He put his hands behind his back and bounced a little on his toes. Aubrey wondered if he'd ever been a training instructor, of the shouting kind or otherwise. 'Our methods are different from those of the army and the navy. Our role is unconventional, flexible, responsive. To that end, some of you here today are to continue with specialised training, some will be allocated to field teams supporting the regular military, while others will be formed into elite three-person units. Each of these units will have a high degree of autonomy.' His grin was not pleasant. 'This is because you will be operating in areas where access to higher echelons may not be possible.'

A low buzz, which Commander Tallis allowed to go on for a moment, then he continued. 'These detachments will be a blend of operatives from the Special Services and the Magic Department.' He paused. 'The Magic Department and the Special Services. Commander Craddock?'

Craddock stepped up to the lectern with a list. 'These people will remain behind. The others will go with their section commander for other assignments.'

Special units, Aubrey thought and he rubbed his hands together. *This is what Craddock mentioned*. He saw Caroline, George and he united again, sent on important tasks together, making the most of their talents. Working behind enemy lines, living off their own wits and own resources, thrown together against all odds, sharing the risks, daring danger and everything it had to throw at them.

All in the service of the country, of course.

Aubrey nodded when his name was read out, and smiled when Caroline and George's were as well. Content, he crossed his arms on his chest and wondered if they were now sitting up, surprised, looking for him.

Woodberry's name wasn't read out, Aubrey noted, and he left with the others whose names hadn't been called, looking somewhat disconsolate. Craddock glanced at Tallis, then went on. 'Orange slips for special unit detachment are now being distributed.' Aubrey saw some of the section commanders working through the rows, pieces of paper in hand. 'You will meet the rest of your unit in the rooms noted, where you will receive briefing on your first assignments.'

Craddock became grave. 'Though it may be difficult for you to see, each mission of each unit is important. You may be puzzled, even bewildered, by some tasks allocated to you, but I must emphasise that the country is relying on you. If you fulfil your mission, you will be contributing to the defence of Albion. Commander Tallis?'

Tallis squared himself. 'I endorse Commander Craddock's remarks. Go with all speed, and with all safety. And come back alive.'

Aubrey was still coping with the chill that Tallis's words brought when a slip of paper was thrust at him. While still reading it, he stood and scanned the room, but both George and Caroline had gone.

Room 7a was on the ground floor, toward the rear of Darnleigh House, and it was where he was to report to a Captain Foster. With some difficulty, Aubrey negotiated the chaos that came from dozens of people trying to find their way in unfamiliar surroundings, for he was constantly asked directions by khaki-clad operatives, all looking formidably fit and vigorous. He was keen to hear from Caroline and George about their training, to see how much of this vim was due to the Special Services regime and how much came from the candidates themselves. Perhaps athletes and manual workers were high on the list of prospective recruits for the Special Services?

He amused himself with visions of Caroline teaching these muscular recruits a thing or two in unarmed combat until he fronted the door marked 7a.

He knocked, sharply, smiling in anticipation.

'Enter.'

Aubrey stepped into the room with what he hoped was the right amount of jauntiness. Not too much, nothing brash, but the step of a confident, well-trained Magic Department operative.

'Aubrey!' George cried, turning around in a chair that faced the single desk. 'Old man!'

A bespectacled, sour-faced captain stood behind the desk and in front of a large map of the Continent. He didn't shout, for which Aubrey was grateful, but chided George nonetheless. 'Steady on, Doyle. This isn't a party.'

Aubrey held out his slip of orange paper. 'Captain Foster. Fitzwilliam, Aubrey, reporting, sir.' Then he smiled at Caroline, who was sitting next to George.

Except she turned and wasn't Caroline at all.

Ten

'GAPING'S A GOOD WAY TO DRAW ATTENTION TO yourself, Fitzwilliam,' Captain Foster said, 'so stop it and sit down.'

Aubrey was so stunned, the captain's voice seemed to come from far away. A veteran planner, Aubrey was experiencing the sensation that things on top of rugs feel when the rug decides to exit horizontally, with speed. His plans, his expectations, his neat order of events that he'd taken for granted had all been thrown into the air.

No Caroline? That was impossible, unwarranted, unnatural! They *belonged* together. Caroline, George and he had been through dangerous adventures and acquitted themselves with honour. Craddock and Tallis knew this. Even Prince Albert, the heir to the throne himself, knew it. Whatever was the Directorate thinking?

He seized on this. Perhaps it was just a mistake. This sort of thing happened – in the hurly-burly of war, communications went astray, documents were lost, identities confused. Surely that was it. All he had to do was point this out, speak to a few people and all would be well. His plans would be back on track, his mission set in motion again.

It was all he could do to stop himself groaning aloud. This sort of thinking was the Old Aubrey, the Aubrey who manipulated people to satisfy his own needs – without asking theirs. Caroline wouldn't want his interfering in her life, not like this.

Slowly, he began to realise that the others in the room were staring at him.

'Are you quite done?' Captain Foster stood behind the desk, leaning forward and propping himself with both arms. His glasses were rimless. His hair was sparse but it was well arranged on his dome of a head.

'Yes, sir,' Aubrey managed. His thoughts still whirling, he fumbled his way into a chair next to George, who was between him and the strange girl.

In the brief glimpse he'd had, it was no wonder George had sat next to her. She was striking – golden hair, and with extraordinary pale blue eyes, the colour of summer sky just above the horizon. Her whole face had been enlivened by the twitch of her lips she gave him. Not quite a smile, but an indication of humour, nonetheless.

She looked nothing like Caroline. It had simply been his expectation, assuming that he'd be reunited with her, that had made him see her in that chair.

'You obviously know Doyle,' Captain Foster said. 'This is Elspeth Mattingly.'

The smile that Elspeth offered him this time was unhesitating, bordering on a grin. 'Fitzwilliam. I've heard a great deal about you, but most of it led me to believe that you were rather more self-possessed than this.'

Aubrey only prevented a grimace with great effort. 'Don't believe what you read in the newspapers.'

'Newspapers? I never read them.' She glanced at George when he gasped, but immediately redirected her disconcertingly even gaze back at Aubrey. 'I have friends at St Alban's. They're impressed with your magical ability.'

'Really?' Aubrey was pleasantly surprised and he felt himself warming to her. Most people knew of him through his father or through various references in the press. He'd learned to bear the burden, but it didn't mean that he enjoyed it. To have it otherwise was refreshing.

'Truly,' she said solemnly. Then she grinned again. 'But don't let it go to your head. My friends are easily impressed.'

'I hate to interrupt,' Captain Foster said. He picked up a clipboard. 'And I'm glad you've got off to such a cosy start, but we have work to do.'

Testily, he went on to outline a new program of training, this time as a team. After they were all kitted out in their Directorate blacks would come more firearms, more map reading, and more communications training, but now it would be supplemented with team exercises.

Nothing like a few nights in a swamp to bind a team together, Aubrey thought as he read through one of the exercises, a simulated incursion at Exmouth Marsh. His eyes widened when he read that some of the ammunition used would be live.

It *definitely* wasn't a game any more.

As they were the only occupants of the motorbus that was taking them to the training facility, Aubrey learned more about Elspeth Mattingly.

'When war was declared, my father insisted that I do what I could. Since it sounded more exciting than languishing in Miss Jarvis's Finishing School I jumped at the chance.' She looked thoughtful for a moment. 'There's no patriot like one who adopts a country, is there?'

'Albion has been good to many newcomers,' Aubrey said.

'It certainly has been to him. He's made his fortune here, and he has connections at the Ministry of Defence, which is why I found myself at Lattimer Hall with Commander Tallis.' She laughed. 'He wasn't convinced, at first, but after I impressed him with a few things, he accepted that my father hadn't been mistaken about my abilities.'

'She's a fencer, old man,' George said. 'You should see her with a sabre.'

She smiled at him. 'You're a dear, George. I would have been bored to death during the training without you.'

Aubrey was still grappling with the notion of someone so petite using the most bloodthirsty of fencing weapons. 'The sabre?'

'Miss Jarvis's School had some unorthodox methods, which was probably a good idea since it dealt with unorthodox pupils.'

'Ah.'

To Aubrey's amazement, she leaned over and prodded him in the chest. 'You're too polite, Aubrey Fitzwilliam, I hope you realise that. You want to ask, but daren't, for propriety's sake.' She grinned and Aubrey couldn't help but grin back while he rubbed the prod spot on his chest. 'So I'll tell you. Miss Jarvis's School was Papa's last hope. It's for notoriously difficult young women and you need to have been thrown out of at least five schools before Miss Jarvis will look at you.' She counted on her fingers. 'I've been expelled from eleven, run away from four, and bought one and closed it down while I was there.'

'She's rich, old man,' George said, chortling.

'Less rich than I was.' She glowered. 'That last school cost a packet. Papa wasn't happy when he saw how little was in my bank account. He was even less happy when he found out that I forged his signature.'

'And thus Miss Jarvis,' Aubrey said. At first he'd been taken aback at the new recruit's unconventional ways, but he couldn't deny that they made her an engaging colleague. Insouciant was the word that seemed to fit her best, as long as he looked past her striking physical characteristics. That golden hair, for instance, waves and curls of it . . .

'And thus Miss Jarvis,' she agreed. 'I was looking to make it number seventeen when all this came up.'

'All this? The war?'

She waved a hand. 'That's right. The war. What a relief. I was on the verge of doing something perfectly dreadful at Miss Jarvis's School just to relieve the boredom, and the next thing you know I'm thrown in with people like George and life is exciting again.'

'Just doing my best for morale. Teamwork, cooperation, that sort of thing.' George plucked a loose thread from his sleeve. 'Important stuff in today's army. Or today's Special Services.'

Aubrey wondered if Elspeth knew about Sophie

Delroy. He'd ask George later, when they were alone. 'How does your mother feel about your joining up, Miss Mattingly?'

She laughed. 'So proper! I think "Elspeth" will do, don't you? Since we're part of the same unit?'

Aubrey swallowed. Her gaze was very direct, and disconcertingly beautiful. 'Of course. Elspeth. I'm Aubrey.'

'I know, remember?' She touched him on the back of the hand and looked directly into his eyes. 'My mother died when I was small. I barely remember her.'

Aubrey knew then that this was further proof that he had an unexpected magical talent: the ability to put his foot in it whenever he was talking with an attractive female. It was eerie how well it worked. It was probably ripe for further research and a paper or two in the leading journals. 'I'm sorry.'

'Sadness and loss are part of life's richness, I always say.'

'That's remarkably philosophical of you.'

She smiled with a hint of challenge. 'I'm a remarkable philosopher.'

'And I'm sure the Directorate has "Highly Developed Philosophising" as one of its most keenly sought-after skills.'

'And I'd call that that a joke, if I were being generous.'

'Nicely done, Elspeth,' George put in. 'Most people can't tell if Aubrey's joking or not. Terrible delivery, he has.'

After this, they shared details of their lives in that slightly awkward, slightly thrilling way that Aubrey enjoyed. It was like opening a new book and plunging into an unfamiliar world.

Elspeth's father was solidly well-off, coming from a family of wine merchants. Being the fourth generation in the firm, he was more of a businessman than a shopkeeper, and his travels on the Continent had meant that Elspeth was quite the polyglot. She spoke ten different languages fluently, and could get by in a handful of others.

In return for this disclosure, she probed him with delightfully naïve questions about spell casting. Those with no magical ability or background often wanted Aubrey to explain the most basic aspects of magic, but in this case he found Elspeth's enquiries both charming and amusing, and was happy to spend time answering them.

An hour flew past in such appealing company and after George recounted a rambling and hilarious story about his training in explosives, he began telling Elspeth about Sophie Delroy.

Aubrey was willing to admit he was not entirely adroit when it came to matters of the opposite sex, but even he knew that telling one young woman how fascinating, intelligent and pretty he found another young woman was a poor way to open negotiations with any hope of a future.

Which means that George is loyal to Sophie, Aubrey thought with relief, *and that he simply enjoys the company of attractive young women.*

Elspeth proved to be an eager recruit. She could barely restrain herself when they arrived at the training facility, putting a hand on his arm and peering through the glass when the omnibus reached the gatehouse. When it pulled up at the commandant's headquarters, she fairly herded Aubrey and George off in her keenness.

'We're going to be the best team in the Directorate,' she announced as they alighted. In the warm sun and faced with such enthusiasm, Aubrey wasn't about to disagree.

The rest of the day was spent on a variety of exercises that were handed out by instructors who appeared to relish the fiendishness of them. Elspeth's linguistic abilities were tested by having to interpret newspaper clippings, business invoices, operational manuals and personal letters, in half a dozen different languages. When translated, these would give George and Aubrey complicated instructions on tasks that involved variously repairing machinery, casting spells or a combination of both.

When the light was fading, and Aubrey and George were tightening the last bolts on a detached ornithopter engine, the captain who'd brought them together strode into the workshop. Aubrey's salute was tired, George's even more so. Elspeth greeted him with a brightness that belied her weariness. 'Captain Foster. Anything else you'd like us to do? A tunnel between Albion and the Continent, perhaps?'

'Hrrrumph.' He pointed with a riding crop. 'You missed that fuel line, Doyle.'

'He's just leaving it until last, sir,' Elspeth said. 'That's what the documents said to do.'

'Hmm. Well, finish it off and then read these.'

Elspeth took the large envelope. 'Details of our Exmouth Marsh mission, sir?'

Captain Foster shook his head. 'There's been a change of plans. Exmouth Marsh is off. You have new orders.'

'Off?' George echoed. He looked unreasonably disappointed, Aubrey thought, at the prospect of missing out on a muddy frolic, complete with mosquitoes and leeches.

'We're accelerating things. You're to be sent on assignment.'

'But we've just started training,' Aubrey said. 'They can't send us into the field yet.'

'Needs must when the devil drives,' Captain Foster said. 'You've been ordered to the Gallian Embassy to observe and assist an experienced team. Tomorrow. It's straightforward, but useful experience.'

Aubrey wiped his hands on a greasy cloth. This was more like it.

Captain Foster frowned. 'Mattingly, you're general liaison and we also want you to talk to their coding department. Fitzwilliam, there's some sort of magical mess that you're supposed to help out with. You'll be reporting to Major Morton, who's already on site working on the unexploded bombs.'

Aubrey looked at George and Elspeth, then back at Captain Foster. 'Bombs?'

'Dropped by one of those skyfleets last night. Magical and non-magical, apparently.'

Aubrey remembered Woodberry's news. 'These attacks have been continuing?'

'We've had a dozen strikes in the last week, but we've kept them quiet. Mostly on the coast, but we've had a number in the capital. Not to worry. Major Morton is our best man for this sort of thing.'

'What about me, sir?' George asked. 'I'm happy to escort these two around, but I can't imagine they're in any physical danger in the heart of Trinovant.'

'You'd be surprised,' Foster said darkly. 'Holmland spies are everywhere these days, but that's not your role.' He smiled in a calculating way. 'You did the extra explosives training, didn't you, Doyle?'

'Yes, sir. And the extra sessions on motor mechanics and electrical machinery.'

'Good, good. You can help Major Morton, too.'

George rubbed the back of his head thoughtfully.

Aubrey was uneasy at the mysterious nature of the tasks, but told himself that he was on the lowest rungs of the service, and questioning orders wasn't what low rungs did.

No, he thought, *low rungs get stepped on*. Then he banished the thought.

George developed a calculating look. 'This may take some time, sir?'

'If you finish before midnight tomorrow, it will be a miracle.'

'So we're to dine at the embassy?'

'I expect so.'

'Good, good.' George beamed. 'We'll manage.'

On the motorbus on the way back to Darnleigh House, they compared notes.

Elspeth pursed her lips. 'Since I'm general liaison, I have to insist that you two behave yourselves. I don't want you to give the Gallians any cause for offence.'

'Well,' Aubrey said, 'I hadn't intended to do anything to –'

'And those uniforms are appallingly dowdy. I don't suppose we could drop in at a tailor on the way?'

'Tailor?' George looked down at his blacks. 'I thought we looked quite spiffing. Much better than khaki.'

Elspeth brushed at Aubrey's shoulder. 'The lines, the fabric . . . It's hopeless. The Gallians are bound to laugh.'

George bridled. 'I say, Elspeth, that's a bit rich.' Then he stopped and punched Aubrey on the arm. 'She's pulling our legs, old man.'

She sat back, trying to stifle a grin. 'I'm remarkably adroit, pulling two legs at once, but there you have it.'

Aubrey was unsettled by this, but he found it a pleasant sort of unsettling. Elspeth Mattingly was certainly a forward young woman. She'd managed to avoid 'prim' by a considerable distance, which Aubrey was quite happy about. Prim unsettled him too, but in an entirely different way.

'We promise that we'll be on our best behaviour. And we'll wear our Albionish garments with pride.' He glanced at George. 'And what was all that about dining at the embassy?'

George rubbed his hands together. 'I've been missing Gallian food after our Lutetian expedition. It strikes me that the Gallian Embassy is bound to have a good dining room. Quite looking forward to it.'

'Do you enjoy Gallian food?' Elspeth asked.

'No need for the qualifying adjective where George is concerned,' Aubrey said. 'George enjoys food.'

'Excellent. I don't trust picky eaters. Food is one of life's great pleasures.'

'Life is meant to be enjoyed,' Aubrey murmured, 'not endured.'

She grasped his arm. 'Oh, I like that! Did you just make it up?'

Aubrey felt himself blushing. 'More or less.'

'Would you mind if I take as my personal motto?'

'Er . . .'

'"Life is meant to be enjoyed, not endured." I'll make that my next tattoo.'

Aubrey's jaw sagged. He stared. 'Tattoo?'

She burst out laughing and had trouble stopping. 'Oh,' she said, sagging against him, gasping for breath, 'oh, I must stop doing that. But it's so hard to resist trying to shock you.' She wiped her eyes. 'You look so eminently shockable, you see.'

'I do? Do I, George?'

George was grinning, cat-wise. 'It's hard for me to tell, old man. The gullibility gets in the way.'

'Elspeth. You don't have a tattoo?'

'A tattoo? Of course not! I'm not a sailor!' She collapsed into laughter again. 'You should have seen your face.'

Aubrey crossed his arms on his chest and snorted. He couldn't take offence, not with someone so . . . so disarming.

THE GALLIAN EMBASSY WAS A PROMINENT GREYSTONE building in what had become the foreign section of Trinovant. As one of the finer property agents might put it, the cluster of embassies and consulates around Todman Square was within easy walking distance of the Prime Minister's offices at No. 4 Credence Lane.

Elspeth approached the guard at the door and impressed him with not just her looks, but with her impeccable Gallian. Aubrey straightened his jacket, made sure the brim of his cap was level, then presented his brand new credentials to the guard, feeling a moment of pride when the guard, after inspecting them, simply waved him in.

He was a member of the Department, credentialed and accepted. The simple recognition of his status by someone else underlined that he had taken a step into a world beyond that he'd previously known. He was no longer a dilettante, pretending to be a part of great events, standing on the sideline and joining in when he thought best. He had left that behind, as the world had left behind its days of peace.

The realisation jolted him. Adulthood was something that belonged to other people, not Aubrey Fitzwilliam and his friends. And yet, here it was, unbidden, with all its accoutrements. When he thought about it, waiting for George's credentials to be examined, he wondered where the supposed freedoms of adulthood were. Where he was standing, all he could see was the heavy weight of responsibility that maturity was bringing.

A beaming Gallian military man bounded down the stairs, his hand extended. He was tall and dark-eyed, with extremely large hands. 'Welcome! I am Captain Bourdin, in charge of embassy security. I am glad you are here. This way. Major Morton is in the courtyard.'

Inside the grand building, it was all light and gilt in the high Gallian fashion of the previous century, but instead of being a palace draped with bored and languishing nobles this was a hive of activity. A horde of harried-looking embassy staff was rushing about. They popped out of doorways, flitted up staircases, bolted out of lifts barely before they'd stopped. They carried boxes, envelopes, folders, maps and books. They argued while walking, arms full of meeting minutes and order forms, and conducted conclaves in alcoves as Aubrey, George and Elspeth passed, following Captain Bourdin as he ploughed through the chaos.

George grinned at the immaculately dressed office girls, and they smiled shyly in return. Elspeth drew close to Aubrey, something that he found he didn't mind at all. 'Have either of you been here before?'

'I haven't,' Aubrey admitted. 'George?'

'No. And dashed sorry about that, too. Would have made a point of it if I'd known.'

Elspeth looked amused. 'Known what, George?'

George opened his mouth, then closed it again before backing up and having another try. 'If I'd known how much Sophie would enjoy this place. So Gallian and all.'

'Splendid save,' Aubrey murmured to George, but had to back against the newel post to let an oily-looking fellow rush past with a box of files. 'Sorry, Mr Fitzwilliam,' he said over his shoulder.

Elspeth turned a querying eye on him. 'You haven't been here before, yet they seem to know you. Your fame precedes you?'

He shrugged. 'Sorry. This sort of thing happens.'

'Ah. Your father.'

'It's helpful sometimes. A bother at others.'

'So I imagine.' She craned her neck and stood on tiptoes, putting a hand on Aubrey's shoulder to balance herself. 'We appear to have lost Captain Bourdin.'

Aubrey looked around. Many people, none of them Captain Bourdin. 'Well, we're supposed to find Major Morton . . .'

Elspeth grinned. 'Wait here, both of you. I know my way around. I'll find out where Captain Bourdin's gone. Or I'll find Major Morton, one or the other.'

'So you've been here before?' Aubrey asked.

'I have a friend who works in the library. She saves the latest Gallian romance novels for me.' She eyed him directly. 'And I don't want you inferring anything from my reading preferences.'

Aubrey blinked. 'Reading preferences?'

'Never mind. We have afternoon tea together and discuss the sighs, the longing looks and the thumpings of the heart under crisp linen bodices.'

Aubrey looked around. *Was it hot in here?*

George, however, was interested in something else. 'Afternoon tea?'

'Oh yes. They have fine pastries here.'

'Did you hear that, old man?' George said. 'I'm sure we need to sample their wares. Do our best for the alliance and all that.'

'I'll take you both when we're done.' Elspeth laughed. 'Can you wait here? I won't be long.' She insinuated herself through the crowd, leaving Aubrey and George behind.

'You know what Caroline would have said,' George said as they shuffled away from the stairs and the flow of clerks and porters. 'She would have said, "Don't move. And do try to stay out of trouble."'

'Elspeth doesn't know us that well.' Aubrey dodged a rolled-up map that was being toted on the shoulder of a young man who appeared to be oblivious to the havoc he was wreaking as he peered from side to side, searching for someone or somewhere.

'Pleasant enough, isn't she?'

'Elspeth? Quite. Able enough, too, if your reports are to be trusted.'

'Believe me, old man, she's top-notch in almost every way. Apart from her judgement.'

'Her judgement?'

'We spent some time together, you know, while we were on field training. Very modern, unchaperoned and all that. In a bunker by ourselves, she told me, quite sweetly, that I wasn't her type.'

'So you're thinking she's probably insane.'

'Very droll, old man, very droll.' George frowned a little. 'It just struck me as a little odd, that's all. I hadn't pressed my suit on her at all. So to speak.'

'She just blurted it out?'

'Hardly. I don't have the impression that our Elspeth blurts anything out that she doesn't want to.' He edged back against the wall to let a porter wheel past a trolley with a single drawer filing cabinet. 'She did go on to ask about you, though.'

'Me?'

'Said she'd admired you from afar.' His face was deadpan. '*That's* when I became worried about her sanity.'

Before Aubrey could follow this further, Elspeth appeared at the top of the stairs and beckoned. 'I think I've found him.'

The corridor was panelled with wood and displayed rather good Gallian watercolours. Sidelong, Aubrey studied Elspeth with renewed interest, but she stopped abruptly at a door halfway along the corridor, and gestured grandly. The light coming through the large arched window at the end of the corridor caught her hair. 'Go ahead. I'll join you in a moment.'

Aubrey raised an eyebrow. She made a gesture of exasperation, throwing up her hands and rolling her eyes. 'Someone from the translation department wants to see me. Trouble with a document. But don't worry, I'll be back before you have a chance to miss me.'

With that, she was off and Aubrey was left bemused.

The door closed behind them, cutting off the buzz of Gallian office rearrangements with a very solid *snick* that Aubrey didn't warm to at all, but his attention was taken up by the alarming sight of a tall, bald man pointing an alarmingly large pistol at him from the other side of an elegant desk.

'Do not move,' the bald man said in Albionish. 'I will not hesitate to kill you on the spot if you do.'

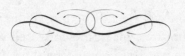

Eleven

HE OFFICE WAS DIMLY LIT BY GASLIGHT, EVEN IN THE middle of the day, because the drapes were drawn over the single tall window. The heavy wood panelling only emphasised the closeness of the confines.

Instant obedience never came easily to Aubrey. He was too willing to question first before agreeing to go along with commands. In the case of people pointing firearms at him and telling him not to move, however, he was able to quell this natural propensity.

At his side, it was George who spoke. 'Who are you? What's going on here?'

The bald man was sweating, Aubrey realised. His head and face shone, and was his hand trembling as it held the pistol? 'Fitzwilliam,' he said flatly. His eyes narrowed, and Aubrey, in a moment of acute alertness, saw the man's finger tighten on the trigger − and he also sensed the magic spells that the pistol was overlaid with.

The equation was clear. If he moved, he was going to be shot, and shot by a magically enhanced weapon. If he didn't move, he was still going to be shot. When it came to choosing, he favoured action over inaction, but before he could move the man grimaced and squeezed the trigger. Immediately, something whipped past Aubrey's right ear with a deadly, low hum. The large mirror on the wall behind him shattered.

Aubrey instinctively ducked, much too late, then hunched at the shower of glass, but his mind was taken up with astonishment. Where was the report of the pistol? It hadn't made a sound at all! Aubrey saw that the bald man was as astonished as he was; the would-be assassin was shaking his head at the revolver, staring at it in disbelief. Then a large vase flung by George struck the man squarely in the chest.

He grunted and doubled over. While hammering came from the door behind them, Aubrey pawed at a side table and sent a carriage clock after George's successful vase strike and was pleased to see it collect the would-be assassin squarely on his shining skull. He screeched, then straightened and waved the pistol. 'I will not miss this time!'

A deafening boom from the doorway interrupted the assassin's plans. He dropped the pistol, sagged in the corner, swore and tried to staunch the flow of blood that was coming from a fresh, and nasty, shoulder wound.

Aubrey whirled. Elspeth stood in the doorway with a large and smoking revolver. She kept it trained on their assailant while George stalked him warily, a brass umbrella stand in his hand. 'Careful, George,' she said. Her voice was even and Aubrey noted how steady her hands were, holding the revolver in a manner that would draw admiring gasps from the shoutiest of military instructors.

'He's not a menace any more.' Without taking his eyes off the bald man, George scooped up his pistol and pocketed it.

As if it were one of Ivey and Wetherall's musical comedies, a trio of armed guards arrived after events had been resolved, almost tripping over themselves in their eagerness to get through the doorway. Aubrey had a giddy moment wondering if he'd ever live to see the day when armed guards appeared in the nick of time rather than too late, then, rather than having his knees give way and his head introduced to the carpet, he sat on one of the chairs. Captain Bourdin appeared, looking both distressed and offended, and pointed a pistol at Elspeth – rather needlessly as she was the target of each of the squad members. 'M'mselle. Please to drop your weapon.'

She looked amused. 'I'll just engage the safety first, if you don't mind. There.'

The revolver thumped to the floor.

'Thank you. Now, you men, see to the cultural attaché before he bleeds to death.'

Aubrey rubbed his forehead. He could feel the effects of nearly being shot starting to assert themselves. His knees were trembling. His stomach was both hollow and cavernous. His mouth was devoid of moisture. He was relieved, naturally, to have survived, and he couldn't help but feel grateful for Elspeth's timely intervention, but he could see a long, complicated explanation ahead.

'AND YOU'RE SURE THE WEAPON IS ENSORCELLED?' CAPTAIN Bourdin asked.

The captain's office was a small, neatly arranged room toward the rear of the embassy. Through the window, Aubrey could see the cordoned-off area of the courtyard that marked the site where Major Morton and his bomb squad were. It was fifty yards away, but Aubrey wondered about the safety of their location. Or was it Gallian bravado, refusing to move away from the scene of danger?

Initially, Bourdin had been outraged at three Albionite guests assaulting the cultural attaché, but as the story emerged his attitude changed remarkably. He became, by turns, mortified, apologetic, then outraged again – but this time the outrage was directed at the would-be assassin.

While his subordinates dragged the wounded official to the infirmary for treatment and interrogation, he'd confided that he'd always suspected the cultural attaché of something or other.

'I didn't get a chance to examine the weapon before your people took it away,' Aubrey said, 'but it was definitely spell-ridden.'

'A silencing spell?' George suggested.

'When he fired, it didn't make a sound. I don't know what other spells it might have had.' *And if he hadn't missed and smashed that mirror instead, no-one outside would have been the wiser.* Aubrey shuddered. He'd been so concerned about international dangers that he'd forgotten the peril that came from simply being the son of the Prime Minister.

'Rather incompetent assassin,' Elspeth pointed out, 'missing the PM's son from that range. I'm glad I didn't miss him. I'd be a laughing stock.'

She looked remarkably cheerful, unfazed by the whole incident. Aubrey realised then that her breezy demeanour was an asset. She was unflappable. Such an attitude would make her a valuable field operative in a crisis. 'I haven't had a chance to thank you,' he said.

She shrugged. 'It was the least I could do. I led you to him, after all.'

'It could happen to anyone,' George said. 'Big place, this, easy to get confused.'

'I know, but I keep thinking of how it would look on my file, losing a colleague in my first liaison officer role. I don't want a reputation for being so careless.'

Aubrey couldn't help but notice that her gaze flitted across him, not challenging directly as had been her wont. Her words were casual, but lacked her usual touch of impudence.

And was that gleam the beginning of tears in her eyes?

He cleared his throat, in a haphazard effort to distract attention from the blush that was creeping to his cheeks. 'This man,' he said to Captain Bourdin. 'Has he made any admissions?'

Captain Bourdin looked at Aubrey then at Elspeth and Aubrey cringed, internally, when the Gallian smiled and raised an eyebrow. 'None so far, Fitzwilliam. But it won't be long before our cultural attaché tells us everything.'

Cultural attaché, Aubrey thought. *You may as well tattoo 'spy' on his forehead.* He pinched the bridge of his nose. A Gallian spy trying to shoot the son of the Albion PM. He wondered how the Holmland intelligence agencies had persuaded him to come over to their side.

'I'm sure that our authorities will be interested in talking to him,' Elspeth said. 'After you're done, you'll get in touch with Commander Tallis? I'm sure he'll be overjoyed to hear about this.'

Captain Bourdin frowned. 'Overjoyed?'

'Sorry. It's Directorate slang. It means "outraged".'

'We will provide a thorough and complete report, m'mselle. And I must thank you for your quick action. It would not do for the son of the Prime Minister of Albion to be hurt in the middle of the Gallian Embassy.'

'Of course,' she said. 'Now, do you think we can continue with our assignment? I'm a stickler for following instructions.'

Aubrey couldn't help smiling. She was nothing if not dedicated. He eyed the bag she clutched. Discreet brown leather, he wondered what other useful equipment it held besides a revolver.

Outside the office, it was still bedlam.

'Anyone would think a war was on,' George remarked, hands in his pockets. 'All this running about, your getting shot and whatnot.'

'Keep that line up your sleeve, George,' Aubrey said. 'Such levity could be useful soon.'

'Gloomy thought, that,' George said, 'but you may be right, old man. You may be right.'

'MAJOR MORTON?' AUBREY CALLED AS THEY APPROACHED THE large crater in the middle of the courtyard. It was a good three yards across and twice that long, with cobblestones scattered in all directions around it, and earth flung against the sides of the embassy buildings. The crater was surrounded by waist-high barricades and the area inside was swarming with black-clad Department operatives.

One of them straightened and squinted. He shook his head, said something to one of the other operatives that Aubrey couldn't make out, then he climbed out of the crater in the courtyard and easily vaulted the barricades. Aubrey fumbled his salute. He still wasn't used to the action and kept forgetting exactly where the brim of his Department cap was. As a result he nearly knocked himself backward, but Major Morton didn't appear to notice.

The major had abandoned his cap, and his thinning sandy hair was dishevelled in the brisk breeze that gusted about the courtyard. He was in his forties, Aubrey guessed, medium height, with shrewd eyes and a narrow nose with such tiny nostrils that it looked as if it could hardly supply enough air to keep a person alive.

'Ah, Fitzwilliam.' His voice was dry and amused, and his salute was languid. 'Doyle. Mattingly. I was told you were on your way. Now, any of you had any experience with compression magic?'

George and Elspeth turned to Aubrey with such perfect timing that Major Morton laughed. 'Only one magic operative in your team, eh?' Major Morton patted the pockets of his black uniform and eventually found a pipe, which he jammed in his mouth.

Immediately, one of the other operatives called out. 'Major Morton, sir! No flames, sir!'

Major Morton sighed and glanced over his shoulder. He took the pipe from his mouth. 'It's empty!' He waved it in the air. 'Good work, though, Maloney!' He turned back to find Aubrey, George and Elspeth doing their best not to look curious, and failing. 'It's part of their job,' he explained, 'to remind me not to strike a match when we're on the job. I forget, sometimes.'

Aubrey wondered how often someone would forget in such a dangerous occupation as bomb disposal. He counted Major Morton's fingers and, to his relief, found that none were missing.

'Now,' the major said, pointing his pipe at Aubrey. 'Compression spells?'

'I have had some field experience, sir. A little.'

'Really? Tell me about it.'

'Sir?'

'I want to hear about your experiences, Fitzwilliam. It may be useful.' He jerked his pipe at the crater. 'I'd welcome anything that could help us with what we have on our hands here. It could go off at any minute.'

Aubrey glanced at the pit. Five yards away. Not far enough. He could see George doing his best not to back off, but Elspeth actually leaned forward to get a better look. 'It fell the night before last, is that right, sir?'

Major Morton smiled. 'Early in the morning, really. About four. We've been working on it ever since, when it became apparent that the Gallians didn't just have an unexploded bomb on their hands, but something magical as well.'

'Something magical that could go off at any minute,' George said.

Major Morton shrugged. 'Or it could go off tomorrow. Or it could turn into a pig and start asking the way to St Swithins Station. Or it could do nothing except make us very, very nervous, like the others these skyfleets have been showering on us these past few weeks.'

Aubrey had been monitoring the spectacular skyfleets, battleships formed of cloud stuff, since Dr Tremaine had sent one after him last year. They had been appearing at irregular intervals all over Albion, but obviously coming from the Continent. They hadn't done anything except sow panic, so this was a new and unwelcome development. The skyfleets had been excellent at spreading confusion and fear, a sense of imminent dread that stopped the normal commerce of everyday living any time a shadow appeared in the sky.

'I dealt with a compression device, sir. In Fisherberg. One that was constructed by the enemy.'

'You did? By Jove, you could be just what we need. Tell me about it.'

Aubrey described the events of finding the compressed lightning spell outside Fisherberg Academy Hall, and how he barely managed to stop it exploding and wrecking the venerable building – a building with Prince Albert inside.

'And what did you do? Remove it?'

'No time for that, sir. I used a few variations on Harland James's technique.'

Major Morton blinked. 'But you're alive.'

'That was one of the main variations, sir, keeping the spell caster alive. The other variation was that it worked. I managed to graft something onto the existing spell with a temporal inversion constant and thus neutralise it. Long enough, anyway, to remove the package safely.'

'You did that?' Major Morton eyed him with something verging on respect. 'But why haven't I heard of this?'

'I'm writing a paper on it, sir,' Aubrey said, and he thought of the thirteen half-written papers on his desk at Maidstone. He *really* needed to finish some of them. 'I just need some more time.'

'Time. We could use some of that, I suspect. Come this way, have a look at what we've found.'

'Go ahead,' George said magnanimously. 'We'll wait here for you.'

'No need,' Major Morton said. 'This was a double bunger.'

'Double bunger?'

'Two loads were dropped.' He pointed with his pipe. 'A regular high explosive bomb landed at that end of the courtyard, the magical bomb at this end. Head down to the high explosive number, there's a good chap. They could use some help.'

'Me?' George said.

'Commander Tallis said it would be useful if you got some practical experience of bomb disposal work.' Major Morton chuckled. 'Don't worry. Spencer and Martin are working on it, our best team. You know what they say about the old and the bold, don't you?'

George tore his gaze away from the far end of the crater. 'Old and bold?'

'"There are old bomb disposal operatives, and there are bold bomb disposal operatives, but there are no old, bold bomb disposal operatives."' He chuckled again. 'Not to worry. Spencer is old, Martin is bold, so you'll get the best of both worlds.'

'Just as long as I don't get blown to bits in either of them,' George said, and he plodded off.

'Now, Mattingly,' Major Morton said. 'You're to meet with the Gallian codes department, to see their methods. It should be useful.'

Elspeth eyed Major Morton with what Aubrey could only describe as considerable affront. 'Does that mean I don't get to work on these bombs?'

Major Morton laughed. 'Good Lord, no.'

'I see.' She fumed a little. 'As liaison officer, I really must object.'

'Object? On what grounds?'

'On the grounds that I'd really like to work on those bombs.'

Major Morton glanced at Aubrey. 'You're new to the military, aren't you?'

'George and I have some experience.'

'Then you understand about old-fashioned things like orders and discipline and such.'

Aubrey could see that Major Morton was going out of his way to be patient. 'Elspeth, I think we need to get on with things as ordered.'

She glared at both of them. 'All right. As long as this isn't a conspiracy to keep females in their place. The world is changing, you know.'

She stormed off, leaving Aubrey to consider that Elspeth and Caroline had at least one thing in common.

With more than one backward glance, Elspeth crossed the courtyard.

'Fine-looking young woman, that,' Major Morton said. 'Great asset to the forces.'

'She just shot someone who tried to kill me,' Aubrey said stiffly.

'Did she now? Plucky as well as pretty. Good show.'

Aubrey wasn't quite sure how he felt about that. He didn't have any argument over Elspeth's prettiness – that was undeniable – and she certainly showed her pluck in confronting the would-be assassin. And she was pleasant to be with.

He snorted. He knew why she made him uncomfortable, despite all that. It was *because* of all that. Pretty, brave, intelligent, capable young women had a way of turning him to jelly, and he had never quite worked out what to do about it, apart from delight in their presence – and feel a pang at their absence.

Caroline.

'This way, Fitzwilliam. Not afraid to get some dirt on your hands, are you?'

'Coming, sir.'

A crumpled canister lay at the bottom of the crater, a few feet long, dark dull metal about as thick as his thigh. On the lip of the crater, Aubrey bent and put his hands on his knees while three operatives used small brushes to ease earth away from the metal. Not all of the canister was exposed, embedded as it was in the wall of the crater.

Aubrey could feel the magic without trying. It pulsed like a heart, malignant and heavy, and it was redolent with a tangle of complex spells. Aubrey worked his mouth, trying to clear the knotty taste that had insinuated itself as the magic played games with his senses.

'Anything familiar there?' Major Morton toyed with his pipe, passing it from hand to hand.

'It's definitely held together tightly, but I can't . . .' Aubrey's voice trailed off. He was looking for any sign of Dr Tremaine's handiwork, but nothing stood out. Nothing specific, that was. The spells crammed into the canister *reminded* him of Dr Tremaine, without his touch, as if they were copies of his efforts.

He straightened. 'How many of these have fallen on Albion?'

Major Morton cocked an eyebrow. 'Now, we don't bandy classified information like that around willy-nilly, you know.'

'It's important.'

'I rather thought it might be.' Major Morton put his pipe in his mouth, chewed on it and then took it out again. 'What if I tell you that several dozen of these magical canisters fell across Albion two nights ago? And about the same number of high explosive bombs?'

Several dozen? Each one would have taken hours to construct. Aubrey couldn't see the rogue sorcerer standing at a conveyor belt casting spell after spell and making sure they were neatly compressed inside metal cylinder after metal cylinder. He wouldn't have the patience for such repetitive stuff.

Without realising it, Aubrey started to hum, deep in his throat. No, he couldn't imagine Dr Tremaine doing that, but . . .

Major Morton nudged his elbow. 'Are you all right, Fitzwilliam?'

'Sir?'

'You were making an awful droning noise.'

'Just thinking, sir.'

'Well, I hope your thinking's of some use. I don't want that earthquake getting loose. Not here, in the middle of Trinovant.'

'Earthquake? I'd assumed it was weather magic.'

'They're a cunning lot, those Holmlanders. They've dropped plenty of compressed weather magic on us, but also a few of these neatly packaged earthquakes. One got loose in Carlstairs on the coast, near the shipyard. Toppled half the cliff into the sea.'

Aubrey looked at the grand old buildings surrounding them. He swallowed. 'So we need to render this one harmless.'

'Ideally, yes. D'you remember the spell you used in Fisherberg?'

Aubrey would never forget that desperate spell casting. It was a matter of defining a temporal inversion constant that would worm its way back through time and latch itself onto the compression spell, adding a few days to the time of its unleashing. Time enough, then, to dispose of this canister safely. A few hundred miles out to sea, Aubrey hoped, on the fastest ornithopter available.

'I have it,' he said.

'Be my guest.' Major Morton raised his voice. 'Maloney, Johnson, Miller, time to move away.'

The operatives in the bottom of the crater looked up, and immediately scrambled out. Aubrey thought they scrambled gratefully, if such a thing were possible.

'Do you want me to come with you?' Major Morton asked Aubrey.

Aubrey shook his head and handed the major his cap. His palms were clammy. Suddenly the crater looked miles deep. The canister was an ominous glint at the faraway bottom. Aubrey shifted his weight from one leg to another, which was enough to set him into motion.

He clambered down the ragged sides of the pit. Loose earth tumbled past him and made his footing uncertain for a moment until he turned and steadied himself with both hands, not caring about how he looked as he slid on his rear. He was prepared to sacrifice dignity for safety, and proceeded to demonstrate that when he reached the bottom by crawling on hands and knees, creeping up on the sinister canister.

He was aware that Major Morton hadn't withdrawn. His pipe was stuck in the corner of his mouth as he circled the crater, matching Aubrey's approach. The man had no nerves, Aubrey decided, and he actually thought the major was grinning.

Aubrey pulled back his sleeves absently. It gave him a sense of being workmanlike, and it had a faint but noticeable settling effect as he studied the canister. From a foot or so away, he could see the line of rivets along one side and the solder that sealed the top. Or the bottom, it was hard to tell with the other end buried in the earth. The surface was scuffed and dented, with a long, bright scrape running along its length.

He took a deep breath. Then he extended his magical awareness.

He grunted and rocked on his hands and knees as the canister came alive in the pseudo-sight that his magical awareness lent him. It was a flare, a roiling of spells held in check by a profoundly woven compression spell. Aubrey gritted his teeth and swayed from side to side in an effort to ascertain what was packed into the canister, what exactly was threatening to explode. He could make out the earthquake spell, shivering as it was in anticipation, but he could also detect intensifying spells, and some that he thought would have the effect of channelling or focusing . . .

Enough, he thought. The nature of the contents of the canister was interesting, but he didn't have time to explore. He needed to clamp down on the whole package.

Following the method he'd established – by necessity –
in the Fisherberg drama, he constructed a neat, terminal
phrase to splice onto the end of the compression spell.
With no time for experimentation or refinement, he
reused the Sumerian version he'd invented in that crisis.
He steadied himself, then pronounced the series of crisp,
slightly harsh, elements, and it was over in seconds. As
soon as he finished, the Sumerian addition inverted itself
and disappeared, tracking back through time to when the
compression spell was originally set in place.

Satisfied, he let out a deep breath. Subtly, the magical
nature of the canister had changed. The enveloping
compression spell appeared less . . . *imminent.*

He straightened until he was kneeling. He wiped his
hands together.

'All done?' the major said cheerily.

'I've added two days to the trigger time,' Aubrey said and
he was quite pleased that his voice neither quavered nor
croaked. 'I'd like to examine it more closely, if I could.'

'Ah. We'll have to see about that. My orders are to get
it out of here quick smart. The Gallians are understandably nervous about having a couple of bombs in their
vicinity.'

Aubrey understood that, if his probing of the canister
was accurate, it wouldn't only have been the Gallian
Embassy that would have suffered if the earthquake had
been released. It would require more study, but he had
an awful suspicion that a way had been found to aim
an earthquake's effects in desired directions – and the
Houses of Parliament weren't that far away.

'Splendid. I'll get the others to cart the thing off with
the high explosive bomb.'

'That's safe, too?'

'Oh, yes, no worries there. Good work, Fitzwilliam. Glad to have had your help. Don't forget that we'll need a full report on your methods, to help disarm the other canisters.'

Aubrey dragged himself out of the crater to see Major Morton had wandered over to the other bomb site, where he was chatting with some more of his people.

He was pleased with himself, but his overwhelming reaction was one of relief. Not simply that he hadn't been killed, but relief that he hadn't let anyone down. Commander Craddock and Major Morton had been relying on him in his new status as a Magic Department operative, but he was acutely conscious of the lives of the people in the embassy and the surrounding streets – and the countless others whose lives may have been affected had an unhappy outcome here caused retribution and a more bloody war. *Where does responsibility end?* he wondered.

He sighed and saw George, walking rather stiff-leggedly toward him. 'Well,' George announced. 'That was an experience.'

Aubrey thought it wise not to draw attention to George's pallor. Normally ruddy-faced, he was definitely pale. 'Did you learn much?'

'They let me cut the red wire.'

'The red wire?'

'The one that might have set the whole thing off, if it was the wrong one.'

'And where were they?'

'They said they were moving to a safe distance. One of them suggested the next county. They wished me luck before they went, though.'

'And they left you alone? To cut the red wire?'

'I'm reasonably sure I was alone. Not that I looked around. Or stretched. Or twitched – they emphasised that twitching was a very bad thing to do.'

'Before they left.'

'Before they left. I did sweat a little, though.'

'I imagine you would.'

'They didn't say anything about not sweating.'

'And what happened when you cut the red wire?'

'Nothing.'

'Nothing? Well, that's good.'

'No, I mean nothing happened because they'd disarmed it before I joined them.'

'Ah.' Aubrey sought for comforting words. 'I suppose they were showing you what it was like, without putting you in any real danger.'

George nodded. Very slowly. 'That must be it. And their laughing, when they came back. That was useful too, I imagine.'

'Most likely. Instructional laughter, probably.'

'I tell you what, old man. I'm going to look for a spot of tea. And some scones. A slice or two of cake wouldn't go astray, either.' He took off his cap, turned it around in his hands and then replaced it on his head. 'We're not messing about here any more, are we?'

'No, we're certainly not messing about. We've jumped in the deep end.' Aubrey took a deep breath. 'Go and get some morning tea, George. I'll find Elspeth and we'll join you.'

Aubrey didn't need any reminder that everything had changed, but the usually sunny George's understanding underlined the way that the world was different.

Adventuring was well and good, but it had had a touch of the carefree, no matter how dangerous the situation. Now, it was different.

After entering via a small conservatory, redolent with palms and philodendrons, Aubrey went searching for stairs leading downward, reasoning that a cryptography department simply *had* to be in the basement. He'd turned several corners, perfecting his Gallian 'excuse me' and 'terribly sorry' as he eased through the crowded corridors, when he realised he'd lost his sense of direction. Was he facing the front of the embassy, or the rear? He was in a nest of activity, an open typing pool surrounded by offices with neat windows for those inside to monitor those at work on the typewriting machines. A dozen young women were hard at work on their machines but, even so, several of them looked up as he passed. He did his best to appear as if he weren't glancing at the papers they were copying, which made him walk with a rather stiff, chin-up gait.

Which meant that he wasn't totally aware of his surroundings as he marched through a door into a smaller area with a young woman working alone at a desk, her back toward him. Still trying to appear as if he knew where he was going, he kept on toward the open door just past her and was glad when she didn't look up. For a moment, he thought of asking her for directions, but he dismissed the thought. He was bound to find the basement sooner or later.

When he opened the door, all he saw on the other side was a windowless office. A lonely desk, an empty hat rack, a filing cabinet and nowhere to go. He rehearsed what he hoped was a rueful and inoffensive smile and prepared to turn on his heel to admit he was lost – only to feel a hefty shove from behind.

He stumbled through the open door, which closed behind him. He whirled – and stared at his latest assailant.

Twelve

'Caroline! Why are you dressed as a typing girl?'

Caroline Hepworth stood with her back to the door, arms crossed on her chest. She wore a plain white blouse, a severe dark skirt and an expression that could only be described as disapproving.

'Because I've *been* a typing girl, Aubrey. My team has been practising covert infiltration. I'm in typing, Walter is in the kitchen, Gregory is inspecting plumbing.'

Aubrey made a mental note to introduce himself to Walter and Gregory. To foster esprit de corps, camaraderie, that sort of thing. 'In an allied embassy?'

Caroline made an impatient noise. 'The Gallians know we're here. It's practice, that's all. Except . . .' She frowned. 'How well do you know Mattingly?'

'Elspeth?'

'When I saw you three blunder in to the embassy, I decided to observe her. For practice.'

'And it wouldn't be useful to follow George or me,' Aubrey said carefully.

'Don't be silly, Aubrey.' Caroline pushed back a stray strand of hair that Aubrey found quite invisible. 'She was the only option. So with an armful of files I shadowed her as she left you and George blocking up the bottom of the stairs.'

'She was looking for Captain Bourdin.'

'That's what she told you?'

Aubrey wouldn't have said that Caroline's slight smile had a hint of triumph, but he wondered if someone else may have.

'Well, we'd lost him . . .'

'She met a man in one of the second-floor offices.'

'She mentioned that she had a friend at the embassy.' Aubrey frowned. Hadn't Elspeth said that her friend was female? And that she worked in the library?

'She did, did she? And did she mention that this friend would like to shoot you?'

'Not in as many words, no.'

'Not in as many words?'

'Not in any words, actually.' Aubrey frowned. 'She met that bald chap?'

'The cultural attaché. They spoke behind closed doors for a few minutes and then she rejoined you.'

'Then took us to meet him.' Aubrey stood still, taking this new datum apart and trying to see how it worked. *Why would Elspeth talk to someone who was an assassin?* 'But she shot him, after he tried to shoot me.'

'It made her look brave, didn't it? Made her more trustworthy?' Caroline's eyes were hard. 'I'd call that a measure of her ruthlessness.'

'Elspeth? Ruthless? But she's so . . .'

'Sweet? Kind? Cuddly?'

'Cuddly? What? Elspeth?'

'Three questions in a row, Aubrey. You're on the verge of blustering.'

'I was going to point out how professional Miss Mattingly has been,' Aubrey said, so stiffly that he was sure he would turn into wood at any second.

'I'm sure she has.'

Aubrey had to bite his tongue quite severely to prevent himself from commenting on Caroline's tone. He had a premonition that such an observation would be a very bad thing indeed. 'I've been keeping a good eye on her.'

'So I've noticed.'

Aubrey hoped that his tongue wasn't actually bleeding by now. 'She's well trained, has useful skills, seems like a fine addition to the security of the nation. I'm sure she has a good reason for talking to that attaché.'

'No doubt. And I'd like to hear it.' Caroline straightened. 'But first I'd like to hear your account of what happened.'

A reasonable, professional request, Aubrey thought, and he launched into what he hoped was a reasonable, professional report about the incident and then about the bomb disposal episode.

'I see,' Caroline said when he finished. She pursed her lips, gazed at the ceiling, and tapped a foot. An enchanting display, Aubrey decided. But entirely professional, he hastened to add. To himself.

'You do?' Aubrey adjusted a collar that felt a little tight.

'Your assassin missed. From a distance of a few yards.'

'You know those cultural attachés. Notoriously poor shots, most of them.'

'Even the ones who are crack marksmen? I checked his military record. He won the Armand Cup last year.'

'For shooting, I imagine, rather than fashion.' Aubrey rubbed his forehead as he remembered. 'He did seem a little startled. And unhappy with his pistol.' *A spell on it, to make sure he missed?*

'Then Mattingly shot him.'

'That's right.'

'So she ended up looking decisive and competent.'

'Indisputably.'

'And you were extraordinarily grateful to her for saving your life.'

'I appreciated her actions, yes.'

'I think her actions were intended to inspire more than appreciation. We need to talk to this Miss Mattingly.' Caroline nodded decisively, then held open the door. 'Nice haircut, Aubrey.'

Aubrey was excruciatingly aware that the disarming incident he'd undergone in the courtyard was as nothing compared to what he had on his hands here. In a moment of godlike apprehension, he suddenly saw all of the thousand ways he could make this situation worse. Outcomes danced in front of his eyes, where he saw Caroline hurt and bewildered, and, alternatively, him hurt and bleeding. He saw lengthy and inadequate explanations. He saw entreaties. He saw imperious retorts and many, many variations where Caroline stormed off, never to be seen again. Of course, most of these outcomes came from his not doing anything, so he was in the most cleft of cleft sticks that he'd ever been in.

So it was with something more than relief that he greeted the door when it burst open and George when he entered excitedly.

'Aubrey! Hello, Caroline! Didn't know you were here. Charming skirt, that. Have you heard the news? The blackguard who took a shot at you, he's escaped.'

Caroline raised an eyebrow at Aubrey. 'An interesting development, wouldn't you say, Aubrey?'

They were eventually able to push through the crowd near the infirmary at the rear of the ground floor, near the conservatory. Gallian excitement had meant that all the important business of preparing for war was suspended while rumour and gossip were passed around with all the authority of the evening newspapers. *Everyone* wanted to see what was going on.

Gallian guards recognised Aubrey and George, but some earnest discussion was needed before Caroline was admitted. Captain Bourdin was alone in the small, sunny room, which smelled of disinfectant and soap. He stood dolefully by a bloodstained hospital trolley. 'The infirmary opens to the courtyard,' he said without any preliminaries. 'He produced a pistol and threatened his way out.'

'I wouldn't have thought he'd be in any condition to run anywhere,' George said, pointing at the bloodstains.

'That is true,' Captain Bourdin said. He was despondent, and Aubrey wondered if he'd be looking for a new job. A shooting in the embassy, and the miscreant escaping soon after? It wouldn't look good on a curriculum vitae. 'He had a confederate waiting in a van outside. It drove, at high speed, past our guards.'

'Sounds as if your gatehouse might need some strengthening,' Aubrey said.

Captain Bourdin shot him a sour look. 'The gatehouse is to prevent people getting in. We did not think we would have to prevent people leaving.'

'This escape,' Caroline said. 'How long after Mattingly spoke to the prisoner did it occur?'

'This is Miss Hepworth,' Aubrey explained to the puzzled Captain Bourdin. 'She belongs to the Directorate.'

'Mattingly,' Caroline repeated. 'She did speak to the prisoner in the infirmary, correct?'

'That is so,' Captain Bourdin said slowly.

'And she also spoke to him before the shooting incident. This would tend to indicate a suspicious level of familiarity. If the prisoner had assistance in his escape from inside the embassy, I know in which direction I'd be looking.'

'Elspeth?' George said. 'She was the one who told me which direction you'd gone, old man.'

Caroline's observations had Aubrey thinking. He'd often wondered at the frame of mind needed to work in the security services, where suspicion was a natural state of affairs – but he could see how it was necessary. In a world where deceit and falsity were prized skills, who could be trusted? Was anyone what he or she seemed?

If Elspeth had been talking to the cultural attaché before the shooting, and if she had been responsible for his pistol being unreliable, then her talking to the same cultural attaché – after she'd shot him – might be curious.

She could have been doing some extra interrogation, he thought, but it rang false, even to him.

He remembered her brown bag. Clearly, it was large enough to hold more than one firearm.

By the look in Caroline's eyes, she had followed the chain and arrived at the same conclusion Aubrey had. 'Miss Mattingly supplied the pistol the attaché used in his attempt to shoot me. And, most probably, the one he used to escape,' he said. 'She is an enemy agent.'

Captain Bourdin scowled. 'Are you sure?'

'Sure enough that I'd advise you to prevent anyone from leaving.'

'Ah.' George held up a hand. 'We may have a problem with that. She's left already.'

'Left?' Aubrey said. 'Why? Where?'

George grimaced. 'On reflection, I may have had something to do with that. I couldn't find a cup of tea anywhere, so I went looking for her. She wasn't in the coding area and I remembered her mentioning her friend in the library. I found my way there, but with no sign of her, I thought I'd see if I could borrow one of those Gallian romance novels she was talking about.'

Everyone stared at him. 'Romance novels,' Captain Bourdin repeated. 'You wanted to read a romance novel?'

George shrugged. 'I have a Gallian friend who enjoys them. I thought I'd see what all the fuss was about.' He shrugged. 'Her letters talk about dark brooding looks and whatnot. Piqued my curiosity.'

'But you don't speak Gallian,' Aubrey pointed out. 'Or read it.'

'Thought I'd give it a go, old man. Might impress Sophie, just having a crack at it like that.'

'But you couldn't,' Captain Bourdin said. 'Not here, not in our library. We do not have these romances you speak of.'

'I found that out quite promptly,' George said. 'Your library is a technical library. Lots of stuff on Gallian history and law and the like. Not much light reading.'

Aubrey's heart sank. Elspeth's duplicity was becoming clear.

'No stories, no fiction at all,' Captain Bourdin said.

'And that's what I told Elspeth when I ran into her,' George said. 'Come to think of it, she look a little flustered, and she didn't unfluster, if you take my meaning, when I asked her about the romance novels.'

'And that's when she remembered that she'd been called back to headquarters?' Caroline asked, one eyebrow raised.

George grinned. 'She said she'd just received a message, if that's what you mean. She told me that we'd all catch up back there.'

'She knew she'd made a false step,' Aubrey said. The detail about the romance novel had probably appealed at the time, but it had brought her undone. For an instant he pondered why she'd wanted to show a romantic side to her nature, but he veered away from that as far too dangerous.

He was still having trouble imagining Elspeth as an enemy agent. He recalled her infectious good spirits, her provocative challenges . . . She was attractive, he couldn't deny that, but now he was starting to question how calculated her persona had been. The little touches on the arm, the outlandish dash she displayed, had him warming to her before he knew it. She was unlike any young women he knew, which was no doubt part of her appeal. With a chill, he wondered who else knew that.

If she were a Holmland agent, she was a deeply embedded one, one whose actions indicated that Aubrey was a person of some interest to Holmland Intelligence. She was ruthless, too, underneath the carefree surface. He doubted that the cultural attaché had agreed to be shot. His surprise at the malfunctioning pistol tended to indicate that he was only aware of part of the plan. He'd been told to assassinate Aubrey, not knowing that he was a dupe whose real role was to make Elspeth Mattingly a hero – and to make Aubrey hugely grateful to her.

With a demeanour designed to please on top of heartfelt gratitude, Elspeth Mattingly would be a bosom companion to Aubrey Fitzwilliam, close enough to be privy to whatever Aubrey knew and then to feed it back to her Holmland masters.

He grimaced at that prospect, but he was sure there had to be more. He imagined Elspeth accompanying George and him on missions, where she'd be relaying plans to the enemy in secret. He saw her teasing him, keeping him delightfully wrong footed, making sure she spent time with him, enough time to be introduced to his family.

Oh my. Aubrey closed his eyes for an instant as the possibilities hit him.

If she played her part well enough, Elspeth Mattingly could meet the Albion Prime Minister, and have access to him in private, unguarded circumstances.

The plan showed all the hallmarks of deep deviousness and complex planning. It fairly smelled of Dr Mordecai Tremaine. A plan that was undone by George Doyle's looking for Gallian romance novels. As soon as that happened, she was quick enough to see that she was undone – and that others would put two and two together quickly enough to make her position untenable.

Thank goodness for George, he thought, not for the first time.

'So she did not plan to leave,' Captain Bourdin said, interrupting Aubrey's thoughts. 'It was spontaneous.'

'I think she wanted to stay.' Caroline glanced pointedly at Aubrey. 'Having embedded herself in the Directorate, I'm sure she was going to do her best to gain the trust of those around her. It would mean she could be privy to sensitive information useful to our enemies.'

Aubrey found himself going back over his conversations with Elspeth and wondering what he'd said. Nothing vital, he hoped.

He made promises to Captain Bourdin to make sure a copy of the report Aubrey compiled for the Department would be forwarded to the Embassy. The unfortunate Bourdin handed Aubrey the ensorcelled pistol, which Aubrey took with some reluctance, even though he under-stood the Department's Forensic team could investigate it much better than any personnel in the Embassy. He probed it enough to confirm that it was indeed embedded with a spell to send rounds astray. The cultural attaché couldn't have hit what he was aiming at, not in a million years.

After slipping the pistol into a satchel, Aubrey shook hands with Captain Bourdin. 'I want to assure you that the Department will take care of things,' he said, doing his best to sound like a decisive leader.

'Things?'

'The would-be assassin. Mattingly. Things like that. The Department prides itself on not leaving loose ends lying about the place.'

'That's it,' George said brightly. 'Think of the Department as a big pair of scissors, determined to take care of those annoying loose ends.'

Before George could strangle the metaphor any more, Aubrey took him by the shoulders and steered him toward the door. 'We must get back to headquarters, captain. Important matters to discuss. Good luck.'

Once outside the Embassy, much to Aubrey's delight, Caroline suggested that they go back together, since Walter and Gregory were busy with cooking and plumbing, and since her pose as a typist had been compromised.

They left Captain Bourdin standing, hands behind his back, dejectedly staring at the empty hospital trolley that could be the remains of his career.

At the gatehouse, a panting young man in a Gallian uniform caught up with them. 'Monsieur Fitzwilliam, a moment.' He stopped, put a hand to his chest and caught his breath. 'Captain Bourdin. He would like a last word with you.'

Aubrey made a face. It had been a long morning. He shrugged at Caroline and George. 'You two go on. I'll catch up.'

The messenger handed Aubrey over to another messenger, who took him to an older woman in one of the back offices, who glanced at the slip of paper (turquoise) the messenger gave her and then she took him right to the end of a narrow corridor on the third floor. 'Wait here,' she said and left Aubrey without even a slip of paper to call his own.

Five minutes later, the door in front of him opened. 'Enter,' a woman's voice ordered.

One step inside, and that was all he knew as huge pain took hold of the back of his head.

As a fuzzy level of awareness returned, Aubrey understood that he was tied to a chair and securely gagged. Or gagged to a chair and securely tied, one or the other. His head was ringing like a bell, so details like that were hard to work out.

The figure standing between him and the door spoke, and he winced. 'I'm sorry, but you're too dangerous to handle any other way.'

'Elspeth,' he said. Or tried to. It came out more like 'Rrgwrwflg,' thanks to the gag, thus proving its efficacy.

She took a revolver out of a satchel that Aubrey dimly realised as his. He had enough wherewithal to wish that ropes weren't so good at binding as they were, but Elspeth shook her head. 'I couldn't leave this here. I might need it to get out of this awful country.'

Aubrey squinted. With an effort, he recognised it as the pistol that had nearly shot him. The pistol that he'd been given by Captain Bourdin. The pistol that had been magically treated to be silent – and to make sure it missed.

She studied him for a moment. 'I suppose I should just shoot you now, you know. I'd be bound to get a medal for it.'

What scared Aubrey most was how businesslike she sounded.

She pointed the pistol at him and he was sure his heart stopped beating. 'On the other hand . . .' She raised the pistol and Aubrey's heart scurried out from wherever it had gone to hide and started beating again, hard. 'If I happen to get captured before I can waltz my way out of here, I might be better off if I don't. Spending the war in one of your internment camps sounds preferable to a hanging. Even with your ghastly weather.'

She crossed the room, and leaned close until all he could see was her large, insistent eyes. She patted his cheek. 'It's a pity that I can't continue this job,' she whispered. 'You really are quite appealing.'

She slipped out and Aubrey surrendered to utter confusion.

'We had our suspicions that she was a Holmland agent,' Commander Tallis said. 'Nothing concrete, but suspicions nonetheless.'

Back at Darnleigh House, Aubrey, George and Caroline faced Commander Tallis and Commander Craddock across a long, metal-topped table. The room was on the third floor, but it had no windows. The walls were undecorated, for Aubrey wouldn't have called the peculiar shade of institutional green paint decoration.

Aubrey's head ached, and his pride, even though neither George nor Caroline had said anything when, after his non-appearance for two hours, they returned to the Gallian Embassy and found him bound and gagged with Elspeth Mattingly long gone.

'So you let her try to kill me just to see if those suspicions were well founded?' Aubrey asked. He was accustomed to the oblique thinking that went on in the realm of security, of plans and plots within plans and plots, so he saw how such a course of events could unfold. It didn't mean that he liked it.

'That was unfortunate. We thought that putting her in a team with you would force her hand but it appears that we inadvertently gave her just what she wanted,' Craddock said. He had a silver letter opener on the table in front of him, perfectly parallel with its edge. 'In any event, we thought she would have done more gradual embedding. Something less dramatic.'

Perhaps she knows something we don't, Aubrey thought. Such a risky display might have been forced upon her, if time was growing short – which was an ominous thought.

'This means, of course, that your team is one member short.' Craddock and Tallis shared a look, and Tallis shifted uncomfortably in his seat. 'It seems inevitable that Miss Hepworth replace our enemy agent.'

'It's the most efficient solution,' Tallis growled.

Caroline stiffened. 'Permission to speak, sirs?'

'I was unaware that you ever made that request.' Craddock picked up the letter opener and held it in both hands.

Tallis glanced at him. 'Permission granted.'

'That would mean my original team would be one person short. I can't let them down like that.'

'I appreciate your loyalty,' Tallis said. 'Rest assured, your team will be taken care of.' Caroline subsided, mollified, as Tallis held up a folder. Aubrey couldn't gauge the extent of her feelings. Was she angry with him? Did she think that he hadn't been suspicious enough of Elspeth because he'd been blinded by her charms? 'Fitzwilliam, you haven't spent any time with the magical surveillance section, have you?'

'Just a familiarisation tour, sir.' The magical surveillance section was such a speciality that the sensitive magicians who were part of it were trained for months before being accepted into its ranks. Being able to detect magical perturbations at a distance was a rare, refined skill and Aubrey had great admiration for those who had it.

'Our best surveillance operatives are concerned,' Craddock said. 'They are detecting some remarkably unusual emanations from north-west Holmland. Near the border with Gallia.'

Aubrey tried to remember a map of the Continent, but George spoke up first. 'From Stalsfrieden?'

'In that area. What do you know about it?'

'A centre for heavy industry,' Caroline said promptly. 'Not armaments, but farm machinery, some lorry building, a few metalworking plants.'

'It's a river port, too,' Aubrey said, in an effort to hold up his end. 'And an important railway hub.'

Tallis grunted and pushed the folder across the desk. 'There's more here.'

George scooped it up. 'Hmm . . . I didn't know it was the centre of Holmland playing card manufacture.'

'I take it that lorry building and playing cards wouldn't cause the sort of perturbations the surveillance people are talking about,' Aubrey said. 'So you're suggesting that something new is happening in Stalsfrieden?'

'New and disturbing,' Tallis said. 'Disturbing enough to make us concerned.'

'When do we leave?' Caroline asked.

Aubrey hesitated. He'd been thinking that their role was consultative here.

'You are a novice team, in the extreme,' Craddock said, pointing with his letter opener. 'Normally, we wouldn't be sending you out for months. In many ways, your training has only begun.'

Aubrey's excitement grew. That didn't sound like a contradiction. They were going on assignment! He clamped down on his enthusiasm, lest he talk them out of it.

'These are unusual times,' Tallis said. 'We've mobilised all our experienced people, they're already scattering themselves throughout Albion and the Continent, monitoring sensitive sites, inserting themselves into suspect organisations.' He sucked a breath in through his teeth. 'If I had my way . . .'

Craddock tapped the desk with the letter opener. 'What our esteemed Commander Tallis is trying to say is that we have little choice but to use inexperienced teams like yourself. With trepidation, of course, but these are straitened times.'

Tallis's face was something like a gargoyle, something like a topographic map as it tried to express his reluctance. 'At the bottom of it all, you are now members of the Albion armed forces, for better or for worse, so it's your duty to respond when needed.' He paused. 'And remember: you are subject to military discipline, but you have the support of the entire Albion fighting forces.'

Commander Craddock took this up. 'Which is a roundabout way of pointing out that the military is a hierarchical beast. From Brigadier Ramsthorn down to the lowliest, rawest recruit, the chain of command is an inviolable thing.'

An inkling nudged Aubrey at that moment, a sense of knowing what Craddock was about to say. It wasn't totally a comfortable feeling and Aubrey was on the verge of actually squirming before he caught himself.

'The upshot of this,' Craddock continued, 'is that before you're let loose, your commission needs clarifying. For each of you. You may have to deal with Gallian officers, and your status must be confirmed.'

'Brevetting you as lieutenants is standard procedure, but don't get big-headed about it,' Tallis said. 'It's the most junior commission we could come up with while still allowing you to hold your head up with the Gallians. Just don't go swaggering about in front of any of our veterans, the ones who've earned their braid.'

Craddock and Tallis shared a look. 'Which leads us to the matter of a unit commander,' Tallis said. 'Despite being irregular and unorthodox, we've decided that a command structure is needed. Fitzwilliam, we've chosen to brevet you as a captain, in charge of these two. Congratulations,' he added, and the word appeared to cost him some effort.

Aubrey was astounded. 'Thank you, sir,' he managed. 'Sirs.'

He glanced at Caroline. Aubrey was sure she would have made an excellent unit commander. He wondered if Craddock and Tallis had considered her.

She nodded at him, coolly, and he was certain she was thinking the same thing. 'Congratulations, Aubrey. I'm sure you'll lead us well.'

Only if I do it very, very carefully. 'I'll do my best.'

'Well done, old man.' George slapped him on the back. 'I'll continue to suppress my obvious leadership capabilities, of course. I don't want to rock the boat.'

'I appreciate it, George.'

Leadership. Official leadership. Aubrey swallowed. Responsibility redoubled.

Craddock studied his letter opener for a moment. 'What is across the border from Stalsfrieden?'

'Divodorum,' George said. 'The vinegar capital of Gallia.'

'It's the home of the University of Divodorum,' Caroline added.

Aubrey considered this. The University of Divodorum wasn't one of Gallia's foremost institutions, but it had been around since the sixteenth century and attracted many foreign students. As with most ancient universities, the town had grown up around it.

'You're to be an advance team,' Craddock said. 'Blend in with the university students, set up a base, and then we'll send across a team of sensitives. Closer to the source of the emanations, they may be able to divine more about what's going on.'

Aubrey frowned. 'Why are we being so clandestine? Why aren't we working with Gallian authorities?'

Tallis made another face. This time, he managed to get frustration, irritation and weariness into his grimace. 'We are. You will have some contact, but we're being very careful about respecting Gallian sovereignty, with the recent brouhaha and all.'

Of course. Dr Tremaine's carefully orchestrated revelation that the long-vacated throne of Gallia actually belonged to the royal family of Albion through a long and tortuous tangling of lineage hadn't torn apart the alliance between the two countries, as Dr Tremaine had no doubt hoped. A number of Gallian patriotic groups were agitating for such, however, with demonstrations and riots, and relations were generally strained.

Which is not a good thing when embarking on a war, Aubrey thought.

'Albion military presence in Gallia might be seen as provocative,' Caroline said. 'Especially among the civilian populace.'

'Exactly,' Craddock said. 'So a secret operation appears best. You will be required to take no action – simply setting up a base and helping the surveillance team once it arrives. Keep the lowest of low profiles.'

Aubrey had a frisson of fear. This was real, going so close to the enemy border.

Craddock leaned forward. 'One more thing: we have reports that the Holmlanders have agents throughout Divodorum.'

Tallis grunted. 'It's what we'd do. Have people cross the border, intelligence gathering, making preparations. You won't know who to trust, so trust nobody.'

'We'll be on our own,' Aubrey said. The creeping apprehension wasn't fear, Aubrey told himself. And if it was fear, it was probably healthy. It would help keep him alert, wary. Alive.

'Apart from one local liaison agent,' Craddock said. Carefully, he placed the letter opener in front of him. Aubrey took note of how it was exactly parallel with the edge of the desk. 'A Gallian who will make himself known to you. He may be useful.'

Aubrey sat back in his chair and put his hands together, rubbing them slowly. He glanced at his friends. Caroline was solemn, but looked determined. She put a hand to the brooch at her collar and then frowned thoughtfully. He could imagine her arranging all the implications of what they'd just been told and then ticking them off once she was satisfied. Very little escaped Caroline. George had his arms crossed and showed not a trace of levity. He looked like someone who'd been told about an impending, unavoidable operation, something to be endured rather than enjoyed.

Aubrey knew exactly how they felt.

Thirteen

THREE DAYS LATER, A FRISKY WIND WHIPPED ACROSS THE Finley Moor airfield and in through the window of the Directorate motorcar. George, as driver, handed their credentials to the guard at the gatehouse and then turned to peer into the back seat. 'The place has expanded, hasn't it, old man?'

Aubrey was sitting with Caroline in the rear of the discreet and powerful vehicle, and had enjoyed the journey from the city immensely. Caroline's closeness was always enjoyable, and the enthusiasm with which she pored over the maps and travel documents was infectious. She was wearing stylish travel clothes – maroon leather gloves, a long gaberdine coat, a neat suit, a felt beret – and she had trouble concealing her excitement now that the mission was underway. She did her best to hide it by adopting a pose of unruffled professionalism, but the grin that escaped when Aubrey questioned small matters in their orders showed how the excitement was bubbling in her.

Aubrey was the same. The weightiness when given the mission had fallen away and was replaced by relief at launching into action instead of merely waiting, stewing in uncertainty.

Caroline gazed through the motorcar window at the huge shapes serenely bobbing at their mooring mast. 'It's been an age since I've been on an airship. Father took us to the Americas on a lecture tour when I was small.'

'These are all military craft,' Aubrey said after scanning the scene through the window. Of course, he had to lean close to Caroline to do so, but he was just being helpful. The airships varied in shape and size, with the newest shining with bright aluminium skins. He wondered what other advances they had. 'They won't be as luxurious as your transcontinental dirigibles.'

'That doesn't matter,' Caroline said without taking her eyes from the window. 'Just to be flying again is enough.'

Their preparations for the mission had been a scramble. Together and apart, they were provisioned and briefed. Visits to the Quartermaster, the Magic Chandler and the Armourer had outfitted them with diverse and clever equipment. Aubrey was still having trouble finding the best position for his handgun. He currently wore it on his left side, under his armpit, as advised by the Armourer, but the bulk of the Symons service revolver made it uncomfortable. George and Caroline didn't seem to have a problem. Caroline no doubt because she was accustomed to concealing firearms about her person, and George because he'd opted for the somewhat experimental

Symons Self-Loader, a new pistol with a seven-round magazine, more compact than the bulky, but reliable, Mark IV revolver Aubrey was carrying.

Other equipment ranged from concealed compasses, hidden map containers, disguised code books and sundry items as requested by each of them. Aubrey had specifically asked for a magical suppression unit, having a conviction that such a thing could be handy, but the Magic Chandler – after consulting Commander Craddock – had declined the request. 'Travel light and make do' was the motto of the mission and the smallest suppression device was the size of a breadbox, despite some rapid advances in spellcraft and technology.

Aubrey took Caroline's left hand. He did it without thinking, which was fortunate, for he wouldn't have if he'd pondered the action. 'That's a new ring.'

'It's only taken you three days to notice,' she said, but she didn't pull her hand away.

Aubrey wanted to tell her that he sometimes became a little fuzzy about details of ornamentation or accessories when he looked at her because she captivated all his attention. It wasn't a bad declaration, but he wondered if it sounded too much like flattery, or fulsomeness, and perhaps something more direct would be better, and as he did, the moment passed. He lapsed into floundering. 'Well, it's been busy, with one thing and another, and I've been trying to memorise our route and code details and –'

'It's from the Armourer.'

'Not from Anderson and Sutch?'

'The jeweller's? No. Look closely.'

The ring was an oval black stone in a silver setting. The band was slender, and it looked good on Caroline, as most things tended to. It could have been gold, for instance, and it still would have . . . He brought himself up short and peered closely. 'It's lovely. Jet?'

'It's enamelled metal. If I prise it up I have a length of very fine wire.'

'Just in case you need to repair a piano?'

'You'd be surprised at what use a length of wire can be put to. Have you heard of garrotting?'

Aubrey shuddered. 'I hope it doesn't come to that.'

'So do I.' She turned the stone ninety degrees. 'And now it's a handy small blade, for use in awkward situations.'

'You're not going to do someone much damage with that.' The blade was the same width as the band, but only a fraction of an inch long.

'It's not for hand-to-hand combat, Aubrey.'

'Then what's it for?'

'I'll find a use for it.'

'Clever gadget.' Aubrey wondered if he'd been short-sighted in merely walking away with a compass inside a hollow heel of his shoe. He never thought he'd be accused of a lack of imagination, but he clearly had a few things to learn about this world of furtive armament. Caroline, on the other hand, had a natural bent for it.

After a formal visit to the base commander, George navigated between the enormous hangars, then crossed the vast open space where the dirigibles were moored. Ground crews were at work. Lorries raced between them and the support buildings, with repair materials, fuel or supplies.

They found their designated craft: the A 205. Aubrey was pleased. This was the latest in the Albion airship fleet, the most modern, the most advanced, and the most recently built. Great ropes had brought it close to the ground, but its bulk still blocked out the sun when they drew close. A uniformed, moustachioed figure stood, arms behind his back, at the open door to the control car suspended beneath the belly of the great ship. As they approached, the engines coughed. 'Quickly now!' he shouted, waving. 'We're casting off as soon as you're aboard!'

As soon as they stepped inside he greeted them enthusiastically. 'Lieutenant Davey! You made good time!' Then, with much shouting and clattering, the gangplank was stowed, the hatch closed, and Lieutenant Davey barked into a speaking tube. Immediately, Aubrey felt a swooping lurch. Caroline clutched his shoulder, eyes bright, and she pointed through the glass observation ports as the airfield dropped away.

The great propellers stuttered, then wound up until they hummed, a blur to the eye. The airship rose speedily toward the clouds, its vertical ascent easily outpacing its lateral movement. As they climbed, the countryside rolled away in all directions. The flatness around Finley Moor became the river valley of the Harwell, then unfolded to become the greenness that lay between the river and the sprawling outskirts of Trinovant. It had taken an hour for George to drive the motorcar from the capital to the airfield, but it looked as if the airship could cross the same distance in minutes.

Except we're going in the other direction, Aubrey thought and, as he did, the great craft did indeed lumber around, swinging its nose to the west. The engines' howl rose in pitch and Aubrey guessed that they were working into a headwind.

'I never get sick of it,' Lieutenant Davey said, straightening from an observation port and dusting his hands together. He was grinning. 'It's like the world is being made afresh each time we fly.' He grinned. 'Come up to the bridge. Captain Bailey wants to discuss your mission.'

Aubrey and his friends followed as he hurried along corridors and stairways that would have been at home on an ocean liner. It was certainly a more comfortable way of flying than the noisy, cramped ornithopters, and undoubtedly safer than the new fixed-wing aircraft.

Aubrey liked Lieutenant Davey's enthusiasm. As well as being infectious and allaying any misgivings they may have had, it was reassuring to see such keenness in the service of the country. Albion would be well served if all its people showed as much gusto as Lieutenant Davey.

Captain Bailey was standing right at the front of the bridge with a pair of field glasses pressed to his face. He was an older man, with a neatly trimmed grey beard. Three other airmen were on the bridge, one doing the helming and the others performing arcane tasks known only to fellow airmen. *Keeping a lookout for flocks of birds?* Aubrey guessed wildly. *Monitoring gas expansion?*

When Davey cleared his throat, Captain Bailey lowered his field glasses. 'Ah, the Directorate people. Good to have you aboard. Miss Hepworth.' He took her hand and bowed over it, very slightly. 'Fitzwilliam, Doyle.' He shook hands. He was a short man, stocky, with alarmingly broad shoulders. Wrestler's shoulders, Aubrey always thought of them as. 'Come into my ready room. Keep it on a seventy degrees north heading, Cheney.'

The helmsman nodded. 'Aye aye, sir.'

The ready room opened off the bridge and was surprisingly spacious. It had a desk, at the rear near a round porthole that let in the late afternoon sun. The front half was more like a comfortable lounge with a suite of low leather armchairs in a circle, surrounding a low table.

'Five o'clock on the dot,' Captain Bailey said, taking one of the armchairs. 'Perfect. What about a spot of tea?'

George beamed and Aubrey knew that the captain of the airship had a friend for life. 'We'd appreciate that,' he said.

The captain leaned to the wall and pulled a cord. 'Tea, and we can decide how we can help you when we reach our target.'

Aubrey hesitated. *Was this a trick question?* 'By landing and letting us off, I suppose.'

Captain Bailey raised an eyebrow. 'Eh? What's that?'

Aubrey looked at Caroline. She shrugged, slightly. 'We thought you were taking us to Divodorum.'

'That's what my orders say. But they don't say anything about landing. The A 205 never lands unless it's at a well-appointed airfield.'

In his mind, Aubrey could see the mission plans shredding and blowing away. He knew that part of being a leader was coping with obstacles, but he'd been hoping that they wouldn't come as soon as this one had. He glanced at the watch on his wrist – having left his family heirloom safely at Maidstone – and saw that they were officially an hour and a half into their mission.

At least the motorcar trip had been uneventful.

'Captain, have you taken out special units before?' Caroline asked.

'It's about all we're doing at the moment. Ferrying them to the Continent, then heading back for the next batch. Always at night.'

'At night?' Aubrey said. 'How do the teams alight?'

'No idea. Once we open the hatch, it's up to them.'

In the silence that followed this revelation, it was George who held up a hand like a hesitant schoolboy. 'And how high up are you when you do this hatch opening?'

'A few thousand feet.'

'A few thousand feet,' George repeated slowly. 'Above the ground, you mean?'

Captain Bailey wrinkled his brow. 'You field operative people have magic, don't you?'

Aubrey sighed. 'We haven't been briefed on such procedures.'

'These arrangements did appear rushed,' Captain Bailey muttered. 'I suppose this means we'll have to turn back, if you don't have the capability to perform a drop.'

Aubrey saw the look of disappointment on Caroline's face, despite her best efforts to hide it. He rallied. Not just for her sake, he told himself. It was for Albion, and duty, and responsibility and all that. 'Not so, Captain. How long will it take to get to our target destination?'

'Close to three hours, with this headwind.'

'I recommend that we proceed. We'll be ready when we get there.'

Fourteen

ESPITE THE A 205 BEING A MILITARY AIRSHIP, IT WAS roomy and well appointed. Aubrey couldn't help thinking that if he had the choice between being a crew member on a dirigible or on a submersible, anyone needing elbow room should definitely choose the dirigible.

Aubrey, Caroline and George were assigned quarters, even though their transit time was short. After being dismissed by the captain, they were ushered through the polished wood and brass corridors by a young airman who keenly pointed out cargo and munitions bays, the wireless telegraphy room, engine rooms and the substantial galley, which nearly turned George aside as they passed, thanks to the savoury aromas issuing from it.

After depositing their meagre bags, they gathered in Aubrey's cabin. The cabin was distinctly nautical in arrangement, with bunks and furniture constructed of aluminium and electric lights in the shape of portholes.

'Aubrey,' Caroline said. 'You're not putting us in an awkward position, are you?'

Such as being dropped from two thousand feet and not being quite sure about effecting a soft landing? He pulled the lightweight chair from the desk and offered it to Caroline. She sat, while George and he perched on the bunk. 'On our recent train trip to Fisherberg . . .' he began.

'On which you carefully didn't invite me.'

Aubrey paused. At the time, he'd tried to communicate with Caroline, but had been unable. In the end, Caroline had found her own way to the Holmland capital anyway, in the company of her mother. But if he pointed out either of these facts he would simply lay himself open to a charge of not trying hard enough. Again.

'I'm sorry for that,' he said, and then added, in a burst of sudden inspiration, 'I should have tried harder.'

'Hmm.'

'In any case, I told you about the events of that journey. About being flung off the train and then running into the band of rebel Veltranians.'

'I searched that train high and low,' George said. 'I had no idea where he'd gone.'

'As if being pushed out of the train wasn't bad enough, it happened just as it was going over a bridge. A very high bridge.' Aubrey paused, remembering his terror. 'It gave me considerable incentive to invent a spell that would ease my descent.'

'I see.' Caroline leaned against the desk. 'And did you use any of the spellcraft you'd being playing around with when we were in Lutetia? When you levitated that whole tower?'

'Some of the elements,' he said. 'Decreasing the effects of gravity, for instance. It's interesting, really, but by decreasing the attractive pull of the earth for a moment I think the earth actually gets heavier. Infinitesimally, but nonetheless –'

Caroline held up a hand. 'Enough, Aubrey. Save it for one of your journals.'

'Ah. Of course.'

'Anything you need, old man?' George asked. 'Magical paraphernalia or the like?'

'Not having much paraphernalia about when I was falling through the air, I made do,' Aubrey said, grinning. 'But I do need one item: a feather.'

George stood. 'So our mission to thwart Holmland begins with a feather hunt on an airship. Wait until my readers hear about this.'

'What on earth are you talking about, George?' Aubrey said.

'You can't write about our work,' Caroline said. 'It's top secret!'

George looked surprisingly smug. 'We all have our talents. My work on the university magazine was recognised by the Special Services people. They said I'd be perfect for a little scheme they've cooked up to help morale. A series of magazine articles about dashing Albionite soldiers and special operatives. Names and details changed, of course.'

'Of course,' Aubrey echoed faintly.

Caroline, however, wasn't so nervous. Her eyes sparkled. 'So, in your story, a feather hunt may become a search for some botanical object or other?'

'Exactly. Or a piece of magic glass or whatever makes

for a good narrative. Nothing dull, whatever the case. Can't have dullness. Not if we're to inspire the nation.'

Given some of the near-fatal scrapes they had found themselves in over the last year or so, Aubrey would have paid good money for a modicum of dullness, but he saw George's point. 'Let's comb this airship for a feather. Can we meet back here in half an hour?'

Aubrey was back after twenty minutes, both disappointed and dismayed. After wandering through crew quarters, officers' areas and in and out of the weapons rooms, he'd even crawled in among the giant gasbags that provided the lift for the dirigible, all without success.

He turned to his notebook.

After he'd returned home from the Fisherberg escapade, he'd made note of all the extemporary magic he'd invented during the efforts to keep Prince Albert safe, as was his wont. He'd learned that unless he actually wrote down these spells, he was bound to forget their intricacies. He'd also found that the simple act of writing actually helped embed the complex elements in his head.

Caroline shook her head at his glum expression when she returned. 'No luck, I'm afraid. You'd better start thinking of alternatives.'

He held up his notebook. 'That's what I'm doing. It's a shame, though. The feather spell worked beautifully.'

'What about the gas in the gasbags?'

Aubrey sat up, nearly clocking his head on the upper bunk. He blinked. 'Caroline, you have permission to crow.'

She raised an eyebrow. Most elegantly, Aubrey decided. 'I do?'

'You do. I thought I was being so clever, reproducing a successful spell, but I was being short-sighted. It's the *principle* that's important here, not the detail. Juggling a few elements, substituting a few variables, that's not difficult once the overall structure of the spell has been hammered out.'

'I won't crow, Aubrey. Not now. I'll save it up for later.'

'When I need some humility?'

'That's correct. I'm sure you would have abandoned the feather business in time, and it's not a huge leap of imagination to start wondering about how this craft stays up in the air.'

Aubrey put his hands together and rubbed them, slowly. 'I find you most useful, Caroline. I hope you understand that.'

Caroline inclined her head, eyes downcast. 'I do understand, Aubrey.' She paused, appearing to consider her words. Aubrey gave her time. 'Ever since we met, Aubrey, my life has changed.'

'Yes?' It was all Aubrey could trust himself to say as he was worried his heart was about to burst.

'The world has grown larger and infinitely more complex. Richer, in a word.'

'Oh?'

'Many things I'd only heard about or read about, I've now actually encountered. It's been frightening.'

'I'm sorry.'

'Let me finish. It's been frightening, but it's also been exhilarating, thrilling and infuriating.' She looked at him solemnly. 'That last is mostly you, of course.'

'Of course.'

'Aubrey, right now, I feel it's time to tell you something. Something important.'

'I'm listening.'

'I –'

The door to the cabin banged open. George stood, outlined in the doorway, brandishing a bright green feather. 'I've found it!'

In terms of unfortunate timing, Aubrey judged that George's entrance was on a par with Mrs and Mrs Unicorn going on a holiday just before the invitation came to join Noah on his ark.

Aubrey swallowed, and with an effort that was the equivalent of swimming through quickly setting concrete, he put a smile on his face. Then he trusted himself to look at Caroline. She had a hand to her throat, the fingers barely brushing her collar. Her eyes glinted. Aubrey was unwilling to believe he saw tears. It must have been the light.

Personal mission status: Aubrey thought with a vast hollowness inside, *failure.*

George wasn't a dullard. He looked from Aubrey to Caroline and back again. 'Ah. You know, I have a sudden urge to go and see cook at work in the galley. Fascinating stuff, that.'

Caroline stood and smiled, most sweetly. 'Thank you, George, but I think your feather is more important.'

'The moment's passed, eh?' George ran a hand through his sandy hair. 'Put my foot in it, haven't I?'

Aubrey couldn't help but laugh at his friend's quick change of demeanour from triumphant to crestfallen. 'George, speaking as an expert in putting feet in wrong places, I can say that you're a mere beginner in the field.

You have years of work ahead of you to achieve my level of malfootedness.'

George studied their faces for a moment, then he shrugged. 'Thank you for your words of wisdom, O Baron of Blunders, O Guru of Gaffes, O Mighty Maestro of Mistakes.'

'My pleasure.' Aubrey pursed his lips. 'Mighty Maestro of Mistakes?'

George dusted off a lapel. 'I'm quite proud of that one.'

'Alliteration is the crutch of the insecure writer, George, you should know that.'

'It is? Who said so?'

'I did. I just made it up.'

'And the feather, George,' Caroline said, turning the conversation aside. 'Where did you find it? I looked everywhere.'

George handed the bright green feather to Aubrey. 'The engineer's mate has a parrot. He didn't know what a foul mouth the bird had, either, until we plucked him.'

With the feather in hand, Aubrey sat at the desk with his notebook and was quickly able to reconstruct his spell. After his discussion with Caroline, he was even able to enhance it, blending it with the levitation spell he'd worked out in Lutetia. This combination, he was sure, would allow him to manage their rate of ascent with some degree of control, which was a blessing. His memory of the moonlight plunge from the Transcontinental Express was one of absolute panic then frantic spell casting followed by an almighty thump at the end. He'd hit the ground hard enough to leave a welter of bruises, but he'd walked away, which was a rather better outcome than appeared likely when he began his descent.

Now, of course, a successful spell was even more important. The mission was contributing to the war effort – which was reason enough – but more paramount was the safety of his friends. Their lives would be in his hands.

AUBREY SQUINTED INTO THE RAIN WHIPPING AT HIS FACE AS he stood at the doorway into the night sky. Even though Captain Bailey had ordered the A 205 to turn into the wind and the crew was doing its best to maintain position, the fitful weather was making things difficult.

At least the foul weather means there's no moon, Aubrey thought. It also meant that most of the citizens of Divodorum would be inside, out of the rain, tucked up nice and warm, and not wondering about mysterious airships wandering about their city.

Aubrey gripped the rails on either side of the exit. Captain Bailey had thought that using the passenger exit was best. Situated as it was right at the bow of the craft, it meant Aubrey could clearly see the terrain below.

He had a tug at his waist. 'Ready, old man? We're freezing back here.'

Aubrey adjusted the rope around his waist. It had been his idea. He didn't want the three of them separating during what he hoped was going to be a controlled descent.

Lieutenant Davey clapped his hands together. 'Best to go now.'

'Really?'

'We're in perfect position.'

Aubrey looked down. Lights twinkled from the houses and businesses of the spread-out city and outskirts. He could make out where the Salia River joined the Mosa River, the confluence being the reason a town grew here in the first place, the Romans knowing a good spot for a trading post when they saw one. For a moment, Aubrey had a vision of an ancient property agent pointing out the delightful river frontage to a centurion, and how the place would be close to schools and shops – when they were eventually built – and deciding not to overquote once the centurion starting fingering his well-used blade.

More sombrely, however, Aubrey took note of more recent developments. North and east of the city he could see earthworks and fortifications. The approach to the city in that direction followed the valley of the Salia River, between beetling ridges of higher land that – some thirty or forty miles away – became the Grentellier Mountains. The open land either side of the road and the river was entrenched and mounded, and sprouted barbed wire much as an ancient ruin would throw up ivy. A fortress loomed on the city side of this build-up. As well as being the centre of the military precinct, it was the gateway to the airfield beyond, where mooring masts stood lonely on the banks of the river.

He wiped his eyes. He was humbled by the confidence George and Caroline had in him. They were perfectly happy throwing themselves out of the dirigible and relying on him. The small bundle of equipment he'd managed to drop successfully, on a previous pass over their position, had been enough for them. Aubrey was their man.

As an alternative, Aubrey had asked Lieutenant Davey about the new parachute devices he'd heard of. The airman had laughed and told him that the airship corps refused to have anything to do with parachutes because if the crew could simply abandon ship, they'd do nothing to save the craft when in difficulty.

Aubrey's opinion of the military mind was confirmed by this. Why have common sense when you can have rules instead?

Aubrey wiped rain from his eyes and tugged on his close-fitting black cap. *I'm confident*, he told himself. *More than that, I'm confident I'm confident.*

Captain Bailey was confident too. His bluff assurances that he'd had dozens of operatives who'd managed such a procedure was meant to be comforting, but was undercut when he'd declared that most of them survived.

Caroline's voice sounded close behind him. 'Time, Aubrey, I should think.'

Aubrey hadn't had any ulterior motive when he arranged his friends on the rope. Naturally, he had to go first. And naturally George was the ideal rearguard man. That meant Caroline had to take the place right behind him. Of course, they'd have to bunch up before they stepped off the ledge . . .

'Put your hands on my shoulders,' he said.

'Like this?'

Exactly like that. And can you move a little closer? 'That's fine. George?'

'Right here, old man.'

They'd dressed warmly, in heavy overcoats, boots and gloves, all black so as not to stand out against the night sky. It didn't stop Aubrey from shivering a little as he contemplated the drop, and he was acutely conscious of the weight of the gold sovereigns strapped around his waist, part of the funds to be used for their mission. He knew, intellectually, that being heavier wouldn't make him fall any faster, but a primitive part of his brain had other ideas and it was the one that was squeezing his panic gland. 'On the count of three, everyone. Right. One, two, THREE!'

An instant of tangling, a roaring whoosh in the ears, the buffeting of wind and hard rain, and Aubrey found he was looking up at the bulk of the airship and wondering why it was moving away from them so quickly. Then his perceptions righted themselves and he realised it wasn't rising – they were falling.

'Aubrey!' Caroline tugged on his arm and her face swam into view. She was wearing an aviator's leather helmet to keep her hair in, and her eyes were huge in the night time. 'The spell!'

He knew he'd forgotten something.

With George flailing away nearby, doing his best impression of a crested grebe, and Caroline undulating gracefully, Aubrey found it difficult to concentrate, but the undeniable – and looming – presence of the earth beneath them gave him the necessary incentive.

He rolled out the Akkadian syllables and inserted a considered value for their rate of descent – then their plummet slowed so dramatically that he nearly lost his supper. George squawked in what Aubrey hoped was a continued approximation of the crested grebe, just in case any of the inhabitants of Divodorum were insomniac skywatchers with good hearing.

When he'd gathered himself sufficiently, and disengaged

his neck from the woollen scarf that had taken on boa constrictor-like qualities, Aubrey quickly estimated how fast they were falling and was relieved to see that the treetops below were relatively stationary. The rain squall had passed, too, and if it weren't for the wind he decided he'd be quite enjoying their position.

He turned to Caroline. Her teeth were white in the darkness. 'Isn't it wonderful, Aubrey! I can see for miles!'

Aubrey was enchanted all over again by a magic much more subtle than his craft. Caroline's unashamed excitement made his heart thump even more than could be accounted for by their plummeting.

George bobbed over, pulling himself closer by the rope around their waists. He jerked a thumb at the ground and looked quizzical. Aubrey sighed. He needed to bring their fall under control.

'Drag yourselves closer!' he shouted. 'I'll get us down!'

THE ROPE SEEMED LIKE A GOOD IDEA AT THE TIME, AUBREY thought as he tried to push his face away from the rough bark of the tree. The rope had tangled around the trunk, trapping him close. 'Caroline! George! Are you all right?'

'Up here, Aubrey.'

With some difficulty, Aubrey levered his head a little away from the trunk and peered up through the leaves. Caroline was perched on a solid branch, looking down with some concern. She'd managed to hook one end of the rope around a projecting limb. While he clung to the trunk, he was taking the weight of the other end, but if he slipped he could drag her off.

'Where's George?'

'Over here, old man, upside down and swinging away.'

Aubrey tried to look to his left, but couldn't move his head in that direction. 'Is anyone hurt? I mean, apart from my bark rash?'

'Uncomfortable,' George said, 'but unharmed.'

'I'm quite comfortable,' Caroline said. 'Can you hold on, Aubrey?'

Aubrey had his arms wrapped around the trunk of the tree. He wasn't quite sliding downward, but he couldn't find anything to grip on to. 'Not for long.'

'Right. I'll just need a minute.'

Aubrey made out a flash in the darkness. The pressure on his rope eased and for a panicked moment, he fell. Then, after barely a foot, he was brought up short and he clutched the trunk, his heart racing.

'There,' Caroline said briskly, as if she were discussing a garden arrangement. 'The rope is secure now. You can climb up. George?'

'Still dangling here.'

'I've cut your rope away from me. I'm now going to drop off my branch while holding it.'

'What? Are you sure?'

'You'll be hauled up to the branch. Do grab it.'

Aubrey had been inching up the trunk, but he nearly let go of his end of the rope. 'Caroline! What about you?'

'Oh, don't worry about me.'

He needn't have. In the darkness, it was hard to make out, but a bulky, cursing shape shot upward, almost colliding with him on its upward passage, and somewhere overhead it thumped into a branch with enough force to make the tree shake. More cursing, then a shower of twigs and leaves fell about Aubrey's head. 'George?'

Silence for a moment, then a forbearing voice. 'I'm safe. Scratched, bruised, and probably green from head to foot, but I'm safe.'

A slim silhouette swooped past, flipped, and landed lightly just above. Light laughter told Aubrey it was Caroline rather than some woodland sprite, although he was sure he could be forgiven if he confused them.

He clenched his teeth and edged up his rope until he joined his friends on the limb Caroline had chosen.

Caroline was sitting, bright-eyed, hands in her lap, aviator helmet just slightly askew. 'Well, here we all are. What's next?'

Fifteen

AFTER BURYING THE ROPE AND FINDING THE BUNDLE of earlier dropped equipment, it was a matter of waiting for dawn and the train and munching chocolate bars for breakfast.

They found an elevated area in the woods, a knoll where a large boulder had pushed its way up through the grass, to monitor the city and the railway. As the night passed, cool and moist, the shapes of the town began to emerge from the blackness. Towers and spires of churches, remnants of the medieval city, the old bridges over the rivers and, as the light grew, buildings made from limestone, common in the area.

Aubrey could make out two significant parts of the city. To the north-east was the fortress, looking outward toward the Holmland border. On the west side of the city, closer to their current position, was the sprawl of the university, a conglomeration of buildings that showed every sign of having grown over the centuries, stretching along the bank of the Mosa River, and penetrating the surrounding streets toward the centre of the town. Even at this early hour, electric lights showed in the university buildings, signs of those either working very late or beginning before anyone else.

The plan was to wait for the morning's first Lutetia–Divodorum passenger train, then to mingle with the people arriving. As Divodorum was an important centre in the north-east region of Gallia, the influx of newcomers to the town was unlikely to cause comment. The suitcases they'd recovered from the equipment drop gave the semblance of ordinariness that Aubrey wanted. They were foreign students, registered and expected, perfectly normal thank you very much.

Aubrey took it as a good sign that the train arrived on time, and their mingling went smoothly. As the passengers alighted and left the station, Aubrey, Caroline and George emerged from the woods nearby, chatting about their non-existent journey and blending in for all they were worth.

Divodorum was an oddity. Only twenty miles from the border with Holmland, it was relatively secure. The wooded and hilly region between the city and the border had long been deemed an unlikely route for the enemy to take. The build-up in fortifications had been routine, according to their briefing papers, and became almost perfunctory once the Holmland alliance had struck east at Muscovia and simultaneously pushed through the Low Countries. A third front? Through Divodorum? Ridiculous.

As such, life went on in the university town much as it

always had – apart from a healthy dose of suspicion that Holmland agents were everywhere.

George was the appointed navigator for this phase and he confidently pointed the way. 'Left at that big lumpy building.'

'The theatre?' Aubrey said.

'That's the one.'

Caroline was walking by his side. She'd abandoned her aviator's helmet – to Aubrey's disappointment as he thought it rather chic – and was wearing a bright red, close-fitting toque hat that matched her bright red suitcase and shoes. He wondered how much of her wide-eyed gazing about was real and how much was assuming the guise of a new student. She leaned close. 'Can you spot the Holmland agents?'

He jerked his head about and, to his astonishment, his hand went to his revolver. 'Holmlanders?'

'A little louder, old man,' George muttered. 'I think a few people back in Albion didn't hear. We turn right at the fountain.'

Aubrey hunched, feeling enemy agents all around, and vowed that he'd keep well away from grabbing at his firearm as a first response. He glanced at Caroline, but she was still pointing at the sights. 'Did you see some-one?' he asked in what he hoped was a low voice.

'No, but I'm alert.'

'There it is,' George said. 'On the corner.'

The boarding house was tired-looking limestone, three storeys, many windowed. Wide stairs and an elaborate canopy over the door suggested that, perhaps, it had known better days.

The landlady was expecting them. After inspecting

Aubrey's letter of introduction she showed them to their rooms. Her suspicions were of a baser kind than suspecting them of being Holmland agents, Aubrey guessed, and it explained why Caroline was given a sunny room on the ground floor, while George and he were put far away – at the other end of the building on the third floor.

From his window, Aubrey could see the university. The clock tower chimed nine o'clock and he was on a mission. For a moment, he revelled in the feeling. He'd had adventures – hair-raising adventures – but they were always happenstance and doing one's best in harum-scarum circumstances. This time, however, he'd been charged with a specific responsibility to undertake. His worth had been measured and found satisfactory. For someone who had spent most of his life striving to prove himself, it was most pleasing.

A knock came at the door. Before he could respond, it opened and George slipped inside with his suitcase. 'Found a place to stow your stuff, old man?'

Aubrey's suitcase was still on his bed, unopened. 'Top of the wardrobe too obvious?'

''Fraid so. Any other suggestions? Apart from under the bed.'

Encoding devices, some basic wireless telegraphy equipment, and a selection of useful tools and weapons weren't the usual accompaniments for students, and their instructions had been to conceal them as soon as possible. Details on exactly how to do this had been left to them. Quite a few other details had been left up to them, covered up with much talk of having to show initiative. It either showed faith in their initiative or a lack of understanding about the actual situation in Divodorum.

Or perhaps it's the way wars unfolded.

'It looks as if under the bed will have to do for now.'

'Good Lord,' George blurted from the window, where he'd wandered. 'I think we have trouble.'

At that moment, Caroline arrived at the door and she joined Aubrey in hurrying to the window. Together, they watched the dirigible that was approaching Divodorum from the south. 'What's Captain Bailey up to?' Caroline said. 'I thought he would have been well clear of the area by now.'

'That's not the A 205.' Aubrey peered over the rooftops. 'That's a Gallian military airship.'

'Can you make out any identification?' Caroline asked.

The great craft rumbled closer to the city, but the way it veered toward the eastern edge of Divodorum tended to confirm their speculation. 'Definitely Gallian,' Aubrey said. 'But first things first: we need to find somewhere to set up our post.'

The primary objective for their mission was to find a building to act as a facility for the second phase team, a building that would be secure enough and private enough for remote sensers to work from.

'So we need to reconnoitre?' George said. 'Splendid.'

Aubrey plucked a map of the city from his suitcase. It didn't need to be hidden – it was the sort of thing that any newcomer to Divodorum would have. He unfolded it and frowned. 'We could go separate ways,' he began, but Caroline had other ideas.

'We should purchase bicycles. A perfect mode of transport for a student. We can cover more ground.'

It was George's turn to frown. 'How long are we likely to be out?'

'Don't worry, George,' Caroline said. 'I've already asked our landlady if she could put together a hamper for us.'

'Really?' George brightened. 'I wouldn't have dared. She looked rather formidable.'

'She's an old dear. Worried, of course, about the war. Her husband died in a skirmish thirty years ago but she won't move. Divodorum is her home, she says, but she wishes they'd finish the earthworks to the north. Oh, and she's sure that the Mayor's assistant is in the pay of the Holmlanders.'

Aubrey groped for an appropriate response. 'You found all that out just now?'

'It's not difficult, Aubrey. It's just a matter of asking a question or two, then nodding sympathetically and listening hard.'

George went out with some of the gold to find a bicycle shop. Caroline took the opportunity to help the landlady in the kitchen – while continuing to gather as much local knowledge as she could.

Which left Aubrey alone, so he took the time to review the mission plans and to make some notes on refinements to the rate of descent spell. Something that would avoid proximity to trees would be a useful addition or, if he couldn't devise such a thing, a quick treatment for bark rash was his next option.

The bicycles George bought were fresh, new and of the best Gallian make. Aubrey felt quite stylish as he mounted the bright blue model he chose, and quite unobtrusive as the student population of Divodorum had apparently decided, as one, to wake up and take to the streets. Most of them were cyclists of one sort or another. Predominantly the daredevil sort, Aubrey decided as they swooped past, gowns and scarves flying.

Navigator George led the way again, with Aubrey and Caroline close behind. They spent a good two hours meandering through the blessedly flat streets, sizing up and discarding properties for a number of reasons – lack of access, lack of electricity, poor condition, too close to other buildings. Aubrey was determined to delay the inevitable next step of approaching property agents. He thought that young people interested in light industrial premises may be unusual enough to draw attention. Curious Gallians were one thing, but more professionally curious Holmlanders would be bound to follow.

Lunch was in a little park near the university, with many students having the same idea and enjoying the sun. Over good bread, cheese and local ham, they discussed the few possibilities and why they weren't really good enough anyway. Nearby, others argued philosophy, art and sport.

War seemed a long way away. Aubrey enjoyed the ease of the lunch but was nagged by their lack of success. He wanted to nail down this part of the mission quickly, finding a base. After that would come the more complicated work of readying it for the team of remote sensers. Aubrey had some plans for this phase that might prove demanding, in time, resources and their personal capabilities, plans to go beyond their mission outline. He wanted to impress the Directorate, and doing more than expected was a useful way of going about it, to his mind.

George pointed with a cheese-laden length of crusty bread. 'I say, isn't that what's-his-name?'

A Gallian officer was striding toward them, ignoring the students lounging on the lawn. He bore down on them with intent, and alarm stirred inside Aubrey. He didn't want a run-in with authorities, not so early in their mission.

'Fitzwilliam!' The officer beamed, and continued in good Albionish. 'You are here!'

Aubrey stood and grasped the Gallian airman's out-stretched hand. 'Hello, Saltin. What brings you to Divodorum?'

'You, of course! Ah, M'mselle Hepworth, Doyle – and is that a Divodorum ham?'

'It certainly is,' George said, 'and a jolly fine one it is. Congratulations on the promotion, Saltin. *Major* Saltin.'

'Join us, Major,' Caroline said, catching Aubrey's eye. 'Please do.'

'Plenty for all,' Aubrey said, divining Caroline's intent. It was far better for Saltin to sit on the ground for a picnic than to stand in the middle of the park, the centre of attention. With the elaborate uniform of the Gallian airship corps, his thick dark hair and his prominent, well-oiled moustache, he was almost the complete anti-student, the opposite of their carefully studied casualness, artfully arranged assemblies of coats and scarves, and hair that was dishevelled just so.

Major Saltin was a prominent member of the Gallian airship corps. Aubrey and George had saved him from certain death when his dirigible exploded while on a goodwill tour of Albion. Full of Gallian energy and charm, he had become an important connection between the Gallian military and Albion intelligence services.

Major Saltin's appetite was as good as George's. He was quick to put together a stylish arrangement of ham, cheese and bread. 'It was your Commander Tallis,' he said between bites, 'who wanted me to meet you, to be your person of liaison. His people communicated with my superiors, who sent the message down the line to me. I flew in this morning.'

Thus explaining the Gallian airship. With some satisfaction, Aubrey ticked that item off his list of things to investigate. 'Did your superior mention the nature of our mission?'

'Mission?' Saltin looked perplexed. 'I thought I was sent to watch over you while you studied at the university. Sir Darius's son deserves such assistance.'

'Not exactly,' Aubrey said carefully. It appeared as if inter-governmental communications weren't all they should be – and it didn't bode well for coordination in future. 'Our task here is war related.'

Saltin made a face. 'The war. A farce. It should all be over in a few weeks.'

'Really?' George leaned forward, neatly balancing half a hard-boiled egg on a slice of bread.

'Holmland troops will march back and forward through the Low Countries, enough to show how brave and shiny they are, then they will go home and the negotiations will start.' Saltin waved a hand. 'That is what people are saying. All will be calm by Christmas.'

He doesn't know about Dr Tremaine, Aubrey thought. He took an olive from a jar that Caroline produced from the hamper. 'Regardless, we have to find a property. A useful property to prepare as a base for some other operatives who will be here soon.'

Saltin thoughtfully munched on his ham and cheese concoction. 'I've visited Divodorum many times. I know people who may be able to help.'

Conversation turned to more mundane matters while the picnic supplies diminished – the weather, the latest fashions, Major Saltin's plans for his moustache. The day was soft and warm, and for a moment Aubrey was able to forget the pressing of the war, with the laughter of nearby students adding to the drowsy comfort of the park. Without raising himself from his prone position, Aubrey could see rowing boats on the river, where couples drifted, absorbed in each other.

It was a way of life he could grow accustomed to. He brushed an ant off the rug. Caroline was telling Major Saltin about dances in Trinovant, while George gazed about the park and made desultory scrawls in a notebook.

After the picnic was packed up, Saltin walked with them toward the fortress, explaining that the area around it was the sort of light industrial district that might have something suitable. As they neared, a column of military lorries and wagons thundered over one of the medieval bridges, sending up dust that hung in the still, warm air. 'We've been told to avoid the Holmland border when flying,' Saltin said while they waited for the dust to settle. 'For the time being. It is a shame, for the Holmlanders are good men, fine pilots.'

'You used to meet them?' Aubrey asked. His boots were filthy and he looked at them with dismay.

'We would often moor at Stalsfrieden, just across the border, and talk about aeronautics.'

Interesting, Aubrey thought. What had Saltin learned? He was no intelligence operative, but even casual conversation could throw up useful information. 'When were you last there?'

'A few weeks ago. Just before this silly war was declared.'

An unspoken conversation flitted between Aubrey, Caroline and George. Even though it consisted mostly of arch looks, raised eyebrows, meaningful nods and pursed lips, the meaning was clear, so Aubrey asked: 'Did you happen to notice anything unusual in Stalsfrieden?'

'Unusual? What do you mean?'

'Did you notice any new buildings? Or unusual movements of heavy transport or the like?'

'Ah, you are after intelligence about Holmland capabilities.' Saltin sighed. 'I am still having trouble thinking that way.'

'We have to,' Caroline pointed out. 'Times have changed.'

'And changed quickly.' Saltin straightened his cap. 'Stalsfrieden always has heavy transport. It is a rail centre for north-west Holmland. I did not notice anything unusual.'

'No new buildings?' George asked.

Saltin shrugged. 'It is a busy place. Much building has been going on for years. Factories, warehouses. Some of the old mills are being turned to new uses. Even the von Grolman complex.' He stopped. 'What did I say?'

It was Aubrey who first found his voice again. 'Von Grolman. That would be Baron von Grolman, the Fisherberg industrialist?'

'You know him? A good man. He hosts Gallian crews at his Stalsfrieden estate many times.' Saltin grinned. 'He knows his wine, too. For a Holmlander.'

Aubrey bit down on this new item of information, already worth its place in a report. Caroline had known

Baron von Grolman for some time as a wealthy friend of her mother. In fact, they'd been staying at his Fisherberg castle when Aubrey had uncovered the plot to replace Prince Albert with a golem. The baron's part in this was not apparent at first, but gradually, it and his association with Dr Tremaine had come to light. While not as prominent a public figure as the Chancellor and his generals, Baron von Grolman's huge fortune – and his desire for more – was a crucial factor in Holmland's warmongering.

'This estate,' George said slowly. 'Is this at the complex you mentioned?'

'No, my friend. The estate is in the woods overlooking the city. Empty, it has been, for many years, until recently. It was a woollen mill, but when the wool trade left Stalsfrieden, it was worthless. It was vacant for years. The baron's father wanted to turn it into a pleasure park, for children, but he lost interest after some work was done.'

'But the baron has opened it again?' Caroline asked.

'As a factory. New buildings have been built, new fences, an electricity generating plant constructed. It is unmistakable. The two towers on the original building make it look like a castle.'

'I'm sure it does,' Aubrey said. 'And I'm sure we'd love to have a look at it.'

'I would take you, if it were not for this war. Still, a few weeks and it will all be over.'

Aubrey – knowing Dr Tremaine's goal and his capabilities – wasn't sure at all, but he wasn't about to disabuse Major Saltin so abruptly.

Caroline took his arm. 'Aubrey.'

He stopped and looked in the direction she was gesturing. A short street stretched off to the left, finishing in a dead end where it reached the river. On one side of the street was a series of warehouses. On the other was a row of two-storey buildings, shops selling hardware-related items, mostly, but right at the end was a long red-brick building with a yard attached and a river frontage. The shops were quiet and shut, and had been for some time, to judge from the boards over the doors and windows. The red brick building, too, looked unoccupied.

'Saltin,' Aubrey said. 'Do you know this place?'

Saltin squinted. 'No, but I have a friend who might.'

The last occupants of the building had been brothers who had started an electroplating business, Saltin reported later that afternoon. A combination of filial mistrust and general business ineptitude meant that after outfitting the place as a workshop and office, it quickly went broke.

Saltin arranged an inspection. With the river frontage came a small private dock for barge delivery, which Aubrey took as a great bonus. George found a considerable basement, too, even if it was a little damp from the presence of the nearby river. Caroline reported good electricity and water supplies, as well as a useful flat roof with good access. With that, they were satisfied.

After a quick discussion with Saltin, Aubrey left the negotiation to him, suggesting a cover story of a brother who was going to set up business in Divodorum.

Aubrey explored the roof while Saltin was gone. With good field glasses, he was sure he'd have a commanding view of the countryside surrounding Divodorum. Even without them, he could see over the fortress and practice fields, the airfield, and – in the other direction – back toward the city, where the river and railway swept away to the south.

Caroline joined him. 'It's perfect,' she murmured. A slight breeze came across the tarred roof and ruffled her hair. Aubrey was glad he was close to her, but saddened that he couldn't be closer. 'I can set up our wireless telegraphy equipment and string an antenna across the roof.'

'Won't that be a little prominent?' he asked.

'I'll lay a horizontal field antenna from corner to corner. No-one will notice unless they come up here.' She peered to the north-east. 'Holmland is just over there.'

'Twenty miles to the border through hills and woods. Stalsfrieden is only a few miles from the other side.'

'Can you sense anything?'

Aubrey shook his head. 'That's not my forte, remote monitoring. I can't feel a thing at this distance.'

'I can.' Caroline shuddered. 'I can feel war.'

Sixteen

THE REST OF THE WEEK WAS GIVEN TO THE TASK OF NOT drawing attention to themselves – while readying their newly leased base for the arrival of the magical surveillance team.

Aubrey was determined to prepare the facility perfectly, to show how well the neophyte team could perform its duties, and to have it ready well within the week allowed for the task.

Of course, what had seemed straightforward – if testing – in Albion, now looked rather more daunting. Aubrey frowned at the list he'd made, not quite sure where to start.

First was a program of making vital purchases. With some misgivings, Aubrey agreed to separating for this. He had doubts about George's managing with his notorious lack of Gallian, but he was convinced by Caroline, who pointed out that a useful team must have members who were able to operate independently.

While these transactions were taking place, they also had to secure the base, making sure that no unwanted visitors could interrupt their delicate work. He sighed. Then there was constructing the area for the remote sensing operatives. It had to be shielded from stray magic, as much as possible, as well as more ordinary distractions like noise, or light, or just about anything, really. Much of this was uncomplicated carpentry, turning part of the basement into a detached area where the remote sensers could concentrate in isolation. Another part of the basement had to be set up as a general workshop. George was a dab hand at that sort of thing, and part of his purchasing responsibility was timber and tools.

The remote sensers were bringing some shielding devices with them, but Aubrey had a notion or two that he wanted to try. He'd managed to bring a few key components, but he'd have to cobble together the rest from what he could turn up in Divodorum.

The plans and blueprints Aubrey had for these machines were cunningly concealed in the maps in the rear of a Green Guide tourist book. Harmless to look at, just the sort of thing a visitor to the city would be expected to have, the pages had been magically treated using a selective application of the Law of Affinity. With the correct activating words, parts of the maps would fade – or disappear entirely. The remaining lines and text showed the plan needed to construct the shielding device. Another uttering of the activating words would restore the map to its innocent original state.

All that was left was to find and purchase the necessary components.

Or the components to the components, Aubrey thought as

he locked the front door of the factory.

Wandering into a shop and asking for a dozen harmonic valves was likely to cause gossip, even if he could find a place that sold such esoteric items. No, he had to construct many of the components from scratch and apply the needed spells in the correct sequence while he was doing so.

The market was Aubrey's first port of call. The Divodorum town square was bustling and crowded, noisy and colourful as stallholders hawked their wares while shoppers scrutinised and occasionally bought them.

Aubrey found a row of stalls offering a surprising array of technical items amid the plumbing necessities and ironmongery. He bought copper wire, insulating material, some small vials of mercury and as much bell metal as he could find. The stall owner was keen to assist Aubrey, and packaged everything in good brown paper, where appropriate, and stowed the rest in a hessian bag. Aubrey swung the bag over his shoulder, gazed at the vigorous commerce of the market, and took stock.

He assumed that uniforms weren't uncommon in Divodorum, given the vicinity of the fortress, but he wondered if the town had seen as many soldiers and airmen as were currently present. Twice on his way to the market he'd had to wait while columns of troops marched through the streets, accompanied by rumbling lorries laden with artillery and – just as importantly – provisions. The amount of provisioning gave Aubrey pause. It showed that someone somewhere was thinking ahead, either to enormous numbers of troops, or to a time when provisions may not be so easily obtained.

Neither option was reassuring.

When Aubrey returned to the factory, Caroline hadn't returned but George was in the yard, unloading a wagon.

'Flour, George?' he said as he approached his friend. He carefully put his bag on a rack just inside the large double doors. 'Butter? Cabbages?'

'Just the ticket,' George said and with a grunt he heaved a crate off the back of the wagon. 'Don't stand back, old man, lend a hand. I have to get this wagon back in an hour.'

'Vinegar, George? And what's that? Olive oil?'

'Just being efficient, old man. We're likely to be holed up here for some time, correct?'

'That's one possibility.'

'So I thought that meals might be a problem.'

'Or we could go hungry.'

George looked as if he'd suggested painting themselves blue and dancing through the streets as a way of remaining clandestine. 'Go hungry? Have you had a blow on the head or something? Go hungry? Can't have that.'

'So I see.'

'The factory has a kitchen – I'm sure you hardly noticed – and I've purchased some basic cooking equipment, some wood for the stove and now, the food.'

Aubrey thought of the lorries taking provisions to the fortress. 'You know, George, I think this may be a very good idea. You'll do the cooking?'

'Of course, old man. Ah, here's Caroline!'

Caroline glided toward them on her bicycle, the front basket of which was stacked so high that Aubrey was worried about her being able to see. He caught the handlebars as she came to a halt. 'Thank you, Aubrey. Can you take that topmost box before it falls?'

'Successful shopping?'

'It's a good start, and I happened to find out something very interesting. Two Holmland agents have been arrested.'

A chill. 'Any details?'

'They were both long-time residents of Divodorum. They had wireless equipment in their houses.'

Aubrey held Caroline's parcel in his fingertips, balanced. Long-time residents meant that Holmland security had been active for some time preparing for war.

It was a reminder, even though none was needed, of the seriousness of their position.

SEVEN DAYS OF HARD WORK RESULTED IN A SECRET ALBION security base that Aubrey was confident would be suitable for even the pickiest of remote sensers.

He stood in front of the factory in the late afternoon sun, hands on hips. He wiped the sweat away from his forehead and appraised their work objectively.

It was good. *And*, he thought, *with a little more work, it could operate even if Divodorum were overrun by the Holmlanders*.

While this wasn't the primary function of such a base, Aubrey knew that such a thing was in the minds of the top brass in Albion – small bands of independent operatives, working behind the lines to make life hard for Holmland occupiers. It would be a dangerous, tense life, and Aubrey hoped it would never come to that – but he couldn't deny that such a challenge appealed.

Caroline's wireless post was secured behind a false wall on the ground floor. The remote sensing facility was in the basement, where George had constructed bunks as well as the monitoring and recording booths, right near Aubrey's tiny encoding office, where he'd work with the compact ciphering machine. The armoury, double-locked and bolted, was set into the floor of Aubrey's office, a masterpiece of George's joinery work.

Sleeping quarters took up the end of the basement away from the remote sensing area. Side by side, divided by neat walls George had erected, each small, private area was spartan, just big enough for a small pallet, with a curtain to screen the straw mattress from the main basement area.

George had also managed some clever electricity theft, organising a hidden connection from a power company cable that ran along the river bank. It meant that if the worst came to the worst, the factory could be boarded up and would give every appearance of being another abandoned building in an area full of vacant premises.

At the moment, it wasn't necessary to be so clandestine. The factory looked just as it was – a facility being renovated, getting ready for new use.

The makeshift shielding was also operating well. The devices Aubrey had sweated over were located precisely about the building. From a distance, he hoped, no magician would notice anything untoward about the factory. Aubrey had tested it, and not a trace of magic leaked through the walls.

That evening, Major Saltin joined them for supper and informed them that his status had changed. 'I am now in charge of the ground crew here at Divodorum,' he announced over a hearty chicken and red wine casserole. 'I will continue to be your liaison.'

'How long?' Aubrey asked.

'Won't you miss flying?' Caroline asked.

Major Saltin shrugged. 'Months, my orders said. It will be a trial, being so earthbound.' He speared a potato. 'But not if the food is always this good. My compliments to the chef.'

'I'm glad you liked it,' George said, 'since it was your chicken. Where did you get it?'

'Friends.' Major Saltin beamed. 'I have many friends.'

Caroline touched her lips with a napkin. 'I should be able to send a message tonight. If you're ready, Aubrey.'

'What time tonight?'

'After midnight. Transmission is easier once the sun has gone down.'

'I'll be ready,' he said, thinking of what he still had to do. 'George, can you lend me a hand?'

'A hand? Of course.'

'I can lend hands as well,' Major Saltin said, 'but do not look to me for any magical assistance.'

'If you're happy to, Saltin,' Aubrey said. 'I'd appreciate it.'

Saltin took off his jacket, hung it over the back of the chair, and rolled up his sleeves. 'Where do we start?'

MIDNIGHT HAD WELL AND TRULY ROLLED PAST BY THE TIME Aubrey, George and Saltin finished the final touches on the remote sensing facility. The smell of sawdust tickled Aubrey's nose, mingling with the slightly oily sensation that came from the shielding magic he'd employed on the devices – something he could only feel because he was inside their range of effect. The devices themselves were installed inside large mantel clocks he'd found at a second-hand shop. All four were different, and it had made his work fiendishly difficult, but – at least at first glance – the clocks looked nothing more suspicious than slightly old-fashioned timepieces.

The booths were made of solid timber, backed with some lead sheeting that George had bought from a plumber. George and Saltin stood inspecting their work with pride. George wiped his brow with the back of his hand. 'Comfortable, secure, private. What more could a remote senser want?'

The booths were along the wall furthest from the river. Only three or four feet wide, side by side, each booth had a solid timber door and a ledge stretching from wall to wall to act as a table. They were a reasonable facsimile of the listening booths in Darnleigh House. No distractions, no decoration, nothing to take the remote sensers away from the focus required for their magical monitoring.

Aubrey was weary, but brightened when Caroline once more came down the stairs to see if they'd finished. 'One more thing,' he begged.

Caroline looked sceptical. 'Your "one more things" have a habit of multiplying. I'll go and warm up the radio equipment.'

'Go ahead. I want to make sure the perimeter security is in place and working.'

Guardian magic was a well-established application of the Law of Entanglement, where a number of similar objects were magically linked, then distributed about the perimeter of a property. If a direct line between the objects was breached, then – using an application of the Law of Intensification – an alarm would sound. Simple and neat, but simple and neat always sounded to Aubrey like an invitation for improvement.

He'd been fiddling with ways to trap intruders, using a more literal interpretation of 'entanglement' – but all he'd ended up with was a number of extremely angry stray cats. He'd tried variation after variation, but for now he was now willing to put this work to one side and simply activate the perimeter alarm.

Aubrey hurried around the exterior of the factory and the yard, stopping every so often to touch the dominoes he'd used for ease of similarity, activating them with a short spell. On the rooftop and along the fence line, twenty-four domino pieces established the line of sight connection, entangling perfectly. With a sigh of relief he touched the last domino, near the gate to the yard, and he rubbed his eyes. They were gritty and smarting, so he took a moment to revel in the cool night air – but he was already composing the message to headquarters as he went inside again.

The report was short and pointed, updating the Directorate on the state of affairs in Divodorum, and about Baron von Grolman's activity in Stalsfrieden. The most important thing was the last line: 'Station 14 is ready to receive the Phase 2 team.'

He crunched the message through the miniature encoding device – about the size of a cigar box – spinning the wheels and keys until a jumble of numbers and letters resulted. He copied these down and raced to Caroline's radio station.

She had already donned her headphones. She took the slip of paper and turned away. After that, all he heard was the tap-tap-tapping of a practised telegraph operator. He imagined the message winging its way across the night sky, through clouds and stars, until it was received by the operators at Lattimer Hall. The Special Services operators – banks of them – were on twenty-four-hour duty receiving messages from all over the world, from Directorate operatives on missions that were both trivial and dangerous. The message would be copied down and handed to runners, who would rush to the coding division. There cipher officers would reverse the process Aubrey had undertaken, turning the complicated string of numbers and letters back into standard Albionish, then direct the message to the correct place.

Caroline turned, gracefully draping one arm over the back of her hard wooden chair. 'Finished. Hot chocolate, anyone?'

Seventeen

WHEN A MESSAGE CAME BACK FROM THE DIRECTORATE with the news that the arrival of the remote sensers would be delayed by three days, Aubrey, George and Caroline had little to do. The base was finalised – Aubrey having abandoned his improvements to the guardian spells around the perimeter – stores were laid in, antennae were tuned, and George had even livened up the basement with a coat of paint, declaring that buttercup yellow always made a place more welcoming.

Another message arrived, advising of another three-day delay.

Aubrey took this in his stride. All the reading he'd done about military command had warned him about bored troops and the mischief they could get up to. While he didn't think this was strictly applicable to Caroline and George – although he did have a passing moment wondering what sort of mischief Caroline would get up to if given the chance – finding worthwhile activity was probably the best thing to do. For him, if for no-one else.

Moving their belongings from the boarding house was an immediate task which was usefully time consuming. Once they were gathered, the delicacy of the living arrangements was something that couldn't be ignored.

A young woman, unchaperoned, with two young men. Living, sleeping in close proximity. The thought of it all made Aubrey extremely concerned. No-one had mentioned it during the construction of the sleeping quarters, but now that personal belongings were making them somewhat more than bare boxes, he felt he had to address the issue.

'Caroline, George,' he said. 'We need to talk about our circumstances.'

'I know,' Caroline said.

'You know? How?'

'For ten minutes you've been staring at the sleeping quarters with that look on your face.'

'That look?'

'The one that says you're trying to do the right thing but you're not quite sure what it is.'

'I see.' He thought about this. 'How many looks do I have?'

'Oh, at least four.'

'What are the other three?'

'I can't tell you,' she said. 'You'd become all self-conscious.'

And I'm not already? 'Thank you. You're kind.'

'Now.' She strode to the sleeping quarters. 'I'm going to try to make this easy for you. Times have changed.

We are living in a modern world. We are in an unusual situation.' She knocked on one of the dividing walls. 'And these walls are extremely solid, thanks to George.'

'My pleasure,' George said. Aubrey noticed that his friend looked highly amused, but he wasn't volunteering to help Aubrey steer this difficult conversation.

'And your point is?' Aubrey asked Caroline.

'Let me worry about my reputation. You don't have to.'

'Ah.'

'And if you're worried about *your* reputation, you're more confused than I thought. Now.' She tapped her foot. 'I'm happy with the way things are and I hope you two are as well.'

That was that. They never spoke of it again. Caroline's attitude convinced him, too, that his mission of the heart had been entirely superseded by a more patriotic one. It was a moment of sadness, but he knew better than to dwell on it. Events moved on without consulting Aubrey Fitzwilliam and Caroline Hepworth.

Immediately, keeping things brisk and professional, Aubrey suggested that some extra intelligence gathering would be worthwhile. Caroline and George greeted this with enthusiasm, so after a fine breakfast (Eggs Benedict and fresh fruit) they took their bicycles out to inspect the fortifications on the north-eastern edge of the town.

They weren't alone. 'Don't they know there's a war on?' Aubrey murmured as they drew up outside the fortress.

'I'm sure they do,' Caroline said. She was wearing a flat straw hat with a black ribbon. Aubrey thought it highlighted her face wonderfully. 'But people have a habit of ignoring anything that's more than a few miles away.'

Many sightseers were strolling about the earthworks not far down the road from the fortress. The rampart was thirty feet high in places, and stretched for miles, north and south, protecting the city from attack from the east.

People swarmed over the earthworks, taking photographs and generally having a splendid time. Grown-ups and children were climbing the heaped-up earth while a horde of dogs circled aimlessly, barking at the wind, the ground and that bird over there that *really* needed a good chasing. Several groups had spread chequered cloths and were picnicking amid the barbed wire, while donkey carts went backward and forward between the town and the formidable rampart – or the superb viewing point offering an unparalleled vista of Divodorum and surrounds, if the hastily printed postcards were to be believed.

Naturally, a gathering like this couldn't be allowed to happen without opportunists appearing, pushing barrows and selling everything from apples to cool drinks to parasols, and they were hard at work on this bright, sunny morning.

Aubrey glanced at the fortress that faced the earthworks. In the tower, three soldiers were lounging about, surveying the carnival scene. Only one of them held a rifle. On the battlements either side of the tower, artillery peeped through the embrasures, but these weren't manned, as far as Aubrey could tell, unless sleeping draped over the barrel was a new and exciting way of being on guard.

'A mixed bag,' Caroline said. 'Serious preparations side by side with complete nonchalance.'

'I don't think the picnickers are serious about war,' Aubrey said.

'Seems not.' George took out a pad and sketched the scene – the river, the road, the fortifications stretching away to where Holmland loomed in the distance. 'I can see this as "Chapter One – A Fool's Paradise". With a little bit of imagination.'

A laugh, then a distinctive voice came from behind them, in delightfully accented Albionish. 'Imagination, George Doyle, is one of your best qualities.'

George nearly dropped his sketch, fumbled for it, then whirled, open-mouthed. 'Sophie! What on earth are you doing here?'

Aubrey thought that question a little unfair. Sophie Delroy, being a Gallian, had more right than George to be in Divodorum. 'Hello, Caroline. Hello, Aubrey,' she said. She was neatly turned out, as usual, in a jacket and skirt combination with a bold blue stripe. 'I cannot wait to hear why you are here, in Divodorum.'

'Steady on, Sophie,' George said, and Aubrey couldn't help noticing how his friend was straightening his tie and adjusting his jacket as he spoke. Ever since George had been introduced to Sophie while they were on their Gallian adventure last year, they had been what George was candid enough to admit were special friends. Petite, perpetually smiling, and stunningly golden-blonde, Sophie had been corresponding with George ever since. Despite few chances to meet, George's admiration for Sophie hadn't waned.

Aubrey had wondered how much of George's enthusiasm for journalism and writing was inspired by Sophie, who had a fierce ambition to work for the greatest Gallian newspapers, exposing corruption, investigating government scandals, and generally doing good.

Aubrey was ready to admit he was pleased to see her as well. Sophie and Caroline got on famously, and he enjoyed Sophie's disarming good humour – as well as her charming way of pronouncing his name so it started with 'Ow'.

She didn't look like someone whose family was experiencing difficulty, as his grandmother had put it. Perhaps it was just something with her parents?

'Sophie,' Caroline said warmly. 'It's good to see you. Are you with *The Sentinel* on this trip?'

'But of course! It is the duty of the press to bring the truth to the people.' She smiled, and Aubrey heard George grunt as if punched in the stomach. 'With so much happening, they are calling on all their writers, no matter how inexperienced.'

Sounds familiar, that, Aubrey thought.

'But it's dangerous, Sophie,' George protested. 'Jolly dangerous.'

'It is? Then why are you here?'

'Vinegar,' George said gamely. 'Divodorum has the best vinegar in all Gallia.'

'And you, all three of you, had a yearning to sample vinegar? You are making fun of me, George.'

'No, honestly, Sophie,' George said. 'It's not like that at all.'

A distant rumbling noise made Aubrey look to the heavens. *Thunder?* 'Are we expecting rain?'

'Aubrey, you try to distract me, to help your friend,' Sophie said, shaking her head. Then, laughing, she had to tuck her curls back under her bonnet. 'But I will not be diverted so easily. The son of the Albion Prime Minister, visiting Divodorum unannounced? This could be a story of great interest to *Sentinel* readers.'

'I don't think so . . .' Aubrey began, but the distant rumbling rolled toward them again.

'Smoke.' Caroline pointed to the north-east, past the earthworks and past the ridge toward the hilly country that lay beyond.

Caroline wasn't the only one who had noticed the plume of black smoke. A spirited argument was going on in the tower above their heads. Aubrey shaded his eyes and saw that it was over who had the use of the single pair of field glasses.

'A lightning strike?' George suggested. 'How far away do you think it is?'

'Not lightning,' Sophie said. Her face was pale, and she jumped when an unearthly howl rose from the fortress. One of the guards in the tower was cranking away for all he was worth on a large siren. 'We have troops stationed over there, a forward post near the village of Remerci.'

George quickly unfolded a map he produced from his bicycle basket. 'Fifteen miles away?'

More thunder, and a second tower of smoke rose, to the north of the first. Suddenly, the party on the earthworks was over. People scrambled to pack up hampers. A man rushed about, ending the donkey rides and leaving children crying. An accordion player, high on the rampart, stopped playing and gazed to the north-east. Then he slung the accordion over his shoulder and ran, barely keeping his balance, down the long, sloping face of the earthworks. When he reached the road back to the city he didn't stop, but kept going, panting and huffing as he loped past.

Aubrey finally said what everyone was thinking, but dared not utter. 'Artillery.'

'But they said the Holmlanders would never attack through Divodorum,' Sophie said. She gazed at the horizon. Three plumes of smoke were now rising.

'Ah,' Aubrey said. 'And these would be the same people who said that Holmland would never invade the Goltans?'

'You have a good point,' Sophie said, but she looked troubled, far from the sunny Sophie Delroy that Aubrey had known.

The massive gates of the fortress swung back. Instead of the coordinated column of military hardware Aubrey expected, a single lorry rolled out. Behind it, a dozen soldiers ran out of the gates, shouting. The lorry stopped and the soldiers – some of whom looked only half-dressed – threw themselves into the back. With a belch of smoke, the lorry lurched onto the road and ground its way past Aubrey and his friends. Picking up speed, it followed the road through the gap in the earthworks.

'I hope someone is going to barricade that gap,' George said. 'It's like leaving the front door open.'

'I'm sure they will,' Aubrey said, thinking that, if the worst came to the worst, he'd do it if no-one else did. A displacement spell, carefully sited on the top of the ramparts, would tip a few tons of earth and rock onto the road.

He was sorting through the elements for such a spell when a glint in the air near one of the columns of smoke made Aubrey squint. 'Is that an ornithopter?'

He looked around. George and Sophie had moved away a little, and were speaking urgently, in whispers. Caroline glanced at them, then answered. 'A scout, I'd say.'

'Or battle observers.'

The thunder had intensified. It was now almost continuous, a bass drum beat that was frightening in its regularity. 'It's no skirmish,' Aubrey said. 'That's dozens of guns.'

He had a heart flutter of fear. The rational part of his brain told him it was a natural response to prospective annihilation, but he found he still had to swallow to keep his insides under control.

Streams of erstwhile picnickers hurried past. Aubrey wholeheartedly agreed with their decision to leave. 'Erstwhile picnicker' would be a poor thing to have carved on a gravestone.

Sophie's voice rose. 'But you must.' Aubrey turned to see George and Sophie in close discussion. She turned and appealed to Aubrey and Caroline. 'Aubrey, all of you, you must leave Divodorum now, with me.'

'Sorry, Sophie. You go. It's probably best. We can't. We have things to do.' As lame excuses went, Aubrey realised, that was probably one of the lamest. Any lamer and it would have been taken out and shot.

The image didn't cheer him at all.

Sophie was on the verge of tears. She was about to speak again when more lorries roared out of the fortress. Most of these were packed with soldiers in rather better state than the first detachment, and most towed artillery pieces ranging from light field guns to heavy howitzers. This was brutality unleashed.

'Sophie!' George cried over the roar of engines. 'We can't leave! You go!'

Sophie glared at the military column, which now included horses and carts, and overladen pack mules trailing behind. Commotion was spreading through the civilian part of the city as the picnickers arrived with the news.

Gallia had been invaded.

Sophie bit her lip. She looked after her countrymen, then at the dust raised by the military column, then at the distant and ominous smoke. 'No,' she said in a small voice, after glancing at George. 'I must stay.'

Aubrey was the one who convinced George that arguing with Sophie could be done while they walked back to the city. While they made progress in that direction, however, George made no progress with Sophie. Once her mind was made up, it appeared, it was set. She refused to be moved by his entreaties, his logic or his passion. Her response was inevitably, and inarguably, 'You are staying, George. So will I.'

Aubrey had always admired his friend's easy manner with females. George liked them and they liked him. He found it straightforward to engage them in a light-hearted manner that most found appealing. Aubrey, however, always found such a thing a mystery.

So it was with some ambivalent satisfaction that Aubrey watched George's becoming more and more tongue-tied as he tried to persuade Sophie to leave. It didn't help, of course, that George enjoyed Sophie's company so much that he actually didn't want her to leave. That sort of double thinking was Aubrey's typical downfall, second-guessing himself constantly.

He imagined George and he would have much to talk about.

They crossed the bridge over the Salia, which was hastily being sandbagged by a squad of local militia. The workers were being shouted at by an extravagantly moustachioed man dressed in a Gallian uniform that was at least forty years old. To emphasise his points he brandished a sword that looked as if it had come from a museum.

Aubrey paused on the city side of the bridge and looked back. The fortress had snapped out of its lethargy and was now the centre of activity. Engineers were sprinting to the earthworks with wheelbarrows. Tractors towed lengths of steel and bales of barbed wire. Soldiers were rushing out of the city toward the fortress, all thoughts of leave abandoned. Aubrey noted their faces. Grim resolve was the standard demeanour of the older troops, while anyone younger – officers and enlisted men alike – had the mixture of bravado and shifty-eyed panic that comes from the unfortunate combination of inexperience and imagination.

The city itself was working up to a state of pandemonium. From appearances, many residents had been waiting for this moment, for fully laden motorcars and carts were already on their way out of the city, heading south and west, away from the artillery noise that was sounding more and more like drum beats. Shops and markets were being besieged both by those fleeing and those staying. Aubrey was grateful for George's preparation. Their base had enough food for weeks, depending on how many it had to support.

And it looks as if we have one more than I expected, Aubrey thought. George was looking dour as he guided the diminutive Sophie through the thronging crowds, using his bicycle as a flying wedge to part the way. With Sophie right behind him, and Aubrey and Caroline following, they made their way past the Post Office, around the cathedral – which was doing brisk business – and back to their base.

The area was even quieter than usual, apart from a line of barges signalling that some people were creative in their fleeing techniques.

Inside, George made coffee while they sat around the battered oval table that was the everyday meeting place on the ground floor. Nothing revealed that the place was a secret base. They'd gone to some lengths to make sure it looked like a solid, if messy, book bindery with ramshackle shelves, bales of paper divided into reams and quires ready for printing, materials for marbling end papers, presses, glue vats, racks of hand tools, sewing tools and gilting tools.

To a casual eye, Aubrey hoped it would be convincing. A not-so-casual observer wouldn't take long to become suspicious, but Aubrey hoped in that time they'd be able to do something about said suspicious observer.

And Sophie? he wondered as he took his seat. *Is she a casual observer or a suspicious one?*

Sophie looked pale and solemn as she sat at the table. She clutched the mug of coffee George gave her as if she were cold, but she didn't put it to her lips. She studied each of them in turn. 'What are we going to do?'

Aubrey knew what they had to do, but he had no idea what they were going to do about her. He caught George's eye, then Caroline's. 'Sophie, we can tell you some things, but there are other things we can't tell you.'

'You are with your security services, aren't you?'

Aubrey stared.

'I told you she was sharp,' George said.

'We're part of a larger team,' Caroline said, without waiting for Aubrey. 'We've been asked to do some reconnaissance in this area.'

'Caroline,' Aubrey said sharply. 'That's enough. I'm in charge of this team and –'

'Aubrey dear, I know that's what they told you, but we won't have any of that nonsense, will we?'

Aubrey stopped. 'Nonsense?' he repeated, but since his mind was still echoing with 'Aubrey dear' he thought that even managing that single word was quite a good effort.

'Nonsense. All that military business about who's in charge and the like. It's much too rigid for my liking. And, I suspect, yours.'

'What?' Aubrey paused. He took a deep breath. Then another. 'In any military situation you must have a chain of command to ensure discipline, morale and –' He was sure there was something else. Was it uniforms?

Aubrey *dear*?

He stumbled on. 'And other important things. I'm a firm believer in it.'

'Are you? So you'd be happy to do whatever I said if I were in command? Without question?'

Aubrey flailed a little, making quite unintelligible noises. George grinned. 'She's got you there, old man.'

'Of course I have,' Caroline said. 'Now, Sophie, while Aubrey is collecting himself, we can't leave Divodorum. At least, not until the others get here.'

'Others?'

'Others from our service.'

'But will they still be coming? When they hear of what has happened?'

'That's a very good question,' George said. 'This might upset things somewhat.'

'Tonight,' Aubrey said, making a grab at seizing the initiative again. 'Caroline. Me. We'll get in touch with headquarters and see what's going on.'

Aubrey *dear*?

THE ARTILLERY BARRAGE KEPT UP ALL DAY. GEORGE PREPARED a lunch that was careful with its use of provisions, but still delicious – quiche, a light salad and fresh bread he'd baked. Sophie talked about the assignments her newspaper had sent her on, mostly designed to pump up morale in the Gallian public. She'd been told to concentrate on happy bands of brothers joining up, factories increasing output of weapons and munitions, young children scavenging scrap metal for the war effort. It all sounded familiar, but with a Gallian twist. She'd noticed, too, that care was being taken to bar some key occupations from enlisting, for example – vignerons and cheesemakers. In Albion, it had been gamekeepers and brewers.

As the day wore on, the thumping of the artillery changed. In counterpoint to the heavy beat of the Holm-land guns came a sharper, more staccato hammering that Aubrey hoped came from Gallian emplacements. They gathered on the roof to see if they could confirm this and were uniformly dismayed to see smoke from a dozen or more fires in the north-west.

'St Ophir, I think,' Sophie said, pointing past the more northerly of the ridges. 'The villages of Plaisance, Mellies,

Brabaque,' she said, moving south one by one. 'I'm sorry, I do not know the rest.'

She shivered and George, without taking his eyes from the horizon, put an arm around her shoulders.

Aubrey marvelled at the effortlessness with which he did it. George didn't hesitate, or ponder, or make a false start. He simply saw Sophie's need and responded in the simplest, most honest way possible.

I wish I could do that, he thought, then corrected himself because he didn't want to put his arm around Sophie, lovely though she was. If the circumstances called for it, if he was the only person around, of course he would do what he could and it would be a pleasure and, he hoped, helpful.

He shook his head. *I'm getting worse. I'm babbling to myself, now.*

Caroline nudged him. 'You're awfully quiet. Are you all right?'

'No,' he said and she took his arm in hers.

'A thoughtful answer.'

A war was approaching them as they stood there, rolling toward them full of blood and metal, but Aubrey found time to feel heartened.

Eighteen

EORGE WENT TO SOPHIE'S HOTEL TO FETCH HER belongings, and reported that Sophie's motorcar had disappeared, along with the driver. He'd joined the exodus from the city, according to the concierge. Many people were streaming out on any road that led east or south. The train station was bedlam, as well, and rumours spread quickly in such an environment. The Holmlanders were on the edge of the city. The Gallian government had given up on defending Divodorum. Special submersibles were coming down the river.

Sophie bought copies of any newspapers she could find. The tenor of the headlines varied wildly, from overwhelmingly optimistic pronouncements about the readiness of Gallian forces to dire warnings about Holmland advances. Aubrey searched for any mention of Albion but scant column inches were devoted to the Gallian ally apart from a small mention that the King was again unwell. Aubrey hoped Bertie was bearing up in trying times.

In the middle of such uncertainty, Aubrey concluded that it was best to keep busy while they waited for radio contact, so they engaged with more hammering and sawing. The aim was to organise somewhere for Sophie to sleep. In a pinch, she could have taken one of the cubicles meant for the remote sensers − when they arrived − but they had the timber and they had the time . . .

Well after midnight, a tired-eyed Caroline turned away from her listening post. 'Finally.' She handed Aubrey a sheet of paper then she stood and stretched, much to Aubrey's delight, for Caroline's stretches were uninhibited and languorous. He was convinced that such a display would be a success on any stage, anytime. 'It's short, whatever it says.'

Aubrey only took a few minutes on the coding machines before he had it. Yawning, he came out to find Caroline, George and Sophie at the oval table, talking in low voices over hot chocolate. 'We can expect our remote sensers tomorrow,' he announced. '1400 hours.'

'Just after lunch?' George said. 'What happened to night-time drop-offs?'

'These operatives are coming by train.' Aubrey frowned at the message. 'Delicate types, some of these remote sensers. They may be afraid of flying.'

'Hmm. They should get remote sensers who are a bit more robust.'

'I don't think there *are* any two-fisted, steely-eyed remote sensers.'

Sophie wrinkled her brow. 'Remote sensers?'

Aubrey paused, aware they were talking about their secret mission. Having Sophie there was already so comfortable and natural that he'd actually forgotten that she wasn't part of the unit.

'I think it might be time to explain,' he said, 'as long as you understand that you can't write about this.'

Sophie shook a finger at him. 'You do not have to worry, Aubrey. George has told me to put away my pen.' She smiled across the table at George, who smiled back. Aubrey thought he looked like someone who was in the middle of a happy dream. 'Most times,' Sophie continued, 'when someone tells me not to write a story, it makes me think that story *needs* to be written. But this time, I understand, and I trust you.'

And we're about to trust you, Aubrey thought. He told the story of their mission.

'The remote sensers,' he concluded, 'are a speciality – a valuable speciality – that means the Department is willing to put up with quirks that they wouldn't otherwise.'

'So they're coming by train.' Caroline stifled a yawn with a hand. 'Sorry. I hope they can get tickets.'

'I'm sure the Directorate will have a way.'

A volley of shells landed in the distance, one after the other, a deadly drumbeat. Sophie looked up. 'They are so close.'

'But getting no closer,' George said.

'Ah,' said Sophie. 'A few hills, through the woods and they are here.'

They fell silent, listening to the artillery trading blows in the night, and Aubrey found he couldn't tell if Sophie were nervous, afraid, or intrigued by the Holmland advance.

THE DISTANT SHELLING CONTINUED ALL THROUGH THE NIGHT. At one stage, unable to sleep, Aubrey slipped out of his cubicle and climbed to the roof. Ominous flashes marked the horizon and he heard heavy thumping that only increased the sense of approaching doom. The Gallian artillery sounded much more sporadic than it had been earlier – and was the barrage closer?

He shivered and went back to bed.

Breakfast was a joint effort. Sophie joined George in the kitchen and the sound of spirited arguing had Aubrey and Caroline sharing concerned looks, but what emerged was a mouth-watering blend, combining George's hearty cooking and Sophie's more refined Gallian approaches. They grinned as they arranged platters on the oval table and Aubrey reasoned that it was tactful not to comment on their appearances. They looked as if they'd been in a flour fight.

After breakfast, Aubrey and George cycled to the fortress to see a ragged column making its way toward them, coming from the battle front. Every lorry was damaged, and all of them were carrying wounded. The soldiers following the lorries were no longer marching – they were limping, the walking wounded. Aubrey counted more bandages than rifles.

Rumbling out of the fortress gates were some undamaged lorries and a few squads of fresh soldiers, but the reinforcements weren't abundant. The state of affairs looked dire, but Aubrey was itching with frustration because he didn't *know* what was going on. 'Let's find

Saltin,' he said to George. 'He may be able to tell us where we stand.'

George frowned. 'Aubrey. We're at war. I don't think a pair of foreigners can just walk into a Gallian military base like that. Not even friendly foreigners.'

Aubrey paused. 'A reasonable point, George. So I'd say that such a thing requires a certain attitude.'

'I'M GLAD WE STOWED THE BICYCLES IN THE WOODS,' George muttered as they approached the gates of the fortress. 'They would have spoiled the whole effect.'

Aubrey nodded, not wanting to draw attention to themselves, even if the soldier on the stretcher they were carrying was far from capable of eavesdropping.

Shuffling along at the rear of the column of wounded had seemed like an innocuous enough idea at the time, especially since Aubrey's disguise spell – drawing on the Law of Sympathy and the Law of Seeming – gave them the temporary appearance of Gallian soldiers. They'd joined the column as it made its way past the woods where the bicycles were hidden, but they were quickly roped into helping with the wounded.

The soldier on the stretcher was unconscious, and Aubrey thought he should be grateful for that, for the head wound under the rough bandage was bleeding. The way his head lolled didn't bode well and Aubrey did his best to walk as steadily as he could to minimise jolting. The soldier's uniform was covered with mud, as if he'd been swimming in it, and one boot was missing.

Aubrey would have been surprised if the soldier were eighteen years old.

Once inside, a quick glance at George told him that they shared the view that skulking off would be an unworthy thing to do, so for hours they worked with harassed medics and doctors, shifting the wounded, bringing food and water, mopping floors and dragging bedding to the industrial laundry, where the floor was red underfoot.

Midday was approaching before the work slackened. By then, Aubrey and George were both working stiffly, like machines, pushed into silence by what they'd seen.

This was what happened in war, Aubrey thought as one of the medics ordered them to take a break. They sat on a step in the sun, across a small courtyard from the infirmary. Someone had planted lavender nearby and the bees were happily bumbling through its purple wonder. *The books go on about the glory and the triumph, but for every moment of heroism, there are a thousand poor sods who end up on the operating table. Or worse.*

George was resting his elbows on his knees, and he cupped his chin in his open hands. 'D'you think,' he said in a voice that was flat, 'that if we brought all the leaders of all the countries together and showed them this, they'd realise what a stupid thing war is?'

'I doubt it. They'd probably march about, congratulating all the wounded on their sacrifice and wondering where the cameras were.'

'I thought as much. So we'd better do what we can to stop this war ourselves.'

'My thoughts precisely.'

THEY FOUND MAJOR SALTIN AT THE AIRFIELD. THE DISGUISING
spell had lapsed, but Aubrey and George were wearing
uniforms they'd found while fetching clean clothes for
the soldiers who were wounded but ready to go back
to the front.

Saltin quickly ushered them into the hangar and then
into an office. It was spacious, with a large window
overlooking the airfield, but its appointments were
modest: a cheap desk, a few mismatched chairs, a cabinet
that looked as if were made of cardboard. The telephone
on the desk was by far the newest item in the room. 'I
did not expect you to still be here! You should leave the
city now, while you still can.'

'We're hearing that a lot, lately,' Aubrey said, taking a
chair gratefully. He could still smell the burning cloth of
uniforms singed in shell blasts. 'I can't say that it suggests
much confidence in the Gallian military response.'

Saltin shrugged. Aubrey noticed the weariness in the
dark circles under the airman's eyes. 'We were not ready
for this.'

'War was declared seven weeks ago and you're not
ready?' George said. 'I don't think an enemy sends letters,
letting you know they're coming.'

'But the Low Countries,' Saltin protested. 'Holmland
and its allies were coming from that direction. No-one
attacks through the Grentellier Mountains.'

'I think it's called strategy.' Aubrey had to raise his voice
more than he wished, because of the ornithopter work
going on in the hangar. 'Tell me, Saltin, what happens if
Divodorum falls?'

Leaning against the wall, Saltin grimaced. 'The entire
Mosa valley is open to the south. Baligne, then Taine,

then Remense. None of these cities is fortified. Lutetia after that.' He hissed. 'Gallia could fall.'

The horror of that prospect held each of them silent for a moment. Aubrey imagined Holmland troops marching up the streets of Lutetia, the people cowed, the alliance in tatters. With Gallia taken, Albion's strongest ally on the Continent would be gone. What would stand between Albion and invasion then?

George scowled. 'Punching through the Low Countries and through north-east Gallia at the same time is a masterstroke,' he said.

'I think the Marchmainers will have something to say once the Holmlanders get through the Low Countries,' Aubrey said.

Saltin straightened at the mention of his home region. 'They shall not pass. Marchmaine may have little love for Lutetia, but we are Gallians all the same.'

'And what about the people of Divodorum?' Aubrey asked.

'It is bad,' Saltin admitted. He pointed through the glass of the door at the battered ornithopter. 'We have few craft available. We sent one out yesterday, in the afternoon, to see what is happening.' He shook his head and growled with displeasure. 'Our pilot was nearly killed. His craft was struck by magically enhanced shells.'

'Was he badly hurt?' Aubrey asked, and he knew he'd never be able to read an account of a battle again without wondering about the reality behind bald statements like 'more than three thousand wounded'.

'He won't fly again.' Saltin's declaration was careful, but his face made it clear that this, to an airman, was the fate to which death was a preferred option. He sighed. 'But he reported that our forces have halted the Holmland advance – for now. They have had heavy casualties, and desperately need reinforcements, but they have dug in and are holding.'

'Reinforcements,' Aubrey repeated.

'They are coming. High Command has sent a division. It arrives today. By train.'

Aubrey had visions of his remote sensing team standing forlorn on the platform in Lutetia, watching as a train pulled out, packed full of soldiers. 'A special troop express?'

'It is the quickest way to get here in numbers.'

'I know of three people who also need to get here. How would I be able to find out if they're on the train?'

'They won't be. All available trains are bringing troops this way. No room for visitors.'

'These aren't visitors. They're essential.'

Saltin considered this. 'You are suggesting that these people are part of your mission here?'

'They're joining us for the next phase.'

Saltin held up a hand. 'Do not tell me. With this, the less I know, the better.' He paced about the office for a moment, frowning. 'The telegraph lines are still open. I can find out from the stationmaster in Lutetia.'

'I'd appreciate it, Saltin.' Aubrey rose. 'And what about you? What are your plans?'

Saltin shrugged. His smile was small and weary, and even his moustache looked the worse for wear. 'Divodorum will resist and I must do my part to help.'

'But you'll be ready to fall back when the time comes.'

'If we need to. If we can.' Major Saltin straightened his jacket, then frowned at the grease still on the back of one hand. 'I have found that it's difficult to know when the time comes. I am sure that many a soldier's last thoughts have been, "I wish I'd left yesterday."'

Nineteen

CYCLING BACK TO THEIR BASE, AUBREY REALISED WHAT had changed dramatically in Divodorum.

'No children, George,' he called as they swooped along the nearly deserted Haussman Street.

'What?' George angled around a dog that was standing in the middle of the road and looking mournful.

'Families have fled. Women and children, at least.'

The city had the feeling of a place with no heart, a place waiting to be put out of its misery. The artillery bombardment in the hills sounded like giant footsteps in the distance, impossible to ignore.

Aubrey cycled on, grimly.

The factory was deserted when they arrived. For a moment, Aubrey stopped dead, looking around the emptiness, unwilling to think the worst, but finding it was presenting itself insistently, like a least favourite uncle at a family reunion.

George flapped a slip of mauve paper at him. 'They've gone to the woods above the station. They want us to join them for lunch.'

Relief was one of the best feelings of all, Aubrey concluded. 'Shouldn't we be rationing our food?'

'If we eat our way through the stores I've put down, that'll mean we've been trapped here for a year. Which would suggest we'd have problems other than food to worry about.'

They found Caroline and Sophie on the grassy knoll overlooking the station, the place Aubrey had first surveyed Divodorum. A blanket was spread out and the two girls were chatting innocently enough, if one overlooked the field glasses sitting on top of the picnic hamper.

George picked them up. 'Hard to explain these, what, if a suspicious Gallian police officer happens by?'

'George, George,' Sophie said. She rummaged in a knapsack and found a slim book. She opened it to show colour plates. 'We are bird watchers, no? I am looking for a warbler. And a crake. And – how do you say this one? – a mallard?'

'Well, I'm convinced,' Aubrey said. 'But what about your fallback, just in case someone else isn't? Your story behind the story? You don't want to be mistaken for Holmlanders.'

'We've been sent by the Central Railway Company,' Caroline said. She slipped off her royal blue jacket to reveal a high-necked white blouse underneath. 'The firm is interested in passenger and freight possibilities in this area after the war, but wants to remain secret because of rumours that a rival company is in the area, sniffing along the same lines.'

Aubrey sat on the blanket and plucked a blade of grass. 'Nicely done.'

While passing platters of cold chicken and salad around, they shared Saltin's news. Sophie had never met the airman, but had heard of him. 'He was a hero after you rescued him, George.'

'Well, I say,' George took a pickled onion from a jar, 'Aubrey was there too. Quite helpful, he was.'

Aubrey let this pass, with a smile. 'If the remote sensers aren't aboard this train, we'll need to decide what to do next. Communication, first, I'd say. Caroline?'

'We can, tonight, but we must be careful. I have the impression that they're out there.'

'The Holmlanders? Of course they are.'

'Listening, I mean, trying to intercept any communications.'

'You can tell that?'

'It's a feeling I get when I'm wearing the headphones.' She looked into the distance, in the direction of the battle front. 'It's like the hollowness of the ether gets bigger, if that makes any sense. I can feel that someone is out there, waiting.'

Aubrey raised an eyebrow. He sometimes had that feeling, when he became aware that Dr Tremaine was in the vicinity, but that was due to the magical connection the rogue sorcerer and he shared ever since their first magical encounter.

He was grateful he wasn't alone. Without George and Caroline, the unease about their circumstances would be oppressive. He could imagine a solo operator actually being glad of capture, relieved at not having to live under such uncertainty any more.

'We'll make the communication short,' Aubrey suggested. A sudden, almost frantic increase in the artillery bombardment made him look to the north-east. The sound hadn't been drawing any closer for some hours, but he couldn't decide what that meant. Was it a stalemate? A Gallian success resulting in a Holmland withdrawal? He rubbed his hands together with frustration.

He went to canvass these possibilities with his friends when he noticed Sophie's expression. While George busied himself with making another sandwich and Caroline searched in the hamper, Sophie had frozen, her face very pale, and she, too, was staring to the north-east at a redoubled barrage of artillery.

Her concern was apparent, but to Aubrey's mind it was more than simply being worried about an imminent invasion. And while he didn't doubt that she was fond of George, did it explain her willingness to remain in such a dangerous place?

'You have another reason for being here,' he suddenly said to her.

She turned, eyes wide. 'What do you mean?'

'In Divodorum. You have another reason for being here.' As he said it, a number of pieces fell into place. 'If your role with *The Sentinel* were so important, you would have been in contact with its office, or the editor. I'm sure he'd be interested in a story from one of his journalists on the front line.'

Sophie's face fell. 'We have been so busy.'

George patted her on the shoulder and gave her his handkerchief. He frowned at Aubrey. 'I say, old man, aren't you being a bit harsh?'

'No, George,' came a tiny voice from the other side of the handkerchief. 'He is right. I should have told you.' She caught her breath and looked up. 'It's my brother, Théo. He has enlisted, and I must see him.'

The tale she told them was complicated yet familiar and Aubrey finally understood what his grandmother had hinted at. Family troubles. Sophie's brother was two years older than she was, but sounded years younger from the way he behaved. For some months he had been growing more and more hostile to his parents, arguing that his father had been treated poorly by his business partners because of some innate – and unspecified – weakness. Finally, he'd stormed out vowing to enlist, against his father's wishes, and to fight for what was rightfully theirs.

'Rightfully ours,' Sophie said wistfully. She twisted George's handkerchief in her hands. 'That's how he said it.'

'It's worrisome,' Aubrey ventured. 'Whenever I hear "rightfully" I hear entitlement and pride.'

'He did not always use language like that,' Sophie said. 'Not before he met . . . her.'

Sophie's unhappiness invested that single word with something approaching contempt. *Unsurprising*, Aubrey thought – not without an ironic sense of his own situation – *a sudden change in a young man after meeting a young woman.*

'Where did he meet her?' George said, filling in the awkward silence as they each contemplated young men and young women.

'Yvette was a fellow music student, at the Conservatorium. She asked him to a political meeting and he was never the same again.'

'What sort of political meeting?' Caroline asked.

'Théo was never very clear about that. I thought it sounded like anarchists, then he began talking as if it were a workers' party. Rabble rousers, is that what you call them? Much talk and little action.'

'We know the type,' Aubrey said. They'd had encounters with groups like that in Albion. With unease, he remembered how they'd been infiltrated by Holmland security and had nearly pulled off a plot to kill the King. This had been the affair that had introduced Aubrey to the world of espionage and secret plots – and the machinations of Dr Mordecai Tremaine, who was the puppet master behind the Army of New Albion. He had manoeuvred these deluded fools and convinced them that exploding a bomb during the King's Birthday Parade was more than a good idea, it was a *patriotic* idea. Aubrey had managed to disrupt this plot, as well as rescue his father from Dr Tremaine's clutches.

'Lots of hot air.' George patted her hand. 'Nothing to worry about.'

'It became very serious. He abandoned all his old friends, he ignored us, and he went off with these new people. Mother and Father are heartbroken.' She paused, and swallowed hard. 'I . . . At first, my father was sure that he had been beguiled.'

'He suspected magic was involved?'

'He thought so, but then dismissed it. Father had some magic, a long time ago. He still reads about it, in journals, in between his work for the government.'

Aubrey had heard enough already to have his curiosity – both professional and personal – leaping into action. He remembered his grandmother's correspondence with

Sophie's father. 'Your father works for the government?'

'Two years ago he was asked to assist, in finance, by those who could see war was very close. He has been very busy.'

'So I imagine. And he believes that Théo has had a spell cast on him? It sounds unlikely.'

Sophie's upper lip quivered. 'But he changed, so much, he was not our Théo. What else could explain such a thing? How could he do anything so foolish?'

Aubrey didn't have to look far to find an example of a young man doing foolish things, even without the help of a mirror. He kept mute and George took up. 'So you've come looking for him?'

'To talk,' Sophie said. 'I must talk to him. He sent me a few letters. He is here, but not so easy to see.'

'Why not?' George said, indignation making his shoulders swell ominously. 'The camp commandant can't very well refuse him a visit from his own sister.'

'It is not that.' Sophie looked to the north-east again at the sound of shelling.

'He's out there,' Caroline guessed. 'You can't see him until he gets back.'

No-one said the 'if' word but it hung in the air, an unwelcome visitor.

Sophie bit her lip and looked away. 'No. It is even worse than that.'

'Worse?' George said. 'What's worse than being hunkered down in an artillery battle?'

'Théo did not enlist in the Gallian army.' Sophie used the handkerchief again. 'Just before war was declared, he went over the border to Stalsfrieden. He joined the Holmland army.'

Aubrey nearly looked around to see who had thrown a bucket of cold water over him, then he realised it was simply the shock of Sophie's announcement. Her brother was a Holmland soldier? Fighting against his own countrymen?

A train whistle sounded. Aubrey leaped to his feet and seized the field glasses.

'Aubrey,' Caroline said fiercely. 'Stop that.'

'Stop what? Stop continuing with our mission?'

'The train can wait. Sophie needs our help.'

I didn't hear her ask for help. 'What can we do?'

'Anything we can,' George said.

'Now, Sophie, I'm sure we can help you find him. Then you can talk some sense into him,' Caroline said.

Aubrey hesitated, then threw caution to the winds. 'So we're going wander about, not just in wartime but in an actual battle, find her brother and then change his mind for him? Make him see the error of his ways? In the middle of the Holmland army? And then bring him home again, through said battlelines?'

George looked at Sophie. 'Do you know exactly where Théo is?'

She shrugged. 'His letters he sent, before war was declared, said he was part of a detachment in Stalsfrieden.'

'Stalsfrieden? Doing what, exactly?' Aubrey asked.

'Guarding. So boring, he said, even though the factory was important.'

'Don't look like that, Aubrey,' George said. 'Stalsfrieden must have plenty of important factories.'

Aubrey agreed, but he had to press. 'Sophie, did Théo say anything else about the factory?'

She frowned and put a finger to her lips. 'He said it was a strange place, and he wrote about something he thought was funny. In the middle of the factory grounds were big animals.'

'I beg your pardon?' Aubrey said.

'Jungle animals. Made of concrete.'

It must be, Aubrey thought. 'Anything else?'

'No. But he wasn't the only one who thought the animals funny. He said that the owner, Baron von Grolman, laughed whenever he walked past them.'

The train whistle sounded, closer.

Aubrey looked at George, who shrugged. Caroline looked thoughtful.

'So your brother is stationed at Baron von Grolman's factory in Stalsfrieden?' Aubrey sighed. 'All right. Let's see what we can do.'

The train whistle sounded again, shrill and echoing from the hills, as the locomotive chuffed and laboured along the tracks. Aubrey swung up the field glasses to see the train coming off the curve to the south and working hard on the approaches to the railway bridge. The ironwork crossed the Mosa, a latticework against the grey and lowering sky, holding the bridge high above the broad expanse of the river. Artillery boomed in a thumping counterpoint to the steam engine. A coal barge slipped underneath the bridge on its way downstream.

Aubrey's gaze lingered on the bridge. It was an example of fine engineering, three long arches. It looked both solid and graceful, with two magnificently curved iron trusses supporting the spans. Three massive piers in local stone stood in the river, impervious to flood.

Aubrey focused more closely on the central pier. On

closer inspection, it was actually an amalgamation of a number of octagonal iron columns and stone blocks. He was impressed by its sturdiness, and the way the materials were interlocked, but he frowned when he spied a number of ominous shapes near water level. They were strikingly out of place, looking makeshift against the elegant construction of the pier, made of wood and metal in various proportions. With growing apprehension, Aubrey counted half a dozen of them surrounding the pier, linked by wire, and he was sure more would be found on the other side.

He ran through a dozen possibilities in his mind, and none of them were good. Before he knew it he was sprinting toward the river and the bridge beyond, unsure of what he was going to do, but knowing that he didn't want to see the train crossing the bridge until the nature of the menacing boxes was determined.

He ran, waving his arms and calling out as he burst through the vegetation on the river bank. The train was on the approaches and steaming mightily since its destination was in sight. Aubrey hallooed, jumped up and down, forgetting all concern for appearances. If it were a mistake, he was sure he could explain his way out of trouble. If it weren't . . .

The train was nearly across when, impossibly, the bridge abruptly rose in the middle.

The noise reached him first, then the blast spun him around and slapped him with a giant hand – a stunning, ear-punishing roar. He was thrown backward into the dense arms of a yellow-flowering broom. He rolled to his feet in time to meet his friends coming down the bank. The trees were still shaking, leaves shredding about them in a storm. Aubrey could feel the earth trembling.

'The bridge!' Aubrey shouted over the ringing in his ears, trying to make his friends understand what had happened. 'They've blown up the train!'

SIRENS, CHURCH BELLS, CRIES OF DISTRESS AND THE BARKING of dogs added to the cacophony. Within minutes, most of the remaining population of Divodorum was rushing toward what had once been the bridge over the Mosa River. Many of them poured out of the station, where hundreds had been waiting.

Appalled and sickened, Aubrey, George, Caroline and Sophie abandoned their picnic gear. They slid and scrambled their way through the woods to the outskirts of the station, where they had a clearer view of the disaster.

The railway tracks stretched from the station a few hundred yards to what had once been a sturdy and much-used bridge. Now, it was a twisted wreck. None of the piers were standing. The approaches were intact but they led to an awful, gaping nothingness.

The acrid smell of high explosives was heavy in the air, which was a haze of smoke, dust and a fine mist of water. He couldn't help wondering how much had been used. Clearly, it had been attached to the central pier and equally clearly – because of the timing – the aim had been not just to bring down the bridge, but to take the train and its passengers down too.

A few small craft were coming down the river toward

where the bridge had been – dinghies, rowing boats, a half-laden barge – but standing next to the bridge abutment Aubrey could see no sign of the train. Stunned into dizziness, he held onto the dressed stone with both hands to stop himself pitching into the river, which was churning with the violence imposed on it, so much steel, concrete, stone and iron plunging into the water.

So many lives.

THEY STAYED ON THE RIVERBANK FOR HOURS, DOING THEIR best to help with the desperate need that witnesses of tragedy so often have – but there was little they could contribute. None of the flotilla of craft that swarmed over the river brought back any survivors.

The army set up an emergency centre just outside the station, complete with field hospital, as people milled about, grey-faced and dazed, sleepwalking while fully awake. Otherwise, the general organisation was haphazard. The few remaining students from the university hovered about the site with goodwill and volunteerism, but were reduced to hand-wringing frustration amid the horror. As much as possible, Aubrey shadowed the Gallian colonel who was in charge, but who spent most of his time looking shattered. Eventually military barges joined the civilian craft. After cruising up and down for some time, they tried using heavy winches and grappling equipment, but after several near-disasters they gave up, the weight of the train wreckage obviously defeating them.

When evening fell, bodies began to be brought ashore and it was time to leave.

Heavy-hearted, speaking in monosyllables, they trudged past the station. George made a few gestures that they all understood and he veered away up through the woods to retrieve their hamper and blanket.

A figure Aubrey recognised came through the crowd by the station. 'Saltin!' he called, waving.

The Gallian major saw who was calling. He pushed toward them and Aubrey saw he was red-eyed, shoulders slumped. 'Fitzwilliam. M'mselles.'

'This is M'mselle Delroy, Saltin.'

'Ah.' Saltin made an effort to regain his usual charm. 'You are the famous daughter of the esteemed Dr Auguste Delroy?'

'I am.'

'It is an honour.'

Aubrey thought there was much to follow up there, but he had more pressing inquiries. 'Saltin, did you find out that information?'

'Information?' Saltin patted his breast pocket. 'But of course. I was given a reply, but I have not read it. The bridge . . .' He took out a piece of paper and his already grim face grew grimmer as he read. 'I'm sorry. Your three agents were on the train. There is no hope for them.'

Twenty

$\mathcal{D}$IVODORUM, ALREADY INFESTED WITH RUMOURS, BEGAN swarming with them. Major Saltin accompanied Aubrey and his friends on the night trek back to their base and, along the way, through streets that were either abandoned or crowded with a second wave of citizens fleeing the city, they overheard snatches of anxious conversations outside cafés and bars where the fearful remaining citizens gathered. Holmland agents were everywhere. Holmland battalions were marching into town in the morning. Holmland airships were about to drop incendiary devices on the city. The two road bridges across the Mosa and the Salia had been found to have explosives wired to them. And, most worryingly, Holmland forces had encircled the town to the south and west. Aubrey didn't know what to believe and what to discard. Rumour was proving to be an efficient worker in the Holmland cause.

Saltin excused himself when they reached the factory. 'I must return to the airfield.' In the pool of light thrown by a single electric lamp outside the front doors, he shook his head. 'Those poor young men.'

'And their families.' Aubrey couldn't bear thinking of the outcry when the news arrived.

'All Gallia will be shocked,' Sophie said. 'But we will be roused by it as well. Holmland may think us weak, but we will surprise them.'

Saltin straightened and nodded decisively. 'You are right, M'mselle.' He yawned and only covered it with an effort, then waved farewell.

Aubrey felt for the airman. He was a good man, doing his best in awful circumstances, but he had a feeling that more people like that would be needed before it was all over.

Aubrey brushed the lock with his magical awareness, enough to sense that it had remained undisturbed. Once inside, he snapped on the electric lights. He rubbed his hands together at the coolness that haunted the factory.

'I'm hungry,' George announced. Aubrey hadn't realised it until his friend said it, but they'd missed their evening meal. Without waiting, George took Sophie to the kitchen.

'Keeping busy can be a good thing,' Caroline said. She sat at the oval table and crossed her arms, hugging herself.

'When in distress? Agreed. And having someone understanding close by is useful, too.'

'I wish we didn't have to keep up appearances.'

'I'm sorry?'

'There's nothing I'd like better right now than to stretch out on a chaise longue. Or a pile of silk cushions.'

The image both disturbed and enchanted Aubrey. 'I'm sorry . . .' He patted his pockets. 'But I don't have anything like that with me. Not at the moment.'

Caroline sighed. 'I'd even pay good money for a hot bath. If there was bath oil included.'

Aubrey wondered why it had suddenly grown so warm. 'I thought the shower bath arrangement we set up worked quite well. Hygienic.'

'Sometimes, Aubrey, one wants more than hygiene.'

Savoury smells began to waft from the kitchen – herbs, garlic, onions – and the clatter of pans gave Aubrey an excuse to turn away, to try to work out what Caroline was hinting at, but he accepted that the pyramids would be worn to nubs in the desert before he could ever hope to reach that state of wisdom.

George and Sophie brought laden trays to the table and served piping hot mushroom omelettes, a green salad and the last of the fresh bread. Sophie was pale with tiredness, but did her best to smile bravely. 'The omelettes, I made. The salad and bread is George.'

Caroline stood and guided Sophie to a chair. 'You poor thing. Sit.'

Aubrey eyes widened as he tucked into the remarkable omelette. It was succulent with mushrooms that were fragrant and earthy, while a hint of – thyme, was it? – added a piquant edge. 'Good work, Sophie.'

She smiled, wanly, and pushed her own omelette around the plate with a fork. Aubrey watched this closely, knowing from experience how a lack of appetite could be a manifestation of inner torment.

'Now, Aubrey,' Caroline said. Aubrey looked at her to see that she, too, was studying Sophie with concern.

'What is it you say about the best remedy for worry?'

Aubrey froze with his fork in mid-air, lettuce glistening with good olive oil. 'The best remedy?' he repeated, trying to buy time. 'Or the only remedy?'

A steely look from Caroline let him know that she knew what he was up to. 'The sovereign remedy, Aubrey.'

'Ah.' He had it. 'The remedy for worry is to do something about it.'

'Something?'

'Just about anything, really. Sitting around and stewing only makes worry worse.'

'So you advise that we should do something instead of sitting here and stewing?'

The banter had a brittleness about it, but Aubrey thought it was a game effort in the circumstances.

'That sounds right,' George said. 'Waiting around like this is wretched.'

Aubrey put down his knife and fork. He steepled his hands in front of him and then dropped them to the table, embarrassed, when he realised it was one of his father's favourite gestures. 'First things first, then. We need to communicate with the Directorate about the loss of the remote sensers, and we need to gather intelligence. To *continue* gathering intelligence. Caroline?'

Aubrey was already forming some plans in this area. He knew that remote sensing was a speciality to which he was unsuited, but he'd had some experience with finding out what was going on at a distance, skills that had come in useful growing up in the Fitzwilliam household when he wanted to know what his parents were saying about him.

'I have it under control. I'll send a report at midnight.' She checked her wrist watch. 'An hour away.'

'I'll work up something and crunch it through the encoder,' Aubrey said, 'as soon as I finish this altogether superb meal.'

'I can do that,' Caroline said.

'No . . .' Aubrey caught himself. He was about to contradict Caroline outright and he'd learned this was rarely a good ploy. 'No need. The encoding device is tricky.'

'I watched you over your shoulder. I can handle it.'

I'm sure you can. 'All right. If you can do that, I can start something where I need two helpers.' He glanced at George. 'Two helpers who will be ready, bright and early, tomorrow morning.'

George responded gratefully. 'And isn't it lucky that you have two people here who are keen and willing?'

LATE THOUGH IT WAS, AUBREY TOOK GEORGE AND SOPHIE down to the workshop area in the basement. It was set up with four benches and magical paraphernalia ready for the remote sensers, but it had remained unused. He ran his fingers through his hair as he studied the equipment they'd managed to procure.

They'd been able to get carboys of chemical reagents, standard stuff like acids and salt mixtures. Lots of glassware – beakers, retorts, distillation tubing. A small high temperature furnace, with a collection of crucibles. Bundles of wires, insulated and bare, of various ratings. Modelling clay. Chalk in powder and stick form. Mirrors. Rubber tubing. A selection of hand tools that had originally been meant for working wood and leather.

Odds and ends, bits and pieces. Shopping for materials that may prove useful in magic was difficult – especially when one didn't know what sort of magic was going to be undertaken. All he could do was make sure that standard ingredients for familiar spells had been procured and safely stored.

It was all fairly ordinary and didn't necessarily look like the workings of a magical cabal. The remote sensers were meant to be bringing the more esoteric stuff.

It meant, as usual, Aubrey was going to have to work with what he had at hand.

'Sophie, tell me about the weather in these parts,' he said as he strolled between the benches. He held his hands behind his back and, almost without being aware of it, began to hum, deep in his throat.

'The weather?'

She glanced at George. He smiled. 'Go on. It will make sense sooner or later.'

She wet her lips with the tip of her tongue. 'I am not from this part of Gallia, you understand, but I am told that summer here is variable.' She turned to George. 'Is that right, variable?' He nodded. She continued. 'We will have sunny days, of course, but the nights can be cool.'

'What about the wind?'

'It can be windy.'

'But from what direction?' Aubrey mused. 'That's what I'm keen to know.'

'From the west, mostly, at this time of year.'

'Splendid. Just what we need.' Aubrey rubbed his hands together. 'Right, George, how long is it since you've made a kite?'

'Box or diamond?'

'You've made a box kite?'

'As a little fellow, on the farm, I went through a kite-making mania, you might say. Became rather an expert.'

'George, you're a wonder.'

'I do my best.'

Sophie yawned, then apologised. 'It has been a long day.'

'I understand,' Aubrey said. 'I'm going to check on Caroline first, but you two should get some sleep.'

The door to Caroline's telegraph station was shut. He could see light through the cracks and he could hear the steady tap-tap-tapping of the key. He crept away, leaving her to it.

When he couldn't find George and Sophie he assumed they'd taken his advice. Their sleeping quarters were dark and quiet.

Which left Aubrey alone. He drew a chair up to the oval table and was immediately seized by an overwhelming yawn that left very little room for anything else. He wiped his eyes, stood up, turned around, then sat down again.

The yawn that took him this time was even more encompassing than the first.

I will not go to sleep, he told himself, *not until I've seen Caroline.*

SUNLIGHT COMING IN THROUGH THE FRONT WINDOW OF the factory made Aubrey lift his head from the table.

He groaned. Then he sat up and groaned again as an ache bloomed in his back. And one in his neck. And his knees then complained because he wasn't paying them and their hurts enough attention.

A slip of ivory-coloured paper on the table – the same sort Caroline used to jot notes when sending or receiving – caught his eye. With as few movements as possible, he picked it up.

You looked so comfortable where you were that I didn't want to disturb you. I'll report in the morning.

Aubrey studied the note, gave it time to sink in, then shuffled off in search of coffee. With a steaming mug in hand, and his body recovering from his uncomfortable sleep, he went to find Caroline – only to see that she was sleeping the sleep of the exhausted, still in her clothes, curled up on her straw mattress, breathing softly and slowly.

He gazed at her for a while, then a while longer. It was only the thought of her waking and finding him mid-gaze that made him leave, reluctantly.

Half an hour later, the kite-making cottage industry was in full swing. George sawed light bamboo into appropriate lengths, Sophie cut brown paper into the required sizes, and Aubrey puzzled over how he was going to achieve the effect he needed.

It was a vague idea to begin with, but one that he believed had promise. It drew on a number of different magical principles, synthesising them in the sort of way that appealed to him. He needed to use the Law of Amplification, and Intensification, and Sympathy, and Contiguity . . . he ticked them off as he fiddled with the tiny mirrors.

'It's all a matter of care,' he said, raising his voice over the sound of George's sawing. 'Can you pass me that hammer, please, Sophie?'

'Take these first, Sophie,' George said and passed several lengths of bamboo across the bench.

'Care is vital in any magical enterprise,' Aubrey continued. 'One element loosely employed can wreak havoc.' He paused. Why was havoc the only thing that was ever wreaked? Could you wreak boredom, for instance? What about wreaking envy?

'Have you finished with that glue pot, Aubrey?' George asked.

'Mmm?' Aubrey blinked, remembering where he was. He stared at the glue pot on the bench nearby. A brush stuck out of it like a flag at the North Pole. 'I wasn't using it.'

'I know. It was a roundabout way of asking you to shove it over here because we have our hands full.'

'Oh. There you go.'

'Care, Aubrey,' Sophie prompted. 'You were – how do you say, George? – droning on about it.'

'Droning on?'

'In an interesting way, old man.'

'Of course.' Aubrey hefted the hammer. 'As I was saying, care is vital for finely functioning magic. Care in preparation, care in execution, care in monitoring. If you care to care, care will care for you, as Professor O'Donnell always said.'

'Was that Ding-Dong O'Donnell, the world's most baffling lecturer?'

'Where did you hear about Ding-Dong O'Donnell?'

'You told me.'

Aubrey spied an empty ammunition box lying in a corner. With a bound, he hauled it up from the floor by one of the handles. 'Just the thing.' The box was made of sturdy wood, with metal clasps and hinges. With it, he wouldn't need the hammer, so he dropped it on the nearest bench.

'Just' the thing for what, Aubrey?' Sophie asked, and Aubrey was glad for her interest. His decision to involve her was working. Left alone, brooding about the fate of her brother would only have been all too easy. Here, she was doing something practical; her natural intelligence and curiosity were asserting themselves.

Aubrey brought the ammunition box close to the bench and trapped it there, level with the surface, with a hip. 'Just the thing for this.'

With a flourish, he swept the pile of mirrors into the box with a crash. Seizing the handles with both hands, he lifted the box onto the bench and shut the lid. While Sophie watched, aghast, he fastened the latches.

'But the mirrors,' she said. 'They are broken.'

'Not broken enough.'

Aubrey shook the box from side to side, up and down, then side to side again. 'I should have thrown the hammer in,' he said, panting.

'I have never seen magic done like this before,' Sophie said.

'Aubrey has a special way about him,' George said. 'You'll get used to it.'

Something Sophie said made Aubrey pause. He stopped his vigorous shaking and dropped the box on the bench. 'You've never seen magic done like this before?'

She shook her head. 'No. It has always been more formal than this.'

'More formal? You've actually seen magic done before?'

Sophie looked at George. 'Sophie did some magical studies, old man. Quite talented, she was.'

'George.' She dimpled. 'It was years ago.'

'You have some magical talent?' Aubrey said.

'I did, but now?' She shrugged. 'I lost interest.'

It baffled Aubrey, but many people who showed early signs of magical ability turned away from it later. It may have been the discipline needed, or the debilitating effects that spell casting sometimes had, but only a few had the necessary combination of ability, determination and perseverance that resulted in competent magicianhood.

'You never lose it,' Aubrey said. 'It's part of you forever. With some practice, you'd get it all back.'

She looked thoughtful. 'I would?'

'Of course. It's like picking up a golf club after years away from the game. You'd be rusty at first, and it would take time, but you'd be hitting it sweetly before you know it.'

'Then tell me, Aubrey, what you are doing, while you do it. Who knows? I could be useful.'

'You already are, my gem,' George assured her.

'Thank you, George, but I want to do what I can.' She put her hands together decisively. 'So, Aubrey, magic is not always formal?'

'Ah, yes,' Aubrey said. 'Sometimes it is. It depends on how you go about it.'

Aubrey knew that his approach to magic was rather different from the norm. Most professors and scholars conducted their magic as if they were holding a funeral service. He'd seen it many times since he'd been at the university and sometimes it made him want to shout out loud. He *always* found it thrilling to be doing magic, and when it was treated with such boring solemnity it made him frustrated to the extreme.

He opened the lid of the box and peeped inside. The mirrors had been reduced to shards and powder. They glinted back at him. Not small enough, though. He tossed in the hammer, then banged the lid down again.

A few more minutes of noise and sweat, and Aubrey had had enough. He looked inside. 'Perfect,' he said, with some relief.

'Now,' he said to Sophie. They hadn't paused in their cutting, tying and gluing, but she was paying attention. 'What I need is something to make a suspension.'

George lashed two lengths of bamboo together. 'I think I know what you're getting at. It'll need to be thick if you want to make mirror paint.'

'And clear, of course.'

Sophie pointed at Aubrey with her scissors. 'But this is impossible. The mirror pieces will not all be facing the same way. They will be random, no?'

'Ordinarily, yes,' Aubrey said. 'Notebook, notebook, notebook . . . Ah, there it is.' He flipped through it until he found fresh pages. 'You see, Sophie, the Law of Constituent Parts maintains that when something is fragmented, each fragment retains characteristics of the whole. In this case, I intend to emphasise their *alignment*. In the original mirrors, they were all facing one way – shiny side one way, dull side the other. With some spellcraft, I can get the pieces to reassert that alignment and all should be well.'

'And that is all?'

'Not exactly, no.' Aubrey heard George snort, but went on, ignoring such commentary. 'Once we have nice, shiny kites, I intend to apply a spell that combines the Law of Completeness, the Law of Inverse Attenuation, the Law of Amplification and . . . several other laws to make the kites receptive to images. After that, I will use a spell relying on the Law of Sympathy and the Law of Entanglement.' He paused for effect. 'So that a mirror we have here will mirror the images that the kite is capturing and enhancing.'

'This is what they teach you at your university?'

'Er, not exactly. This is something of my own.'

'Something you've done before?'

'Not in its entirety.'

George snorted again. 'Not to any extent at all, am I right, old man?'

'That may be the case.' Aubrey grinned. 'But the principle is sound, don't you think?'

'You convinced me,' George said, 'but you could read a spell out of a Christmas cracker and I'd be impressed.'

Sophie looked from George to Aubrey and back again. 'So he is making this up?'

'As he goes along,' George said. 'Not to worry. He usually makes it work. In the end.' George rubbed his chin and studied the array of finished kites: two large box kites and three diamond kites, all with their lacquer drying. 'I take it then, old man, you want to fly the kites from our roof and come as close as possible to the battle lines?'

'I was getting around to that.'

'You realise, of course, that the height and distance of a kite is dependent on its lifting power?'

Aubrey affected an airy wave. 'So obvious, I would have thought, as not to require noting.'

'And the weight it has to lift includes the string? Which gets heavier the longer it is?'

Aubrey bounced through the implications of this. 'String isn't exactly what I had in mind.'

'You didn't? Pray tell, what were you planning to use instead of string? Something that is lighter, but stronger, I hope.'

'Find me a spider, would you?'

WITH A ROLL OF DESTICKIED SPIDER SILK, THANKS TO THE Law of Contiguity and an inverted application of the Law of Cohesion, they were nearly ready.

The challenge of working with such limited ingredients gave Aubrey great enjoyment, but it was tempered by the constant, intrusive memory of the events of the previous day. His concentration was interrupted a number of times by flashes where he saw the bridge erupt, and memories of the half-glimpsed, broken train plunging to its doom. He recalled the panic among the onlookers, the valiant but vain efforts to help. Because of this, he twice bungled his thread-making spell, which meant that George and Sophie had to hunt up more cobwebs in the dusty recesses of the factory, a duty they didn't seem to mind. Sophie's attentiveness and perceptive questions were helpful and also kept Aubrey on his game. Nothing like explaining something to an intelligent audience to help one's own thought processes.

While they were off hunting up the spider silk – or whatever they were doing – an unhappy Caroline appeared.

'Why didn't you wake me?'

Because you looked so comfortable where you were, he only prevented himself from saying with a huge effort. 'Sorry. I thought you were awake.'

She glanced at him, then frowned, then went to speak, rethought, frowned again, then shook her head. 'That doesn't make any sense at all.'

No, but it's giving you time to calm down. 'It doesn't? I beg your pardon. We're busy kite-making here.'

'Kite-making?' She narrowed her eyes. 'You're deliberately throwing up non sequiturs, aren't you?'

Yes. 'No, honestly, we're making kites. I had an idea about intelligence gathering. Let me explain.'

He had to give Caroline credit. She gradually put aside her annoyance at not being wakened to listen to his plan for the kites – and she was good enough to be impressed.

She picked up one of the spare bamboo struts and examined it. 'So we'll have some idea of what's happening at the battlefront, without too much risk?'

'If it works.'

'I'm sure it will. Most of your lunatic schemes seem to, one way or another.'

'That's me. Aubrey Fitzwilliam: purveyor of lunatic schemes to the rich and famous.'

They caught and held gazes for a moment – a still heartbound moment – and then Caroline waved the bamboo strut and the moment was gone. 'Don't you want to know about the message to the Directorate?'

'The Directorate?' Aubrey's putty-like brain coughed and wheezed into action. 'Of course, the message to the Directorate.'

'I sent it, but I'm not happy. It took a long time – there was much to report – and I have the feeling that it may have been intercepted.'

Aubrey shrugged. 'It shouldn't matter. That code is unbreakable.'

'Famous last words.' She rolled her shoulders and stretched. 'But it's not the code-breaking that I'm most worried about. It's triangulation.'

Aubrey grimaced. 'Of course. The longer you're broadcasting, the easier it is for the Holmlanders to get a fix on our position.'

'If they're looking for us. I may simply be over-reacting.'

'In this case, I'd most definitely prefer to overreact than underreact. Underreacting is likely to get us some unwelcome visitors hammering on the door.'

In the middle of the tiredness and tension, Aubrey realised that he was very comfortable with Caroline. Then, with a start, he wondered how that happened. Being with Caroline had always been exhilarating, but he would never have claimed it was comfortable. Comfortable suggested old slippers and cardigans, and he could never imagine Caroline in a cardigan.

Their relationship had changed. In their earnest efforts to remain good friends, they'd become just that. Good, comfortable friends. Cocoa and ginger nut friends. How are you and very well thank you friends. It was an eminently practical and workable way of living, but Aubrey felt as if he'd lost a diamond and found a hundredweight of coal.

'Sorry?' he said, realising that Caroline had continued speaking while he was wool-gathering.

'I said that I asked the Directorate for an urgent response, but all I was told was to wait for further instructions. Again.'

'I can't imagine they'll be able to send another remote sensing team straight away. If the rest of the Directorate is stretched thin, I'd say that the remote sensing department must be stretched almost transparent.'

It was close to dawn, after a frustrating night of waiting at her station, when Caroline received her response. This time, Aubrey was awake and alert, thanks to seven cups of very strong coffee, each one regularly spaced through the night-time hours. The message was terse, and Caroline had to ask for a repeat transmission, as the brevity made her think the message had been interrupted.

'HOLD POSITION,' Aubrey read after decoding. 'GATHER INTELLIGENCE.'

Caroline made a face. 'A distinct lack of imagination there.'

'No,' Aubrey said distantly. Without thinking, he rolled up the piece of paper and tapped it in his hand like a baton. 'Tomorrow, we'll follow orders and test our intelligence-gathering kites.'

'And then?'

'Hold our position. Gather intelligence.'

Twenty-one

A WEEK — SEVEN FRUSTRATING, MADDENING DAYS — later, no further news had arrived from the Directorate. Aubrey wished the message had given some sort of time expectation. 'GATHER INTELLIGENCE FOR THREE DAYS' or 'HOLD POSITION FOR A FORTNIGHT' would have been preferable. The lack of certainty was frustrating but, he was starting to understand, it was the military way of doing things.

The makeshift kite intelligence-gathering devices worked well. More or less. Dazzling to look at, especially in the full sun, the kites flew high and true in the consistent breeze from the west. The spider silk was strong, if a little difficult to handle due to its extreme thinness. Leather gloves were definitely needed when handling the line, even after George had rigged a clever hand-cranked spooling mechanism on the roof.

The mirror dish that had been linked magically to

the kite surface, however, was problematic. It was a large, shallow dish a few feet across, made from a concrete bird bath Aubrey had found standing forlorn in a corner of the yard. Aubrey could look into it for a maximum of an hour, and Sophie not at all. The image in the bowl was hugely unsteady, despite everything Aubrey tried to stabilise it. Looking into it provoked nausea and headaches within minutes. The first viewing, with all four crowded around it on the roof of the factory, showed the Gallian countryside, heavily wooded and ridged, as soon as Aubrey completed his binding spell. Then, almost immediately, the image swooped sickeningly, even though the kite itself appeared quite placid, high above Divodorum. Soon, Sophie had to flee, decidedly green in the face. George and Caroline held out for longer, but eventually Aubrey was left alone, clutching the sides of the bowl, forehead sweaty, insides a turmoil, trying to make sense of what he saw. With a sketchpad nearby, he endured the shuddering image for nearly an hour before he staggered away to gather himself.

All that day, Aubrey alternated between working on intensifying spells, levitation spells and balancing spells and steeling himself for another bout with the surveillance bowl. At the end of the day he thought he had an impression of the actual placement of forces on both sides, but he also felt as if he'd been adrift in a bathtub in the middle of a hurricane.

A week of it and he was sure that joining the undead would be an actual improvement on how he felt. He lost weight, as he couldn't stomach food at all. Caroline took it upon herself to act almost as an animal trainer; she forced him to take some of Sophie's clear chicken broth at regular intervals. Sleep was a welcome visitor, but when he finally pitched onto his pallet each night, it swayed and swooped beneath him, so ingrained was the nauseating motion.

He did find time, however, to marvel at how unintimidating this physical malaise was. He was reasonably certain he wasn't about to die from it – especially with Caroline's eagle eye on the case – and the distressing physical symptoms certainly weren't signs of his soul wrenching away from his body and leaving him spiritually torn apart. All in all, his projectile vomiting and dry retching were relatively minor discomforts to one whose body and soul had once been on the verge of separating.

He took arid pleasure in the notes he'd compiled, the maps he'd sketched. These would be priceless to the Directorate and the Army. Within a few days, Aubrey had divined the dispersal of Holmland forces in this area, the battlelines, the trenches, the supply routes. This was intelligence gold.

While he was engaged in this, the others were busy. Caroline spent time perfecting the antenna array and restructuring her telegraph cubicle area. George and Sophie kept meals coming as well as doing more work on the factory floor, making it appear even more like a recently active bookbindery. They also spent time in the basement, improving the facilities for what everyone was still expecting to be an influx of Directorate operatives.

George and Sophie were also the main excursionists. They were the ones who went into Divodorum to shop and to reconnoitre a town that they reported as being resolute, terrified – and half-deserted. Reinforcements hadn't appeared, according to talk, as the main Holmland push was to the north-west and all Gallian forces were being rushed in that direction.

After one of these excursions, Sophie gleefully showed Aubrey a small globe of light she'd conjured, the first spell she'd cast for years. She confided that it had taken numerous attempts, but Aubrey praised her efforts and pointed out some useful refinements for her to practise. When she left, excitedly seeking George, he promised himself he'd organise an instructional program for her – when he had time. It would be useful to have someone else on the team who could cast spells.

They had tried to communicate with Major Saltin, only to find that an airship had arrived from Lutetia with orders for him to assume command. George reported, gloomily, that on a reconnaissance mission over the battlelines it had been shot down. While it apparently hadn't exploded, it had come to ground some miles into Holmland, with no news of survivors.

Aubrey was saddened by this news. Major Saltin had been a stalwart, a comforting presence in the area. He would be much missed.

The only optimistic piece of news that George and Sophie managed to garner was the rumour that Albion troops were on their way to relieve Divodorum.

George and Sophie heard this repeated in more than one place. Albion forces were on the way, with thousands of soldiers, hundreds of artillery pieces and tons of equipment. They would save the day.

Which was useful, for a neighbourhood on the eastern edge of Divodorum had actually sustained shelling from long-range guns. After that one instance, it wasn't repeated – but the event was ominous and morale sapping.

Each night, alone in the dark, Caroline listened, intent on the ghostly whispers that flew across the ether. Each night, the same message came: 'HOLD POSITION. GATHER INTELLIGENCE.'

AUBREY STUDIED THE MAP HE'D SPREAD ON THE TABLE. He'd painstakingly pencilled in the battle lines, the troop and artillery emplacements and the trenches that both sides had dug – at least, to the best of his ability. He was sure that the kite surveillance would be a useful method of gaining intelligence in the future, but right now it was frustrating. He needed a few months of uninterrupted time, a bank of experts to consult, weeks of experimentation before he could effectively refine his procedures.

From the corner of his eye, he could see Caroline examining him as he studied the map. She was dressed in the no-nonsense silk fighting suit under the short leather jacket she'd come to favour. Her hair was pulled back and tied with what looked like a piece of insulated wire. The whole effect was devastating but, then again, he couldn't remember any outfit of hers that hadn't devastated him.

She crossed her arms. 'We're not going to stay here, are we?'

He straightened, rubbing the small of his back. He had no idea how generals managed, bent over maps all day. 'We've learned about as much as we can from the kites.'

'So you're going to get all twitchy at any minute.'

'I'm patience personified, but I understand if you're getting a little housebound. Factorybound. Hideoutbound.'

'Need I point out that we haven't learned anything about this factory that we were sent to find out about?' She stabbed a finger at the map. 'Stalsfrieden.'

'Two points about that. Firstly, we *weren't* sent to find out about it. That was a job for the remote sensers.'

'Pooh.'

'I beg your pardon?'

She narrowed her eyes dangerously. 'You heard me.'

'I heard; I simply didn't believe it.'

'Harrumph,' she said, adding to Aubrey's incredulity. 'I was about to say that while it may have *technically* been the job of the remote sensers to find out about this Stalsfrieden factory, it was actually the job of this base. The base you're in charge of. Also technically. Your second point?'

Aubrey rocked in place, buffeted by the force of Caroline's argument. 'Second?'

'To follow "firstly".'

'Of course.' He did his best to retrack his derailed train of thought. 'Secondly, Stalsfrieden is twenty miles on the other side of the Holmland border. Which is on the other side of the Holmland army.' He eyed her nervously. 'You're going to pooh again, aren't you?'

'Perhaps. Your point deserved it.' Instead, she tapped her foot and glared at the map. 'Well, you're not going to let a small thing like a Holmland army stop us, are you?'

And so, that night they found themselves with George and Sophie creeping through the woods to the north of Divodorum and peering down on the battlefield they were skirting on their way to Stalsfrieden.

Originally, Aubrey had tried to convince George and Sophie to stay behind, but Sophie had united support from George and Caroline. Unspoken was the thought that they would be close to where her brother was, and Aubrey could see a spontaneous side mission waiting to spring upon him. He also knew the inevitable when he saw it. The romance of reuniting a family would appeal to Caroline, while George had only grown closer to Sophie.

Aubrey was sweating under his black balaclava, part of the all-black outfit each of them agreed to wear. Caroline and Sophie wore the sensible trousers and pullovers far more stylishly than any quartermaster could have imagined, Aubrey guessed, and he was sure that Caroline would have her silk fighting suit handy as well. Sophie thought wearing the balaclava was silly, until George pointed out how her blonde hair was a beacon in the darkness, easily seen at a distance. Caroline wore her leather aviator's helmet to good effect.

He lay on his stomach, feeling his revolver poking into his side, and peered across the panorama that was spread in front of them. With Caroline, George and Sophie likewise prone, he brought up the field glasses, metal casing carefully blackened to avoid tell-tale glinting.

A mile down the heavily wooded slope was the bulk of the Gallian force. Aubrey could pick out camp fires and tents, but most of the soldiers had dug in – a long double line of trenches stretched for hundreds of yards to either side. Barbed wire was the feature of the Gallian emplacements, stretched and bundled, ragged and well placed, a warning and a saviour. The rear line of trenches was reinforced, and in places had a rough parapet made of sandbags. The front line, however, looked crude and hasty, more like a series of ragged fox holes than a resolute emplacement.

Nearly half a mile behind the trenches was the artillery – or what was left of the artillery. Aubrey swept the field glasses along what had been the pride of the Gallian gunners, but could only find one field gun that wasn't shattered or overturned. Sandbags were scattered and earthwork emplacements destroyed.

The other side of the Gallian trenches was a bare, chewed-up area, three or four miles in extent, leading to the Holmland emplacement, which was almost a mirror image of the Gallian – trenches, barbed wire, but the artillery was ominously unharmed.

Aubrey had a moment, a tiny frozen moment when the future spread out in front of him. He saw the scene he was looking at repeated, and repeated again and again, across the Continent, across the world, as Dr Tremaine drove towards his goal.

The rogue sorcerer wanted blood. He needed a sacrifice on a scale unheard of, and duplicating this battleground was the way to do it. A meat grinder, a slaughterhouse, a mass killing ground where people died and died and died. Guns and barbed wire and mud and blood. Countrysides pounded until they were unrecognisable. Whole populations fleeing. Machines wiping whole armies away.

And for what? Manoeuvred by Dr Tremaine they might be, but whole countries had committed themselves to war because of ancient grudges, foolish ambition and simple, stupid misunderstandings. Was any of this worth the sacrifice of one life, let alone thousands?

Aubrey knew that the events leading up to the declaration of war would be pored over in the future, argued and debated. In the end, the way the war started didn't matter. It was the way the war ended that was important – and he was determined to do what he could to bring that about.

Aubrey lowered the field glasses and shook his head. This was no skirmish. The forces on either side had dug in for the long haul.

'Which way is Stalsfrieden?' he murmured, hoping he wouldn't have to pull off his boot and consult his compass.

George pointed. 'If we climb that ridge, we can skirt the battlelines and then we should be able to follow the river valley right up to the border.'

'After that?'

'Ingenuity will be required, I'd say,' Caroline said. 'I hope you have something up your sleeve, Aubrey.'

'Théo could have been down there,' Sophie said softly. 'I hope he is safe where he is.'

'I'm sorry, Sophie,' Aubrey said and he took a look back at the trenches. Pinpoints of light glinted all along the battlelines, making them look like stretches of stardust, 'but I don't think any of us will be safe until this is all over.'

Twenty-two

*A*TESTING FIVE DAYS LATER — FIVE DAYS DURING which George's woodsman's skills and Aubrey's concealment magic had been much in demand thanks to Holmland patrols — Aubrey was glad night was drawing in quickly to add extra security to their hiding place. Lying on his belly, scanning the eastern outskirts of Stalsfrieden, safe in the thick canopy of one of the huge willow trees on the bank of the Salia, he was relieved to have made it this far.

Aubrey hadn't told his friends that the magical air bubble that had enclosed them in their underwater border crossing had been experimental, as he didn't want to worry them while they were under the surface. He'd been continuously monitoring its integrity as the river current swept them along, right under the border bridge, and well past the Holmland border military emplacements. They'd fetched up on the northern bank of the river and now, Stalsfrieden stood before them.

Stalsfrieden was a sizeable city, twice the size of Divodorum. From his briefing documents, Aubrey knew its importance was determined by its nearby coal and iron deposits, so no matter how much it may have wanted to grow up into an arts or religious community, it had no option but to become a sturdy contributor to Holmland's industrial might.

Yet Aubrey was puzzled by a singular lack. 'Where do you think all the people are?' he whispered.

'I was wondering the same thing.' Caroline had the field glasses, a smaller, more compact version suitable for travelling. She swept them over the streets and buildings. 'All I can see are soldiers. A curfew?'

Even close to midnight as it was, a column was rumbling through the main western exit of the city, bound for the border and the Divodorum front. Aubrey was struck, and sobered by, the difference between a Gallian column and a Holmland column. The Holmland column moved briskly, whether lorries or marching troops, with an undeniable air of purpose. The artillery and the lorries themselves looked as if they'd just rolled off the assembly line. No horses or mules or camp stragglers. This was an entirely businesslike affair – and Aubrey hadn't seen a break in the column in the hour they'd been watching. He imagined such a scene repeated on the eastern front, and in the Low Countries. Holmland's military build-up had been even more thorough than the most pessimistic Albionite had thought. It pointed to a failure in intelligence-gathering.

And that's something to be looked at when this is all over, Aubrey thought, *if we're able to.*

The thought gave him pause. He had great respect for Commander Craddock, and Commander Tallis was a fine organiser, but could it be that they were both part of an old world? The world was changing drastically. Perhaps a new approach to intelligence gathering was needed, something more comprehensive and systematic.

His thoughts were interrupted by Sophie's reaching past George and tapping him on the arm. 'I have been counting.' She pointed to the dirt in front of her. 'Fourteen civilians is all I have seen.'

'Fourteen?' Aubrey frowned. He could see lights about the city indicating that it wasn't deserted, but the only figures in the streets were clearly soldiers. The riverside docks were busy, but all the workers were wearing Holmland uniforms as they manhandled barrels and sacks from barges to the wharfs, watched by a solitary, unhappy civilian barge captain. Wagons and lorries were being driven by soldiers and were loaded by soldiers. Officers wandered about and directed these efforts or stood under street lamps, smoking.

Stalsfrieden was a city that had been taken over by the military. It might be different during the day, once the curfew was relaxed, but Aubrey wasn't sure. The whole city looked as if it had been handed over to the war effort.

Aubrey motioned to the others. Quietly, they withdrew and worked their way down the bank away from the city until they found a densely wooded pocket where a determined streamlet forced its way through the overgrown boulders to join the river. It was gloomy and well sheltered from the wind that came off the river.

'And where is the baron's facility?' Caroline asked eventually. Not risking a light, they shared the cold rations they'd packed – ham, bread, cheese. If he had to survive on any cold rations, Aubrey decided as he sampled the delicious ham, he'd prefer they were Gallian cold rations.

'Saltin said it was to the north,' George answered.

'The other side of the town,' Sophie murmured.

Aubrey gazed into the darkness. A barge chugged past, its engines labouring against the current. A single figure stood in the wheelhouse, a light turning him into a glowing figure in the night, gliding in an illuminated world all of his own. 'The facility is a little more north-east than north. Can we get there tonight?'

'Look,' George said, 'I don't know about you lot, but I'm tired. I say we rest here and skirt around the town in the morning.'

It made good sense. Aubrey had been straining not to yawn for some time, but he knew his responsibility. 'I'll take first watch. Two hours, then I'll wake George.'

THE NEXT MORNING, THEIR CAREFUL JOURNEY AROUND THE outside of Stalsfrieden meant flitting through woody out-crops, crossing a frustrating rocky spur that was surprisingly muddy, and avoiding the occasional farmhouse where dogs were only too willing to let the neighbourhood know that strangers were about. It was a mixture of countryside and more urban areas where houses had grown up around the major roads leading to and from the city. The idea of a dawn journey proved optimistic as it took them most of the morning to get to the industrial part of the city, to judge from the increasing amount of smoke. Aubrey wrinkled his nose at the telltale odours of manufacturing and engineering: tannery residue, mysterious chemicals and the stuff euphemistically labelled 'organic waste'. As they scuttled along one of the gullies that broke up the landscape, his eyes were on the ground as much as ahead, for he had an aversion to stepping in organic waste.

Along the way, they saw more evidence of civilians, but they were still outnumbered by soldiers, who were even present on the farms, organising deliveries of foodstuffs.

The industrial area grew until the intrusions of woods and undeveloped areas were infrequent. Activity increased, with lorries and carts much more frequent – but all driven by soldiers. Smoke and steam hung over this quarter of the city. The fumes and the clattering, banging noise that came from every small workshop and factory combined with the lowering sky to emphasise that this was a great machine dedicated to pumping up the engines of war.

Night was falling by the time they found Baron von Grolman's factory. They surveyed it from a wooded rise about half a mile away, with professional curiosity – apart from Sophie, who looked at it with both longing and determination. At the front was the original building, a hulking three storeys flanked by two towers that managed to be both squat and beetling, a triumph of ham-fisted architecture. It was built of stone that may once have been light coloured, but was now so grey that it was almost black, and streaked here and there with even darker smears. Every window was bleary.

Joined to the original building were two wings which projected back into the grounds of the extensive complex, then the newer additions began. Chimneys sprouted from these, and to judge from their outpourings, Aubrey was prepared to wager that the factory was dedicated to making the most eye-watering, nose-scouring smells in the world, probably as a battlefield weapon, or as an example to schoolboys everywhere about how to make the perfect stink bomb. One chimney was a particular offender, belching greasy black smoke that seemed to have the specific job of turning the stomach.

A railway spur ran into the complex, a sidetrack from the main route, which was trending southward, to the heart of Holmland. It could only mean that heavy industry was taking place in the complex, requiring the delivery capability that only the railway could provide.

The entire complex was alive, even in the night. It was boring ahead with its noisy business, unchecked by darkness. Most of buildings were alive with electric light, and it flooded the façade and grounds in an almost arrogant display of industrial power.

'Théo,' Sophie breathed. 'What are you doing in such a place?'

It was a good question, but Aubrey really wanted to know what the place itself was doing. It was apparently a centre of activity and Holmland was investing substantial resources here, but what was happening?

'Are you sure this is the right place?' George asked. The wire fence that ran around the complex was at least fifteen feet high and topped with barbed wire. Tall guard towers stood at each corner.

'I can feel the magic from here.'

He wasn't a trained remote senser, but every magician had some degree of magical awareness, based on natural ability and honed by practice. He could feel powerful magic fairly radiating from the factory and it was actually causing perturbations in the magical firmament. It rattled his senses, a storm of confusion in touch, taste, sight, hearing and smell that he had to shake off in order to concentrate. It was a kind he couldn't pin down, but he thought it had a touch of animation magic, pattern magic, and traces of half a dozen others he knew – plus an equal number he had no idea about. He was in no doubt, however, that it had Dr Tremaine's hands all over it. Magic and heavy industry together. Who knew what sort of devilry he was planning?

'Aubrey,' George said.

'Mmm?'

'We have visitors.'

Aubrey looked over his shoulder and his heart sank. A dozen black-clad figures stood about in the shadows, but with the attitude of trained combatants rather than vicars out for a late night nature ramble. Hostile, but professional, their lack of obvious weapons wasn't at all encouraging. They had the air of people who had several implements of mayhem secreted about their body, and were dying for a chance to use them.

'You will be tied up,' one of them growled in Holmlandish that, to Aubrey's ear, was overlaid with a thick foreign accent. Were they foreigners in the Holmland army? Or did the lack of uniform indicate they had they been surprised by someone else entirely? 'Do not make a sound, if you value your life.'

Getting to his feet, he caught and held Caroline's eye and he gave a minute shake of his head. He'd seen how the strangers were spread out, carefully not screening each other from line of sight. He'd also caught a whiff, a faint tang of disturbing magic. Caroline could take a few of them, he was sure, and George could account for more, but there were too many, too many.

At that moment, he was acutely aware of the revolver under his armpit. It almost sang to him and it was hard to resist: 'Now! Use me now!'

He shuddered. To a man with a hammer, every problem looks like a nail. To a man with a pistol, every problem looks like a target. He understood, then, as he stood there with hostile parties descending on him, the allure of the firearm – and the way it often made things worse instead of better.

'I'm armed,' he said, making sure his hands were up above his head. 'Make sure you take it. Left side, under my pullover.'

Better off without that temptation. Of course, it made the hostiles even more suspicious, and this only increased at the number of weapons they found on Caroline. George coughed up a few, and Aubrey was surprised to see that Sophie had nearly as many as Caroline, including a lethal-looking stiletto.

Wrists bound, he was roped to the others. They were urged through the woods away from the factory, deeper into the countryside, along what turned into a small ravine before becoming a stream that cut well into the landscape. In the defile, it was eye-bafflingly black, but a few steps was all it took before Aubrey's hair stood up on the back of his head.

'Do not step in the water,' came the hushed order.

Aubrey searched, but couldn't see a thing, let alone water – but he could feel the heavy presence of malignant magic. It made his skin crawl with shapeless, unformed dread.

'It's too dark,' he whispered. 'We can't see.'

A jerk on the rope stopped them short, with someone (Sophie?) colliding with his back. He was anxious about her, so he did his best to project steady, calm authority. Caroline and George were somewhat accustomed to danger and to plans taking unexpected turnings, but Sophie couldn't have anticipated this. Although she was made from stern stuff, being waylaid by ominous strangers and dragged through mad magic couldn't have been part of her outlook.

A small light the size of a bee appeared just ahead of them. Aubrey nearly whistled in admiration before he caught himself. He hadn't felt a thing, and yet one of the nearby strangers – he could now see their shadowy shapes surrounding them – had summoned it to help their way. Deft, skilled magic.

The muck at the bottom of the gully gleamed in the soft beelight, but it gleamed with the unhealthiness that Aubrey associated with the eyes of cave-dwelling fish. It didn't flow, either, at least not in the regular manner of water. It heaved and shivered, as though it couldn't quite make up its mind if it were solid or fluid, but knew that it had to keep moving down the gradient. It stank, needless to say, but it was the rolling waves of magic that came off it that turned Aubrey's stomach.

He turned to see that it was indeed Sophie directly behind him. Her eyes were wide, but she nodded gamely at him. He indicated the water with a nod and then a shake of his head, but he was sure that no-one in their right mind would step into that stuff if they had a choice.

The farmhouse they came to was only a mile or so from the factory, which loomed on top of what Aubrey saw now was a slight ridge and smoked and steamed away, sailing above its surrounds like an ocean liner ploughing through a sea of forest. He thought it looked ominous, and it brought to mind Dr Tremaine's showy, threatening skyfleet.

He couldn't contemplate this for long, however, as he was dragged through the doorway of the farmhouse.

He'd been expecting an abandoned ruin, such was the way his mind was working after the experiences of the night, so he was surprised to see it furnished with simple but comfortable fittings. They'd come in through the kitchen, which was warm thanks to the large iron stove taking up most of one wall. A round wooden table was surrounded by chairs. Cooking implements and utensils hung from racks suspended from the ceiling. It looked so much like an ordinary farm kitchen that Aubrey was automatically suspicious.

Then a well-concealed trapdoor in the floor banged back and Aubrey sighed. *Basements. It's always basements.*

He rarely had good experiences underground. He recalled the incidents with the hydraulic railway (nearly drowned in a flood), the Bank of Albion vault (nearly killed by Dr Tremaine) and the buried Roman shrine (nearly crushed by malevolent magic). No, if he ever built a house, it wouldn't have a basement. He'd build it on rock. Better still, it would be a tree house, totally detached from the ground.

This basement, at least, was dry. They were ordered to sit, bound, on the stone floor while the strangers dispersed, still mysterious, still silent apart from the one that Aubrey assumed was the leader. At least he was the one who spoke.

'It is lucky we found you,' he growled, his hands on his hips.

Aubrey looked around at the stone walls. 'It depends on what you mean by luck.'

'Yes?

'Well, if you mean the sort of luck where strangers abduct you while you're going about your business, then I suppose we've hit the jackpot. If you mean the sort of luck that actually has a good outcome, then I must beg to disagree.'

'Enough,' came another, rather familiar, voice. 'It is him. I was not sure at first, but such nonsense shows it is him.'

One of the strangers unwound the scarf from her face. The white-blonde hair and large eyes were enough to make Aubrey stare – and to think they weren't going to die. 'Madame Zelinka. It's good to see you.'

Twenty-three

ALL IN ALL, AUBREY JUDGED, IT WAS MUCH BETTER falling in with Madame Zelinka's Enlightened Ones than a patrol of Holmlanders. At least, that's what he hoped, and he tried to remember if he'd offended or otherwise made an enemy out of her.

Aubrey, George and Caroline had encountered Madame Zelinka in Fisherberg. Her secretive order had been attempting to cope with malignant magical residue left behind after one of Dr Tremaine's experiments. This was the ancient responsibility of the Order of Enlightened Ones, neutralising the accidental by-blows of magic before they festered and produced their own horrors. After Aubrey had managed to counteract a particularly nasty outbreak – one that had killed an Enlightened One – Madame Zelinka had disappeared abruptly.

His fears that he'd transgressed in some way were dispelled when, after a few awkward minutes, she shook her head. 'Unbind them. They are harmless, but I want to know what they are doing here, interfering with our work.'

Aubrey saw Caroline bristle at being described at harmless, but she caught his look and subsided. 'Much appreciated.' He rubbed his wrists and stood. 'Any chance of a cup of tea?'

Madame Zelinka smiled a little at that. A touch frosty, but definitely on the way to a thaw. 'We will have tea. Katya.'

One of the Enlightened Ones detached herself from the silent onlookers and disappeared into the further reaches of the basement. Madame Zelinka gestured at the long table that took up much of the space in the basement and Aubrey sensed a shifting in the tension in the air. When they were sitting down, it wasn't frosty any more. Not quite warm, but it was approaching mild.

While mugs were distributed, the other Enlightened Ones shed coats and scarves. Aubrey introduced Sophie to Madame Zelinka, but he was careful to scan the range of faces that were intent on him and his companions.

The even dozen of Enlightened Ones were of all sorts, a multiplicity of nationalities that Aubrey had only seen hints of at great academic seminars or symposia. Madame Zelinka came from somewhere east of the Continent, one of the shifting regions in dispute with Muscovia. The silent man on her left had the aquiline features and shockingly white hair that announced his origins were north of Muscovia, in Zeme, the land of lakes and forests. In the others, he saw men and women from the far Orient, from either side of the African continent, from the islands of the Great Ocean, and from the heights of the Andean mountains. These last spoke a clipped language that intrigued Aubrey and he wished he could listen to it more carefully. It was accompanied by much hand-waving and he assumed it was designed to facilitate communication between those not sharing a common language.

But another possibility occurred to him and made him itch with impatience. It was simplified, but could it simply be primitive? Did the Enlightened Ones, with their ancient heritage, have access to languages not known elsewhere?

The last of Madame Zelinka's companions to remove his concealing cap and scarf was the man sitting on her right. When he did, Aubrey only dimly heard Caroline's gasp and George's stifled oath, because it was as if someone had just hit him behind the ear with a mallet.

'Is that any way to greet an old friend, Fitzwilliam? You look like a codfish.'

Aubrey struggled, but eventually put words together. 'Von Stralick. I should have guessed.'

'Really?' Von Stralick looked disappointed.

Aubrey was rallying after the shock of the Holmland spy's appearance. 'I should have guessed because you have a habit of turning up when least expected.'

'And here I am.' Von Stralick beamed, but Aubrey thought the usually immaculately groomed Holmlander looked worn and tired. His hair was worn long, as usual, to hide his missing ear, but it looked as if it needed a good trim. His moustache, too, looked more utilitarian than ornamental. 'Ah, the delightful Miss Hepworth.' He stood and bowed to Caroline. 'And who is your friend? Is that Miss Delroy? My reports said you were beautiful, my dear, but they missed the mark by a long way. You are most striking.'

'Steady on, von Stralick,' George growled.

'Ah,' von Stralick said, 'it's . . . please don't remind me . . . I'll have it in a minute or two.'

'It's no time to play games, von Stralick,' Aubrey said.

Von Stralick sighed. 'I apologise, Doyle. It was petty of me, but we have had little chance for levity here. No sense of humour, these Holmland patrols.'

'I can't imagine they have,' Aubrey said.

Von Stralick sipped his tea. 'Do you know what would have happened if we hadn't saved you from being snapped up by one that was on its way?'

Aubrey went cold. 'We didn't see a patrol.'

'They're quite good,' Von Stralick said. 'And they know the terrain.'

'What would have happened?' George said evenly.

Von Stralick shrugged. 'It wasn't a rhetorical question. We've lost people and we have no idea of their fate.'

Aubrey sat back. He'd last seen von Stralick in Fisher-berg, at the disastrous symposium. The Holmlander's status was more than ambivalent. He'd fallen out with the Holmland intelligence service after his superiors had been removed, and he'd abandoned his attempts to win favour with Baron von Grolman once he realised that the baron was working hand in hand with Dr Tremaine. Aubrey wondered if von Stralick's actions assisting Aubrey and his friends had further compromised his position.

'Wait,' Aubrey said, holding up both hands. 'You might want to know what we're doing here –'

'It had occurred to us,' von Stralick said. He sat, and Aubrey couldn't help but notice how close he was to the imperious Madame Zelinka. And how she shifted her position so she was even closer to him.

Amazing, he thought, but steered himself to the matter at hand. 'But I want to know what you're doing here.' *Even though I've just seen at least part of the reason.*

Madame Zelinka had an arresting beauty, and could only have been a year or two older than von Stralick, while he was dashing, intelligent and remarkably adaptable. A good couple?

'Self-interest,' von Stralick said proudly. 'Look no further than that, Fitzwilliam. I intend to make a great deal of money from this exercise. I believe that while the Enlightened Ones are clearing up other people's messes, I may have a chance to put my hands on a few items for which the highest bidders will be very high indeed.'

Aubrey had doubts that von Stralick was as selfish as that, but he also knew that if he dared suggest that von Stralick was doing anything that had a whiff of altruism about it, he would blanch and recoil in horror.

'And how did you two . . . meet?' George asked.

Von Stralick took Madame Zelinka's hand. 'Your Commander Craddock was responsible.' She clasped his hand fiercely. 'I still find that remarkable.'

Aubrey looked around for the bus that just run him over. *Remarkable?* he thought at the prospect of Commander Craddock acting as a matchmaker. *'Inconceivable' fits better.* It was like imagining Dr Tremaine having second thoughts, renouncing his plans for worldwide slaughter and becoming a dentist instead.

'Pompey thought we could work together,' Madame Zelinka said. 'He said we had much to offer each other.'

'Wait.' Aubrey held out a hand. The other, he put to his brow. He was dizzy. 'Pompey. You're not saying that Commander Craddock's first name is Pompey, are you?'

'I didn't know he had a first name,' George said. 'I thought he was like a dog.'

Aubrey couldn't believe what his friend was saying. 'Dogs have first names. They just don't have last names.'

'What are you talking about, old man? My old terrier was called Morris. That was his last name, obviously. Short and sharp.'

'He was part of your family, wasn't he? His full name was Morris Doyle.'

'I'm sorry,' Caroline interrupted. 'I think more important matters are at hand.'

Sophie nodded solemnly. 'I have been warned about Albion men and their dogs. They take them very seriously.'

Aubrey was about to launch into an explanation of why this was so – citing the importance of stick throwing in the development of national character – but caught Caroline's warning glance. He put the matter aside for later.

'Pompey Craddock,' von Stralick said with relish, enjoying the effect it had on Aubrey. 'Pompey Craddock is a fine, perceptive man.'

With a superhuman effort, Aubrey stopped himself from pursuing this line of thought and stuck to the idea of Craddock seeing some utility in the coming together of Madame Zelinka and Hugo von Stralick. Some utility apart from being a strange sort of experiment.

Von Stralick knew his way around the Holmland intelligence community. Despite being an outcast since the falling from grace of his mentor, he had contacts aplenty and had garnered a great deal of information about key people in government. He had hinted to Aubrey in the past that he kept what he called useful documents on file, secrets that a number of important figures wouldn't want revealed. In a war where the notion of weaponry was being redefined almost daily, such information could be in a weapon class of its own.

Allied to this was von Stralick's antipathy to Dr Tremaine, who he held responsible for the death of his mentor. This ill will had to be harnessed correctly, however. Von Stralick might declare that patriotism was an old-fashioned concept, but he was a Holmlander through and through. He saw the current Chancellor and his crew as misguided, unfortunate and ultimately dangerous but he didn't feel that the Holmland people should be held responsible for the idiots who led them, voting and representation being the flawed systems they were, in his estimation.

And Madame Zelinka? Aubrey assumed Craddock knew more about the Enlightened Ones than he did, but a powerful mystical organisation that was hostile to Dr Tremaine, seeing him as reckless in the extreme, could only be a useful partner.

Aubrey asked himself why Craddock didn't work directly with the Enlightened Ones and he had the distinct feeling that there was more beneath the skin of this particular rice pudding than met the eye.

'So,' von Stralick continued, 'we have an unholy alliance here. Our Baron von Grolman and your Dr Tremaine united for the Holmland war effort, pursuing nefarious, top secret plans.'

'So it would seem,' Aubrey said. 'You wouldn't have any idea exactly what they're up to, would you?'

'Exactly? No, I wouldn't say we know exactly. But look at this.' He signalled to one of the other Enlightened Ones. A tall Oriental woman handed a wooden box the size of a large bible to von Stralick. He thanked her. 'We captured this sample from a rail delivery two days ago.'

'I assume the train would be armed,' Caroline said. 'For a delivery to a top secret facility, it would stand to reason. How did you get the sample?'

Madame Zelinka pursed her lips. 'Some of our people have expertise in shrouding magic. The train slows down for a sharp bend a mile or so to the south. They were on and off before anyone knew it.'

Von Stralick grinned. 'Katya is quite bloodthirsty, too. Something about revenge for Holmland aggression in Veltrania.'

Veltrania. Aubrey glanced at the tea-bringing Katya, a slim, serious-looking woman in her thirties. She had prominent cheekbones. Aubrey wondered if she knew Rodolfo and his people.

Von Stralick put the box on his lap and fiddled with the top before removing it with a sound of satisfaction.

'Clay,' Caroline said. She looked at Aubrey, waiting.

'It's more than just clay.' Aubrey could feel it from where he was, playing on his skin like a swarm of tiny insects. 'It's potentialised clay.' He looked through the basement wall, through the ceiling, through the farmhouse to where Baron von Grolman's factory was waiting. 'They're making golems.'

Twenty-four

THIS ANNOUNCEMENT PROMPTED A BUZZ FROM THE Enlightened Ones. 'We thought so,' Madame Zelinka said. 'None of us has skill with golem magic, but Katya thought she recognised the material.'

'Potentialised clay,' Sophie said. 'What is that?'

Aubrey held out a hand, as if he were warming it by a fire. 'I can feel the magic that this clay has already been imbued with.' He didn't tell them that it was a sonorous droning, like a hive of extremely large bees. The confusing mix of sensations, where touch and sound could meld, where taste and sight could interweave, was an aspect of magical awareness that was hard to explain to those not endowed. 'It's heavily steeped in spells. The Law of Animation, the Law of Elastic Deformation, the Law of . . .' His voice dwindled. He reached out and broke off a thumbnail-sized piece of clay. 'It's special,' he finished lamely. *And it's certainly Dr Tremaine's work*, he thought. *It has the hallmarks of his magic.*

Aubrey was able to admit he admired Dr Tremaine's genius. It was extremely clever, working like this. Potentialising the clay in bulk allowed the rogue sorcerer to divide his efforts. He could roam about, tending to his plots and schemes, while the factory churned out golem after golem without his having to be there.

Aubrey was rolling the clay into a ball between his fingertips when a thought came to him and he stopped, frozen. 'You said this came from a train.'

'Indeed,' Madame Zelinka said. 'I know this is not our task, but Katya wouldn't be stopped.'

'A train.'

'That is what I said.'

Aubrey's mind was measuring. 'How many carriages?'

'Six.' It was Katya who spoke, in deeply guttural Albionish.

'Six carriages full of clay?'

'Yes.'

'That's a lot of golems,' George said, saying aloud what everyone was thinking.

'It wasn't the only train this week,' von Stralick said. 'Three others have made deliveries.'

Aubrey started rolling the clay again as he thought. Such an amount of potentialised clay. Combine it with the revolutionary golem-making machinery that allowed non-magicians to manufacture golems and it had the making of . . .

'George, what does an army need most of?'

'Dashed if I know, old man. Food?'

'Infantry,' Caroline said. 'Foot soldiers, ground troops, call them what you will.'

'With enough infantry,' Aubrey said, absently working the clay in his hands, 'generals can keep throwing troops at an enemy until they're overwhelmed. Especially if they're fit and trained troops.'

'Finding infantry is harder and harder, as wars wear on,' Caroline said slowly and Aubrey knew she had it. She looked at him with fear in her eyes. 'But how will we know if we're right?'

'Right about what?' Sophie said, looking from one to the other. 'What are you talking about?'

'That factory could be making golem soldiers,' Aubrey said.

'A golem army,' Caroline said.

The basement became a much grimmer place. The Enlightened Ones protested and argued, but Aubrey could see that none of them were Holmland supporters. Even so, some were sceptical.

'How can we find out for sure?' George asked.

Aubrey held up the piece of clay. It was now a rough, four-limbed creature. 'Send a golem to catch a golem, I always say.'

BASIC GOLEM MAKING HAD BEEN SOMETHING AUBREY HAD experimented with in the past. It had come in handy when he needed to explore the burnt church in the Mire. With a supply of potentialised clay at hand, it was the perfect stratagem. Explore, reconnoitre, report, then plan.

The limited amount of clay was not a handicap. Aubrey had never been able to master the intricacies of building full-sized human golems. He'd quickly learned that his best expression was in tiny mannikins, hand-sized figures with limited capabilities. Movement, observation and reporting was the limit of their endeavour, but within that they were surprisingly resourceful, able to overcome obstacles in their way, brimming with the desire to fulfil whatever mission Aubrey had charged them with.

Firstly, he had to neutralise the clay, to remove any possibility of Dr Tremaine's magic interfering with his. Neutralising was usually a straightforward process, something every young magician learned when beginning magical studies, but Aubrey was left sweating and shaking by the time he rendered the clay harmless. Dr Tremaine's magic was stubborn.

Not resting, he pushed on. George and Caroline took von Stralick and Madame Zelinka aside, and together they pored over a large map spread on the table. Most of the Enlightened Ones spread themselves about the farm, wearing stolen Holmland military uniforms so as not to appear out of place as they busied themselves, but three or four of them hovered in the basement, watching him working. In them, he saw the professional regard that magicians shared, and he was also pleased at Sophie's attention. She had a habit of holding one of her gold ear-studs when concentrating. While he was working, both gold orbs were being brought to a high polish.

He tore fist-sized chunks of clay from the box until Sophie took over that task, rolling the clay into manageable pieces. The rest was up to him.

He retrieved his golem spell from his memory, turned it around and inspected it only to find, as was his wont, that he wanted to make improvements. Sophie found paper and pencil and he'd soon scrawled out the spell components so he could study them while he gnawed on the pencil.

Three full versions later, and half a dozen minor embellishments, he had a spell he was happy with. It was tighter, with less room for error, and he'd built in an element of connectivity so he could feel the whereabouts of each mannikin at a distance.

Then it was a matter of making little human-shaped figures. Not much artistic skill was required, which was fortunate as Aubrey understood his limits in this area. Head, arms, legs was all that was needed, roughly in proportion. He inscribed each mannikin with an animating symbol on its forehead. This was a flourish, for the spell would take care of all the necessary animating, but the symbol did tend to ground the spell, keeping it within the confines of the clay bodies that he was working with.

They had enough clay for thirty-two, a number Aubrey judged had no auspicious or inauspicious connotations, so he was happy with it. The mannikins lay in two rows on a length of canvas that von Stralick produced. He rubbed his hands together and ran through the spell in his mind. Caroline handed him a wet cloth and he thanked her absently.

He cleared his throat and was aware of Sophie and the watching Enlightened Ones, so he did his best to uphold the great traditions of Albionite spell casting. He strove to look calm, dignified, very much in control – not someone who hadn't bathed for five days and who had a substantial amount of clay smeared all over him.

He began in his best Etruscan, and several of the Enlightened Ones smiled in recognition. He was careful not to hurry, and he counted a beat in his head to help him roll through each element in measured, round tones.

A final, modest signature element, and he was done.

The mannikin nearest to him quivered. A shiver ran through the next, and the next, running along the row, as if they were connected with wires. The first mannikin swelled, its rough limbs filling out and becoming more solid. Just as its neighbour began the same swelling process, the first mannikin bent in the middle and sat up, trembling. A few seconds later — where Aubrey had the distinct impression it was gathering its wits, what little of them it had — and it stood and swayed slightly, the first of his golem squad.

Aubrey heard some murmurs of approval from the Enlightened Ones, but most of his attention was on monitoring the progress of the spell. Ten minutes later and the golems were all ready. They stood solemnly like so many faceless gingerbread men.

Aubrey took a deep breath. A complicated spell, made all the more complicated by the numbers he was juggling, and he could feel the toll it had taken. Some of his weariness was no doubt due to the lateness of the hour, and the long, taxing day they'd been through, but the spell had had an effect. His limbs were weary, and he was sure his hands would be trembling if he wasn't holding them together. As he stood there inspecting his work, he could sense each of the golems and their physical location, even if he closed his eyes. The connection element was working.

He was embarking on a dangerous strategy. Another dangerous strategy. The connection ran both ways – it could be traced back to him, revealing his location, leading the enemy to their position. Sending the mannikins was potentially compromising their security and jeopardising their ability to observe the facility in secret.

He knew this. He knew it was a risk – but the reward of detailed information about the inner workings of the factory was great enough for him to proceed. The mannikins would have to be furtive, clinging to shadows and avoiding notice at all times. He wanted them to be mice in the wainscoting, not elephants barging through the jungle.

'Follow,' he said, keeping his commands simple, knowing that this was essential for golems of this order.

Without looking back, aiming for an air of utter confidence, he led the mannikins up the stairs, through the trapdoor, and through the farmhouse until he could point at the factory steaming away above the tree tops to the north. He took a deep breath and pointed. 'Go. Observe. Report back to me. Don't be seen by anyone.'

The mannikins, as one, leaned in the direction of the factory, then back toward Aubrey, like grain in the wind. Then they set off, running stiff-legged though the night. They ran in slightly different directions, through the grassy field, then plunging into the woods that separated the farm from the factory.

Aubrey dusted his hands together. 'Now, we wait.'

WAITING WAS ALWAYS FRUSTRATING FOR AUBREY, AND AFTER three hours with no appearance from his mannikins, he was on edge. He began to find the kitchen increasingly small, especially after Caroline narrowed her eyes at his finger-drumming and foot-jiggling. After the first hour, when it became apparent that no quick mannikin return was imminent, some of the Enlightened Ones retired. Those unwilling or unable to sleep stayed in the kitchen and talked in the candlelight, low voices discussing families, magic and war. Caroline took up a position by Aubrey's side as the talk moved and flowed through loved ones left behind, to the mandate and heritage of the Enlightened Ones, then into discussion of Dr Tremaine and his motives, expanding into magic in general. Aubrey asked about the pidgin used to communicate among Enlightened Ones of different backgrounds, which launched a discussion of the connection between magic and language that made Caroline yawn. She apologised, and did her best to stay with what became a technical discussion. Aubrey was startled, however, a moment later, to feel her head against his upper arm. He immediately lost track of the finer distinctions between Babylonian and Sumerian and he stopped talking, just in case he was lapsing into unintelligibility. Carefully, he sneaked a glance at Caroline's restful face and immediately, he was lost in admiring how the hair curled around her ears and the sweep of her eyelashes, closed in well-earned sleep.

'Fitzwilliam.' Aubrey carefully turned to see von Stralick. The Holmlander's smile was without malice. Aubrey looked around. The other Enlightened Ones had gone. How long had he been looking at Caroline? 'We are going to get some sleep. You should, too.'

'I will,' Aubrey whispered. His arm was numb from being in the one position for so long, but nothing on earth could have made him move it. 'I thought I might inspect the perimeter before I do. How many are on watch?'

'Four. Approach them carefully.' Von Stralick touched his forehead. 'I forgot. Your Doyle and the delightful Delroy girl are out there as well.'

'They are?'

'They volunteered. Our people have been here on alert for two weeks. I thought you newcomers could help share the burden.'

'Of course.'

Von Stralick saluted with only a touch of irony and left Aubrey and Caroline alone, with a single candle for light.

Happiness sometimes came unasked for and unlooked for, Aubrey decided. Sweaty, dirty, in danger and at war wasn't the sort of situation he'd anticipated would bring about contentment, but he knew it was the addition of Caroline to that equation that made the difference. She made his heart beat faster, his breath come more awkwardly, his throat tighten, but the physiological effects were only part of how she moved him.

He liked to think – he liked to hope – that they had a connection. Not a magical one, unless it was the ordinary yet miraculous magic that wove its way through all human history. No, it was the connection that set two people apart from the others about them. It was the connection that outlasted and overrode exasperation, irritation and frustration. It worked on conscious levels of liking how someone looked, but it also wrapped the two of them up in a million ways impossible to disentangle from each other. It was a connection that, in some ways, could best be defined by its absence: he ached when he wasn't with her.

He wanted her to feel the same.

He sat bolt upright, every muscle taut. 'Connection.'

Caroline hardly moved. She opened one eye. 'I may get tired of asking this one day,' she said sleepily, 'but are you all right, Aubrey?'

'I feel it. The connection.'

She sat up, rubbing sleep from her eyes. Her hair was in magnificent disarray. She stretched and yawned. 'Aren't you connected to your mannikins? Isn't that what you're feeling?'

Aubrey shook his head impatiently and started pacing as excitement bubbled inside him. 'No, it's not that. I can still feel them, but this is different.' He stopped. He tilted his head back and stared at the ceiling. 'It's him.'

Caroline's hands curled slowly into fists. 'Tremaine?'

'Yes. I can feel him.' Aubrey ground his teeth. His first certainty was fading. Could it be the magic he'd been performing with the mannikins, leaving him sensitive to other connections?

'Where is he?' Caroline said.

She was sitting upright and doing her best to remain calm, but her burning hatred for Dr Tremaine had never diminished. Her eyes were bright and hard as her desire for revenge on the man who killed her father.

Aubrey couldn't refuse her. 'He's in the factory. His presence is . . . everywhere.'

'Why? I thought you said the whole idea of the clay and the machinery was so he could go about his evil ways elsewhere, while others finished the golem work.'

'You're asking me to divine Dr Tremaine's thoughts?'

Caroline nodded sharply, acknowledging Aubrey's point. 'So how are we going to get in there?'

'Into the factory?' That wasn't the plan. Reconnoitre, observe, then report, *that* was the plan. When Aubrey's mannikins came back he was sure he'd have enough information to satisfy the Directorate. Any action after that would be up to the planning bigwigs.

'We can't walk away.' Caroline stood and crossed her arms, hands clutching elbows. 'He's here, we're here, and we have allies. It's a good chance to strike a blow against Holmland. Imagine if we can remove him.' Aubrey wisely didn't question Caroline on exactly what that meant. 'Holmland would be thrown into disarray. We could stop the war before it really starts.'

Quibbling with Caroline when she was in this mood was a delicate affair. He doubted, for instance, that she'd appreciate it if he pointed out that the relatives of the soldiers and civilians already killed in the Low Countries would be convinced that the war had started. 'Taking him would certainly thwart his plans.'

'Oh yes,' Caroline said softly. 'It would do that.'

Aubrey wondered if he would be the same if the situations were reversed. When his father had been abducted by Dr Tremaine, he had been outraged at the affront. He'd rushed to do something to get back at the man, but his anger had cooled once his father had been rescued. His attitude to Dr Tremaine after that was shifting, not quite fixed. The rogue sorcerer's gusto and utter self-confidence had undeniable appeal. He was never struck by the self-doubt that crept up on Aubrey when he least needed it.

What a gift to go through life undisturbed by such nigglings, he thought. *How clear everything must seem.*

But Dr Tremaine was without conscience, in a way that was shuddersome. Aubrey had wondered whether the man was truly human, so unconcerned was he for other people. When he disposed of them, it wasn't with cruelty, or spite, it was with a casual lack of regard. Aubrey doubted if he could remember the names of any of them.

Through their magical connection, Aubrey knew how deeply this attitude ran. It wasn't a pose. It wasn't a guise. He simply had no sympathy with other people on any level at all.

Aubrey shivered at the contemplation of such a condition. Was such a person actually human? Anyone who had so little connection – and there was that word again – was frightening. It meant he was capable of anything, and would feel as little concern about sending hundreds of thousands to their deaths as he would demolishing a potting shed.

Aubrey could admire the wide-reaching intellect of Dr Tremaine, but he could never admire the man. He was dangerous on a level that was beyond any other single person. Even the leaders of nations were pawns in his cosmic game.

Caroline hated Dr Tremaine for a simple reason: he had killed her father. Sometimes a simple response was enough.

'Let's wait until we have more information,' he said, hating both how priggish and how feeble that sounded. 'If Dr Tremaine is in the factory, we can report, wait for reinforcements, then move on him. We can round up Sophie's brother then, too.'

'More information,' Caroline murmured. 'Yes, that's standard procedure, isn't it?'

'The mannikins shouldn't be long, I'm sure. Then we can decide.'

She patted him on the arm. 'You're right, Aubrey. Now, where are George and Sophie? Perhaps we could see about some breakfast.'

Aubrey realised, then, that dawn was breaking. His eyes were gritty. He yawned. 'I might see about catching an hour of sleep, first, if that's all right.'

'By all means.'

Caroline patted his arm again, looking thoughtful and rumpled in a way that made Aubrey's heart nudge his breast bone. She wandered out through the kitchen door and into the farm yard, touched gold and pink in the dawn.

Twenty-five

$\mathcal{T}$HE NEXT MORNING, HE DISCOVERED WHAT 'BONE weary' truly meant. It wasn't just his muscles that were complaining, every single part of his skeleton was picketing for a nice, long holiday. Hunched over, he limped to the kitchen to find that the mannikins were waiting for him. He groaned as they bounced about at his presence.

He desperately wanted to sit down for a moment to gather himself, with a cup of tea as a restorative, but mannikins didn't last forever. The animating spells for such low-level golems had a duration determined by the clay. With time and movement, the creatures simply wore out, their joints fraying and failing. Overcoming these problems was one of the main challenges of creating and maintaining the higher order golems – a Dr Tremaine speciality.

Von Stralick climbed out of the trapdoor to the basement. He was dressed in what looked like army khakis, but with no emblems or insignia. 'Ah, little dolls.'

'Mannikins.'

'How quaint. Mannikins. I hope they have news for us. Did you see that the factory is busy this morning? Producing more spell muck for us to clean up, no doubt.'

'It's probably because Dr Tremaine is managing the operation.'

Von Stralick's easy demeanour disappeared. 'Dr Tremaine?' he said harshly. 'He is here?'

'I can sense him.'

Von Stralick scowled in the direction of the factory. 'We thought he was elsewhere.'

'He has a habit of getting about unobtrusively.'

'This . . . this changes the situation.' Von Stralick cast another glance toward the factory, tugged at the hair covering his missing ear. 'What is he doing there?' he wondered, and he raised an eyebrow. 'Ask your dolls. What have they seen?'

Aubrey felt a fool, crouched in the kitchen of a Holmland farmhouse communing with a squad of four-inch-tall clay people while a collection of assorted magicians from around the world stood guard, but he decided it would make a nice episode in his memoirs.

Sometimes, in difficult circumstances, he liked the idea of writing his memoirs. Not because he desperately wanted people to read about his life, but because if he wrote them it meant that he'd lived through whatever dangerous predicament he was currently in.

The reporting back was on the same sort of level as the little golems themselves. It wasn't a detailed military report complete with diagrams and troop numbers. It was more an impression of what each mannikin experienced. As a result, it took some time for them to work through their recollections, and it took Aubrey more time to sift through the dross to find nuggets.

As he worked through the mannikins he became more and more concerned. Each one recounted the same experience from different vantage points (under benches, in rafters, in between banks of shadowy machinery) and they affirmed what he'd guessed at.

Baron von Grolman's factory was making golems on a scale unheard of – enough golems for an army – thanks to Dr Tremaine's magic and machinery

He was frustrated by the lack of detail in the mannikins' reporting, even though it was what he'd expected. They recognised that huge creatures were being made, and that clay was part of the process, but that was all. Exact numbers, dimensions, capabilities were too much for the tiny scouts.

Aubrey's head was aching with the glut of sensation and image that he'd taken on board, and he was sickened by what he'd been shown. He straightened, but before the quizzical von Stralick could ask, George rushed around the corner of the milking shed nearby. 'Have either of you seen Sophie?' he panted.

'Sophie?' Aubrey echoed. 'No.'

'She's gone off somewhere.' George ran a hand through his hair, then grimaced. Aubrey had rarely seen his placid friend so upset. 'I don't like to think about her out there on her own, so close to the factory. Holmland patrols are out there.'

'I don't think you have to worry,' von Stralick said. 'Katya said she saw her with Miss Hepworth.'

The alarm bells that sounded in Aubrey's head were so loud he was actually worried that the sound would leak out of his ears and startle the others. He slapped his forehead. He was an idiot! He should have been more suspicious of Caroline's easy acquiescence when he'd left her to get some sleep. 'With Caroline? Heading in which direction?'

'Miss Hepworth told Katya she wanted a closer look at von Grolman's place. Your Miss Delroy joined her at that moment and –' He looked at both of them carefully. 'They appeared to argue, according to Katya.'

'Argue?' George said. 'Caroline and Sophie? What about?'

'Katya did not hear every word, but there was much pointing in the direction of the factory. And Miss Delroy was concerned about a relative.'

Aubrey and George exchanged looks. George, to Aubrey's eyes, looked as close to frantic as he'd ever seen.

'Do not worry about them,' von Stralick said. 'They appeared to reach some compromise, for they did go off together.'

George frowned. 'We are going after them, aren't we, old man?'

'Straight away,' Aubrey said. 'Hugo?'

Von Stralick rubbed his chin. 'I cannot. We have our work to do. The residue we've found will need much spellcraft, apparently.' He coughed discreetly into his hand. 'We will be here, when you return.'

Aubrey silently thanked von Stralick for not using 'if'. 'George? Ten minutes to get a few things ready?'

'I'll be ready in five.'

I<small>T WAS</small> K<small>ATYA WHO GUIDED THEM THROUGH THE FOREST</small>, but Aubrey was aware of other presences nearby. Nothing magical, just good scouting, only revealing themselves in a few half-glimpses of figures darting from tree to tree.

The hundred yards or so of woods surrounding the factory was uncomfortable work: belly crawling through a mess of ivy, bracken and clumps of bushes that were unidentifiable despite being proudly and defiantly prickly. These were the fringe dwellers of the vegetative world, the ones that would slink out of a line-up, unrecognised, with the witness behind the glass saying, 'Sorry, officer, but they all look the same to me.'

Katya led them to a place that she was sure – from some arcane sort of woodcraft, Aubrey assumed – was the launching place for Caroline and Sophie's assault on the factory. She waved away their thanks and said they could thank her by killing many, many Holmlanders – something which made Aubrey most ambivalent – before fading away with her colleagues.

From the edge of the undergrowth, they looked across fifty yards of cleared area to the chain link fence. Although it was at the rear of the property, half a mile or more from the main road, the fence was in good repair. The barbed wire on top looked formidably new and sharp.

They'd approached the south side of the facility. In the early morning light, the complex was all clangour and activity. None of the soldiers Aubrey saw moving between buildings was tarrying, and he wondered if one of them was Théo. They moved on the trot or better, while lorries both heavy and light tore along with no regard for the soldiers, who appeared accustomed to leaping aside at their approach.

The main road ran past the western end of the complex, and a fortified gatehouse guarded the approach to the original building. Some distance behind the old buildings was an open expanse, with a large squat construction on the south side. Bundles of cables ran from this building to the others, looping from strategically placed poles. Aubrey tentatively marked the squat building as the location of an electricity generator.

North of the open expanse was a cluster of buildings, the centre of most of the activity and the source of most of the smoke and steam. These buildings were new and Aubrey guessed they were the heart of the manufacturing. If golems were being manufactured they would probably be stored in the huge warehouse building that bulked large behind the factories. If he could judge distances properly, the warehouse was also the receiving and dispatch end of the railway spur. Beyond it, and overtopping it, were huge black heaps of coal, one after the other, stretching the entire length of the far side of the immense structure.

Abutting the eastern edge of the open area were buildings that could only be huts for the soldiers. They stretched off in rows to the back of the property. If they were needed to house all of the soldiers, it gave Aubrey pause. This was a substantial military investment.

He rolled onto one elbow and, while he was stowing his field glasses, he studied George, who continued to observe through his own binoculars.

'Right, George,' he said. 'Before we get going, I think we need to clear up something.'

'We do? What is it, old man?

'What's wrong with you, George?'

'Wrong?' George answered without lowering his binoculars.

'Ever since we discovered Sophie had gone, your face has been so long you've had trouble not tripping on it. You've been sighing like a traction engine. If you looked any more like a consumptive poet you'd have to join their union.'

George lowered his field glasses. 'Hello, Mr Pot, I'm Mr Kettle. What colour are we?'

'You may have a point. But you must admit that I've some practice in this, while it may – dare I suggest it – be a novelty for you.'

George frowned. 'Maybe.'

'So what's causing it? Sophie hasn't run off. She's just over there. Somewhere. Behind barbed wire and in the middle of an enemy military industrial complex, admittedly, but she's not lost to you.'

George chewed this over. 'That's assuming, of course, that her intentions were honourable in the first place.'

Aubrey had to work this one through for a while then he stared at George, incredulous. 'You think that Sophie was just using you to get to her brother.'

The silence was so stony Aubrey could have used it to pave half a dozen streets. 'You can see how one could come to that conclusion,' George finally said. 'She was trapped on the border, no way to get to her brother, and we lob into the area. Now, I'm not saying that she latched onto me with a plan immediately in mind, but when we started talking about heading across the border, she made sure of coming along.'

'By . . . being nice to you?' Aubrey ventured.

'If you're insinuating anything, old man, I'd be very careful if I were you.'

'George, you know I'm not. And I'm convinced you're not thinking clearly.' He paused. 'May I speak frankly?'

'If you must.' George's face was bleak.

'Well, if I'm speaking frankly, I need to tell you that Sophie Delroy is wonderful, and she is obviously, evidently and wholly enamoured of you. As she should be.'

'Really?'

'George, you fathead, of course she is.'

'She's not just using me?' George looked away for a moment. 'I couldn't stand that. She's . . . special.'

Aubrey had never heard George talk like this. He liked girls. All girls. Lots of girls. He always had the highest opinion of them. Apparently, though, there was something special about Sophie.

'George, you can grump about thinking the worst, or you can have faith in someone you appear to admire so much.'

George lay the binoculars on the ground. Carefully, he picked a blade of grass and ran it through his fingers. 'Don't you have doubts, old man?'

'Doubts? Not many people don't have doubts. The trick is not to listen to them.'

'All right.' George threw the blade of grass over his shoulder. 'Let's make a pact.' He stood and brushed himself off, then he stuck out his hand. 'Let's promise each other not to listen to those doubts.'

Aubrey climbed to his feet, took his friend's hand and shook. 'Not unless they're reasonable doubts.'

George growled. 'Aubrey.'

'Right. Sorry. I mean: let's do the best we possibly can for those around us.'

'A noble aim. Now, how do we get into that place?'

Aubrey had been wondering if a night approach may be best, but he was sure the light towers situated at the corners and halfway along the boundaries would have powerful beams and equally powerful machine guns.

Think, Aubrey, think.

Standard tactics came to him – a diversion, tunnelling, fence breaching – but he had a suspicion that this place might be well prepared for such approaches.

He lay on the leaf-covered dirt again, the better to steady his field glasses. They were the best the Department could supply, by the hands of the renowned Crouch Bros. The lenses were each hand ground and the brothers Crouch had moved with the times, incorporating some neat stabilising spells in the frame of binoculars, so Aubrey had a firm, steady range of view. This allowed him to see the double box arrangement atop the nearest corner of the fence, attached to the guard tower legs, about twenty feet.

'I thought so,' he muttered. He lowered the field glasses.

'So did I,' George responded, shaking his head.

Aubrey stared. 'You what?'

'I thought so too, old man.' George paused a moment and seemed to enjoy Aubrey's puzzlement. 'You see, old man, I like to keep you on your toes. Sometimes, when I'm supposed to give a compliant "What did you think?" response, I prefer to throw in a googly.'

Aubrey couldn't help but smile a little. George gave every appearance of being a solid, unsurprising sort of chap, but Aubrey knew from experience that this was far from the truth. His still waters ran deep indeed, and his mind worked in quick and sometimes capricious ways – and he had recovered some of his equanimity.

Aubrey was lucky to have him as a friend.

'Thanks, George. I fell for it completely.'

'Excellent. Now, what were you saying?'

'This facility is even more important than we suspected. It's guarded.'

'I can see that, old man. Those big towers do stand out.' George shrugged, a tricky job when lying on one's stomach. 'You know, you're going to have to work harder in the "startling revelation" area. Good build-up, but a bit of a letdown afterwards, rather. I was getting all tense and now I'm left flat as a pancake.'

'That's not what I mean. Under the towers and –' He picked up the field glasses again and scanned the rear fence. 'About halfway along. Magical detection devices.' He adjusted the focus, very slightly. The devices looked larger than usual. 'And I think they're not just for physical intrusion, they're also capable of detecting magic.'

Aubrey chewed his lip. If this was the case, the devices must be extremely sophisticated. They had to be capable of filtering out authorised magic, otherwise whatever was going on inside the buildings would be setting them off all the time. And such differentiating was an advance indeed, as he'd seen nothing like this in Albion.

'Aubrey,' George said, interrupting his thoughts. 'How did Sophie and Caroline get inside the place?'

'Dr Tremaine's imprint is all over this factory. He's in there somewhere.'

George winced. 'You told Caroline that Dr Tremaine was in there? That'd explain why she was so keen to get in.'

'I've put her in harm's way,' Aubrey said. It pained him.

'Don't think like that, old man. Caroline wouldn't like it. Suggests she's helpless, in more ways than one.' George pointed. 'More important than worrying over that is the question of how Sophie and Caroline got in to the place.'

'I hope Sophie didn't try any magical means.' In fact, Aubrey was reasonably sure she hadn't. He hadn't heard any alarms and the factory didn't show any signs of a place that had recently been magically breached.

George thumped the ground in front of him. 'We should have asked Katya.'

A voice came from nowhere. 'They went through the front gate.'

If Aubrey had been standing, he would have given the world high jump record a distinct nudge. Katya insinuated herself out of a dense tangle of shrubbery with nary a rustle, emphasising to him what a city fellow he was. She crawled close to them. 'They went in the front gate.'

'Just like that?' George said. 'Bold as brass?'

'They joined the soldiers who came this morning. Sophie performed some magic and they were in.'

'Magic?' Aubrey was startled. She must have used something extremely passive. He was already thinking of the possibilities. Some sort of passive concealment magic was most likely. Or a semblance spell? He needed to know more about Sophie's capabilities.

Katya brought them to the spot where lorries full

of soldiers ground their way around a bend and up a slight rise before reaching the factory gates. The lorries slowed here, she explained, and Caroline and Sophie had slipped themselves into the rear of the last in a column of three.

'We can do that,' Aubrey said and he was confident he could, especially since their effort in slipping into the fortress at Divodorum had required the same sort of disguising magic. It was good, sound special unit magic.

'I WILL WAIT,' KATYA SAID AS THEY TOOK UP A VANTAGE point behind some thickly growing hazels, 'and report back to von Stralick and Zelinka.'

'I'd appreciate that,' Aubrey said, and he felt a flutter in his stomach. At least someone should know where they'd gone.

George took some time checking his revolver. Aubrey, feeling a little foolish, followed suit. He'd been prepared to leave the firearm behind, never having felt totally comfortable with it, but George had insisted on his bringing it.

It wasn't long before the noise of an overladen lorry came toward them. 'Two only,' Katya told them after disappearing for a moment. 'Go to the last.'

'Ready?' Aubrey said to George.

'As rain.'

'What?'

'Let's go.'

George scrambled through the brush, nearly leaving Aubrey behind – because Aubrey hadn't yet cast the disguising spell. 'George!' he called, but the roar of the lorries drowned out his voice. A mixed blessing, for it hadn't alerted any soldiers, but George was ploughing through the brush, heedless of his lack of disguise. Aubrey rushed his spell as fast as he could, then put his head down and had to hurry to follow. Branches slashed at him, twigs plucked at his jacket, then he was through.

The rear of the lorry was canvas-covered. The back opened onto darkness and it was pulling away from them up the slight hill. George dug in, sprinting. An unfamiliar George, now looking remarkably like a Holmlander infantryman in full kit – navy blue jacket, cap, trousers, heavy boots. Aubrey's legs went slightly rubbery with the casting of the spell as if he'd already completed a nippy mile-and-a-half cross country. He had a moment of horror when he thought he wasn't going to make it.

The lorry lurched over a bump, just as George reached the backboard and hauled himself inside. Immediately, he leaned out and stretched his hand.

Aubrey gritted his teeth and found some strength. He pushed himself forward, feeling that awful moment when his stride was about to go to pieces. He was convinced he'd lose all momentum – just as George clasped his outstretched hand.

For an instant, Aubrey's feet left the ground and he was suspended in mid-air, most precariously, then George dragged him into the rear of the lorry where he lay on his back, panting.

While he regained his breath, he congratulated himself on how convincing his disguising spell was. His clumsy arrival hadn't caused any consternation. None of the dozen or so figures in the dimness under the canvas had moved.

No-one questioned him, no bayonets were brandished in his face, no coarse laughter chaffed at him. All they had to do now was to sit tight and the lorry would take them right through the gates and into the factory. Their uniforms were perfect, just like the other soldiers who were quietly sitting in the back of the lorry, right down to the clumsy bandage wrapped around Aubrey's arm. Their faces were composites, blended versions of the features around them, fitting in neatly.

He began to feel extremely uneasy. 'What's going on here?' he muttered to George, who helped him to a spare space on one of the benches on either side.

George leaned close and Aubrey saw that he had a bandage on his head, under his awkwardly sitting cap. 'We're in a hospital transport, old man. At least, that's what it looks like.'

Aubrey surreptitiously glanced around the lorry. Each of the soldiers was wounded. Bandaged limbs and heads, blood-stained uniforms, but Aubrey had trouble believing that the wounds were entirely responsible for the bone-lessness and the grey pallor in the faces surrounding him, especially since none of them had head wounds.

Young faces, too, he realised. It gave him a wrench to see they were about his age, youths who should be making their way in a world unblighted by war. These were the fodder for the insatiable appetite of the war monster that had been unleashed. So young, so many, and with the war so new.

He wrinkled his nose. A faint vibration was lodged there, irritating but not to the point of sneezing. He sniffed, but it buzzed and he realised he was detecting low-level magic. He frowned, looking around at the blank faces, the unseeing eyes, the chins resting on chests, and he realised with a start that the entire squad was enspelled.

He shook the shoulder of the soldier on the other side of the lorry, a fair-headed youth with one arm in a bloody sling. While George watched with some alarm, the Holmlander's head lolled from side to side like a rag doll. Aubrey lifted the soldier's good hand. When he let go it fell, unresisted.

Aubrey sat back and wiped his hands together. 'It's clever,' he said after a moment's thoughtful contemplation of the canvas roof, remembering various descriptions in texts he'd read.

'Some sort of trance?' George asked. His expression was one of caution tinged with definite distaste.

'Our Dr Tremaine has come up with a new application of the Law of Patterns, is my guess. These poor wretches are entranced by a repeating pattern, caught in following an endless loop, so to speak. They follow it to the end, but find that they're at the beginning again. The effect, as you pointed out, is much like a trance.'

'For what purpose?'

'So they can be loaded onto lorries and shipped wherever needed.'

'But who'd need wounded battlers like this?' George swept an arm around the interior of the lorry. 'They should be in hospital!'

'They should, indeed.' Aubrey was quiet for a moment. 'But it appears that someone has plans for them.'

'In a factory.' George's face was bleak. 'Dr Tremaine is making me *very* angry.'

'There's no mistaking his magic.' Aubrey hesitated. Even though the spell was clearly Dr Tremaine's it had an odd cast. It wasn't *fresh*.

George frowned. 'Let me see if I have this straight, being magic stuff and all. These poor fellows have been put into a trance by Dr Tremaine's magic.'

'Correct.'

'And we're currently rolling with them toward Baron von Grolman's factory.'

'Most apparently.'

'Where Dr Tremaine is.'

'Ah.' Aubrey thought for a moment. How could these benighted soldiers have been enspelled by Dr Tremaine if Dr Tremaine was in the factory they were being shipped *to* instead of *from*? 'I suppose he could have whipped over to wherever these fellows came from, cast his spells, then whipped straight back here.'

'That's a lot of whipping. Even for Dr Tremaine.'

'And von Stralick said they hadn't noticed him coming. Or going.'

Aubrey frowned. Had Dr Tremaine discovered a way to cast spells over a great distance? Or was it something even more fantastic – had he managed to package spells so others could activate them? In a way, it was a variation of the principle that governed potentialised clay. For a man who needed to be everywhere, it could be a revolutionary discovery. *Another* Dr Tremaine revolutionary discovery.

'Thank you, George, for throwing that little sparkler into the pot.'

'Least I can do, old man.'

As they drew closer to the factory, Aubrey could feel Dr Tremaine everywhere. His presence was stamped on the whole complex. It fairly radiated with markers of his spellwork, both residual and active, and it all became confused with the multiple connections Aubrey had formed with his mannikins.

Aubrey's head started to ache. The life of a spy was taking some getting used to.

WHEN THE LORRY PASSED THROUGH THE ENTRANCE, AUBREY felt a slight tingle, which announced they were crossing the magically guarded perimeter. No alarm sounded at the ensorcelled soldiers, so Aubrey assumed that the detection level had been set high enough to allow such to pass – which explained why Sophie's disguising magic had gone unnoticed.

He was impressed. She'd shown a light touch for someone out of practice. He wondered how good she could be if she really put her mind to magic.

The lorry followed the leader and pulled into the loading area of the enormous warehouse, alongside the railway line. Immediately, two armed soldiers appeared and peered inside. 'Ten in here,' one of them called.

'Act like them,' Aubrey whispered to George, who nodded. The backboard of the lorry banged down. The soldiers showed no reluctance, nor any untoward cruelty, as they manoeuvred the wounded out of the lorry and assembled them in rows. It was as if they were moving furniture. Aubrey and George adopted the dazed, preoccupied expression they'd noted, shuffling with arms dangling at their sides, mouths slack, heads bobbing, and they were herded with the others.

When a large man entered the loading bay and stood in the light coming through the open double doors, Aubrey desperately wanted to draw George's attention. He stumbled and nudged his friend, cocking his head in what he hoped was a hintful way in the direction of the man, who was studying a clipboard given to him by a respectful – and unwounded – captain of the Holmland infantry.

Baron von Grolman. The barrel-chested, bald industrialist studied the clipboard and pulled at a lip. Then, startlingly, he lifted his head and smiled expansively, like a man who has just seen a long-lost friend.

A white burst of radiance filled the loading area. It made Aubrey blink, and at first he thought it was a spell of some kind, then he caught the familiar stink of flash powder. Baron von Grolman scowled at his clipboard while the photographer slid another plate into his camera.

Aubrey had difficulty in coming to terms with how bizarre he found the whole scene. The soldiers who were swarming about the loading bay treated the baron with respect but that was only half the picture. They were on best behaviour, snapping out salutes and making sure that all commands were carried out with gusto as they organised shambling, pliant, wounded infantrymen. While this was carried out under the watchful eye of Baron von Grolman, a photographer was regularly interrupting proceedings to snap pictures. He was a cheerful young chap, the only civilian Aubrey had so far seen in the complex, and he had no hesitation in calling for soldiers – or the baron himself – to stop and adopt a pose suitable for his next photograph.

It was like being at a wedding, or an important birthday

party, instead of in a factory involved in secret military work.

An opportunity is an opportunity, Aubrey thought. The photographer arranged the baron so he appeared to be joking with one of the lorry drivers. When the flash went off, Aubrey added a subtle intensifying spell. The result was blinding. The baron swore, and shouts and cries came from the soldiers nearby. The photographer was immediately apologetic. In the confusion, Aubrey dragged George behind the nearest lorry. Within seconds, they emerged, but now they looked smart and clean in the uniform of Holmland lieutenants. No bandages, nothing to associate them with the entranced cargo.

Carefully, Aubrey reached into the cabin of the rearmost lorry. He pulled out a sheaf of papers and a lantern. He gave the lantern to George and with the papers in his hands they looked as if they had a purpose. It didn't matter that George was carrying a lantern in the middle of the day; carrying *something* made it less likely they'd be questioned than if they were empty-handed.

Aubrey glanced at the papers. It didn't really matter what they were, but he was intrigued to see that he'd picked up invoices, shipping manifests and delivery dockets, with duplicates in best military fashion. All of them confirmed that the lorry had been in Fisherberg – but its cargo had come from the battlelines on the border with Muscovia. Each of the unfortunate wounded had been transported through Fisherberg for 'treatment', before being sent on to Stalsfrieden.

While in Fisherberg, Aubrey thought, *they've been specially prepared by putting them into this trance, thanks to Dr Tremaine's spells at a distance.*

It was both efficient and ghastly, with the typical Tremaine indifference to suffering.

The soldiers in charge were obviously accustomed to dealing with the entranced wounded. They barely had to speak. Aubrey and George followed at the rear, Aubrey making great show of counting heads as they went, while wooden batons were used sparingly, guiding the wounded out of the loading bay, across a short gravelled area and into the heart of the complex: the factory itself.

Aubrey was startled. He'd been expecting they'd be taken to an infirmary faculty, or a hospital, or some sort of medical facility. This was industry on a grand scale. Through the battering noise, he could smell hot metal and the distinctive tang of ozone. Looking upward, Aubrey could make out exposed beams and girders, skylights, caged electric lights, chains and gantries.

The vast space was full of machinery – great blocky shapes like enormous cabinets – cabling, chains and conduits hanging from gantries overhead, humming conveyor belts, clanking shuttles and hoppers. Iron walkways ran around the perimeter, high up, for maintenance and supervision. Aubrey's eye immediately went to what looked like an office or control room, up in the heights. Well lit in the industrial gloom, it would provide the perfect bird's-eye view of whatever was going on in the infernal place.

It was an overwhelming place. Noise and stench. Hammering, crackling, hissing and pounding. Ozone, burnt rubber, hot metal and the cloying, nauseating smell of organic waste.

All of this assaulted him, but Aubrey also became aware

that whatever process was going on in the cavernous building, it incorporated powerful magic.

The magic roared at him as they stood there, actually making him squint, as if he were facing a gritty wind. Then it slackened and played on his hearing, tickling with unkind fingers made of ice and bitterness.

The magic was not constant. It ebbed and veered, and was hard to grasp.

Aubrey took in as much of the surroundings as he could, already preparing for a report. Soldiers hurried past, disappearing through gaps in the massive pipes, or mounting the walkways up high. Moving with less haste and more deliberation, however, were white-coated civilians. Their coats didn't cover uniforms, just the rumpled suits and askew ties Aubrey had come to associate with academics or theoreticians. While they may have been barbers on a field trip, Aubrey was prepared to wager that they were more likely to be either scientists or magical researchers. *Or perhaps both*, he thought as he noted how each of the white coats was accompanied by a fully-armed uniformed soldier.

Subtly, knowing that George would follow his lead, Aubrey lingered as the wounded were led away into the factory. He waited for a pair of white coats to walk past, then consulted his papers, shaking his head in disgust. He was pleased that his disguising spell was working well, for he'd added an extra variable based on the Law of Familiarity, where scrutiny can be manipulated to become acceptance, based on plausible appearance. It was a delicate application because the effect had to be subtle. Trying to apply it to someone or something that was egregiously out of place was doomed to failure. Therefore, as well as looking like Holmland soldiers, the more Aubrey and George could behave like them the more chance of their presence going unremarked.

The weight of the revolver rubbed just under his armpit. Some may have found it reassuring; Aubrey found it disconcerting. A revolver tended to imply shooting people, something he wasn't altogether in favour of. As an option, he had it near the bottom of his list, just above 'being shot'.

Aubrey and George moved away from the entrance and stood with their backs to a bright red fire alarm. George hung his lantern from a hook on the wall, crossed his arms on his chest and looked sidelong at Aubrey. 'I'm hoping that you've worked out a way to find Sophie and Caroline.'

A frenzied din hammered from the depths of the factory. The sound of metal on metal was deafening.

'An aspect of the Law of Contiguity would appear to be best.'

'I'm glad. Sooner rather than later would be excellent.'

'That's the problem. I'd *like* to use the Law of Contiguity, but I'd need something belonging to either Caroline or Sophie. Something that has been in close contact with either of them.'

'Why didn't you say so?' George reached under his jacket, fumbled about for a minute, then brought out a fine silver ring. 'Here. It's Sophie's.'

Aubrey stared at the ring in his palm. 'She gave it to you?'

'A few days ago, after we slogged through that marsh.

It wouldn't fit on my finger, and we had a laugh about that, so I strung it on a shoelace.'

'A shoelace.'

'Needs be, old man. I'll organise something more suitable when we're home.'

The unspoken provisos and conditions that went with that declaration hovered about them, but Aubrey was thinking more about how lucky George was to have such a token. He readily admitted to being envious of his friend, but happy for him at the same time. With the only ring Caroline wore, if she gave it to him he'd probably slice his own finger off.

If she gave it to him.

Aubrey cast the spell with no hesitation, keeping his voice low, with George keeping a discreet look-out. With the busyness about them, however, no-one wasted any time on wondering what two perfectly ordinary lieutenants were up to. Too many other things to do.

As soon as Aubrey completed the spell, he closed his hand on the ring, and was rewarded by feeling its tugging. 'She's in here.'

The sound of a thousand motorcars being pushed off a tall building made them both jump, and before they were quite settled it happened again. Two white coats wandered past, shouting at each other about reducing valves, oblivious to the hideous noise.

'I see,' George said, shrugging. 'If she's in here – with Caroline, I hope – how are we going to get her out?'

'By getting everyone else out first.' Aubrey took two steps to the red box on the wall. He seized the hand crank, agreed with the sign that this was an emergency, and wound it for all he was worth.

It was a very good siren. It had to be, Aubrey supposed, to cut through the noise that owned the place. Aubrey's cranking was picked up and amplified through some neat magic, and a banshee howl sprang out of the speaker horns high on the walls. The alarm didn't just cut through, it sliced the factory noise to pieces and then danced on the shreds. It had an edge to it that you could shave with, as long as you didn't mind its teeth-jarring, bone-numbing quality.

Aubrey clapped his hands to his ears and stopped cranking, but the siren didn't diminish. It rose, echoing across the factory floor and sending workers running for the exits.

'Well drilled!' Aubrey shouted.

George had his hands over his ears. His face was screwed up. 'Like my head!'

'We won't have long!' Aubrey signalled, and George followed. They had to push through the soldiers and white coats who were headed in the other direction, but Aubrey found that a well-wielded toolbox at kneecap level was a wonderful path clearer.

They worked their way past benches where soldiers had flung down tools. Lathes and punches were still whirring, shaping brass and steel. Waves of heat came from industrial ovens they passed. The far end of the building was taken up with huge machines that nearly reached the roof, but iron pillars and great brick chimneys made it hard to see their purpose.

Whitecoats and soldiers fled the factory with an alacrity that suggested they'd experienced an unpleasant state of affairs or two in recent times. It didn't take long before Aubrey and George gazed about, alone, while the siren wailed away, echoing madly.

George flinched. 'Can you do anything about that noise?'

Aubrey sympathised. His head felt as if it were being rasped out from the inside. He studied the fire alarm and thought of the work he'd done back at Stonelea School on amplifying voices in Clough Hall via an inverted application of the Law of Attenuation. If he could just add to that . . .

He cranked the handle. He spoke some careful Akkadian. The siren rose in pitch, then swallowed itself in a pained, electrical squawk.

The silence was wonderful. They pushed into the factory, looking for Caroline and Sophie.

The immense factory floor was divided into sections, with conveyor belts and chutes running between them. Some parts were obvious in their function, with banks of lathes and metal-working machinery indicating light engineering works, but other parts were less apparent. Those stone walls in the rear corner, for instance, didn't match the rest of the architecture. Two walls making a small room which was separate from the factory floor? It looked as if it were an addition, and a secure addition to judge from the heavy brass door – which had been left ajar by whoever had been inside when the sirens went off.

A secure facility within a secure facility that was making something useful to the Holmland military. Aubrey considered exactly how difficult it would be for him to ignore the open door, and it actually made him dizzy.

Of course I'm going to investigate, he thought. *It would be wrong not to.*

George followed him, avoiding the belts and chains that hung from the walkways.

Aubrey raised an eyebrow at how thick the walls of the secure chamber were. Double walls made of large stone blocks, reinforced with steel bars. Whatever was in here was extremely valuable.

Or extremely dangerous, a small voice at the back of his mind said. He stopped at the entrance. A dusty, oily smell came to him, and it brought to mind trains and locomotives, but this smell was sharper. Carefully, he reached around and fumbled for an electric light.

Racks. The entire chamber was lined with wooden racks. Resting in the racks, in separate concave niches, were hundreds of metal cylinders about the length of his forearm and four or five inches in diameter.

In the centre of the room was a manhole. A large brass cover over a circular hole in the wooden floor. It was locked with a heavy padlock, brass again.

George, leaning over his shoulder, frowned. 'Why brass?'

It hadn't occurred to Aubrey, but once George had thrown up the question, it intrigued him. Surely steel would have been cheaper and quicker to machine. 'It looks good?'

George eased Aubrey aside and stepped into the chamber. He picked up one of the cylinders. 'They're light.' He tilted it from side to side, then shook it. 'Empty.'

Brass. Aubrey had it on the tip of his tongue. Something about brass. 'What's brass used for?'

'Musical instruments. It has a lovely tone.' George placed the cylinder back in the rack, and Aubrey realised he was relieved he had. 'Some plumbing fittings, things you don't want to rust.'

Aubrey examined the room. Featureless, apart from the

electric light, the manhole and the racks of cylinders. The floor was wooden, which was interesting, as the walls and the ceiling were made of stone. 'Anything else?'

'Lots of things, old man. Brass is jolly useful. It doesn't spark, for instance.'

The hairs on the back of Aubrey's neck rose. 'Step outside, George. Carefully. And don't knock any of those cylinders.'

George heard Aubrey's tone of voice, and he was out of the chamber in a flash. 'Are they dangerous?'

'No. But they're stored in a double stone-walled, reinforced chamber. With a wooden floor, just in case they're dropped. And they're made of brass, so as not to cause sparks. I'd say that someone is taking precautions against explosions, wouldn't you?'

George paled. 'I gave one of them a good shaking.'

'It was empty, you said.' *Empty. Waiting to be filled with something?*

'So it seemed. Famous last words, "I'm sure it's empty."' George snorted, then he pointed. 'Are those machines the same as the one you commandeered from Fisherberg?'

Aubrey turned. 'Golem makers.'

Twenty-six

Racks of pipe fittings separated them from the large, blocky machines that George had spotted. They had to step over discarded implements, dropped in the haste to escape the imaginary fire. Aubrey didn't blame the workers. Factory fires had caused huge loss of life in Albion and around the world where factory owners put profits ahead of safety. Crowding workers into poorly ventilated, appallingly lit facilities was only the start. Add highly inflammable materials and the lack of easy exit, and the results were nearly always disastrous. Aubrey had heard of workers trapped by flames choosing to leap from tall buildings, rather than waiting for a fiery end.

'Clay,' George said and Aubrey saw that his friend was standing in front of a large bin set against a brick wall. It was nearly a small room, four or five yards across, open at the front to allow access, and it was half-full.

Glancing around first to make sure they were alone,

Aubrey joined his friend. He flexed his hands and a lively glittering slipped over his skin. He squatted and took some of the clay between his fingers. 'It's potentialised clay, the same as the sample Madame Zelinka's friends found.'

'Two and two coming together?' George asked him as he straightened and wiped his hands on his trousers.

'So it would seem.' He approached the nearest machine. It looked substantially different from the one he'd seen under the palace in the heart of Fisherberg – and the one he'd managed to procure and ship to Albion.

This machine was about ten feet tall, and solid as a pile driver. Huge cables ran from the ceiling, connecting it to what must be a substantial electricity supply. The front of the machine could have looked crowded, but to Aubrey's eyes it was an elegant display of dials, levers and wheels, featuring brass that had been polished to a high finish. Two large brass handles showed where the drawer and the hopper were, but Aubrey paused, scratching his chin. The more he studied the machine, the more different it looked. The conveyor belt entering one side, for instance, looked big enough to transport a motorcar. The previous model of golem maker had nothing like that.

Aubrey peered at a bank of switches. They were labelled in Holmlandish, but the labels didn't make anything clear at all. 'Process 1', 'Splice', 'Optimise'. And what did 'Overgrossing' mean?

George had taken up station at the nearest window, making sure he couldn't be seen from outside. 'All clear?' Aubrey asked.

'They're assembling on the parade ground. Nice, neat ranks. No movement this way.'

They still had some time, but Aubrey started as the pocket of his jacket began flapping, all by itself.

'Stay where you are,' came a commanding voice. Aubrey stiffened, but the voice immediately added, with a slight note of disappointment, 'Oh, it's you.'

'Hello, Caroline,' George said. 'Sophie! I'm glad we found you.'

Caroline and Sophie were both wearing the black pyjama suits that were Caroline's fighting outfits, the design suggested by an Oriental friend of Caroline's father. The sleeves and legs of Sophie's were rolled up. Caroline had a pistol, but it vanished when she recognised Aubrey and George.

Aubrey put his hand into his jacket pocket and grasped the leaping ring. With a quick whisper, he cancelled the spell, and was about to hand the ring back to George when he saw that this was not a good time to interrupt.

Sophie took a hesitant step toward George. Her eyes were shining. George looked pained, then abashed, then he held out his hands to her.

The doubts that Aubrey had been harbouring disappeared. He hadn't liked thinking that Sophie had simply been using George to gain access to the facility and her brother – but the doubts George raised had been niggling at him.

I'm spending too much time in this world, he thought. *I see duplicity everywhere I look.*

Sophie took George's hands and she dropped her gaze, before lifting it again and adding her other hand to the arrangement, squeezing his tightly.

Aubrey was happy for his friend, and for Sophie. They

stood for a moment, wordless, and Aubrey had the feeling that words were superfluous.

He knew that their hearts were thumping, painfully, and that it was hard to breathe, as if their chests were being squeezed. He understood that where they touched, the clasping of hands, was something extraordinary – but something to be experienced again and again.

At least, that's how it was for him with Caroline. When he allowed himself. When it caught him by surprise. When it swept him away despite all his best intentions to honour the pact of reserve they'd agreed on.

He took off his cap and ran his hand through his unfamiliar short hair, feeling it thick and sleek like fur, and stole a glance, only to see that Caroline was looking at him carefully. Although she had no magical ability, he was convinced that – at times – she was able to read his mind, so he coughed, rubbed his face with his hands and made a great show of seeing the controls of the machine for the first time. Not his best spot of acting, but he hoped it was a reasonable piece of improvisation.

He crouched and tapped a knob that looked as if it had something to do with pressure, and was about to go looking for a steam inlet, when he understood – in a way that approached magic, but wasn't – that Caroline was standing behind him. Closely behind him.

'Aubrey.'

He straightened and spent some time dusting off his trousers and the sleeves of his jacket. It didn't matter that it was obvious what he was doing, or that Caroline knew exactly what was going on.

'Leave the pattern on,' she said lightly.

'I beg your pardon?'

'It's what my father always used to say if we were scrubbing something too hard. Leave the pattern on. It's a joke.'

'Ah. Forgive me if I don't laugh.'

She took his arm. 'I will if you come with me.'

Anywhere! his traitor mouth nearly blurted, but he managed to nod. 'You've found something?'

'You're looking for a steam pipe, aren't you? I think it's on the other side of this apparatus.' She glanced at where George and Sophie were speaking in low tones, hands clasped between them at chin height. Chin height on Sophie. Somewhere near mid-chest on George.

Sometimes it took a cricket bat to the back of the head, but on this occasion Aubrey saw what was going on straight away. 'Right. Steam pipe. Indeed.'

His head started to angle toward the murmuring couple again but Caroline put a finger on his cheek and turned it away. 'Now, Aubrey.'

He followed Caroline willingly, still feeling the spot where Caroline had touched him as a bloom of warmth that he was quite happy to become accustomed to.

Behind the machine the electric lights were poorly positioned and shadows reigned, hiding details and making everything look ominous. Even so, he could make out a large bore pipe that entered the rear, well lagged to keep the heat in.

'Where were you?' he said as he squatted at the junction of the brass shut-off valve.

'We found our way in here early, when there weren't many people around. It must have been a change of shift, for it started to get crowded. Too crowded. We stood out.'

'No females,' Aubrey said. All the soldiers and white coats he'd seen were male.

'Quite, and Sophie's magic was fading so we found a place to hide. An old boiler, destined for scrap, I'd imagine. We crept inside and waited our chance.'

'Which I provided.' Aubrey had visions of the boiler being carted away with Caroline and Sophie inside. He shuddered.

'We would have thought of something if you hadn't appeared.'

'I'm sure you would. I didn't mean to imply that you were helpless. Or anything like helpless.' Aubrey bit his tongue. It was the simplest solution to his babbling. It was getting so well scarred that it barely hurt, but it served its purpose nonetheless. He took a breath. 'And George and Sophie are now reunited.'

'She was distraught, leaving him like that. She thought he'd assume that she had simply been using him to get to her brother.'

'Ah. Yes. Well.'

'He did?'

'He had his moments.'

Caroline sighed. 'Foolish.'

'I'm glad to hear that she wasn't just using him,' Aubrey said. 'That's what I told George.'

'Well, she *does* want to find her brother, and running into us was a stroke of luck, but she definitely has feelings for George.'

'Feelings? Like that one you get when you put your keys down and can't quite remember where?'

'You know what I mean.'

'I do.'

'And you can stop projecting this onto anyone else's situation.'

'Are you thinking of anyone in particular?'

'Yes.'

'I see.' He nudged this around for a moment. 'Heavy-duty valve, this, wouldn't you say?'

'I'd say that you know a heavy-duty steam valve when you see one.' She looked at him and he tried not to show that he was aware of her scrutiny. He instantly felt awkward, as he always did when she studied him. Mainly it was because when she did, he immediately tried to make every movement impressive – or at least acceptable – to her, resulting in self-consciousness. He started to monitor every gesture, every facial expression, every word, and ending up being critical about himself because he wasn't better than he was.

It was a shortcut to complete madness. He was glad when she spoke. 'Have you worked out what this machine does?'

He stood and wiped his hands together. 'You've noticed that it's different from the one we captured?'

'I've noticed enough to know it's different, but not how.'

'I have some idea, but we may have to see it in action before I can work it out fully.'

'Hmm.'

'You obviously haven't found Dr Tremaine. Or Sophie's brother.'

'Théo? It's proved a little more difficult than we imagined.'

'We could have helped, you know. If you'd waited.'

'I thought you wouldn't. Not part of the mission.'

'Some missions don't always go as planned.' He winced as he remembered another mission that had definitely gone awry.

'So if I had waited, you would have come with us?'

'Was there any real doubt?'

Caroline stiffened. 'I've jeopardised our mission.'

'Let's just say you showed extraordinary initiative. I'm sure that's what's going in the report.'

'But I didn't pay any attention. I was headstrong, with him so close, or so I thought, I had to do something, after what he did to my father, I couldn't . . .'

'Caroline?'

'Yes?'

'You're babbling.'

Her eyes widening, she put a hand to her mouth. 'Oh.'

'Never mind. It happens to the best of us.' Aubrey turned away.

Caroline was eminently sensible, which was one of the many things Aubrey loved about her. Of course, she was eminently non-sensible at times and he loved that too. And her stubborn, contrary, froward ways.

His jaw dropped. *When did I start using the 'love' word?*

'Did I say something, Aubrey? You look as if you're getting ready to swallow a pumpkin.'

He shook his head mutely.

She held up a hand. 'I think George and Sophie have had enough time for their reconciliation. Then we can see what we can do about our triple objectives.'

'Triple?'

'Finding Dr Tremaine. Finding Théo. Going home.'

GEORGE WAS LOOKING RATHER PLEASED WITH HIMSELF, AND he seemed a few inches taller as well. Aubrey had the notion that his friend was probably bulletproof, at least for a while. Sophie was made of energy, taking notes as George described the controls of one of the golem machines.

'I haven't seen any golems around here, old man,' George said when Aubrey and Caroline appeared from behind the machine block.

'They could have been shopped out,' Sophie said. 'Shipped out. They may be building more.'

Noises from the entrance end of the factory could only mean one thing. Aubrey gazed at the machines with longing. He would love to have a few days, a few *weeks* to plumb their intricacies, but . . .

'We have to go.'

'We cannot,' Sophie said, distressed. 'Not without Théo.'

Caroline took her arm. 'We won't leave without finding him.'

'But where?' George asked. 'We've been looking, and so have you . . .'

Caroline caught Aubrey's eye. 'We need to share our findings.'

'Excellent idea,' Aubrey said. 'Superb. I'll just ask these Holmland gentlemen who are approaching for a place we can use for a plenary session.'

Caroline smiled. 'We found somewhere, Aubrey. This way.'

Which is how Aubrey found himself with his friends, safe and secure in the belly of a giant concrete elephant.

Twenty-seven

EXITING THE FACTORY WAS A MATTER OF CAREFUL slinking. This was assisted by the arguing going on in the ranks of first Holmlanders to re-enter. Accusations accompanied finger-pointing among Holmland officers and Aubrey was relieved to hear that the argument centred about the way the fire alarms were unreliable and subject to misuse.

Caroline and Sophie flitted from pillar to press to stamping machine, neatly avoiding the soldiers and white coats who were generally relaxed, giving every sign of having enjoyed the break. Aubrey and George followed as best as they could.

The giant concrete animals were in the garden behind the original building. Aubrey imagined that in the past they'd been brightly painted and impressive, but neglect had left them weather-beaten and sad, despite their monumental size. Once upon a time, these beasts were marvelled at, gazed at in awe, but they had come upon hard times. Paint flaked from a lion the size of a small bungalow. The giraffe could peer into the third story of the buildings around it, but the only colour it had left was a patch of yellow on its rump. The zebra, the crocodile, the elephant and the rest of the stony menagerie stood in their grey loneliness, doing their best to be dignified.

They were huge, and the – artist, sculptor, construction engineer? – had gone to some pains to make them as jolly as possible. All of the animals had seen better days, but Aubrey could see how they once would have charmed children. The elephant was enormous, twice the size of a real beast, but the small skull-cap (once crimson) gave it a jaunty rather than a formidable air. The other animals had similar embellishments, which removed any hint of danger and replaced it with jollity.

Some effort had been given to the maintenance of the gardens. The lawn was well kept, the flower beds sported mature rose bushes, and waist-high box hedges divided the area into distinct regions, with benches so weary strollers could rest and admire the preposterous concrete animals.

They used the hedges for cover until they reached the tree trunk legs of the elephant. 'This way,' Caroline said.

Without hesitating, she jumped straight up and seized an iron rung that was set in the leg, a few feet over their heads. Aubrey gaped as she climbed ten feet before clinging by one arm and using a slim tool to open the locked trapdoor in the belly of the elephant.

Sophie looked at George. 'Please?'

He smiled, then took her by the waist and lifted her to the first rung.

Soon, they were gathered inside the concrete elephant, trap door shut, the only light coming through the glass panels that were its eyes.

'Has anyone anything to eat?' George asked.

THE INTERIOR OF THE ELEPHANT WAS CAPACIOUS, AS LARGE as a room. Aubrey could stand upright, and even George had headroom. It wasn't, however, cosy. The concrete was bare, uncomfortable to sit on and smelled of mildew – but it did provide them with a good view down the length of the garden and out over the parade ground toward the barracks.

'Sophie found it,' Caroline explained. 'We were crossing the gardens and a squad came from the old building, which was our destination. With soldiers coming from both wings we were trapped, until Sophie looked up.'

'Before leaving Lutetia,' Sophie said, 'I did some research in the archives of *The Sentinel*. When it was made, the baron's father held a banquet inside this elephant.'

George looked around their confines. 'A rather small banquet, wouldn't you say?'

'Six friends, but the old baron brought a proper table and candles. It was most grand.'

'When it was safe, we crept out and went looking for Théo,' Caroline said.

Sophie explained their searching, and confirmed that the blocky building on the south side was indeed the generator. They had been working their way toward the barracks when they'd been diverted into the factory.

'Where we found you,' Caroline said.

'Thank goodness,' Aubrey said. 'But if we're going to find Théo, let's see if we can be a bit more sensible in our searching this time.'

'Your meaning?' Caroline said.

'Let's wait until night.'

AFTER THEY'D SHARED THE DETAILS OF THEIR TIME IN THE factory complex – Caroline was outraged at the treatment of the wounded soldiers – George didn't complain about hunger, not more than a dozen times or so before deciding to nap, for which Aubrey was grateful. Sophie took up a position looking out of the elephant eyes, lying on her stomach with her chin on her hands. Caroline stretched out, languorously, and went to sleep.

Aubrey sat on the trapdoor – reasoning it might make it harder for anyone to surprise them – and thought about leadership.

Hiding in the middle of hostile forces, separated from the Albion command structure, with no-one to consult for order, it gave him a new appreciation of the role. Ultimately, despite what Caroline said, he was responsible for the lives of his friends. In the end, after reporting, he would be held accountable. Were all the other commanders, in a multitude of situations and in all branches of the service, aware of this burden? If one thought too much about it, he imagined it could become paralysing, and the commander who didn't do anything was a nightmare in any battle situation.

Of course, he could hardly consider himself the regular sort of commander. Not in this clandestine mode of operating, and not with the team he was lucky enough to be in charge of. The idea of unquestioning obedience from Caroline and George was laughable. While they might charge side by side with him into the Valley of Death, if he asked them to, most likely Caroline would need some clarifying of what he was after with said charge, and would suggest an alternative, probably involving some obscure but deadly skill or other he was unaware she possessed. George would be happy enough, but would most likely drop in an observation that would make Aubrey reconsider the whole escapade – and while Aubrey was doing that, George would clean up the Valley of Death problem by himself, just to be helpful.

He shrugged. Different sorts of leadership for different sorts of people being led. He was happy with that.

'Aubrey. How did you find us?'

Aubrey blinked. Caroline had lifted herself on one elbow and was wide awake. 'I used this.'

Aubrey took Sophie's ring from his pocket.

'My ring!' Sophie cried. 'George, you do not have it!'

George came awake quickly. He took in Sophie's disappointed face, then looked at Aubrey, who was dangling the ring by its shoelace and immediately saw what was going on. 'It was an emergency, Sophie. Let me explain.'

After the explanation was offered and accepted, Sophie helped George retie the shoelace around his neck, tut-tutting at George's fumbling efforts.

'So,' Caroline said once the ring was in its rightful place again, 'if you had something of Théo's, you could lead us to him?'

'I don't see why not,' Aubrey said. 'Sophie, do you have

anything of your brother's? It would be best if it was something that had been in close proximity to him for some time.'

Her face fell. 'I am sorry. Nothing. If I had known . . .'

'Never mind,' Aubrey said, thinking hard. He was conscious that Caroline was watching him, and he was glad he had nothing complicated to do, like walking. 'The Law of Similarity.'

Sophie blinked. 'Similarity? I am not familiar with this.'

'On a fundamental level, Sophie, you and your brother are alike.'

'We are very different people, I must tell you that.'

'I'm not talking about personality. On a biological level, I mean.'

'Apart from his being a male,' George pointed out.

'Yes, there is that.' Occasionally, he regretted his need to explain things to people. Sometimes he thought it would be better if he simply said, 'It's magic', and left it at that. 'But all things considered, Sophie and Théo are more alike than non-siblings are alike. So I can use the Law of Similarity to formulate a spell that will guide us where Théo is.'

'Like that brick in Lutetia?' George said. 'You used that to find out where the Heart of Gold was.'

Sophie's eyes went wide. 'The Heart of Gold? George, you haven't told me of this.'

George shifted uncomfortably. 'Well, there are a few things I haven't told you about. Quite a few.'

Sophie looked askance for a moment, then patted him on the knee and smiled. 'You will have to tell me later.'

Aubrey cleared his throat. 'Well, yes. But that was using the Law of Constituent Parts, which is more relevant to inanimate objects than . . .' He saw two of them frowning at him, while one was intensely interested. 'And I can see that this isn't important right now. What say I cast this spell and we can get on with things?'

George shrugged. 'If you say so. I'm just getting jolly interested in all this magic stuff, with you and Sophie being so clever and all. Right, Caroline?'

'I leave magic to Aubrey,' she said firmly.

Aubrey flashed a grateful look at her. She returned a wry half-smile that made something bump oddly inside him. Pancreas, he guessed wildly. Or those whatchmacallits. Thymus.

'Ready, Aubrey?' Caroline prompted.

'Me? Of course. Ready as rain.'

'What?'

'It's one of George's. Now, Sophie, move over here. Can you sit cross-legged? Good.'

He reviewed the Law of Similarity. It described a wide range of phenomena, and it had been one of the first laws to be described in rational, empirical terms. As such, its applications were well-established and had been eagerly shared through reputable magical journals. Of course, many banged-together, jury-rigged applications of the Law of Similarity were formulated every day by practising magicians for ordinary purposes and forgotten just as quickly – as Aubrey was about to demonstrate.

He touched his hand to Sophie's forehead. She closed her eyes, and he pushed aside a strand of her golden hair.

He was about to make Sophie into the human equivalent of a lodestone. The similarity between her brother and her (*another connection*, he thought) would be enhanced and she would be able to orient herself on his presence – and she'd be able to take them to him.

It was a minor spell, he decided after he'd lined up the elements in his mind. He wouldn't be debilitated at all by it, nor would Sophie suffer any after-effects. It would only last a few hours without renewing, though, so he hoped that Théo would be easy to find. Otherwise they'd have to start all over again, and using the same spell twice so soon would begin to have some cost.

Aubrey pronounced his spell carefully, aware of George's silent scrutiny, and as soon as he finished, Sophie's eyes flew open. 'Oh!' She put a hand to her chest. 'Théo. He's here.'

'I'm relieved to hear that.' *I didn't fancy wandering all over Holmland.* 'Where?'

'Not far.' She pointed. 'Over there. Where the soldiers live.'

'The barracks.' Aubrey scratched his head. He hadn't quite worked out this bit.

'I don't fancy smuggling Sophie in so she can walk along the bunks until we find her brother,' George said.

'No need for that,' Aubrey said. 'Caroline, how do we encourage many people to leave a building very quickly?'

Caroline grinned the wicked grin she kept for special occasions. Aubrey added it to his enormous list of things to like about her. 'Oh, I have a way that might work. And it works best at night.'

Twenty-eight

AUBREY HAD BEEN HOPING THAT THE FACTORY'S ACTIVITIES would diminish as the day gave way to night, but all that happened was that electric lights snapped on all over the complex, keeping the darkness at bay. The industrial din continued, and the chimneys belched away unchecked. He began to wonder if this was a sign of urgency. Was there an important date approaching? An imminent commitment of the output of the factory? Aubrey grimaced as he thought of hundreds of golems unexpectedly appearing on the battlefront at Divodorum.

Sophie gasped. Brilliant light flooded the interior of the elephant. 'Look! Come and see!'

It was crowded, somewhat delightfully, but they all managed to take up a position lying on their stomachs to peer through the eyes.

'I say,' George breathed. 'Drilling? At this time of night? What on earth are they up to?'

Aubrey didn't answer. His attention was on the parade ground, where half a dozen fully uniformed Holmland officers had gathered.

The parade ground was flanked on the west by the barracks, the long huts that Aubrey assumed were the soldiers' quarters. On the north was the main factory building, where the golem-making machinery was pounding away. To the south was the electricity generation station.

The officers were looking toward the factory and the warehouse situated behind it, where the train loaded and unloaded.

Caroline tapped his shoulder and pointed. Baron von Grolman, wearing a long black coat and carrying a silver-topped cane, was hurrying past the concrete animals. Aubrey couldn't help but tense when the baron passed their position, and he saw the industrialist spare a glance at the elephant before rushing on, chuckling.

Aubrey found his field glasses, and with their help he was able to see the baron greeting the officers with arms outstretched, every inch the expansive, welcoming host. He proceeded to point at various buildings of the complex with his cane, no doubt explaining the functions of each. Some of the officers were sceptical, to judge from their posture (arms crossed, leaning away from the baron) but others were enthusiastic – nodding and asking questions.

Aubrey noted the amount of gold braid on the uniforms. These weren't just officers – they were generals, at the least.

The baron stood back and pointed across the parade ground at the warehouse. With a voice that echoed, he cried, 'Behold!'

In the distance, past the far side of the parade ground,

Aubrey spied two soldiers dragging back the doors on the warehouse. The officers with the baron moved apart, the better to see, then the baron herded them to the western edge of the parade ground, where they stood with their backs to the gardens. Aubrey grimaced. He would have liked to see their faces.

'Good Lord!' George burst out. Aubrey swivelled the field glasses. Clanking from the warehouse was a sight that made him grip the binoculars so hard it hurt.

A vast billow of steam rolled from the warehouse entrance. Emerging from the cloud was an impossible figure. At first, Aubrey thought it was a giant golem fifteen or twenty feet tall, but then it resolved itself into a metal nightmare that glittered under the electric lights. It was human shaped, but its angular limbs were made of brass struts. It body was a metal mesh, an armature behind which cables clearly slid and gears whirred. Red eyes gleamed in the metal head.

'It's a monster,' Sophie breathed.

'If it is,' Aubrey said with horrible certainty, 'it's a monster made here.'

A second figure, identical to the first, swaggered out of the warehouse. Its arms swayed loosely, nearly down to its knees, and Aubrey, with a jolt, realised he should be noting details for the Directorate. Their mission had become more than vital. He had to get news of this development to Albion, for he knew that these giant creatures were weapons that could win the war for Holmland.

More of the ponderous figures marched from the warehouse, one after the other, grinding and clanking their way, while the first to emerge trod remorselessly to the centre of the parade ground.

Aubrey began to refine his initial impression. At first, they appeared to be mechanical men. He was frustrated that he couldn't make out the inner details more clearly. Was that copper? And what were those globes? Those dull, non-metal sections? *Automatons*, he thought, but he immediately knew that wasn't right. These weren't machines, not in the way he usually thought of machines. He'd never seen a machine that moved so fluidly, so easily. Their limbs bent and straightened with an almost animal-like grace. Even though they must have been as heavy as an omnibus, they stalked across the parade ground in good form, leaving a trail of steam behind them.

Steam? Aubrey frowned and adjusted the focus on his field glasses.

Projecting up over the head of each of these creatures was a chimney that sprouted from the spine. 'Impossible,' he breathed.

'What is it, Aubrey?' Caroline said, her voice tense.

'These creatures are steam-driven. But they can't be. Where would the boiler go? They're not big enough . . .'

His voice trailed off. Take something impossible, then insert a magical genius into the picture. Dr Tremaine could have, for instance, used reinforcing spells on a miniature boiler, increasing the pressure . . .

'Thermal magic?' Sophie murmured.

'Sorry?'

'Could a heat spell be used? Instead of the firebox a steam engine would require?'

Aubrey went to argue, but stopped and thought for a moment. 'In theory, yes.'

'It would have to be contained in dimensionality, of course.' Sophie touched an ear-stud, pensively. 'It could be reduced to a single point of intense heat that way. Perhaps.'

'Perhaps? Almost certainly.' Aubrey looked at the clanking monstrosity and then back at Sophie. 'You seem to remember quite a bit of your magic studies.'

'Magic never leaves you,' she said. 'It is – how do you say it, George?'

'In your blood?'

'The blood. It is there.'

'Aubrey,' Caroline said. She'd managed to prise George's field glasses from him. 'What sort of a head is that?'

It wasn't a head, not as heads were usually thought of. It was a bright metal box set on the creature's lumpish neck. The box was square, with glowing red eyes and dark patches, one on either side. Ears, if Aubrey had to guess. But he wouldn't swear to it. This creation was unlike anything he'd ever seen, so normal rules did not apply.

A horrible thought came to him. He shied away from it as too gruesome, too inhuman, but he found himself circling it, unwilling to let go.

'The neck, Aubrey,' Caroline said, offering glad distraction. 'What is that made of?'

She had a good eye. Aubrey scanned the milling creatures, moving from one to the next. In each one, the neck didn't fit with the rest of the gleaming construction. Connecting the head and the shoulders was a dull, lumpy, non-reflecting region, quite out of place.

Thinking hard, he lowered the field glasses. Immediately, Sophie took them from his hands. 'May I?'

'Be my guest,' Aubrey mumbled, his thoughts elsewhere.

No, he thought again, and he tried to tell himself that he wouldn't contemplate such a thing, that he refused to. His humanity rejected such a thing – but he knew that even if he rejected such a thing, Dr Tremaine wouldn't. Not if such a thing served his ends.

'It's a hybrid,' he whispered.

He became aware that everyone was staring at him. 'Aubrey,' Caroline said. 'You've gone pale.'

'Dr Tremaine hasn't just made golems, he's blended golem with machines. He's made *enhanced* golems.'

'Why?' Sophie asked. 'What is the benefit?'

Aubrey put both hands to his head. He was sure he was missing something. 'I don't know. The endurance of golems married with the power of machines?'

That wasn't it. There had to be more.

'They're monstrosities,' Caroline said, '*whatever* is animating them.'

Caroline was right. It was the animating principle that was important here. Aubrey studied the parade ground. More of the mechanical hybrids were emerging from the warehouse, steaming as they stamped their way into ranks. He counted two dozen, three dozen, four dozen before he lost count. 'It's ghastly,' Aubrey agreed, but part of his mind was still trying to work out exactly how it had been done. 'I need to get closer to see exactly what's going on.'

'I don't think right now is the best time for that,' George said. 'Rather public, if you get my meaning.'

A hundred of the mechanical soldiers were clustered on the parade grounds, stubby chimneys steaming relentlessly. The clashing and whirring even came to them where they were inside the concrete elephant, so

Aubrey wondered how loud it would be on the parade ground. He imagined it could be a useful battleground effect, inducing terror long before the mechanical soldiers actually appeared.

Baron von Grolman waved his cane, and immediately the parade ground was ceilinged with black smoke as the giants clanked into action, their chimneys belching furiously. Then, they marched about at double-time, reeling around until they faced the dignitaries in perfect ranks, motionless, a company of terrifying mechanical warriors.

Baron von Grolman handed over to a uniformed soldier, whose bellowing signalled that he could only be a sergeant-major, and an exhibition drill began. With motion that was stuttering to begin with, but became smoother as they went, the mechanical soldiers were on display.

They marched at single time, then double time, wheeling in perfect formation when they reached the end of the parade ground, and heading back in the direction they'd come with never a falter, never a misstep in the ranks.

Something was puzzling Aubrey as he watched, then he had it. It was all being done with no commands. The sergeant-major stood stock still to one side of the parade grounds, his hands behind his back, but unlike every other NCO Aubrey had ever known, he didn't shout once he'd set the company in motion.

The mechanical soldiers broke into teams of three or four and were busy with ropes and timber that had been wheeled out on a flat-bed trolley, constructing . . . what, exactly?

The answer didn't come easily, for the mechanical soldiers weren't all constructing the same thing. With deliberate haste, each team was lashing, tying ropes at angles – but all busy on different tasks.

'They're building a bridge,' Caroline said, and Aubrey immediately saw she was right. Some were putting together massive pylons made of multiple spars, some were building stretchers and bearers, others were making stanchions, others were organising suspension leads. When put together, they'd have a bridge with a span of more than fifty yards. It was a remarkable feat of coordination, especially given that the teams had to negotiate their resources from a central pool of timber and tackle, which they did smoothly and with no fuss – which was something a golem could never do, and this gave Aubrey pause.

Then the lights went out.

It only took a few minutes, however, before the teams had used frayed ropes, shattered timbers and sparks to start fires enough for the watching audience to see, after which the floodlights snapped back on.

Soon a neat rope and timber bridge stretched across the quadrangle.

'Twenty minutes,' Sophie said, and Aubrey was glad someone had been alert enough to time the extraordinary effort.

'They're not golems,' Aubrey said flatly. 'Golems couldn't do that.' Repetitive work, intense focus, endurance, *that's* golem territory. Team work? Adaptability? Unheard of.

Aubrey realised that they were looking at super soldiers. Strong, fast, and adaptable. A battalion of these monstrosities would sweep through the defenders of Divodorum as if they weren't there.

Two impulses warred in him: to find out more, and to take what they already knew back to Albion.

'They're finishing,' George said. 'The bridge is all packed away.' Aubrey scrambled to see what was going on.

'Not that one,' Sophie pointed.

At the rear of the parade ground, one of the mechanical soldiers was bent at the waist. Its arms dangled nearly to the ground.

'What's wrong with it?' Caroline asked.

The rest of the mechanical soldiers were back in ranks and were marching off the parade ground. Their chimneys steamed purposefully. Baron von Grolman pointed his cane after them, no doubt explaining more features of his creations. Aubrey doubted that the baron would need to possess a silver tongue. His mechanical soldiers were impressive enough to sell themselves.

The baron shepherded the dignitaries away from the parade ground toward the old buildings. They went past the concrete elephant, close enough for Aubrey to see their faces. The generals were impressed. Some tried to hide it, but the others were talking keenly with the baron, asking questions about maintenance and transport.

On the parade ground, the sergeant-major was left behind with the sole remaining mechanical warrior. He marched over and stood with his hands on his hips, shaking his head.

Aubrey narrowed his eyes. Nothing was coming from its chimney – no smoke, no steam. Was that the problem?

The sergeant-major turned toward the warehouse. He roared, and Aubrey clearly heard his voice, even over the mechanical rumble of the last of the mechanical soldiers. He was shouting for coal.

'Impossible,' Caroline said. 'You couldn't feed these things on coal. They'd have to drag a tender around with them.'

'A tender the size of an omnibus,' George muttered.

Aubrey didn't respond. He had a suspicion that their clever enemy had concocted a way around that limitation. After all, they should have moved with the ponderousness of steam engines. Clearly, magic had been used to new and frighteningly efficient effect, as Sophie had suggested.

A white-coated civilian ran from the warehouse. Aubrey wouldn't have been surprised if he'd pushed a wheelbarrow, or even carried a bucket, but he was startled to see that the man was carrying a brass cylinder about the length of his forearm – and a pair of tongs.

'We've seen those cylinders before,' George said to Sophie and Caroline. 'In the factory.'

'But they were empty. Now we might get to see what they're used to transport,' Aubrey said.

The sergeant-major, no fool apparently, stood back while the hapless white coat clamped the cylinder and the tongs under one arm, then with the other reached into the chest cavity of the metal warrior. A series of movements – opening a hatch? – then the white coat straightened.

His next movements spoke of extreme care. He slowly unscrewed the top of the cylinder, then placed the cylinder on the ground with exquisite caution, making sure it was steady, pausing, waiting with every tiny movement. Finally, when he was sure it was stable, he took the tongs. Delicately, he reached into the cylinder and withdrew a small black object, the size and shape of a golf ball.

George adjusted his field glasses and whistled. 'That's coal?'

'It can't be ordinary coal,' Aubrey said. His mind was spinning. He was already thinking of ways in which coal could be compressed, enriched, but every one of them was crazily dangerous. The Law of Amplification? The Law of Compression? 'It must be enhanced coal, the same way these are enhanced golems.'

The white coat managed the difficult task of leaning away while thrusting the laden tongs into the chest cavity of the mechanical soldier. A jerk or two of his shoulders and he withdrew with every sign of relief.

A blast of smoke shot from the mechanical soldier's chimney. It straightened. Its arms swung like pendulums, making the white coat and the sergeant-major fling themselves aside. It twisted at the hips, then set off after the last of its comrades.

The sergeant-major climbed to his feet and dusted himself off sourly. The white coat stared after the retreating mechanical soldier, then stood and absently wiped the tongs on his coat.

The sergeant-major recoiled, shouting. Instantly, the white coat whipped off his coat and flung it on the ground – just before it burst into flame. As he stamped on it, the sergeant-major berated him roundly.

'Astounding,' George said. He lowered his field glasses.

'Super soldiers and super coal,' Caroline said. She looked grim.

More than ever, the mission weighed on Aubrey. Holmland's military build-up had long been feared, but its magical preparations were proving to be equally formidable. Could Albion and its allies hope to combat such terror?

Forewarned is forearmed, he thought. 'We'll get this back to the Directorate. But before we do, we have to find Théo.'

'So it's time to get some people out of a building, quickly,' Caroline said.

Aubrey held up a finger. 'It's time to abandon the elephant.'

'Which isn't a phrase we get to use enough, to my mind,' George said as he lifted the trapdoor.

'Keep it for your next dinner party,' Aubrey suggested. '"I'm sorry, Duchess, but it's time to abandon the elephant."'

Caroline stifled a laugh and Aubrey was inordinately pleased.

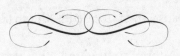

Twenty-nine

GEORGE LED THEM VIA A CIRCUITOUS ROUTE. HE TOOK them through a maze of sheds and workshops, dark and quiet at this time, for which Aubrey was grateful. Then they skirted the building that held the electrical generator. Aubrey could feel the turbine at work, with the concrete underfoot vibrating and an almost tangible hum in the air.

They kept to the shadows, listening before moving. Sophie was no handicap either, moving silently and proving to have excellent night vision. She was the one who pointed out a guard who was leaning against a supply hut, asleep and unmoving, an observation that prevented them from bumping right into him.

The barracks was a collection of long, single-storeyed timber buildings raised on piles. They looked new, to Aubrey's eye, and he noted how each one of them was linked by electrical wires. The windows were dark, but each building was easily big enough to sleep fifty.

They crept close, then stopped in the shadows of a lone oak tree.

'Caroline?' Aubrey whispered. 'Do you need any help?'

'I'd be happy of it. Follow me.'

With that, they slipped off, shadows among shadows.

FIFTEEN MINUTES LATER, AFTER THEY'D COMPLETED THEIR mischief and climbed the oak tree, Aubrey found that it was festooned with coloured electric light globes, a remnant of a celebration from happier days. He hoped that they had been disconnected.

From their position in the branches, he shook his head in admiration at the chaos below. 'Nicely done, Caroline. The actual fire was a master stroke.'

At the far end of the barracks, a metal drum was ablaze with the most noxious and smoke-producing materials they'd been able to find, grandly topped off with what George assured them was a damp dog blanket.

The result was a horde of Holmland soldiers bolting from the front doors, stumbling and wheezing, pouring down the stairs into the open air. When someone activated the fire alarm for the second time that day, the commotion was complete.

'There!' Sophie pointed, so eagerly that George had to throw out an arm to stop her slipping from their perch. 'There! It is Théo!'

Aubrey had to trust the spell was helping her identification. In the gloom and smoke, all the soldiers looked the same, but he saw the way that Sophie kept shifting her position, tracking one particular infantryman as they bumped and blundered before one – smarter, or less smoke-dazed than the others – managed to stagger through the smoke to find its source. He kicked it over, shouting for help.

'Excellent,' George said, 'but now we've found him, how are we going to spirit him out of here?'

'I wonder if these soldiers ever go to the town,' Caroline said. 'We might be able to separate Théo from the others.'

'Separate him,' Aubrey mused. 'That's the trick, isn't it?' He peered through the leaves. The milling about was dying down as NCOs reasserted their control. 'Sophie, what's your brother's health like?'

Sophie frowned, then she glanced at George and Caroline, who both shrugged. 'Aubrey's irrelevant questions sometimes aren't,' Caroline explained.

Sophie didn't look entirely convinced. 'Théo is strong, even though he is small.'

'Childhood illnesses? Accidents?'

'He had bleeding noses when he was little, but not any more.'

Aubrey rubbed his forehead. 'And his teeth?'

'Teeth?' Sophie shook her head in bewilderment. 'I do not know. Why is it important?'

'Teeth are good,' Aubrey said, rubbing his hands together. 'I can do something with teeth.'

FROM THEIR POSITION IN THE ONCE-FESTIVE OAK TREE, THEY could hear the groans. Piteous, heart-wrenching groans that made Sophie greatly distressed. 'Oh, I did not know it would be so!' she said softly as they watched the figure being helped down the stairs of one of the huts by two comrades.

'Did you have to give Théo such a corker of a tooth-ache?' George said to Aubrey. 'The poor fellow looks completely knocked about.'

Medical magic not being one of Aubrey's specialities, he was actually quite pleased with the result. He'd been able to invert a pain-relieving spell and keep its location confined to a single tooth, with only Sophie's orientation and distance estimate to guide him. Building in a sympathy element so it would home in on Théo and not some poor unfortunate nearby was also quite a coup, so Aubrey was a little miffed at the criticism.

'It won't last,' he assured Sophie. 'An hour at the outside. Just enough to get him to the infirmary.'

'Where we can talk to him,' Caroline said. 'A neat plan, Aubrey.'

The criticism was forgotten as he warmed to her praise. Even while he noted the effect it had on him, he was promising himself to do his best to earn more. 'And shall we follow, then?'

George snorted and tapped the trunk with a fist. 'I know it should be Prince Albert saying this, but as far as secret refuges go, this was an excellent branch office.'

'Hush,' Caroline said at the groans that followed George's dreadful pun, but Aubrey saw her smiling. 'If we're going to shadow Théo, then let's do it quietly.'

THEY WATCHED AND FOLLOWED, TWITCHINGLY ALERT FOR THE appearance of sentries, guards, giant soldiers, insomniacs, astronomers or any other unexpected night strollers. Aubrey wouldn't have been surprised to stumble upon smugglers, nightwatchmen or bat-fanciers, such was the outlandish nature of the goings-on at the complex thus far.

The groaning Théo was taken to one of the wings of the old building, past the concrete animals. After some hammering on the door, a light came on and the trio was admitted. Soon after, Théo's comrades emerged and hurried back toward the barracks. The light stayed on in the infirmary and Aubrey suggested that they hide in the nearby garden while they waited for Théo to be treated and the physician to retire again.

This was signalled by the light going out in the infirmary. They waited another ten minutes, to be sure, then it was Caroline's deft work on the lock that gave them egress – only to find Théo stretched out on the bed, insensible in the moonlight that spilled through the uncurtained window.

'Théo!' Sophie gasped, then she clapped her hands over her mouth at George's fervent hushing. She rushed to the bed – the only occupied bed in the four-bed infirmary – just as Théo began snoring.

He was unmistakeably a relative of Sophie. He was short, and his blond hair and fine features were a masculine version of the Delroy physiognomy.

Aubrey kept an eye on the only other door in the sparsely outfitted room, but his mind was working. He'd been expecting to find wards full of wounded soldiers, the poor souls he'd seen transported and delivered to the factory, but the infirmary was tiny. Four beds only, it was doing its best to be unwelcoming, without going to the actual extent of having a 'Malingerers Not Wanted' sign.

So where are those wounded soldiers?

Caroline knelt at Théo's bed and rolled back one of his eyelids. 'It appears that your brother has been given some treatment.'

'Treatment?' George pushed up Théo's sleeve. 'Some sort of opiate jab, it looks like. He must have been persuasive.'

And my spell might have been a little more painful that I expected, Aubrey thought. *Some more work needed on that spell before using it again, perhaps.*

'So what shall we do?' Sophie was concerned but determined. 'We cannot leave him now we have found him. Not like this.'

'This looks like my cup of tea,' George said, rubbing his hands together. With a grunt and a heave, he lifted Théo and positioned him across his shoulders. 'Tally-ho.'

Théo was no great weight, but Aubrey knew that George would have borne the burden even if Théo had been a giant. He wasn't going to let Sophie down.

'Which way?' George said, jauntily. 'Back to the farmhouse or would we like to go dancing first?'

'Do we have enough information, Aubrey?' Caroline asked.

A tricky question. 'One never has enough information. I'd like to get a closer look at those super soldiers.' He weighed up the options. 'George, do you think you could get Théo into our elephant? Could you and Sophie wait for us there?'

'Can do, old man. How long will you be?'

Aubrey raised an eyebrow at Caroline, conferring. 'An hour?'

'I've seen the layout of this place, and the way it's guarded. We'll need two.'

'Two hours,' George repeated. He glanced at the still-comatose Théo. 'Then we really must be leaving.'

'Agreed,' Aubrey said.

George grinned. 'Just because I know how things can go astray, I have a suggestion. In two hours, the power will go out.'

'I beg your pardon?'

'You see, old man, sometimes I think you work better with a deadline. A sense of urgency, if you will. Left to your own devices, you're likely to wander all over this place until the cows come home.'

'There isn't any danger of that,' Caroline pointed out. 'I'll be with him.'

'I appreciate that,' George said. 'And if anyone is likely to keep Aubrey under control, it's you, Caroline. But on the other hand, just in case things get a bit sticky, it might be handy to know that the lights are about to go out.'

'It could be useful,' Caroline allowed.

'Wait,' Aubrey said. 'Exactly how are you going to achieve this?'

'Never mind,' George said. 'Leave the details to Sophie and me.'

Aubrey sighed. Faced with such confidence, who was he to argue?

Thirty

CAROLINE WAS AN EXPERT AT GETTING INTO SECURE places. Aubrey was happy to follow her as she led the way through a facility that was rather more active than Aubrey would have preferred. He supposed they should take some of the blame, with Caroline's fire having the same effect as hitting a wasp's nest with a stick.

Nevertheless, after some shadowy lurking, a considerable amount of belly crawling, and a hair-raising wall scramble or two, she brought them to the far side of the warehouse, away from the invitingly open double doors that faced the parade ground.

For a moment, they stood with their backs to the corrugated metal. The north perimeter fence was fifty yards away, with the deep woods just on the other side. The nearest guard tower was a good distance away at the front of the complex. Aubrey could just make out the upper storeys of the old buildings. The chimneys of the factory building were smoking away, and he could see the other guard towers on the perimeter fence, but their position was well away from most of the lights in the facility. They were swallowed up by darkness.

'Too good to be true,' she said in answer to Aubrey's whispered query as to why they hadn't sneaked in through the double doors. 'It must be guarded.'

'So how are we getting in?'

'Where there's a train,' she said, trotting off, following the long side of the warehouse, 'there must be . . . Here we are.'

If Caroline moved more than a few yards away, it was hard to see her. Yet, some distance ahead, Aubrey could make out something blacker than the blackness around them, a mound higher than their heads, with a familiar, nose-tickling smell.

'Coal,' he said.

'Correct. And where there's coal outside a building, there must be a way to get it inside the building. I was prepared to look for a water tower if we had to, but I think scrambling in via a coal hopper would be easier than swimming underwater, in darkness, through a water inlet pipe.'

'Good thinking.' He paused. 'There is a lot of coal here, wouldn't you say? Rather more than would be needed to refuel a locomotive?'

Caroline craned her neck. 'You're thinking that it's needed for something else? For the manufacture of your enhanced coal?'

'From the amount of coal here, I'd say this facility is the source of it.' He wrinkled his nose at the tickly coal smell. 'If the plan is to ship those mechanical soldiers by train to wherever is needed, then they'll need to ship the fuel as well. Make it here, pop it in the cylinders, and off it goes. Neat, efficient, and very much the Holmland way.'

Caroline clambered up the side of the huge mound of coal and peered over the top. Then she slid back down in a controlled and elegant manner that Aubrey could not have hoped to duplicate in a million years. She stood and started to dust her hands together before realising that she was so filthy it would make little difference. She made a small moue of disapproval, then as Aubrey watched, fascinated, she dismissed it from her mind. He knew it wouldn't bother her from that moment on.

'What are you looking at?' she said.

Caught, he lunged for an answer and came up trumps. 'I'm not sure. It's so dark . . .'

'Hmm.' She turned toward the wall of coal. 'This way.'

Aubrey did his best and kept up without disgracing himself too much, squeezing through a hatch in the wall to find that a locomotive was standing quietly under a row of electric lights, its nose against the massive wooden bumpers at the end of the track. By crouching, Aubrey could see that on the other side, a platform was built up for easy loading and unloading.

A dozen goods carriages were attached to the locomotive, all open and empty.

Caroline tapped him on the shoulder. She pointed. One, two, three guards. None of them looked particularly alert, but none of them was asleep, either. Caroline gestured and he followed her, duck walking, keeping low, shielded by the locomotive, waiting for the right moment until they were able to dart into the body of the warehouse.

Once inside, Aubrey had an awful moment of déjà vu. He was immediately taken back to Lutetia, the ghastly photographer's lair where poor, soul-deprived victims were stored in racks, one on top of the other like forgotten spare parts.

Racks stretched into the distance, a hundred yards or more away, and towering twenty or thirty feet high. Aubrey did a quick calculation and realised there were over eight hundred racks in the space. In each, as far as they could see, was one of the mechanical soldiers, silent, motionless, gargantuan.

Staggered by the implications, Aubrey wandered along the rows. This was an army, ready to ship anywhere at any time. He could imagine trainloads of the mechanical soldiers, stacked efficiently and uncomplainingly, rattling to the nearest front, ready to create mayhem. No need for elaborate barracks, or mess halls, or provisioning. No need for uniforms, medics or quartermasters.

Caroline peered at the nearest giant warrior with nothing but curiosity. Her lack of fear gave Aubrey every incentive to do his best to keep his disquiet well hidden, even though he'd already decided that if any of the things moved as much as one brass-plated finger, he'd grab Caroline by the arm and they'd be off.

He licked his lips, then thought clearly for a second. 'Let's move away from here.'

'Too close to the entrance?' So, despite Aubrey's misgivings, they crept deeper into the body of the warehouse.

When Aubrey judged they were far enough from the entrance to minimise being stumbled upon, he began a close inspection.

As he suspected, even though mechanical was the best description, he could now see that sizeable parts of the internal workings were actually made of clay. Potentialised clay was actually embedded in the torso. Gingerly, he probed with a finger and revised his first guess. The clay wasn't just implanted into the workings, it linked cables and joints, providing buffers for some metal parts and protecting others.

He found what could be a miniature firebox and boiler. It was cold, but it was intensely embedded with spells that he would have liked to investigate further. He squinted to see that part of the inner workings were tightly wound with copper wire. Was electricity incorporated into these creatures, harnessed as an animating principle, as well as steam?

But the animating principle was still uncertain. Electricity, steam and potentialised clay wasn't enough to create creatures capable of such tasks as he'd seen. Something else had to be included, something more flexible, more capable.

The size of the thing was impressive. It was even bigger than Aubrey had thought. It was closer to twenty feet tall than fifteen, and was clearly capable of great power. Aubrey could see the massive feet crushing anything in its path, and the arms swinging like scythes.

Each creature looked identical, an army of purpose-built duplicates.

He spent some time over the creature's hands. He was appalled at how functional they were. They were designed to grip, to seize, to crush, and with immense force. It was breathtaking engineering, and would have been extraordinary in a single example, but he was surrounded by hundreds. All, as far as he could see, equally well made. Every part was exquisitely machined. Every surface highly polished – apart from the soot around the stubby chimney stack. Every seam welded to perfection.

Except for the neck.

Aubrey frowned. The neck of the creature was a mess and was entirely out of place. It looked like nothing as much as a failed flower pot, something that had fallen off the potter's wheel and splodged on the floor. It connected the clean, ingenious head and the rest of the creature, but the connection was crude and inelegant compared to the rest of the design.

With some squeamishness, Aubrey prodded at the seam where the clay joined the metal head and the hair at the back of his neck stirred. 'The clay goes right up inside the head,' he muttered.

'And what does that mean?' Caroline whispered.

'I don't know. I can't tell what's inside the metal skull.'

'Can you take it to pieces?'

Aubrey shuddered. He was quite prepared to tamper with the unknown, but he was very nervous about trying to remove the head of a giant mechanical warrior when a few hundred of its comrades were lying nearby.

Caroline had given him an idea.

The doughy neck was made of potentialised clay – potentialised clay that had been activated. It had been transformed and was undertaking some sort of magical task. If he could shape his magical awareness properly, with the utmost control, he might be able to divine exactly what it was doing – which should give him some indication of what was inside the metal head.

He had a suspicion that the workings of the head

could tell him a great deal about the construction and capabilities of the mechanical warriors – and their animating principle.

'I'm going to have to concentrate hard to investigate,' he said to Caroline. 'I won't exactly be aware of our surroundings.'

She smiled, wryly. 'Don't worry. I'll keep watch for both of us.'

Aubrey crouched down beside the mechanical soldier, as close to the neck and head as he could manage. He studied it for a moment, then he closed his eyes, took a deep breath, and extended his magical awareness.

Immediately, he had the pseudo-vision that a honed magical awareness provided. The world around him became vague and formless, apart from magical artefacts – and he was surrounded by them.

Every mechanical soldier was alive with magic – Dr Tremaine magic. It spread through every component, following every cable and running over every surface. The magic was dull red, making it look as if the hundreds of mechanical soldiers were red hot as they slept in their racks.

He moved his hand until it was hovering over the creature's neck, right where it joined the metal head. Quickly, he sensed elements that were applications of the Law of Cohesion and the Law of Elastic Deformation – and an unusual twist of the Law of Completeness. All of these would make sense if the clay was useful in joining disparate components, parts that wouldn't work well together otherwise. Then he hissed. He was sensing subtle, powerful spells, and some aspects reminded him of . . .

Death magic. Aubrey had run foul of death magic in

the past, and it had left him teetering on the brink of annihilation until he had found a cure. He had a healthy respect for death magic, so healthy that he wanted nothing to do with it.

Yet this wasn't pure death magic. It had some of its flavour, but it was more involved with preservation and, intriguingly, connection – *again*. The clay was serving the function of preserving and linking something to the mechanical components of the construct. Something important, but what?

Aubrey probed more, carefully, with all the delicacy he could muster.

Then his eyes shot open, and he recoiled, hissing. He spat, trying to clear his mouth of the taste of corruption that had filled it.

He stared at the creature with horror, until he became aware that Caroline was grasping him by the shoulder. 'What is it?' she whispered in his ear, concerned and urgent.

'The creature.' He stumbled over the words. He was having trouble with his tongue. 'The thing.'

'Slow down, Aubrey. Slow down. Breathe deeply.'

He did what he was told until his heart was calmer, merely thumping along instead of racing out of control.

'Now.' Caroline held his shoulders. 'What have you found?'

'We must go. We have to let them know.'

'We will, don't worry. But what have you found?'

Aubrey swallowed, took a deep, deep breath, and found what he hoped was his poise. 'I know where the wounded soldiers have gone. Part of them, at least.' He rapped the mechanical soldier on the head. 'There's a human brain in here.'

AUBREY EXPLAINED, IN TIGHT, CLIPPED SENTENCES, WHAT he'd found. The more he used dispassionate language, the more he was able to control his horror. Caroline was appalled, but her revulsion quickly turned to anger. 'What can we do?'

'We must get back to George and Sophie.'

'But these creatures, the havoc they will create.' She swallowed. 'I can't help thinking of the poor people, trapped inside all that metal.'

'I don't think they're aware of their plight. Dr Tremaine has used the brain as a component, a superb component, to control the rest of the creature. It's extraordinary.'

Caroline narrowed her eyes. 'You almost sound as if you admire him.'

'I do?' Aubrey reflected, and to his horror he realised that he *had* been verging on admiration for the man and his creation. The breathtaking daring of such a thing . . .

Don't be ridiculous, he thought. *The man is a villain. An unprincipled, arrogant villain.*

'I have an idea,' he said, finally. 'I may have a way to stop these creatures.'

'That's better. Something involving large explosions, I hope.'

'Something more subtle than that. I need to get to the brass cylinders again. The enhanced coal.'

Caroline didn't argue, which was perhaps a measure of her profound shock. She found one of the ways connecting the warehouse and the factory – and also found two white coats. These donned, Aubrey hoped, would give anyone at least a moment's pause before suspecting them outright. He knew that in a single moment, Caroline could achieve wonders of mayhem. He could brandish his pistol, too, given enough time.

It made them a formidable pair and he hoped anyone encountering them would realise it.

The factory was subdued, not the overwhelmingly noisy place of earlier in the day, but it wasn't silent. Hoists were moving and at least one conveyor belt was in action. Electricity flashed and hissed. The personnel on duty were absorbed in tasks or dozing, which made their passage remarkably easy.

The door to the stone chamber was closed this time, and Aubrey cursed as they studied it from their hiding place in a tangle of pipes that emerged from the wall nearby.

'I can get us in,' Caroline said.

'But what about whoever's inside?'

'No-one's inside. Look closely: two locks, one in the door, and a padlock looped around the handle and through the eyebolt in the wall. You can't lock yourself inside like that.'

'But someone on the outside could lock you in.'

'Aubrey, it's a matter of weighing up the odds. We're taking a risk just being here, but the odds of someone being locked in a bunker are low, if you think about it.'

'Right. I'll keep watch while you go to work.'

He didn't have to watch for long. Caroline approached the door confidently in her white coat. The padlock went quickly. The lock in the door was more complex, to judge by her frowning, but soon it yielded.

Caroline didn't look back toward Aubrey's hiding place. She briskly stepped inside and left the door ajar.

Aubrey waited until he counted sixty, slowly. Then he scanned the surroundings, climbed out of the pipes, crossed to the stone chamber and slipped inside.

Caroline was crouching over the manhole, which she'd opened. 'I assume,' she said after glancing over her shoulder, 'that your plan involves destroying these transportation cylinders so the mechanical soldiers can't be refuelled.'

Aubrey couldn't answer for a moment. The magic that poured from the pit in the floor was staggering. It spewed from the open mouth like a fountain.

He came to the pit and leaned close, squinting. His ordinary senses told him that it was simply thousands of small black balls. His magical senses, however, were assaulted by the web of spells that was embedded in the orbs of enhanced coal. Tartan patterns played on his skin. He heard colours – red, silver, black. His mouth was full of music, discordant and loud.

'If we destroy the cylinders . . .' Aubrey shook his head in an effort to clear it. 'They can make more. It's not an answer.'

Caroline straightened. She took one of the cylinders from the rack and unscrewed the top. Inside, Aubrey was intrigued to see that it was packed with loose, spun material. Rock-wool?

She put the open cylinder on the floor, then took another from the rack. 'It may not be an answer, but it's a start.'

With that, she used one cylinder to hammer the other, destroying the thread and making it impossible to close. The chamber rang. 'Unless you're thinking of using that enhanced coal to blow up this place, this may be the best we can do.'

Aubrey looked at the hundreds of cylinders. He thought of George's helpful deadline and knew it would take too long to batter each one of the cylinders so that they'd be unusable. 'I have a better idea.' He knelt and peered into the pit again. 'If this place is the source and repository for enhanced coal, then we could have a chance here.'

'I hope it's a chance that we can take quickly. I don't want to be here any longer than we have to.'

An idea had been nudging Aubrey, demanding his attention; he finally yielded and gave it his full attention. He realised that a number of considerations had come together without his really thinking about it. The unexploded spell in the Gallian embassy had contributed, as had the attempt to stop the symposium in Fisherberg, but his cogitations had gone back further than that, drawing on every encounter with spell compression and interaction.

He wanted to construct a tiny spell, one that was hard to notice – but one that had the ability to reproduce itself. A *spawning* spell.

Aubrey was convinced that such a thing was possible, even though he'd never heard of it being done. The Law of Constituent Parts, the Law of Essence, the Law of Seeming, the Law of Origins, the Law of Separation and dozens more all danced about the concept of identity and being. If he could bring them together with derivatives of the Law of Similarity and an application of the Law of Contiguity, then he could have something. One half of the spell would be the infectious factor, the other would be the part that would do the damage.

He wanted to infect the enhanced coal so that pieces in proximity would pass on the spell to each other. Any new enhanced coal in this pit would be infected by the rest. Any enhanced coal taken elsewhere would spread the infection.

The damaging part? He rubbed his hands together. A tiny, imperceptible spell that would lie dormant until triggered.

Aubrey considered the trigger and decided that a thermal point would be best. Nothing too early, or else the spell may be detected. No, it had to be when the mechanical soldiers were marching into battle, steaming at their most furious.

Then the spell would spring into action.

A startled gasp came from behind him. He turned to see Caroline lunge at the door, fling it open, drag a white coat inside and render him unconscious with a hold that Aubrey was sure hadn't been part of Directorate training. 'Well done,' he breathed.

'Not quite. The other one escaped.' She sighed. 'I wish they didn't travel in pairs.'

'I suppose I'd better make this quick, then.'

'If you don't mind.'

Caroline smiled at him briskly, every inch the calm, professional colleague. It made his heart ache.

With an effort, he reapplied himself to his work.

Aubrey chose the Chaldean language as best for this sort of synthesis. He ran through the elements in his head, wishing he had time to draft the spell on paper. It was going to be complex, and the implications of Ravi's First and Second Principles of Magic resounded in his head: the more powerful the spell, the more complex the spell construction, and the more complex the spell construction, the more effort is required from the spell caster.

What he was attempting really required careful planning, a team of magicians and a corps of assistants to help with recovery. Seeing as he had no choice, he plunged in.

In a split second, he achieved the sort of focus that told him he was casting a very complicated spell indeed. The surroundings almost faded away, so intensely was he concentrating on a single ball of enhanced coal . . . that one right there . . .

Caroline's voice came to him softly, distantly: 'Aubrey, I just have to slip out for a moment.'

He wanted to stop, to ask her where she was going, but cutting off the spell mid-stream would be a disaster. He'd have to find the strength and the wherewithal to start again – and he wasn't sure if they'd have the time.

He kept going, delineating the constants for dimensionality and duration.

A shot sounded and it was immediately answered by another, louder firearm. Somewhere, metal rang. He ignored it.

Compression, affinity, cohesion. He itemised each element, couching them with the appropriate variables, taking great care with his pronunciation.

More shots. Sporadic, not volley firing. He took some small comfort in that.

The end of the spell was close. All he needed was to delimit the sequence of the spell concerning attenuation, then insert the elements for attraction and he'd be done – once he put his final signature element at the end.

When the last syllables dropped from his lips, a wave of exhaustion hit him. The muscles in his legs and back trembled, then threatened to cramp, and he had to steady himself against the floor with one hand. He closed his eyes, and snapped them open again. Falling asleep would be a very bad idea.

With as much haste as he could summon, he dragged the cover over the pit and locked it. He had enough time to totter to the racks and starting fumbling with the cylinders in an effort to make it seem as if they were the object of his attention. A harsh Holmlandish voice came from behind. 'Take him.'

He did his best to whirl around, but he was afraid it was more of a crotchety unfolding than the panther-like movement he'd been hoping for.

Outlined in the doorway was Baron von Grolman, standing behind four armed troopers, each holding a rifle at the ready.

'Caroline!' he cried.

'Aubrey!'

Caroline appeared, hurling herself at the four troopers who stood in front of the baron. This distraction gave Aubrey a chance. He pulled out his revolver in one smooth movement – and stood, wondering what to do.

Caroline was in the middle of a tangle of arms and legs. He couldn't just blast away, and he wasn't sure he would even if she wasn't there.

The hesitation was enough. One of the Holmlanders saw him, shouted a warning, and then – with commendable bravery – threw himself at Aubrey.

Aubrey hurdled the brave Holmlander then aimed his revolver at the roof and squeezed off three quick shots.

The noise was deafening and all the Holmlanders threw themselves to the ground. Aubrey was stunned. His ears rang but he kept his wits. He burst through the door and found Caroline throwing a Holmlander over her hip. Baron von Grolman was crouched behind a heavy steel workbench. 'Stop them!' he cried.

Aubrey grabbed her hand. 'This way!'

She didn't argue. Aubrey sprinted off, waving his revolver at anyone who appeared. White coats quickly dived back into their workshops. Soldiers backed away, but soon they were trailing a band of Holmlanders determined to take them.

Panting, Aubrey darted left and right whenever a turning appeared, past stamping machines and presses, past metal pouring sluices and industrial ovens, past assembly lines with limbs of mechanical soldiers waiting for clay impregnation.

Clay. That was what Aubrey was looking for. He spun them around one of the golem-making machines and they were faced by the huge bin of potentialised clay George had discovered on their earlier expedition.

Aubrey gave Caroline his revolver. 'Here,' he panted, 'hold them off.'

Caroline reached for him, then dropped her hand. She nodded, sharply, then quickly scaled a hanging rope of chain before taking up position, lying prone on the golem-making machine.

Immediately, she fired a shot, and Aubrey knew he had little time.

He wanted to infect the clay as well. This was a good time to be a belt and braces man, leaving nothing to chance. Contaminating the enhanced coal with his spawning spell was good, but if he could do the same with the clay, the mechanical warriors themselves could pass on the contamination, simply by being in close contact. If he could adjust his parameters appropriately, simply lying in racks such as he saw could be enough. In their headlong flight through the factory, he'd been constructing such a variant.

He dropped to his knees in front of the clay bin and launched into the spell.

The second time around, it wasn't quite as difficult, but the spell still left him dizzy. He staggered to his feet to see a dozen Holmland soldiers charging toward him, past a fuming acid bath. Behind them, Baron von Grolman urged them forward.

He stood, eyeing the man in the vanguard – a large, blond soldier who looked terrified – looking for an opportunity to shift his weight and knock the man aside.

At that moment, Caroline Hepworth threw herself from the top of the golem maker, bowling over four of Holmlanders before rolling, coming to her feet, and dispatching another with a lightning-fast strike to his sternum.

For an instant, one of those distilled split seconds where everything stands still, she grinned at him across the mayhem she'd created. She was tall and slim in her fighting suit. He had enough time to notice how one cuff had unrolled, and that she had a scratch on the back of her hand that was bleeding.

He couldn't imagine anyone more perfect.

He grinned back at her, then another Holmlander was on him, swinging a rifle butt. Aubrey ducked, tripped his attacker, then waded in and was hand-to-hand fighting.

His combat skills had been enhanced by his training with the Directorate, and he did his best to be as scientific as he could. To judge from the grunts and cries of pain, he had some success, but as more and more Holmlanders appeared, he knew he was doomed. No bayonets were used, for which he was grateful, but the rifle butt that caught him in the side set him back, and the troopers had no qualms about using boots, either.

In the end, it was numbers. Two dozen armed, veteran soldiers were simply too many. Aubrey was sure he had a loose tooth, and his ribs were bruised if not cracked. Caroline had left a swathe of unconscious troopers, but eventually they'd managed to throw ropes around her.

Baron von Grolman limped through the press of injured Holmlanders to where Aubrey and Caroline were each being restrained by a pair of the brawniest veterans. 'I'm glad I found you,' he said in good Albionish. 'You rats have caused enough mischief, scuttling about my factory.'

Thirty-one

WHEN AUBREY LAST ENCOUNTERED BARON VON Grolman, he had been every inch the hospitable Holmlander, jolly and generous. A very different Baron von Grolman faced them over the desk in the office they'd been dragged to. Cold eyed, deliberate, incisive, this was a man, Aubrey decided, who could work with Dr Tremaine.

After the fracas, they'd been bound and, in Aubrey's case, gagged, so it was Caroline who took it up to the industrialist.

'My mother would die of shame,' she said, 'if she could see what you're up to.'

The baron winced at this. 'I like your mother. In the past, it did me good, to be seen with such a renowned artist. But now, I never have to step inside an art gallery again, which is a great relief.'

The baron's office was in the north wing of the original

buildings, and – to judge from the exposed beam that divided the room in half – had once been two rooms before it was converted into this long, narrow space. The office wasn't grand. It was a workaday place with a large desk over which the baron studied them. Behind the desk, a large window looked out over the railway line and the northern boundary fence to the dark and inviting woods beyond. A clock hung on the wall, a telephone stood on the desk, while vertical racks of plans and blueprints took up the other wall.

From the time on the clock, Aubrey was able to see that half of George's allocated two hours had gone.

'What are you going to do to us?' Caroline demanded.

'You're better off not knowing.'

'As enemy combatants, we are entitled to be treated correctly.'

The baron actually chuckled. 'I'm afraid not, my dear. You two are clearly spies, not enemy combatants.' He glanced at Aubrey. 'One of whom is a magician.'

Aubrey was heartened at the mention of 'two'. It meant that George and Sophie were undetected.

'Spies?'

'You are wearing no uniform, you have no identification, you are from the enemy. That is the usual definition of spy. Different rules apply to spies. Spies are interrogated, and then they are dealt with.'

'We aren't spies,' Caroline said.

'Yes you are.' The baron plucked a document from the pile in front of him and peered at it. 'You and young Fitzwilliam are operatives of your Security Intelligence Directorate. You have been specially trained and sent on a mission to find out about my factory.'

The baron's voice was flat, as if he were reading from a furniture catalogue.

'What nonsense,' Caroline said gamely. 'We've simply come to find a friend's brother.'

Aubrey's spirits rose, and for a moment he was able to ignore the ropey taste of the gag in his mouth. This was good thinking – a part truth. As long as Caroline didn't give away the presence of George and Sophie, it could work.

'Our intelligence is good. You are spies.' The baron tapped the document.

'Your intelligence is flawed. Who would say such a thing?'

'Someone who knew. Someone who has benefited from your Directorate training. Someone who will help guide our interrogators, since she knows the questions to ask.'

He rapped the desk and the door behind him opened. In walked Elspeth Mattingly.

Aubrey's efforts to loosen his gag dried up; he was stunned into immobility. The irony of his situation asserted itself when he realised that he was in exactly the same plight as when Elspeth last saw him – bound to a chair.

She glanced at Caroline and, with a sunny smile, studied Aubrey for a moment before frowning. 'But where is George?'

'Doyle?' the Baron said. 'Is he here too?'

'Teams of three was the standard arrangement.'

The baron sniffed. 'It is no matter. He will be found.' He beamed at her. 'Soon you will start on them, my dear. Are you eager?'

'Baron, I can't wait.' She put a finger to her cheek. 'Who will be first? Ah, decisions, decisions!'

The baron glanced at Aubrey. 'She is very good at what she does. Good at interrogation, but better at gaining trust. I'm sure you agree.'

Aubrey did his best to remain impassive.

Caroline jumped in. 'You've trusted her too, Baron, which is a great mistake.'

Elspeth laughed. 'Everyone trusts me. I make sure of it.'

Caroline gazed at her coolly. 'I didn't.'

For an instant, Elspeth's sunniness slipped and an expression of utter calculation flitted across her face. Aubrey blinked, but it was gone. She waved an airy hand at Caroline. 'Well, people like you wouldn't.'

Baron von Grolman raised an eyebrow. He found a rough fingernail and picked at it. 'I'm keen to hear why Miss Hepworth thinks it a mistake to trust you, Elspeth.'

Caroline was silent for a moment and Aubrey could see her weighing up what to say. 'She was detected as one of your agents very early on. Every piece of information she has gained was deliberately fed to her, full of falsehoods.'

Aubrey tensed. Caroline was playing a dangerous game.

The baron held up his fingernail in front of his eyes, happy with his work. 'What you are saying now could be full of the same falsehoods. Or different ones.' He sighed. 'This world is full of uncertainties, is it not?'

Elspeth nodded. 'Never a truer word was spoken, Baron. Many a more interesting one, but we can't have everything.'

The Baron smiled at her in an avuncular way. 'So, to make certain where we are uncertain, the questioning will need to be most direct.'

'Direct?' Elspeth said. 'I'd better sharpen my instruments then.' She looked tenderly at Aubrey, came close and loosened his gag. 'I want you to know that you're in very good hands.'

Aubrey looked at her beautiful, smiling face and realised that she was loving every minute of this – and looking forward to what was to come. He swallowed a fear-induced lump in his throat and blurted out a question that had been nagging at him. 'Last time, in the embassy, you had me helpless. Why didn't you kill me?'

Elspeth darted a glance at the Baron, then she shrugged. 'My orders didn't say anything about killing you, silly boy, so I didn't. But now? Baron?'

He snorted. 'Do what you must.'

After rearranging his gag, she left in an obscene combination of haste and excitement and he was relieved to sit back and watch as Caroline took to the baron.

Sitting there under Baron von Grolman's placid gaze, as Caroline upbraided him for his attitude and behaviour, Aubrey had a moment of utter dismay. He knew that at times he had been carried away in the thrill of the adventures in which he'd become involved. He couldn't deny the excitement he'd had in successfully duping dangerous foes, or in inventing new magical methods under great duress, or rescuing his friends from peril. It was exhilarating. But now, the other side of the coin had been turned toward him. Failure didn't only mean ignominy – although that would be bad enough. Failure meant death.

As someone who had spent considerable time actually staring death in the face, thanks to being left on that precipice by his remarkably hare-brained experiment with forbidden magic, Aubrey had a healthy respect for death. Yes, he knew it was a natural process and other platitudes, but it was a natural process that he really didn't want hastened in any way. He preferred to imagine a long happy life ahead of him.

He had a prickle of sweat in his palms. He did his best to flex his hands but his captors had been efficient and left him with very little play.

He tried to read the time without looking directly at the clock on the wall. Was there forty minutes left?

While, with some effort, he could contemplate his own extinction, the prospect of Caroline being no more both outraged and distressed him. A universe without Caroline Hepworth in it? It was wrong, so wrong that he emitted a groan that the gag couldn't stifle. Both Caroline and the baron interrupted their arguing to look at him.

'This is just business,' the baron continued after satisfying himself that Aubrey wasn't beginning a spell. 'Nothing more. War is good for such a person as me. My factories will be happy, my suppliers will be happy, I will be happy.'

'That makes you worse than the generals,' Caroline said. 'They, at least, have some sense of duty and honour.'

'Delusions. I have self-interest at heart and I make no quibble about it.'

'Like Dr Tremaine?'

Aubrey was fascinated to see that the baron actually shifted uncomfortably at the mention of the rogue sorcerer. 'He has his interests, I have mine.'

'And we know what happens to people who work for Dr Tremaine,' Caroline bore in. 'We've seen the results.'

'I do not work for Tremaine. We are partners.'

'Of course he'd tell you that.'

'His expertise with magic, my expertise with manu-facturing. It is a good arrangement.'

'Dr Tremaine will get what he wants, that's certain.'

Baron von Grolman stared at her sourly, then he rapped on the desk again. 'Take them away,' he said when the door behind him opened.

'I shall,' came an amused voice. Aubrey sat bolt upright, as much as he could. 'All in good time.'

Dr Tremaine entered the room and was immediately the centre of attention. Baron von Grolman nodded at him in a disgruntled fashion. Caroline glared daggers at him. Aubrey wondered if his eyes were deceiving him.

Dr Tremaine looked happy and healthy, as if he'd spent time on a tropical island rather than manoeuvring the world into war. He wore a dark blue cutaway frock coat, with a white shirt and an eye-catching red paisley cravat. He carried a cane – with no sign of the Tremaine pearl.

'Tell me, Baron,' Dr Tremaine said, his voice rich with delight at his partner's discomfort, 'when were you going to let me know you'd found the intruders?'

The baron adjusted his bulk slightly, as if he knew it were a hopeless effort. He narrowed his eyes. 'You were busy, Tremaine, doing your business with the coal essence. I know how you hate interruptions.'

'Not as much as those who do the interrupting, once I've reminded them of my aversion to them.' He peered across the room. 'I knew Fitzwilliam had come to pester me again. And he's brought the girl.'

Aubrey could feel Caroline's cold fury from where he

was. He would not, ever, have wanted to be the object of Caroline Hepworth's anger.

Once again, however, she surprised him. With steely calm, she addressed the rogue sorcerer. 'I'm happy that you've forgotten who I am. The less time I spend in that horror you call a mind, the better.'

'Hah!' Dr Tremaine perched on the corner of the desk, much to the irritation of Baron von Grolman. 'Your father would have been proud of you!'

'Don't mention my father. Your lips sully his name.'

'He's dead, you know, so it doesn't really matter.'

He turned to the baron and launched into a discussion of train schedules and clay shipments, and so missed Caroline's shock, and the look she shot him once she'd recovered. Aubrey wished he was able to capture that look, for top military magicians would be very interested in its weaponry applications. He waggled his head at her, trying to hook her attention. She rolled her eyes at his feeble efforts at indicating their bonds. *Of course she would have thought of that*, he thought. If only he could cast the spell to harden his tongue to a cutting edge, so he could sever the gag to allow him to cast a spell to harden his tongue . . .

'I'll take them off your hands, von Grolman,' Dr Tremaine said.

'I want them,' the baron said. Again, he shifted uneasily in his seat. 'I have the interrogators ready.'

'The Mattingly girl is there?'

'You know about her?'

'Of course I know about her. She's one of mine. I used her to dupe Delroy's son into joining the Holmland army. Imagine that.'

Aubrey went to gasp, but the gag made him choke. Dr Tremaine glanced at him.

'Delroy?' the baron said, stunned. 'You have a hold on him?'

'The boy is here. I'll go to work on him soon, and then we'll have someone neatly placed to bring down the Gallian government.'

The baron stared at Dr Tremaine for some time. 'I knew she was one of yours,' he said eventually. 'That's why I found her useful.'

Dr Tremaine laughed. 'You lie so wonderfully poorly, von Grolman. That's why I'm happy for you to work with me.'

For an instant, Aubrey thought he saw the baron's gaze flit around the room, a mouse trapped in a corner by a cat. Then he composed himself by lacing his hands on his chest. Aubrey begrudgingly awarded the baron some points here. He hadn't achieved his fortune by being a weakling. The baron knew he was dancing with a tiger – but Aubrey thought he may have been making the mistake of assuming he was leading.

Aubrey had a hint of hope. Could there be something here? Some dissent, some difference of outlook that he could work on?

Difficult, he thought, *tied up and gagged like this*. He wrenched at where his hands were lashed to the chair frame, but the wood and the rope were solid.

'Perhaps you should get back to the train-loading platform, Tremaine,' the Baron said. 'Don't you want to gloat over your invincible warriors?'

'Gloating is a sign of weakness, von Grolman, try to remember that. I'll let your people manage the loading of the golems. I'm sure they can handle things well enough.'

'The interrogator –' the baron began, but Dr Tremaine cut him off short.

'Can wait. I want to talk to these two now.'

Baron von Grolman licked his lips, quickly, his tongue moving in and out like a snake. 'As you wish, Tremaine. No need to make a fuss.'

Dr Tremaine stood. 'Other people make fusses, von Grolman. I don't.' He gestured, and a slim knife appeared in his hand. 'Now, girl, I'm going to slice through the ropes around your feet. Don't attempt to kick me. I'm assured it's painful trying to walk on a broken leg.'

Caroline stiffened, but resisted the impulse as Dr Tremaine went to work. 'I'm leaving your hands bound,' he said, straightening. 'For your good, not mine. Call me sentimental.'

Caroline rallied. 'Once I've finished making my list, I'll call you many things.'

'Excellent. Now, Fitzwilliam. The same applies to you, of course, but I'll leave that gag on. Not just because you look foolish and it makes me laugh, but because I want to do away with the faint possibility of your working magic that could actually interfere with my plans.'

The baron drummed his fingers on his desk while Dr Tremaine shepherded Caroline and Aubrey out. The last Aubrey saw of him, he was reaching for the telephone, and a brief moment of pity came to him. In a better, kinder world, he would have had the chance to sit Baron von Grolman down and offer him some advice: 'Look, Baron, the only thing to do is to drop everything and run. Run fast and run far. Change your name, your appearance, your habits and hope that Dr Tremaine forgets all about you.'

Aubrey was amazed that the baron hadn't come to that conclusion for himself. It confounded him that so many people thought they could work with the rogue sorcerer and walk away safely, whereas Aubrey saw it as similar to working with nitro-glycerine. Take all precautions: heavy gloves, metal tongs, keep your distance, and you'd still never know when it could go off.

Dr Tremaine walked behind them, issuing instructions, 'Left here' or 'Straight ahead', when they came to intersecting corridors. This part of the complex was obviously residential, for the baron and his people, with some administrative function, and it was quieter than the manufacturing section, so Aubrey was able to hear a strange, unfamiliar noise. Aubrey frowned as Dr Tremaine nudged them through a doorway and through the gardens, past the concrete giraffe and back into the factory, and then his eyes widened.

Dr Tremaine was whistling.

It was soft, but the rogue sorcerer was whistling as he went. He accompanied it by tapping his cane on handy iron stanchions, columns and balustrades while he herded them up stairs and along walkways to a control room overlooking the factory floor.

Dr Tremaine was a virtuoso whistler, Aubrey realised, but it didn't surprise him. As well as being an unparalleled magical genius, the man was a concert standard baritone, a sculptor whose miniatures were much sought after, and a bare-knuckle fighter banned from competition for being entirely too good, and they were only a few of his accomplishments.

He was whistling a chorus from Ivey and Wetherall's *Major Majority*, the musical farce that was all the rage in Trinovant since its premiere two months ago.

Aubrey stared. *Two months ago? Then how did Dr Tremaine come to hear it?*

The control room could have been an office for a minor clerk or bookkeeper. It was cramped, with pigeon holes and key hooks taking up the wall opposite the entrance, and it smelled of dust and paper. Three telephones were lined up on the long bench under the window. The wall that overlooked the factory floor was entirely made of glass.

Dr Tremaine gazed outward, admiring his handiwork, then he gestured at the two wooden chairs while he leaned against the empty peg board that was the back wall.

'Now,' he said, 'it goes like this. I'm going to remove your gag so you can respond. But first.'

Dr Tremaine struck his cane on the floor, hard, then twisted it. The head separated, and he was holding a sword. 'Not magic, just good craftsmanship,' he said, running a finger along the flat of the blade. He held the point just under Aubrey's chin, tickling his Adam's apple.

'Don't imagine you can spit out a spell faster than I can wield this beauty. And don't think that my wrist will be bound to grow weary and the point will drop for a moment into which you can cast a spell you're no doubt preparing.'

Aubrey went to shake his head, thought better of it, went to nod, thought better of it, then swallowed, and regretted it as his skin feathered against the steel.

Dr Tremaine smiled broadly and released the gag with his other hand. The sword stayed steady.

'What do you want?' Aubrey croaked. He wanted to spit out rope fibres, but he stopped himself.

'Aubrey,' Caroline said.

'Let him speak,' Dr Tremaine said. 'I have some time, and I find that amusement is in short supply when I'm surrounded by Holmlanders.'

'I'm not here to amuse you,' Aubrey said. 'I'm here because I'm a nuisance to you.'

Dr Tremaine sighed. 'You disappoint me – which, by the way, is generally not a good thing to do. You've made the same mistake that many people do. They imagine that I'm actually interested in them and their little lives. It gives them a sense of self-importance, I gather, to think that Dr Tremaine, the most feared man in the world, is concerned about them.'

'And you're not?'

'Only in the same way that I'm concerned about the moth that's flitting about the electric light.'

'What moth?'

Dr Tremaine gestured. A bright flash, and a tiny, ashy shape fell to the table.

'That moth.'

Aubrey swallowed again, and felt the tip of the sword. 'Neatly done, if a little showy.'

'Ah. Everyone's a critic.'

Aubrey bridled. 'You say you're not worried about me? Then what about the stormfleet? And when you turned me into a mindless assassin?'

'Those? I'd almost forgotten them. Minor stuff, designed to inconvenience you and thereby inconvenience the Albion Prime Minister.' He wagged a finger. 'You see yourself as important. I see you as a tiny part of my plans, an infinitesimal tooth on a minute gear in one ordinary corner of the vast, interlocking and magnificent machine that I have built to serve my ends.'

'Your quest for immortality. A small quest for someone so ambitious.'

'I have no ambitions. I simply have so much to do that one life is too absurdly short. Which leads me to what I want from you.'

Aubrey opened his mouth to point out that this could be seen as contradictory, his being both nugatory and useful at once, but decided that since Dr Tremaine had the better of him, it might not be a good time to go down that path. 'Go on.'

'You're aware of this connection we have, of course.'

'It wasn't my fault.'

'I'm not interested in whose fault it was. I've spent some time analysing it and it looks as if it was a freak accident, a blending of our magics at a time when we were both vulnerable.' He laughed. 'Imagine that. For an instant, I was actually vulnerable – and all that happened is that I have this flimsy connection with you.'

'It's erratic,' Aubrey ventured.

'I know. Erratic, ghostly, unreliable, but mildly interesting nonetheless. In some circumstances, I can sense your presence. Not from any distance, but it has proved useful. I knew you were lurking about, for instance.'

'You didn't come looking for me?'

'Looking for you? I left you to the baron. I knew you'd trip yourself up in time.' He chuckled, and Aubrey thought it was a measure of the man that one minute he was making offhand death threats, and the next he was enjoying a joke.

'So you want to destroy the connection,' Aubrey said.

Dr Tremaine started, but the tip of the blade at Aubrey's throat didn't move. 'That's not it at all. I want to study it and reproduce it because I want to connect with Sylvia.'

Sylvia. Dr Tremaine's much-loved sister, the only one in the world he cared for. Aubrey and Caroline had encountered Sylvia in a coma, induced by Dr Tremaine in an effort to preserve her life from the terminal illness that had been wracking her.

'She's here?' Aubrey asked.

'She's somewhere delightful, somewhere of her own choosing. Cured now, of course.'

That, in part, had been Aubrey's doing. Not that he looked for any thanks. 'So you want to connect so you can monitor her.'

'Monitor? I want to be sure she is safe. I want to take the feeble thing you produced and improve it so I know all about her at all times.'

Aubrey wondered if Dr Tremaine had bothered to ask his sister if this is what she wanted. He saw that the same thought had occurred to Caroline. 'And what will happen to her once you're immortal?' Caroline asked him. 'You'll be leaving her behind.'

Dr Tremaine shook his head. 'That's the beauty of my machine for the future. It can change, it can be adapted, it can have bright new components bolted on. In this case, once I had recovered Sylvia, it meant that she, too, would need the Ritual of the Way performed.'

Aubrey went cold. 'So that means your blood sacrifice will need to be doubled.'

'That's right, yes.' Dr Tremaine withdrew the sword, but before Aubrey could react he flipped it to his left hand and then it was back at his throat. 'Practice, practice, practice. Just being good isn't enough, you know?'

'Stop,' Caroline said, half rising from her chair before a cock of Dr Tremaine's head toward Aubrey stilled her. 'You've just said you want hundreds of thousands more people to die. Just to fuel your personal aims.'

'To my mind, at least it's better than fuelling the personal aims of a handful of stupid generals and politicians. At least my aim is an aim that will resound for the ages.' He paused, thoughtfully. 'Of course, being immortal I can make sure of that.'

Aubrey was exhausted. It had been a long day and Dr Tremaine's revelation didn't surprise him. From his point of view, with his single-minded view of the world, it made perfect sense. 'And that's it? What happens once you've worked out what this connection is all about?'

Another chuckle. 'I could lie, tell you that is the totality of my need for you, and then roll out my next task, but I choose not to. I'm going to be straightforward.'

'That must be refreshing,' Caroline said.

'Ah, she jokes! A witticism trips from those lovely lips! Here I was, assuming it would be the boy who endeavoured to keep up spirits with a quip. You must be learning from him.'

'Don't be foolish,' Caroline said but Aubrey couldn't help notice that her cheeks were flaming. In other circumstances it would be a delightful sight but . . . He reconsidered. No, it was delightful, even in this unfortunate situation.

Dr Tremaine studied her, then he glanced at Aubrey, then back at Caroline. A smile crept to his face. Aubrey prepared himself for the rogue sorcerer's taunting, but all

Dr Tremaine did was raise an eyebrow and tilt his head at Aubrey. It astonished him. A murdering genius, having some delicacy with affairs of the heart? Who would have guessed it?

At that moment, the door banged open and Baron von Grolman stood there. 'I have an idea,' he said. 'We can use the boy.'

Thirty-two

Dr Tremaine turned his head — but the sword still hovered at Aubrey's throat. 'You've interrupted me, von Grolman,' he said in a voice full of wonder.

'Sorry, Tremaine, but I wanted to catch you before it was too late.'

That's has an unspoken implication that I'm not altogether happy with, Aubrey thought. He went to speak, but Dr Tremaine moved the sword tip infinitesimally.

'And what *is* so important that you burst in here like that?' Dr Tremaine said to the baron.

The baron clasped his hands together. He was sweating, beads appearing on his broad forehead. 'I've just realised what a godsend we have here, Tremaine.'

'You've just realised? Are you sure someone hasn't been in your ear? The Mattingly girl?'

To Aubrey, the baron's blustering denial was as good as an admission, and from Dr Tremaine's amused expression, he thought so as well. 'Look, Tremaine,' the baron said eventually, desperately trying to wrest back the initiative, 'you understand that we have the son of the Albion Prime Minister here, don't you?'

'There is little I don't understand, von Grolman, but do go on.'

'Imagine what the effect would be on the Albion populace if he defected.'

Aubrey couldn't help himself. He blurted. 'Defected?'

The baron ignored him. 'We photograph him, shaking hands with you, inspecting Holmland troops, conferring with the generals I've brought here. It would destroy his father, for a start.'

Dr Tremaine smiled. At the sight of that smile, Aubrey immediately wanted to be on another continent, and couldn't understand why the baron wasn't running for his life. 'Von Grolman,' Dr Tremaine said, 'I like this. It's underhand and grubby, just the sort of thing I've come to expect from you. But I fail to see what you will get out of it, which makes me suspicious.'

The baron swallowed. 'Partners shouldn't be suspicious of each other, Tremaine. I'm being open.'

'Yes, you are. So just to make sure, tell me how you'll benefit from this little plan.'

'I am a patriot. This will help us win the war.'

'Now you're starting to disappoint me . . .'

'I have access to certain shares,' the baron groped for a handkerchief in his pocket and used it to mop his brow, 'in companies that are owned by Sir Darius. If I sell these now and buy them back later when the price tumbles, I'll make a fortune.'

Dr Tremaine turned to Aubrey and Caroline. 'Finance.

It's a magic of its own and I have little time or inclination for it.'

'It could be your undoing,' Caroline said, but Aubrey could see that her heart wasn't in it.

'I doubt it. I have a man who takes care of such things for me.'

Caroline perked up at this. 'Excellent.'

'Excellent?'

'They're the ones – after the embezzling and running off with all your money – about whom you say, "But I trusted him completely."'

Dr Tremaine laughed. 'You're right, I always read that in the paper. But my man can't run off, you see. I've placed a small locative spell on him. He can't move outside the room I've placed him in without his heart stopping.'

The baron paled and his hand crept to his chest. 'Well, Tremaine, what do you think about my plan for the boy?'

'I have a potential problem with this scenario, delicious though it sounds. I don't think that young Fitzwilliam will cooperate.'

'Turn traitor?' Caroline said. 'I should think not!'

'Not willingly, perhaps,' the baron said, and colour began to return to his cheeks. 'But with the right sort of lever, much can be achieved, no?'

'No,' Caroline said.

'I will ask him. Tremaine, let him answer.'

Dr Tremaine moved the sword tip away a little. He was immensely amused by what was going on, as if it were a divertissement arranged purely for him. 'He is yours, von Grolman.'

The baron moved until he was facing Aubrey squarely. He leaned over, hands on his knees, until his face was at

Aubrey's level. 'Now, Fitzwilliam, I want to make this very clear. Unless you cooperate, I will kill her immediately.'

The baron straightened and pushed back his jacket. He removed an Oberndorf pistol from his waistband with a grunt of relief. He armed it and pointed it at Caroline.

Who laughed. Her eyes held only contempt, not fear, and Aubrey loved her for it. 'Aubrey, don't you dare.'

It was permission. Caroline had just given him permission to stand fast, to ignore whatever they would do to her. In training, they had been warned about interrogation. The promises made, the threats, the bribes, the tactics used. Worse than physical harm, a grey-haired colonel lectured, was the possibility of harm to a loved one.

The fate of a someone dear versus the fate of the country.

He shrugged. 'What do you want me to do?'

THUS FOLLOWED A GALLING ROUND THAT AUBREY WOULD rather forget. Shaking hands with a smiling Dr Tremaine. Dr Tremaine with a casual arm draped over Aubrey's shoulders. Aubrey examining the mechanical soldier-making machinery (carefully arranged at an angle to show little detail of the actual apparatus). Aubrey inspecting a row of the gigantic creatures, accompanied by recognisable members of the Holmland High Command and, most horribly, Aubrey inspecting a handful of Gallian prisoners who had been obviously and shockingly beaten. Here, he found it almost impossible to keep his demeanour acceptable. The baron stood next to the photographer for all the shots, requiring Aubrey to do it again when he wasn't satisfied with his expression, which had to be either delight or approval or – at appropriate times – awe. Each expression was designed to let all Albion know that the Holmland war effort was so mighty that resistance was a poor option.

Between photo arrangements, guards gagged him and he had time to reflect on the scene in the control room once he'd agreed to cooperate.

Caroline had been shocked and angry at his acquiescence and managed to rise from the chair, flinging off her bonds and kicking the baron in his vast belly before Dr Tremaine subdued her. Aubrey had an inkling that Dr Tremaine had actually waited before moving, allowing Caroline to lash at the baron first, to judge from his grin.

After that, Caroline had subsided, smouldering, but as Aubrey passed her, shepherded by the baron on the way to the door, she looked at him pleadingly. She muffled a sob and she reached out for him. He took her hand in both of his, and she immediately completed the grasp with her other hand.

'Enough,' the baron said. 'This way.'

He bustled Aubrey through the door, but Aubrey hardly noticed. Caroline's little performance had fooled the baron, and for a moment Aubrey had been swept away in it, but when she'd withdrawn her hands, she'd made sure to leave her ring in his, complete with cutting edge.

It was an eminently practical display. A ruse, nothing more, and he was a little wistful at that.

The baron's photographer was obviously delighted with his job. Even in the prison cells, surrounded by suffering, he was continually prodding Aubrey to turn his face to the camera, or straighten his head, or adjust his jacket. He spoke good Albionish and kept up a commentary, telling Aubrey what he was doing and how Aubrey could look his best.

Aubrey complied with what he hoped looked like pained reluctance, while checking the time at every chance. He was grateful for the Holmland mania for efficiency. Clocks were liberally distributed throughout the complex, like police officers in the streets of Trinovant.

Fifteen minutes. He had fifteen minutes to get himself into a position where George's distraction would be of use.

While they were on the factory floor he looked for loose cables. When riding the lift he sized up opportunities to disarm guards. He summed up the best routes out of the complex and, when outside, he checked the perimeter fence for blind spots between towers, or shadowed areas, or overhanging trees.

'Stop!' the baron called as they made their way through the garden back toward the administration wing. 'Here. Let us have a photograph of him here.'

The photographer gazed around and grinned. 'Perfect, Baron von Grolman. The buildings, the gardens . . . You have a good eye.'

'I have a good eye for an opportunity. I want him against the animals. We can tell the Albionites that Fitzwilliam is enjoying himself at our Holmland fun fairs.'

Aubrey gazed up at the giant concrete zebra. Its stripes were faded and flaking in places, but he supposed that wouldn't show up in the photograph.

'The tiger would be perfect,' the photographer

suggested. 'You stand with him, Baron von Grolman, and point up at it.'

'Like this?'

'Mr Fitzwilliam, if you please, do look in the direction the baron is pointing. Remember that scowling isn't the look we're after. Be impressed. Try opening your mouth and eyes wide.'

Aubrey took a deep breath and did his best to comply.

'And hold that pose . . .' A brilliant flare of flash powder. 'Capital! What's next, Baron?'

Baron von Grolman looked at Aubrey and smirked. 'I think that's enough, don't you?'

Aubrey went to answer, but Dr Tremaine, standing to one side, admonished him and held up a wicked throwing knife. 'Tcha! No speaking, Fitzwilliam.'

Gagged again. When they came back to Baron von Grolman's office Caroline was gone. Aubrey raised an eyebrow and a glance passed between the baron and Dr Tremaine. 'She's safe,' the baron said. 'Don't worry.'

Nothing about von Grolman convinced Aubrey that he was telling the truth. Not his words, his tone of voice, his facial expressions, his stance.

He allowed his gaze to slide over the clock on the wall and he bit hard on the rope. Ten minutes!

He pointed to his gag. Dr Tremaine nodded, but produced his throwing knife and held it to Aubrey's throat. One of the guards undid the rope and withdrew the by now filthy gag. 'I want to get this over and done with,' he said slowly. 'When can we examine this magical connection?'

'Eager, aren't you?'

Aubrey shrugged. 'I'm curious. I want to know more about it.'

'You have the passion, don't you?'

Aubrey realised that he didn't have to pretend. He couldn't talk about magic this way to many people. His professors were mostly fusty theoreticians. His non-magical friends could never know what it was like to wrestle with the fundamental force that pervaded the universe, shaping it to one's will, using language to codify and control it.

It was thrilling.

'It burns.' Aubrey looked directly into Dr Tremaine's eyes. 'I lie awake, thinking about ways to work it. I dream about alternatives. I imagine what it could do.'

Dr Tremaine grunted. 'Leave me here with him, von Grolman. I've a mind to do some magic.'

The baron was vexed. 'Are you sure? Shouldn't I leave some guards?'

'Don't be tiresome. If I can't manage him, then a few guards aren't going to help. Besides, Fitzwilliam is going to cooperate, aren't you, boy?'

'He will if he wants to see his sweetheart again.'

Aubrey could have quibbled with that, as he had some trouble thinking of Caroline as a sweetheart – it sounded too soft and sugary – but he kept mum. 'And when *will* I see her again?'

Another significant glance between the baron and Dr Tremaine. 'We can't let you go, of course,' the baron said, 'but we think you'll be happy enough under house arrest in Fisherberg. We'll set you up somewhere comfortable with your ladylove. Nice and convenient, and we'll know where you are, for when we need to use you for more propaganda.'

Aubrey grimaced. The baron looked satisfied at that, but the grimace wasn't for the reason the baron thought. For the fleetest of fleeting moments, Aubrey found himself thinking that that fate wasn't so bad after all. A comfortable house, with Caroline, and not having to worry any more about trying to save the world. With a sigh, he banished the mirage, for mirage he was sure it was. Dr Tremaine may not care much about Aubrey and his fate, but he was certain that the baron wouldn't want to see Aubrey – or Caroline – still on hand to talk to whoever may want to listen.

Not to mention Caroline's contempt at agreeing to such a life.

No, things weren't going to turn out all right. Not without his doing something.

The baron left, the guards left, and Aubrey was left with Dr Tremaine, who sighed. 'You see what I have to work with?' He laughed, then flipped his knife up in the air and caught it again. 'I'll take the photographic plates with me when I go to Fisherberg tonight, just to make sure they're properly used. Now, move over there, boy, near the window.'

Thirty-three

AUBREY DID AS HE WAS TOLD. OUTSIDE, THE DARKNESS of the woods beckoned, but now to get to the door, he'd have to vault the desk as well as get past Dr Tremaine.

Tremaine started banging drawers open and closed. 'Now, expel any hopes you have. I'm not about to share my plans or reveal my weaknesses. I'm not going to turn my back on you or allow you one chance to test yourself against me.' He fixed Aubrey with a stony look. 'Understand: I'm going to use you, then discard you.'

'I'm glad that's settled,' Aubrey said. 'Otherwise I'd think you were ill.'

Dr Tremaine roared with laughter. 'Good effort, Fitzwilliam, you nearly reached panache.' He pulled a magnifying glass from a drawer. 'Now, don't move.'

Aubrey could feel the magic coming from the magnifying glass, a form of amplification on top of a spell derived from the Law of Origins. His hands itched. He wanted to examine it to see if Dr Tremaine had invented the same sort of application he had for his own magic magnifying glass.

Dr Tremaine bowed his head and, for an instant, Aubrey thought he had a chance, but the rogue sorcerer looked up and a brief smile crossed his lips. 'Don't.' Then he shifted his shoulders and stretched his neck. He extended his hands, shaking his cuffs back from his wrists, and launched into a spell.

Aubrey actually took a step backward as Dr Tremaine's words rolled over him, and he felt the chill of the window at his back. When the magic struck him, it was like being hit by a summer storm. He had to narrow his eyes as the ex-Sorcerer Royal brought his will to bear and wrought great magic.

Within moments, Aubrey was reminded that he was in the presence of a master. He'd experienced it before and every encounter only reinforced it. With no doubt, no uncertainty and no lack of raw talent, Dr Tremaine routinely attempted magic that no-one ever had before.

Aubrey did his best to take mental notes, but try as he might he couldn't place the language Dr Tremaine was using. It matched none that he knew, none of the ancient languages that were used in an attempt to get close to the natural language of magic.

The language was clipped and staccato, each syllable pure in its integrity. Aubrey knew that Dr Tremaine must be extolling elements for duration and intensity, for range and for effect, but what *were* they? What *else* was he using to grapple and shape raw magic to his will?

Aubrey experienced it then, the not-quite-itch that was the connection between Dr Tremaine and him. It was both a physical and non-physical sensation, where he felt it as absence *and* presence. As the sorcerer completed his spell the feeling intensified and Aubrey, with his magical awareness, was jolted by the connection. When he concentrated, the rest of the office dimmed and the cord that ran from his chest to Dr Tremaine's became more solid and appreciable. It was still insubstantial, a softly glowing mirror shine, but it was the strongest he'd ever beheld it.

'Well, boy?' Dr Tremaine said and the sense of his words echoed along the cord, along with a taste of Dr Tremaine's feelings – not disdain, but an almost detached lack of concern. 'This is what has perturbed you for these months. Unremarkable, really.'

In the unreality of their shared experience, Aubrey's voice sounded hollow in his own ears. 'It's like the golden cord, the one that –'

'The one that held your body and soul together before whatever lucky accident has recently reunited them.'

Aubrey was about to contradict that hotly when he realised it was true. It *had* been a lucky accident. Despite all his research and clandestine experiments, he hadn't been able to reunite his body and soul, and it was only the clash of two aspects of Dr Tremaine's magic – the neutralised Beccaria Cage and the magical residue from Tremaine's weather magic – that had welded his body and soul together.

'The language you used.' Aubrey stopped, but his curiosity wouldn't allow him not to go on. 'I didn't recognise it.'

Dr Tremaine took his attention from the connector, glancing at Aubrey for an instant. 'You wouldn't have. It's new.'

'What?'

'Your Professor Mansfield has been very helpful. And that Lanka Ravi chap.'

Aubrey was taken aback. Professor Mansfield, his missing lecturer in Ancient Languages. Lanka Ravi, the mysterious genius. 'Wait. You're telling me that Ravi isn't dead?'

Dr Tremaine slowly moved the magnifying glass along the cord and didn't look up. 'It was a useful story. It prevented people looking for him.'

'No. He and Professor Mansfield wouldn't help you. They wouldn't.'

'I'm very persuasive. Especially when I know about their families.'

Ruthless perhaps wasn't the correct word for Dr Tremaine, Aubrey realised. Ruthless implied an ability to countermand one's conscience. He had serious doubts about Dr Tremaine having had a conscience to begin with.

'You're constructing an artificial language.'

'You're not altogether dim, are you?' Dr Tremaine grunted and tossed the magnifying glass on the desk with a dreadful lack of care. 'The Ritual of the Way has failed in the past because of the failures of language. Even the purest, most ancient languages have inherent ambiguities. My magical language, although based on a selection of ancient tongues, will be free of that.'

Aubrey's head whirled with the implications of this. Professor Mansfield had been abducted, with the Rashid

Stone. And add Lanka Ravi. Dr Tremaine had a pair of formidable intelligences at his call.

'Now,' Dr Tremaine said. 'Quiet. Don't interrupt me again.'

The room continued to shimmer and shift around them. It was as if Dr Tremaine and he were the only real parts of a tiny universe, the rest being merely shadows, devoid of colour and substance, hints of reality rather than reality itself. To Aubrey's pseudo-sight, the office walls became ghostly. The desk, the filing cabinets, the letter racks were translucent, shadows of what they were.

Dr Tremaine ignored him. The great sorcerer was frowning, a hand rubbing his chin, as he studied the connection. His magical awareness was fixed on it in his efforts to understand its composition. The ferocity of his attention was staggering, as if simply by an act of will he could parse the connection, apprehend all its constituents, grasp its making, and immediately concoct improvements and devise other applications.

Aubrey hesitated. This was his chance, but he couldn't bring himself to move. Part of him simply wanted to stand back and watch the master magician at work. Some of this was selfish, simply wanting to learn from a unique practitioner, but most of it was born of automatic respect.

Magicians respected magicians, colleague to colleague, initiate to initiate. Good magic was approved of, clever spell casting was appreciated, articles were published in journals to spread knowledge. Of course there was jealousy, but the field of magic was renowned for its collegiality. Magicians readily shared findings, understanding that a group approach in the exploration of magical fields was best.

In Dr Tremaine, Aubrey had the chance to watch a once-in-a-lifetime magician – perhaps the magician of the ages – so he stood and watched when he may have been able to do something.

Dr Tremaine's fearsome scowl increased, if anything. He reached out, hand extended, and grasped the insubstantial connection.

Aubrey gasped and stumbled forward, his eyes wide. It was impossible – such connections were intangible – but Dr Tremaine had actually taken *hold* of it.

'Steady, boy,' Dr Tremaine growled absently, as he raised the connector to his eyes to examine it more closely. Aubrey's amazement was nudged up another notch when Dr Tremaine actually sniffed at it before looking thoughtful.

The tug of the connector had set Aubrey back like a solid blow in the midriff. It had reminded him, uncomfortably, of the constant battle he'd had to hold his body and soul together. The wrenching hadn't been just a physical thing. It was a spiritual buffet, something that affected him on a level beyond the mere bodily.

He had an idea. So simple, it was, and yet it was only because of his unique situation that he could see it.

Connection. The whole self-evident truth about connections was that they work in two ways. If Aubrey could duplicate Dr Tremaine's extraordinary handling of their connection, he may be able to do more than knock him off balance.

Aubrey had something in his favour. Out of the battling to keep his body and soul connected, he had a special appreciation of the phenomenon – and because he'd suffered, he had a tolerance for the discomfort involved.

So if anything he did rebounded on him, he was sure he would be able to endure it – and his hope was that Dr Tremaine may not be so inured.

The connector was about the thickness of a fire hose. It hovered between them, undulating slightly as if weightless, and with a ghostliness about it that signalled its preternatural qualities. It was like an object that had moved while being photographed, making it slightly blurred. Nonetheless, it was familiar. It belonged to him. It had an *Aubreyness* about it that he could feel, but it was mixed with the overpowering presence of Dr Tremaine.

He recalled that Dr Tremaine hadn't uttered a spell before he grasped the connector. This suggested that the ability to do so must be inherent, part of the natural expression of the connection itself and the people it connected.

Aubrey glanced at Dr Tremaine. He had lowered the connector and had placed both hands in front of him. He was rubbing them together slowly. His eyes didn't move from contemplating the connector itself.

Slowly, Aubrey shifted his stance. Tiny, tiny movements, nothing to concern anyone, and soon he was turned sideways to Dr Tremaine, his body shielding what he was about to do next.

Without taking his eyes from the connector, he extended his left hand. Delicately, he touched it with his fingers – and had to steel himself against the flood of sensation. Mingled with a welter of confusion, he had the sensation of utter familiarity. This was something that belonged to him, as recognisable as his own nose.

He grasped the connector more firmly, barely daring to breathe. Then, with his other hand, he scratched his head.

Such an innocent movement, he hoped that Dr Tremaine – if he were aware at all – would see it for what it was. Harmless. Not threatening in any way – so Aubrey could drop his hand from his head to join the other one grasping the connector.

At that, Dr Tremaine looked up – in time to see Aubrey to seize the connector and heave.

Aubrey had steadied himself, ready for the effort, and he put his back into it, dragging for all he was worth. Dr Tremaine was taken completely by surprise. He bellowed, pulled forward and entirely off balance. Before he could use his extraordinary reflexes to recover himself, though, Aubrey snapped the connector like a whip.

A great curve hurtled along the connector and Dr Tremaine's forward staggering motion was instantly arrested. He was flung backward and crashed into the wall behind him.

The connector dissolved – and Aubrey had his chance.

The exposed beam that divided the room in half was integral to supporting the weight of the two storeys on top of it. Using the most powerful magic he could summon quickly, Aubrey altered its dimensions. In an instant, the beam became a single point – and thereby incapable of holding the weight of the building above it.

So, as Aubrey leaped for the door, the building collapsed.

The thunderous crash behind him sent a billow of dust through the door and a gust of displaced air that threw him off his feet, but by then he had enough momentum to roll, come to his feet, and continue running. He hunched his shoulders as he went, fully expecting a shot or a bolt of snarling magic, but it was from in front that he had to worry, as four Holmland troops rushed around the corner ahead of him.

Without losing a beat he kept running. 'Hurry!' he cried in Holmlandish and pointing back the way he'd come. 'The ceiling collapsed! People are trapped!'

When in a place of fear and doubt, he thought, *a man who is certain is bound to be followed.* The guards didn't spare him a glance. They hurried past, eager to do their duty.

Then the lights went out and Aubrey cheered.

Not the best idea, he thought as he heard voices shouting nearby. Drawing attention to oneself by cheering in the middle of a disaster was the sort of thing that attracted attention, but the darkness – in this case – was his friend.

He set off, with Caroline on his mind. While he ran, a man on a much adapted, much disrupted mission, he helped matters by shouting 'Fire!', 'Intruders!' and 'Beer!' at regular intervals whenever a startled face showed itself.

Some time later – five minutes? ten? – he parked himself in a closed doorway for a moment, to catch his breath and appraise the situation while confused Holmlanders rushed up and down, shouting. He fumbled in his pocket for Caroline's ring. While her efforts to get it to him were eminently practical in terms of rope slicing, he had another, equally practical, use for it.

He could use it to find her.

Once outside, he had a moment of wonder when he saw the results of his spell. In the light from the other wings and the rising sun, he could see that the entire eastern end of the administration wing had collapsed into a mass of rubble. Giant wooden beams protruded from the ruin of plaster, brick and tile. Water gushed from a lonely pipe, while dozens of Holmlanders ran about in shock.

The enspelled ring led Aubrey to a room in the original building, high up in one of the towers. A short corridor, four cells, two opening on either side, and two guards who Aubrey was sure were nervously wondering what the uproar was all about. From the concealment of the stairwell, Aubrey cast a small spell that shifted the air away from the faces of each of the guards, thanks to the Law of Transference. The eyes of one rolled up, then the other, and they slid down the wall, unconscious. Aubrey cancelled the spell and used the keys from the belt of one of the guards to free Caroline.

She was ready, standing at the door, alert and ravishing in her intensity. 'Aubrey.'

'Caroline.'

'You're unharmed?'

'Yes. And you?'

'I'm well, thank you.'

'That's splendid.'

With a touch of asperity, she raised an eyebrow. 'Now we've established our excellent standard of health, may we escape?'

'Ah. One moment.' Aubrey held out her ring. 'It's yours. I used it to find you.'

An odd expression crossed Caroline's face. Aubrey's heart expanded, then contracted in an aching motion. She shook her head. 'Keep it. You never know.'

'Good idea.'

'Speaking of ideas, have you a plan for getting out of here?'

He grinned. 'Oh, you're going to like this one.'

Thirty-four

'SO WE'RE SAFE FOR THE MOMENT,' CAROLINE SAID, HER back against the concrete. She peered through the elephant's eyes at the chaos, firelight adding a weird orange cast to the proceedings. Near the ruin, Aubrey could see the baron raging about, trying to restore order while organising the troops to fight the fire that Aubrey's hasty wall removal had brought about. 'What's your plan?'

'George, that generator won't be fixed soon?'

George grinned. 'I shouldn't say so. Not with the amount of ironmongery Sophie managed to get into the turbine.'

'While you fought off three of their operators,' Sophie said admiringly. She had taken up position next to the still-unconscious Théo. 'I did what I could.'

'I don't expect the fourth fellow was expecting your elbow jab to his forehead. I'm sure he's regretting grabbing you from behind like that.'

Sophie rubbed the aforementioned elbow. 'We dragged them all from the building before the generator expired,' she explained. 'I'm glad.'

So was Aubrey. He had no interest in slaughter. He quickly told George and Sophie what they'd found in the warehouse. Their faces hardened when he explained how the brains of the wounded soldiers had been harnessed to both animate the creatures and make them so formidable.

'We can't let this go on,' George said.

'It shan't,' Caroline said. 'Aubrey has taken care of that.'

'Good show. But we still need to report this back to Albion.'

'And so we shall,' Aubrey promised.

'And getting out of here will take magic?' Caroline prodded.

'Animation magic,' Aubrey said. 'George, do you remember when we rescued Major Saltin from that crippled dirigible?'

'Close shave, that one. Especially when our ornithopter nearly went down. You had to turn it into a bird.'

'Precisely,' Aubrey said. That sort of animation magic wasn't commonplace, and Aubrey wouldn't even have attempted it if not for the desperate circumstances. *Which we once more seem to be in.*

'Oh,' Caroline said. 'I have a feeling we may be entering the realm of the ridiculous.'

Aubrey rubbed his hands together. The encounter with Dr Tremaine had sapped him, but he really had no choice. 'The Law of Similarity states that things that are alike can be encouraged to assert their likeness, given the correct application of magic. Combine it with the Law of Familiarity, and the possibilities are endless.'

'An ornithopter is like a bird,' Sophie said. 'So it became a bird.'

'Something like a bird, anyway.' Aubrey said. 'I think I've ironed out a few wrinkles with that spell. Caroline, can you please keep an eye on what's going on out there?'

Aubrey had been constructing the spell ever since the plan came to him, so he was ready. The spell was in Etruscan. He was particularly careful with the elements for range and dimensionality. This was a strain for he was encompassing multiple objects at once, but he managed it through sheer grit and finished with a discreet signature element.

'Good Lord.' George was looking over Caroline's shoulder. 'The zebra. It moved.'

'The crocodile did too.' Caroline turned to Aubrey. 'You've animated the other concrete animals.'

'Look at the penguin!' Sophie cried.

Suddenly, they were thrown sideways. Aubrey was ready and caught himself with a hand against the concrete flanks of the elephant. 'Not just the others. I thought I may as well go the whole hog, as our colonial cousins might say.'

Another lurch. The concrete walls trembled. The elephant shook, and then it jolted, with one great thump. Immediately, it rolled back a little, then it rocked again, side to side, before tottering forward.

With ponderous footsteps, the concrete elephant began to walk.

Aubrey beamed at the success of his spell and he caught Caroline's eye. She grinned at him. 'The last elephant ride

I had was in Siam,' she said, 'but I was on the outside, not the inside.'

Aubrey hunched up so he could better look forward through the beast's eyes. After making sure Théo was secure, Sophie huddled close to George and all four of them could see the pandemonium that Aubrey's spell had produced.

All the concrete animals were moving. The giraffe was marching slowly and stiff-leggedly. It was as if it were a toy and a cosmically sized but invisible child's hand were propelling it in clumsy motion. Soldiers were dashing away on either side as it blundered until it collided with the remaining wall of the administration wing. It swung from side to side for a moment, still marching directly into the wall, before it slid aside and began tromping south. One flank dragged against the building, wrenching window frames apart and creating a screeching din. Several soldiers fired rifles at it, more as a gesture of outrage than with any prospect of doing it harm. Bullets ricocheted from its concrete hide and hummed off in dangerously unpredictable directions.

The concrete crocodile was swarming directly through the garden, with rather sinuous grace for a concrete creature. Its tail swayed from side to side as it scattered Holmlanders without actually connecting with any of them. The way it snapped its jaws, regular as clockwork, was encouragement enough to flee the area and many of the soldiers took up the invitation, backing away or simply turning tail and running.

The gorilla, the tiger, the lion and the polar bear were all in motion, adding their particular beastly overlay to the bizarre scene. Outlined against the flames of the burning building, the tiger looked as if it had leaped from a furnace. The lion tottered forward, demolishing a lorry that had been full of terrified troops who scattered at the beast's approach. The polar bear bumped into the giraffe and sent them both off on an angle toward the factory, which caused more panic. The gorilla was asserting its apeness by attempting to scale one of the towers on the original building. A radio mast was clearly in its sights.

The penguin merely stood in place, rocking from side to side. Aubrey wished he could nip over and give it a push to get it started.

'I say, old man.' George steadied himself as the elephant crushed a large metal bin with a dreadful squealing noise. Its motion was a violent rocking, like a small boat on a storm-tossed sea. 'How do you steer this thing?'

'Steer?' Aubrey said vaguely. The elephant was heading directly for the solitary tree at the end of the garden: a slender cypress. 'Ah, yes. Steer.'

This was going to be tricky. Aubrey hadn't built in any fine control. Such a thing would be a challenge, for it would mean organising the legs on either side to take larger or smaller steps to turn left or right, depending on which direction . . .

'Hold on!' George cried.

The elephant didn't strike the tree head-on, something for which Aubrey was grateful, after he picked himself up. It glanced off and was sent in a new direction toward the barracks – barracks which had been partially reduced to splinters by the passage of the crocodile, which was now in the process of ploughing through the chain mesh fence, and the tiger, which looked as if it were limping. Nearby, one of the guard towers had collapsed, thanks to being rammed by the zebra, which had since veered off in a large spiral and was circling the factory, homing in on the gap in the warehouse where the train was waiting. This was apparent to someone in relative command, for the zebra was under a concerted fusillade of rifle fire – not that it made any difference. One soldier, braver than the rest, had sent a speeding lorry at the zebra, leaping out just before it collided. The zebra's off foreleg buckled for a moment, but then it swung and the lorry was thrown aside like an insect.

Aubrey turned his attention to the barracks, now only a few yards away. Two guardsmen stood in front of the huts, waving their arms as if they could scare the elephant away. When they realised the concrete beast wasn't so easily distracted, they flung themselves aside at the last minute and the elephant crashed into the side of the nearest hut.

This time, the four friends were ready and braced themselves, George sparing a hand to steady Théo in place. They were shaken but not hurt. The elephant slowed a little, but then it pushed forward. Over the sounds of small-arms fire, shouting and the splintering of timber came the deep-bellied groan of a building surrendering the struggle. The entire long side of the hut gave up and collapsed inward, which meant that the corrugated iron roof slid backward, helping to tear the far wall from its foundations.

The elephant was unperturbed by this and crunched on through timber and glass, leaving destruction in its path.

Ahead was the fence, partly demolished by the crocodile. Away from the buildings, the elephant was ignored as it broached the fence and bumbled onward toward the woods to the south of the complex.

'Shall we?' Caroline said, indicating the hatch.

It was a scramble, but they laughed with a giddy combination of relief and triumph, clinging to each other and helping as the elephant lurched from side to side. Aubrey held onto an ear and lowered Caroline, then helped George with Sophie's comatose brother. Sophie laughed as George swung her down before he leapt to her side. For a moment, Aubrey paused, swaying with the lumbering gait of the concrete creature, feeling like a captain abandoning his ship. Then he, too, laughed and tumbled to a soft, grassy landing.

They looked back toward Baron von Grolman's factory. The administration wing was still on fire, and it was spreading to the factory. The tiger was butting up against the train on one side, while the zebra had rebounded from it and was making toward the gatehouse. It was gathering the most attention, as a crushed and breached gatehouse was not what a secure facility needed. The gorilla had managed to climb the radio mast, but it had toppled under the weight of the concrete ape, which had plummeted right through the roof of the old building.

'Where's the crocodile?' Aubrey asked.

'Over there,' Caroline pointed, 'on the west. It's making for the town.'

'It will probably fall in the river first,' said Sophie and Aubrey was saddened by this, but he brightened when he thought of the concrete animal, gamely ploughing along at the bottom of the river, not needing to breathe, making headway for as long as the spell lasted.

The other animals were wreaking havoc, in a way that Aubrey could only have dreamed of. Both wings of the original buildings were ablaze. Half of the barracks were demolished. The factory and warehouse, however, were battered but not damaged in any significant way.

Without warning, the original building exploded.

Aubrey threw an arm up in front of his face, but was still blinded for an instant. George let out an oath. Behind them, the elephant rocked a little but then resumed its inexorable progress toward the woods.

All the original buildings were now on fire, and a patter of debris fell about them, testimony to the force of the explosion. 'A fuel tank?' Caroline wondered aloud.

'Perhaps a store of the enhanced coal,' Aubrey suggested.

'Maybe the gorilla fell on it,' George said.

They reached the trees. Aubrey squinted. Dark figures were flitting through the trees. 'Company,' he muttered.

'Welcome company?' George peered at the woods.

Aubrey smiled. 'It's Katya and her crew.'

Thirty-five

THEY GATHERED IN THE SHADE OF THE WOODS WHILE Théo recovered.

When he woke, he was pale and red-eyed, but quickly took in his surroundings – and was shocked to find his sister there. 'Sophie?'

'Théo.' Kneeling beside him, she was on the verge of tears, but took his hand and gathered herself. 'I came for you.'

He stared about him. 'Who are these people?'

Sophie made the introductions. 'They helped rescue you from that place.'

'But I am now a deserter.' Théo frowned. 'Who gave you the right to do this? I made up my mind and you think you know better?'

'Théo,' Sophie said wearily and Aubrey knew that he was seeing the latest in a long history of sibling arguments.

'Holmland is the future.' Théo sat up and his voice grew shrill. 'The Holmland army has none of your aristocratic preferment! It is one of opportunity.'

'Steady on, fellow,' George said. 'You were just about to have the opportunity of having your brain scooped out and popped into a clankenmonster.'

Théo stared. 'What are you saying?'

It took the rest of the hour under the watchful eye of Katya before Théo was convinced, and it was only Aubrey's revelation of Dr Tremaine's actions in sending Elspeth to lead Théo astray that tipped the balance. Along the way he went through denial and then sullenness before a dawning realisation of the fate he'd narrowly avoided came home to him.

'Yvette,' he cried, his head in his hands. 'Yvette.'

Aubrey couldn't help it. He had to probe to satisfy the gnawing curiosity he had. 'Yvette was the young woman who introduced you to politics? And suggested your joining the Holmlanders?'

'I loved her,' he sobbed. 'She loved me.'

'I'm sure,' Aubrey murmured. Elspeth Mattingly – if that was her name – had done a fine job on Théo. Aubrey marked her down as a dangerous operative. He flinched a little, understanding only too well how Théo would have been attracted to her.

Théo wasn't an unintelligent lad, Aubrey decided as he watched this slow dawning. Somewhat petulant, perhaps, and unwilling to accept that his sister loved him dearly, risking her own life to save his, but Aubrey thought he detected the frustration of thwarted ambition in the young man's arguing.

He turned away and watched the elephant trundling

off to the north. Aubrey waved, not without regrets. 'Goodbye, noble beast, you served us well.'

'It's concrete, Aubrey,' Caroline said.

Aubrey affected a downcast face. 'I know. That's why it's so hard.' He paused. 'Saying goodbye, I mean.'

'Hmm.'

After Théo had lapsed into sombre reflection, Katya affirmed that they had been responsible for the final explosion in the complex. A few of the more active Enlightened Ones had infiltrated the drains weeks ago – the Enlightened Ones having considerable experience with drains – and laid caches of high explosive.

'You won't let Madame Zelinka know?' she said. 'She holds to the code of neutrality.'

'But you don't?' Aubrey asked.

'Some of us have long memories. Rodolfo always said never forget.'

'Rodolfo?' Aubrey smiled. 'You do know Rodolfo!'

'Rodolfo is my cousin. He is in hiding. It was his brother who assassinated Duke Josef.'

'Oh.' The murky world of Goltan politics was almost impossible to fathom. 'But wasn't Rodolfo *against* assassination? Wasn't he trying to stop such actions?'

'He is his brother's brother. That is enough for the authorities.'

'Who are now mostly pro-Holmland, since the invasion,' Sophie pointed out.

The discussion on the way to the farmhouse didn't make the Goltan situation much clearer to Aubrey, and he only half-listened as it bounced about him. He had other matters on his mind.

Madame Zelinka and von Stralick were sitting at the

kitchen table. The Holmlander jumped to his feet when he saw them. While the other Enlightened Ones crowded around cheering – and after Théo had been introduced – von Stralick stood with his hands on his hips and shook his head. 'I do not believe it. You are all alive.'

Chairs were provided for Aubrey and the others. Mugs of tea were thrust on them. Aubrey savoured the aroma for a moment with closed eyes.

'Hugo was sure he had seen the last of you,' Madame Zelinka said. 'He wanted to go after you but I persuaded him to wait.' She paused. 'Then I wanted to leave, but he persuaded me to stay.'

'But now . . .' Von Stralick spread his hands.

'Now we need to get back to Albion and report,' Caroline said.

'We have plenty to tell them,' George said. Then he blinked. 'Sophie. I suppose you'll take Théo home?'

Sophie, anguished, looked at her brother. 'Théo?'

Théo studied the floor for a moment, his hands behind his back, before answering. 'I think I would like that.'

'We can cross the border together,' Caroline said, 'but then we must go on without you. We need to get to Albion.'

'George?' Sophie's voice and gaze were steady.

George looked at her, then at Aubrey, then at Caroline, before looking at Sophie again. 'Can you bring your family to Trinovant? They may be safer there if Holmland crashes through.'

Sophie brightened, and her hand stole out and took her brother's.

'I will do that,' Théo said firmly. 'They must not stay in Gallia. If Holmland invades, Father will be in great danger.'

George scowled. 'Perhaps I should go with you . . .'

Aubrey interrupted. He put a hand to his chest and rubbed it. 'Dr Tremaine is heading west. Further into Holmland.'

'What?' Caroline said. 'How do you know that?'

Aubrey looked down. Since Dr Tremaine had undertaken his investigation of the connection in the factory, it had been stronger. He shook his head. No – not stronger. He was more *conscious* of it, but it was maddeningly erratic in its presence, almost disappearing at times before reappearing, clear and strong, for short periods of time. 'I felt it. The connector. It was stronger there for a minute.' He concentrated. 'He's about ten miles away, moving fast.' He looked at all of them. 'I have to go after him.'

Naturally, in a room of opinionated individuals, this was like dropping a stone in a pond full of ducks.

'You can't!' Caroline cried, louder than the others. 'We have to report to the Directorate.'

'I must.'

George glanced sharply at him then, and Aubrey was sure he'd noticed the pronoun, but Caroline went on before he could say anything. 'Aubrey, you're being ridiculous!'

'I don't think so.' He rubbed his brow. He was tugged in all directions, and had to resist. 'It's Father, and the country.'

George frowned. 'There's something else, isn't there?'

Trust George to see to the heart of the matter. 'It's the Ritual of the Way. I'm sure that Dr Tremaine is getting close to having it ready for the first great battle.' He explained about the artificial magical language Tremaine was developing. 'If I can stop that, I may be able to stop his plans entirely. Without his driving it, the Holmland war effort will fall apart.' He sighed. 'And I can't let Professor Mansfield languish in his clutches.'

Caroline was breathing very deeply, her arms crossed, giving every sign of being on the edge of a fearful rage. 'If you don't come back to Albion with us and those photographs are made public, your name will be ruined.'

'I've thought about that. It's why I need you to convince Father to disown me before they do.'

Uproar, again, as he explained about the photographs and what he wanted to do.

After a babble of shock and discord subsided, Aubrey shrugged wearily. 'It's the only thing to do, strategically. Of course, I'd prefer that he knows the truth, but he must keep that private. As Prime Minister, he must declare me a traitor.'

More protests, louder than ever. Aubrey waited. 'It's the only way. A pre-emptive move like this will shore up his position as a strong leader and forestall any accusation of his covering up for me.' He shrugged. 'He *must* do it before the newspapers receive a mysterious envelope full of photographs. If he denounces me first, it will give him enough to survive any calls for his resignation.' He held up both hands. 'Caroline, Father will listen to you. Convince him. George? You too. Send a telegraph message if you can, but talking him face to face will be necessary, I'd imagine.'

'But Aubrey!' Caroline said, her voice catching in her throat. Then she stopped herself and took a deep breath. 'You're right, of course. Sophie, we can organise our journey so we find your parents first.'

Sophie had been following this carefully. 'Théo will come with us. He will help.'

Théo nodded.

Von Stralick, too, had been watching carefully. 'This looks like a time for some drastic rearranging.' He stood, then took Madame Zelinka's hand. He kissed it. 'My dear, I have to take leave of you. It seems I have an opportunity to even the score with that madman Tremaine.'

Madame Zelinka was grave. 'As it must be. We will be reunited.'

'Of course. Now, Fitzwilliam, you will need assistance to get to Tremaine's stronghold.'

Aubrey rocked on his heels. 'You know where it is?'

'I know where it *was*. I was not a valued member of the Holmland intelligence services without learning a few things. One of those was to accumulate little bits of information that might come in handy later. To protect oneself, of course.'

'Hugo. I'd be glad of any help. But we should leave right away.'

'Naturally.'

George stood, then took Aubrey's hand and shook it. 'Take care, old man.'

Sophie went to George's side and linked her arm with his. 'Thank you, Aubrey, for your help. I am grateful.'

Madame Zelinka unrolled a map on the table and conferred with her Enlightened Ones. Aubrey tried to see what they were pointing at but Caroline caught his eye. 'Aubrey. Can I speak to you outside?'

Aubrey would have been lying if he'd said he agreed without trepidation. Caroline led the way without looking back, while he followed, finding that whatever he did, his hands were out of place. They were awkward by his sides, uncomfortable in his pockets, strange when his arms were crossed on his chest. He briefly wondered if should try simply holding them up and surrendering when he realised that Caroline had stopped and was leaning against the ramshackle dairy, studying him evenly.

'Aubrey.' She nodded. 'Aubrey.'

'Caroline,' he said carefully, reluctantly engaging in this over-obvious identification exchange.

'Aubrey,' she said a third time. Then she took three rapid steps and, before he could move, she seized him by the shoulders, then she clasped both hands on the sides of his head.

She kissed him soundly.

'There,' she said, or may have. Aubrey's hearing had gone strange. The world was coming to him through the sounds of giant bells and rushing winds. In his unsteady vision Caroline gazed at him, utterly, utterly controlled despite the moistness of her eyes and the quivering of her lips. He almost couldn't bear it when she pushed back a stray wisp of her hair. 'Now, do what you have to do and then come back. No silly nonsense, you hear? Or I'll have to come and get you.'

Then she turned on her heel and marched in the direction of the farmhouse.

Aubrey put out a hand to prop himself up against the dairy. The timber was rough, needed paint, was warm in the sun. He understood, then, that his self-imposed mission to win Caroline had been taken out of his hands. He couldn't decide if it was inoperative, lost, or merely ill-founded in the first place. Then he remembered the kiss and knew that all along, while he thought he knew what he was doing, he had actually had no idea at all.

Von Stralick was discreetly lingering at the door to the farmhouse. Aubrey gestured to him. 'We should go.'

'Of course. We have a mission to attend to.'

Aubrey sighed and thought of lost opportunities. 'Don't call it that, Hugo. Please don't call it that.'

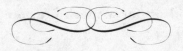

About the
Author

Michael Pryor has published more than twenty fantasy books and over forty short stories, from literary fiction to science fiction to slapstick humour. Michael has been shortlisted six times for the Aurealis Awards (including for *Blaze of Glory* and *Heart of Gold*), has been nominated for a Ditmar award and longlisted for the Gold Inky award, and five of his books have been Children's Book Council of Australia Notable Books (including *Word of Honour* and *Time of Trial*). He is currently writing the final book in the Laws of Magic series.

For more information about Michael and his books, please visit www.michaelpryor.com.au.

Read on for a sneak preview of

The Laws of Magic Book Six: Hour of Need

'*Y*OU'RE THE ONE WHO BETRAYED US!' HE CROAKED. 'I always knew it was you!'

Aubrey flinched as the accusation echoed on the rock walls that had been their home for almost a month. Slowly, he climbed to his feet, trying not to startle the wild-eyed Holmlander. A restraining spell was on his lips but he was unwilling to use magic unless he had to, not with the magic detectors around the estate below, so close, so sensitive.

'Traitor!' von Stralick snarled at him. 'You, and the rest of them! Everywhere!'

'I'm not a traitor, Hugo.'

'Traitor.' Clawing at the air like an animal, Hugo von Stralick, the ex-Holmland spy, advanced. 'We have photographs.'

Aubrey hesitated, and was dismayed to see von Stralick had a rock in his hand. 'Put it down, Hugo. You're sick.'

'Hah! Sick, am I?'

A grunt, then the stone thumped into the wall not far from Aubrey. He sighed. Von Stralick may have been sick, but enough was enough. Aubrey caught him around the waist and shuffled him backward. A feeble blow or two landed on Aubrey's back, then von Stralick faltered, groaning. His knees buckled and Aubrey had to move quickly to avoid falling on top of him.

'Traitor,' von Stralick murmured as he lay stretched out on the rocky floor of the cave.

Aubrey groped for his electric torch to find that the Holmlander's eyes had closed. His face was pale, a disturbing chalky-white. He was shivering, too, and when Aubrey touched his forehead he was dismayed at how hot it was.

Alarmed, he dragged von Stralick back to the pile of tree branches that was his bed.

Aubrey arranged him as comfortably as he could, picked up the notebook he'd been using to work on his spellcraft from where he'd accidentally kicked it during the struggle, then sat by his side. The Holmlander's lips moved, a meaningless stream of half-words and names, as if he were alternately reading from a street directory and a poorly compiled dictionary. Aubrey had thought von Stralick had been getting better, but it had obviously been wishful thinking. The fever and the delirium hadn't broken. For nearly two weeks, von Stralick had been ill, and Aubrey was now starting to worry that the ex-Holmland spy was going to die.

What had begun as a mission to find Dr Tremaine's estate and to confront the rogue sorcerer had become frustration after frustration. Careful initial observation had been necessary, for Aubrey wasn't about to move on the rogue sorcerer without meticulous preparation, but after von Stralick had collapsed with fever, Aubrey had no choice but to nurse his companion. As von Stralick's illness worsened, this meant that Aubrey had much time on his hands – but using this rare gift, he had formulated a daring move that could end with war with a single stroke.

The crag that overlooked Dr Tremaine's retreat was high in the Alemmani Mountains. It caught the wind, no matter from what direction it came, and it constantly reminded Aubrey that this place was the natural home of ice and snow, and probably bears and wolves. 'Forbidding' was possibly the kindest thing that could be said about it, but its dramatic outlook probably appealed to the rogue sorcerer. That, and the relative isolation.

Their three-hundred-mile cross-country scramble had taken them more than a fortnight. They'd become expert in avoiding Holmland troops, but Aubrey had come to understand that 'living off the land' sounded altogether grander than the reality, which was actually spending hours scrounging for food and water. He never thought he would have seen the day when his mouth watered at the prospect of the larger of the two grubs they'd found. Occasionally, while pawing at the leaf mould in the darkness of woods, he'd wished he'd studied mycology instead of magic, just so he could have known the difference between the edible mushrooms and the attractive ones that drive people mad.

Dr Tremaine's stronghold was a local landmark. From its position right on the edge of an impressive granite cliff, it had a view over the mountains and the woods that surrounded it, then the open expanses of farmland. The city of Bardenford was perhaps twenty miles away, clearly seen by day or by night. The retreat wasn't cut off, however. A tarmac road had been rammed through the forest, switching backwards and forwards up the face of the mountain until it arrived at the gatehouse. The road was wide enough for supply lorries, and comfortable enough for town cars – including that of the Chancellor, who had visited twice since Aubrey and von Stralick had been there.

Within the walls of the estate were a number of buildings. One clearly housed an electrical generator, from the thick cables and the unceasing whine. Another sported a tall chimney and could be a foundry or furnace of some kind. The purpose of the scatter of other structures – clearly newer than the main house, and perhaps temporary – was uncertain, but Aubrey wouldn't have minded wagering that at least one was a laboratory. The others? Living quarters? Workshops? Prisons?

On their journey, four days after leaving Stalsfrieden behind, it had been von Stralick who had insisted on finding some news. While Aubrey hid in what turned out to be a mosquito-infested bog, von Stralick, after doing his best to improve his bedraggled appearance, strolled into the reasonably sized town of Pagen and bought a newspaper.

Aubrey had been sickened by the triumphant

headlines that crowed over his father's humiliation. The more sensationalist newspapers were full of glee at the Prime Minister's disgrace. More correctly, of course, it was Aubrey's disgrace: 'the traitor son of Albion'. He took some solace in that it confirmed that Caroline and George had arrived home safely, because Sir Darius had implemented Aubrey's plan: he had denounced him before the Holmlanders could publish their photographs.

Aubrey was now, officially, the blackest of black villains in Albion. He was the son of privilege who had turned his back on everything the nation had done for him. He could almost hear the cries for his blood, the press running riot; he only hoped that his father's pre-emptive action meant that he could stand firm, positioning himself as the wronged father of an ungrateful son, and that the public would feel sorry for him.

Aubrey wasn't confident, however, that this would mean that he would be treated as a hero in Holmland. Traitors rarely were and, besides, he was sure that Dr Tremaine had him on a list of people of interest. If he dared to make himself public, a cell was no doubt waiting for him somewhere secret and unofficial.

Or perhaps a more dire fate would be his, to judge from what he'd glimpsed of the activities of Dr Tremaine's retreat.

Aubrey glanced at von Stralick, who had ceased his muttered outpouring and appeared to be sleeping more soundly. The Holmlander's condition had begun as a simple cold, a few days after finding the cave in the crag. It had worsened gradually until he'd collapsed while on surveillance duty. In the ten days since then, Aubrey had been dividing his time between tending him, finding food and water, and working on the spells that could win the war.

Cut off as they were, the lack of information frustrated Aubrey. He was desperate to know what was going on. What about the siege of Divodorum? What were George and Caroline up to? Sophie and Théo?

At least he had some hint about the success of his sabotage at Baron von Grolman's factory in Stalsfrieden. Yesterday, a lorry had made a canvas-shrouded delivery. When it unloaded, Aubrey had been instantly on his feet.

Three Holmland soldiers were needed to manhandle the ominous metal shape from the back of the lorry. They stood it upright on a trolley and it towered over them. It took all their effort, but the monstrous golem-machine hybrid was eventually wheeled into one of the temporary buildings to the north of the main house.

Aubrey had been sure that his efforts to destroy the hideous creations, back in Stalsfrieden, had been successful. The contagious spell would infect golem after golem, embedded as it was in the enhanced coal that was the vital, energising element in the creatures. If the spell hadn't been successful, Dr Tremaine would have hundreds of ghastly mechanised soldiers ready to storm through Allied lines and lead a Holmland assault on Gallia.

But why had a single mechanised golem been brought to Dr Tremaine's retreat?

Movement below had caught Aubrey's eye and, when he had the binoculars focused again, he saw Dr Tremaine striding across from the main house and entering the building where the mechanised golem had been taken.

A tense hour later, Dr Tremaine had shouldered through

one of the gates at the rear of the main building, his arms full of metalwork. He strode to the edge of the cliff and, with one disgusted motion, flung the pieces wide. They fell in a glittering arc, but Aubrey had time to see a box-like head and what was unmistakably a stubby chimney.

Aubrey was relieved. To judge by Dr Tremaine's displeasure, it appeared as if Aubrey's spell had worked. The rogue sorcerer had little patience with anything that didn't live up to his expectations. Having failed a test, the golem suffered the consequences.

In between tending to von Stralick and working on the raft of interlocking spells that he hoped would achieve his goal, more than once his mind had drifted to Caroline and the way she'd farewelled him after the Stalsfrieden mission. He'd examined it from a dozen different points of view, a *hundred* different points of view. He'd probed it, dissected it, weighed and analysed it. Then he'd abandoned any effort at a scientific approach and he began to alternate between wild optimism and unutterable pessimism, both states being totally resistant to evidence. With little effort, he was able to construe Caroline's actions as pity, as irritation, even as forgetfulness, before he'd veer around and start thinking they might be signs of actual affection. This being the conclusion he hoped for most, it was naturally the one he was quickest to discount.

Of course, he'd accepted that his mission – his personal mission to win Caroline – had gone by the board. Matters of the heart were out of his hands, overtaken by matters military and political. Out of his hands? He had to laugh at that, without much humour. As if matters of the heart were ever in his hands.

Wearily Aubrey put aside the spellcraft notebook. He rubbed his eyes, glanced at von Stralick, then at Dr Tremaine's retreat. Even at this time of night, it was alive with lights and activity. He reached for the surveillance notebook, checked his watch and made an entry, then flipped back through the pages of observations he'd made, just in case he could communicate them to the Directorate.

And just in case your spells don't work, a traitorous voice whispered at the back of his mind.

He lingered over the entries for the people who he'd seen brought to the stronghold. Aubrey had found it hard to believe the number of well-known magicians who were bundled into one of the outbuildings. He recognised Maud Connolly, Parvo Ahonen, Charles Beecher and a score or more other prominent theoreticians and scholars. None of them showed any signs of delight at being there, unless manacles and gags had suddenly become fashion items rather than devices of restraint.

This influx of magical practitioners and theoreticians was alarming, especially when Aubrey added Professor Mansfield and Lanka Ravi to their numbers. Dr Tremaine had mentioned that he had these two luminaries in his keeping, which meant that he was assembling a formidable array of magical talent, but to what end? Aubrey couldn't imagine many of them – the Albionites and Gallians, most obviously – cooperating with the ex-Sorcerer Royal. Was he simply removing them from the possibility of helping the allied cause?

It did explain the disappearances of prominent magical people over the previous few months, and Aubrey's record keeping could help the analysts who pondered these things. More intelligence, more information, pooled together, might throw up a conclusion.

Aubrey had even seen Professor Bromhead, Trismegistus chair of magic at the University of Greythorn for twenty years, when he was first brought to the complex, struggling and kicking. A few days later, Aubrey had seen him in a walled garden to the west of the complex. He'd been wandering about, attended by an armed guard. Aubrey hadn't recognised Bromhead at first and he had focused on the lonely figure simply because of a strange device attached to his face. It was a cross between a muzzle, a helmet and a clamp, a metal and wire contraption enveloping the man's head, but particularly strong around his mouth and jaw. After some careful focusing of the binoculars, Aubrey was finally able to make out who it was, and he understood that at least part of the function of the device was to stop Professor Bromhead from speaking – and to stop him from casting a spell.

Each of the savants who arrived – some in the middle of the night – appeared later in the walled garden, guarded and wearing the same cage, confirming their identity as magicians, even the ones who Aubrey didn't know by sight. Over the next weeks, they were taken on this exercise time for an hour every second day, but otherwise they were hidden away in the clutch of outbuildings to the east of the sprawling two-storey hunting lodge.

Over the month of Aubrey's enforced vigil, Dr Tremaine had come and gone, sometimes several times in one day, mostly driving himself in a bright red, open-topped roadster. Aubrey had come to recognise the scream of the motor as it hurtled along the road in a way no other driver dared. When Dr Tremaine was present, prominent

Holmlanders often visited. As well as the Chancellor, all of the Army High Command and the Navy Board were present two nights ago, only leaving well after midnight. Two hours later, Dr Tremaine had leaped into his roadster and shot down the road after them.

At times, Aubrey wondered if the man slept at all.

If Aubrey didn't understand what was happening in the retreat, he at least knew something – that Dr Tremaine used the formidable estate as a base and a site for magical operations of an as-yet-unspecified nature. The tell-tale wafts of magic that prickled Aubrey's magical senses were enough to let him know that.

Aubrey lifted von Stralick's head and held the canteen to his lips. Water dribbled out of his mouth, but Aubrey thought he swallowed a little. He sighed at the prospect of the water wasted, knowing he'd have to gather more, spending hours holding the canteen to the rock crevices to catch the remnants of the frequent rain that swept across the heights. When he was so close to finalising the construction of his spells, he hated losing time like that.

The weather was trying. In this northern part of Holmland, summer had hurried off the stage and autumn had well and truly taken its place. The nights had become decidedly chilly, the rain more frequent, the days noticeably shorter. None of this helped von Stralick's condition.

Aubrey studied von Stralick's face. The spy's teeth were bared as he shivered, and Aubrey decided he had no choice but to risk a gentle heat spell.

He'd been avoiding magic. With Dr Tremaine so close, he didn't want to do anything to alert the rogue sorcerer to their presence, not before he was ready to implement the spells he'd spent so much time over. With von Stralick this ill, however, it seemed as if he had little choice.

He composed himself and reworked a basic Thermal Magic spell, adjusting the parameters for location and dimension to encompass von Stralick's wasted frame. Aubrey tugged his filthy jacket around him as he took care with the intensity variable, too, to provide a gentle warmth rather than a roasting heat.

Von Stralick's shivering faded as the spell began to work. Aubrey nodded and ran a hand through his hair – hair that had long forgotten its military cut and was starting to resemble a shaggy pelt. He was remotely glad that the only human being in close proximity was insensible, for he was sure he smelled dreadful. If he looked anything like von Stralick's red-eyed, grimy, dishevelled appearance, he was ready to apply for a position as understudy to the Wild Man of Borneo.

Aubrey monitored the heat spell, and was pleased. Von Stralick had settled. His lips were still, his breathing steady. Aubrey chewed his lip for a moment, then touched the Holmlander's forehead. It was much cooler, and he allowed himself to hope that some sort of crisis had passed, and that he was able to cast magic without detection.

He picked up his spellcraft notebook. His pencil was worn to a stub, but the break from his magic preparation had been useful. He saw now that it was nearly finished.

LATE THE NEXT MORNING, BARELY BREATHING, AUBREY Fitzwilliam held Dr Tremaine in the sights of the Oberndorf rifle. The rogue sorcerer was perfectly positioned, standing on the road outside the gates of his cliff-top retreat. Aubrey swallowed, acutely conscious that all his spellwork and preparation had led to this: he had one chance to remove Dr Tremaine and put an end to his warmongering. A careful, steady squeeze of the trigger and it would all be over.

A sound came from behind him. Aubrey was lying on his stomach at the entrance of the cave. The noise had to be von Stralick, sleeping much more comfortably now.

Aubrey waited a moment, but when no more noise came to him, he wiped sweat from his forehead with a finger and looked to re-centre his sights. It was time to shoot Dr Tremaine with a very special projectile.

Aubrey knew that a standard bullet wasn't going to stop Dr Tremaine; Aubrey had seen him walk away after being shot at close range. Something extraordinary was called for.

Aubrey had brought together all his thinking about magic, all of the reading, experimenting and theorising, to construct the complex array of spells which had replaced the bullet in the sole cartridge they had. This magic was some of the most intricate that Aubrey had ever attempted, bringing together elements from a number of wildly different spells Aubrey had worked with in the past. Hour after hour, in between tending a suffering von Stralick, he'd taken apart compression spells, intensification spells, amplification spells, spells that juggled aspects of Familiarity, Entanglement, Attraction, combining them and recombining them, splicing, reworking until he was able to make a spell-ridden object smaller than his fingernail, but as deadly as anything he'd ever created.

Much of the spell was based on his study of the

transformed Beccaria Cage that was now armouring his body and soul against premature separation. He'd also incorporated characteristics of the ensorcelled pearl that had been both a refuge and prison for Dr Tremaine's sister, Sylvia. The result was a highly compressed binding spell, overlaid with homing spells to counter any misalignment in the old Oberndorf – or in Aubrey's aiming.

When the spell struck its target, if all of Aubrey's hopes were true, Dr Tremaine would be caged in a magical prison, a prison that combined the strengths of the Beccaria Cage and the Tremaine Pearl. Once the projectile struck, the prison would be unleashed, then it would compress itself and its contents until it was the size of a marble. The reverse entanglement spell would activate, and the prison would be reeled in, landing back with Aubrey. Dr Tremaine would be imprisoned, neutralised, and Aubrey could return him to Albion for trial.

All Aubrey had to do was to squeeze the trigger. One shot, and he could go home, could restore his name, knowing the Holmland war effort would collapse without Dr Tremaine's guiding hand.

Ignoring second thoughts, doubts and qualms, he settled himself in his prone position and regripped the rifle, making sure it was stable on the flat rock he was using as a firing platform. He found Dr Tremaine with the sighting post and adjusted until it was aligned with the notch. He took a breath, let it out slowly, then drew in another and held it.

The war was about to end.

Don't miss the thrilling final book in The Laws of Magic series – coming in early 2011!